Eclectica Publishing Intl LLC Titles

Eclectica Magazine
Best Fiction

Celebrating 20 Years Online

Eclectica Magazine
Best Fiction

Celebrating 20 Years Online

Selected from *www.eclectica.org*
October 1996 through February 2016
by Tom Dooley

*With an Introduction by Tom Dooley
and a Foreword by Ron Currie*

E ECLECTICA PUBLISHING INTL LLC
ALBUQUERQUE, NEW MEXICO

In memory of Paul Silverman, 1940-2009,
and dedicated to another departed dreamer, Dennis Dooley.

Acknowledgments

Thanks to...

Julie, Lise, and Evans, who endure a mighty disruption to our lives so *Eclectica* might live.

Chris Lott, without whom there would be no *Eclectica*.

Ron Currie, for his generous foreword.

The 113 contributors to our Kickstarter campaign, who footed the bill for this and three other volumes.

Victor Ehikhamenor, who kindly provided the image for this volume's cover, and whose writing and artwork have been a rich addition to *Eclectica* over the years.

Charles Yu, Melvin Sterne, and Thom Didato, for blurbing this book, the latter two for founding two seminal online publications.

David Schutt, Paul Kelley, Ruth Hoar, Julie King, Tom Churchill, Joe Williams, Larry McEnerney, and Richard Stern, who at different times and in different ways contributed to the development of my appreciation for and understanding of the written word in general, the art of fiction more specifically, and the short story in particular.

Tamara Brenno-Uribarri and Anne Leigh Parrish, who as fiction editors helped select many of these pieces.

The many editors, authors, and supporters not already mentioned above, who have helped keep the boat afloat for two decades.

Contents

Foreword

IT'S THE YEAR 2000. George W. Bush has, with an assist from roughly 10,000 Florida lawyers and the Supreme Court, stolen the presidency from Al Gore. The human genome has recently been mapped. The unimaginable horror of 9/11 is still quite unimaginable. And the Internet, just a few years earlier the strange and mysterious domain of government worker bees and hardcore tech nerds, is beginning to demonstrate just how ubiquitous it will become.

On a more personal note, I had just been sprung from the nuthouse and was still deeply depressed and despairing in the way only hypersensitive 20-somethings are capable of being. It's not overstating it to say I hated my life: crap job, no education or prospects, much frustrated ambition to be a writer. Hardly anything unusual about these circumstances for most aspiring artists, but as with most aspiring artists, I and my suffering seemed special to me. As Greg Dulli put it, "Nobody bleeds the way I do." There's a term for this state of mind in 12-step programs: Terminal Uniqueness. It's not pretty, and it's not sexy. But there I was.

A large portion of this self-pity sprung from the fact that I had not, despite tremendous efforts, been able to publish so much as a single short story. The simple explanation for this fact was I hadn't yet written anything good enough to publish. But naturally I *thought* I had, believed in my very bones I had, and so the ongoing, uniform rejection from the shining lights of the literary magazine world—the reviews *Iowa, Kenyon,* and *Paris,* among others—seemed a great, nay historic, injustice.

But along with the rest of the world, the fiefdom of lit mags was undergoing fundamental and disruptive changes as a result of the Web's growing presence in our lives. Every day, it seemed, new virtual publishing venues were springing up. To the fusty Ivory Tower crowd, these online-only magazines were little more than vanity projects, nothing to be taken seriously. Certainly none of these "magazines" would ever find itself invited to the *Best American Short Stories* party.

But as is still the case now, there was a lot more good writing going on than there were places for it to be published, so for those of us who could not get a golden ticket from the hoary gatekeepers at *Ploughshares,* those of us who would never have the privilege of bussing Joyce Carol Oates' table at Bread Loaf, the explosion of lit mags on the Internet was a lifeline, offering hope where it had previously not existed. To be fair, some of these outlets were not very good, and many (even some of the good ones) not long-lived. One exception to both rules, however, was a place called *Eclectica Magazine,* which at the dawn of Dubya, had already been around for an improbable, amazing four years.

I'll put it plainly: I was ready to give up writing. I'd become (nearly) convinced I didn't have the chops to make a go of it and never would, that if I continued I'd only keep beating my head against the wall, keep chipping away at an already too-small portion of self-regard. I was cooked, demoralized, plain beaten. I'd go back to school, get a degree in some sensible field, stop being poor and miserable, and forget there was ever a time when I wanted to be a writer.

Back in those days, submitting stories to magazines was a decidedly analog process that took right around forever. Plus it *cost money.* There were manuscripts to print over and over again, manila and business-size envelopes to buy, postage to be paid both for sending out the story and for its return. If you were at all serious about submitting your work, these expenses were not inconsiderable—all told, sending out ten copies of a particular story might cost you $20, and then you waited, month upon agonizing month, for the response to arrive in a Self-Addressed Stamped Envelope, or SASE. The SASE almost always carried a rejection, made all the more painful by the fact that the envelope bore your own handwriting, as though you'd rejected yourself, somehow. The entire process was an exercise in slow-motion masochism, even if we all entered into it willingly.

And this was another way in which online magazines were changing the game. They quite logically accepted *electronic* submissions (no paper! no postage!) and took, on average, less than half the time to respond. Thus came an email, a mere several weeks after I submitted, from the editors at *Eclectica*, telling me how much they'd enjoyed my story "The Marlboro Man Died of Heartache," and that, moreover, they would very much like to publish it.

Wait. What?

'Twas true—they wanted to *publish* that fucker. This thing I'd written. Publish it! Welcome to bizarro world, where up was down, black was white, and cats lived comfortably with dogs.

In this era of the casual overstatement, let me say it would be impossible to overstate the positive effect this little bit of affirmation had on me. After years of struggling in silence, of being rejected by almost every magazine on the planet, someone had finally reached out a hand and said, "Hey man, that's pretty good. Mind if we take the time and trouble to show it to other people?" Conclusion: maybe I wasn't crazy to try and make a go of this writing thing. Maybe I did have what it took to make it (whatever "make it" might mean).

What I didn't understand at the time was that *Eclectica*, along with a very small handful of online magazines possessed of both solid editorial acumen and staying power, had transformed the lit mag world long before that world would deign to acknowledge its transformation. Imagine not forcing poor writers to spend money they don't have on paper and postage! Imagine offering them something other than a sniff and a form rejection! Imagine putting together the best writing you can find, publishing it to the widest audience you can find, and doing all of that for 20 years, and you'll have the slightest inkling of what *Eclectica* is about, and has been about from the very beginning.

In 2016, the SASE is as anachronistic as the bag phone—bad news for the United States Postal Service, good news for writers just getting their sea legs. In 2016, even the most venerable of literary magazines accepts electronic submissions, and have for some time. And in 2016, 99% of that online lit mag vanguard is long, long gone. But *Eclectica,* still the scrappy, online-only publication it's always been, is still here.

Ron Currie is the author of *God is Dead, Everything Matters!,* and *Flimsy Little Plastic Miracles.* A new book, *The One-Eyed Man,* will be released by Viking in 2017. His fiction has also appeared in *Glimmer Train, The Sun, Other Voices, The Nervous Breakdown,* and *Night Train,* and his story "Memento Mori," for which he was named a Spotlight Author in 2001, appeared in *Eclectica Best Fiction Volume 1.*

Introduction

A LOT CAN HAPPEN in 20 years. Relationships can run their course. Loved ones and pets can pass away. Cars can be traded in or sold. One might move to a new apartment or a new state, buy and sell a house, change jobs or careers, earn a degree. Kids might arrive in a timespan like that, maybe even grow up and depart. Hairlines recede and waistlines expand, eyesight and hearing weaken, joints stiffen. Entire TV series come and go, as do actors' careers, singers' popularities, cultural trends and artistic movements. Presidential administrations, wars, terrorist attacks and genocides and atrocities, revolutions, disasters, outbreaks... technology changes everyone's lives, and then changes them again.

Reflecting on the intervening years since Chris Lott suggested the two of us start an online literary publication in 1996, I realize all those things not only *can* happen in two decades, but they *have* happened—much of the personal and specific stuff very specifically and personally, to me. Very little remains of the life I led when I was 26 years old, but I have continued—and continue—to devote whatever spare time I have to putting together a virtual issue of *Eclectica Magazine* every three months.

After the first seven years, we had published so many outstanding pieces of short fiction, I felt compelled to produce a "best of" anthology. Putting together that book was satisfying, but here it is nearly twice again as many years later, and the archives are bursting at the seams. The time has come to shine a light on not just some great stories, but also the nonfiction and poetry that helped make *Eclectica* one of the most respected, longest running electronic lit-mags on the

Internet. But even three volumes can't do justice to 20 years, so we added a fourth devoted to speculative literature.

The stories in this, the fiction volume, are not intended to appear in any particular order, but nonetheless, as is often the case, thematic patterns emerge after the fact anyway, the way we see animal outlines in random smatterings of stars. I'm struck rereading the collection by how the first two stories, Chika Unigwe's "Dreams" and Elena Tuparevska's "Skopje 2011," present very different and yet similar portraits of women, ditto how "Dreams" and the last story in the book, Sefi Atta's "A Union on Indpendence Day," do the same more specifically for two African women. I'm further struck by how far ranging and deeply penetrating a catalogue of humanity and the human experience these and the rest of the stories here present. I feel license to borrow from O'Henry series editor Larry Dark, who said this in the introduction to his 1998 anthology:

> The story lives, I tell you. And the [33] you find here are the proof. They are full of life, death, love, humor, passion, hubris, blood, guts, dirt, God, war, mystery, fear, and longing.

I didn't explicitly set out to present such a catalogue; my intentions were to select the absolute best tales we've published in the past 20 years that didn't already appear in the first volume and aren't in the Speculative volume. In the interest of providing as wide a cross section of our contributors as possible, I chose to also exclude authors who appear in those other books. Certainly Alex Keegan, Stanley Jenkins, David Taylor, and many others have published multiple stories in *Eclectica* worthy of any "best of" collection, and I urge readers to seek out their work in the online archives.

One of the great things about editing *Eclectica*, and now about putting together these anthologies, has been getting to know some (and, I hope in the coming months, more) of the authors. Online publishing, existing as it does in the virtual world, doesn't always grant the opportunity to cultivate friendships face to face, unless it's Facebook to Facebook. Many of these authors live continents away, and social media gives us a chance to share our lives sometimes more immediately and personally than if we lived next door to each other. I've LOL'ed at Ron Currie's ascerbic wit, marveled at Victor Ehikhamenor's art installations, enjoyed political discussions with Ray Norsworthy and Will Lasky. I haven't yet had the pleasure of meeting Anne Leigh Parrish, but I was blessed to have her co-edit *Eclectica's* fiction section for three and a half years. I haven't met Tom Hubschman, either, but he has been a fixture in my life longer than my children have, and I'd like to think reading his work over the years has made me smarter and kinder. Happily, Tim Keane was passing through Albuquerque this summer, and we were able to meet up for drinks, fish and chips, and conversation at the perhaps appropriately named Two Fools Tavern. I look forward to more such encounters in the coming months as we all come together in whatever ways we're able to promote this book and its siblings.

I wouldn't have kept doing this all these years if it weren't for the authors. When I was a kid, not long after reading Beverly Cleary's *The Mouse on the Motorcycle,* I wanted to grow up to be a writer. When I was in high school, I naturally dreamed of publishing short stories in *The New Yorker* and *Atlantic Monthly.* When I went to college, I set out to major in creative writing, although when I transferred to the University of Chicago, I had to "settle" for English Literature because that august institution didn't offer something so frivolous for people to major in as creative writing. After college had pretty much beaten writerly ambitions out of me, Chris Lott proposed we start an online literary publication, which he claimed was partly a gambit to get me to write more, or at that point, anything. What editing *Eclectica* did, though, was help me realize I don't actually, *really* want to write, or at least, I don't want to do it badly enough to actually *do* it. What I want is to discover authors and stories and share them with others. Ultimately, it's not about taking credit for the find, it's about knowing someone else also loves a story I'm crazy about. I do the same thing with music, TV shows, movies. I'm still trying to talk my besieged 76-year-old mother into watching *The Walking Dead,* and I'm still psyched I hooked her on *The Shield.*

If I'm mentioning authors, I have to say it's been gratifying to see so many former contributors make an impact on the print publishing world, like Caroline Kepnes, one of whose eight appearances in *Eclectica* is represented in this volume, and who has remained as generous and accessible as she was before Stephen King called her work "totally original." Ditto the aforementioned Ron Currie, who kept in touch even after the *New York Times* called him "startlingly talented," and who took the time to provide the foreword to this volume, for which I'm especially grateful given his busy schedule these days as he gears up for the release of his third novel and fourth book, *The One-Eyed Man.*

Years ago, I wrote an Introduction to our first *Best Fiction* anthology where I talked about these stories as the authors' children first, mine second. That my challenge in selecting those works wasn't so much in deciding what to include, but in coming to terms with what to leave out. All still true, but now with a gestation period measured in decades. It's been a very personal process, and gratifying, to bring forth something akin to what Updike called his own selection of stories in the *Best American Short Stories of the Century:* "...this brave little flotilla, the best of the best."

It's fair to wonder, will there be another 20 years? When will we publish the next batch of anthologies? I hope the answer to the first question is yes, and the second, soon, but it's always a good policy to live in the now. It may very well be we've already experienced the golden age of Internet publishing, or at least, the golden era of *Eclectica Magazine:* this intrepid era when writers like Ron Currie, whether out of desperation or pioneering spirit, took a chance on a new medium, a new virtual frontier, and an upstart electronic "magazine" thrown together by a couple fools in their spare time. Like Hell's Kitchen or the French Quarter, the Internet may have gentrified and lost its low rent, starving artist appeal. For my part, I'm willing to keep plugging away at it, though, evolving perhaps, but evolving slowly because I think there's something to be said for seeing what can be built with patience and discernment over a very long time.

Ron stated in his foreword to this volume that there will always be more good writing than there are places for it to be published. In truth, sometimes the sheer volume of online publications makes it feel like we may be approaching a time when there are actually more places for writing to be published than there is writing, good or otherwise, and worse, than there are readers. Stephen King once suggested in an *Atlantic* interview that most of the people reading short stories in small press publications (and I think it would be fair to add poetry and really any literary genre to this statement) are aspiring authors trying to figure out what is publishable and where to submit.

Maybe that's not the worst thing, to have a bunch of writers as your readers. It does suggest a degree of participation, of ownership, of community. Certainly this book wouldn't have been possible without the financial backing of the authors contained within it and their friends and relatives. The next 20 years and next set of anthologies, if and when achieved, will almost certainly be constructed the same way.

Ultimately, whether you're a contributor or potential submitter, a friend or relative, or a good old-fashioned, unencumbered reader who came to be holding this book serendipitously or deliberately, the work is going to have to speak for itself. Without a hint of objectivity, I hereby present 33 stories I believe don't just speak, but sing the praises of their authors, the pleasures of short fiction, and the possibilities of the Internet, perhaps even as yet a largely undiscovered literary territory.

CHIKA UNIGWE

Dreams

From January/February 2004

HE HAS HAIR like mango fibers, sparse and white. His hands are like you expect: sandpaper. But as he touches, you do not flinch, not even when he rubs the sandpaper against your bare arms. His touch reminds you of the cleanser that keeps your face spot-free. The cleanser hurts, but no beauty comes without its pains. Everybody knows that. Or ought to at least.

When he licks your ears and makes kissing noises (except they come out sounding like a bottlecap scratching a cement floor), you do not move away in repulsion. Instead, you smile and count your blessings. He cannot see your smile is no more than an *ochi eze*—the sort of smile that hurts at the jaws, a smile that stays on the surface like froth on milk. He sees your teeth gleaming in the light and smiles back, exposing a full set of his own. They sit awkwardly in his wrinkled mouth, seeming to be too much for that cavity. His lips barely cover them. He reminds you of a rabbit. You wonder for a minute if the teeth are all his. You wonder if he has bought them like he buys everything else in his life. He tells you he paid a huge bride price on his wife, tells you about the three cows he slaughtered for the wedding, about the sacks of rice he had imported from Thailand especially for the ceremony, about the bales of lace from Vienna he gave his mother-in-law and the 24 karat gold chain he bought from a Jewish merchant in Antwerp for his wife. You know all about his cars (the Mercedes, the Peugeot 505, the Land Rover and the Land Cruiser he just imported from Belgium). Brand new, he says. Not *tokunbo*, those second-hand cars littering the streets. You know all about his houses (the ones in London and New York, the apartments in Enugu and Onitsha, and the mansion he is building in his village, which has 15 self-contained bedrooms and a lawn tennis court).

He thinks he makes you happy. And maybe, in a way he does. Happiness is not a static quality. Its parameters change, swelling or shrinking. This is a lesson you have learned. It is one you are still learning as a matter of fact. What made you happy a few years ago is no longer there. Now, you are teaching yourself to be made happy by other things. So maybe the sandpaper hands grate your taut arms, but you are close to your goal. And that makes you happy. You give him another smile, the floating on the surface one, not coming deep from your heart. It has been awhile since you smiled from your heart, anyway. You do not know if you are capable of doing that anymore. Besides, it is easier to smile this way, even though it hurts at the jaws. It is a smile that comes without you having to search too deep for a reason. It is instantly gratifying to the receiver.

Obi was the first and only man you fell in love with. You married him, and your life was a fairy tale: a husband with a smile like a full moon. His smile lit up a room, lit up your universe. That smile stole your heart the first time he sent it to you across a crowded wedding reception. He said fate brought you together when you told him you had stumbled into the wrong room. Your second cousin's reception was in the hall on the upper floor. Somehow, not having listened properly to your mother's hurried directions, you ended up in this hall. You did not mind. You never did like your second cousin much, but you did like this man with a thin mustache above his upper lip. He had a low, rumbling voice, and when he told you in that low rumble that fate brought you together, you fell in love with the word "fate." Fate is beautiful. It pushes you into the wrong hall to meet the man you stumble into love with. You would explain to your mother later why you did not turn up at your cousin's wedding. She would scold you and tell you off for missing it. She would warn you how everybody would think it was because you were jealous. After all, the cousin whose wedding you missed was three years younger than you, and you were still yet to get a marriage proposal.

Indeed, your mother cried and beat her chest and asked her gods why she was burdened with a daughter like you. What did she do in her former life to earn this punishment? She lamented you were a bad child, a disgrace, and how, she asked, could you hope to find a husband if you missed weddings where so many eligible men were present? Did you not know your cousin had at least four brothers-in-law of marriageable age? *Ewo*, her gods had given her the worst daughter ever. She said and did all these things, but you did not mind. You did not care because you were confident fate was taking care of you.

The day you mentioned to your mother that there was a man interested in marrying you, she danced around your small sitting room. She waved a handkerchief in the air and sang praises to her gods who had finally smiled on her:

chim di mma chim di mma onye si na chim adighi mma bia fulu ife o melu m ooo chim ooo, tanku you

She held you close in happiness, pressing your nose against her neck (your mother was a few inches taller than you), and you feared she would suffocate you with her happiness. The happiness filled her arms with a surprising strength, and it was a while before you could extricate yourself from her embrace. You were embarrassed. It had been so long since she had hugged you. In fact, it had been such a long time that even though you tried to remember the last time, you could not.

The day she met Obi, she told you he would make you very happy, that mothers know such things. She made him yam porridge with spinach leaves, and even though he did not like yam, he ate to make your mother happy. He knew one does not reject a prospective mother-in-law's first meal! And especially not if she has killed a whole chicken. She hung around while he ate, asking him questions about his family, what he did, where he lived. Obi answered between mouthfuls. It was not really your mother's place to question a prospective son-in-law, but she took on the duty because there was no man to challenge her. Your father was dead and you had no brothers. She would tell your paternal uncles you had a suitor, and they would ask their own questions and perform their own investigations. But that would be later.

When he left, your mother told you he did not eat like a greedy man. He did not fill his mouth with food so much so it was impossible for him to talk. Greedy men do not make good husbands, she said, and you wondered if that was why she made the food, to test him.

After a meeting with your uncles, Obi paid your bride-price and took wine to your people. You did not want a huge traditional wedding. You wanted to save the money for a modern wedding instead. You want the city to talk about it.

Your wedding day was a drizzly Saturday. Your mother worried it was bad luck to marry in the rain, but you cast her worries away with a high laugh and the back of your palm, telling her it was merely superstition. You were beyond superstition. It had no power over you. Your mother smiled, but her eyes still looked worried.

She was in a red George wrapper and a white lace blouse with sleeves that puffed up to her ears. They were Obi's presents to her, her first set of new clothes in years. You loved her very much, and you did not want her happiness marred by the rain. You smiled at her and told her not to worry, that nothing could possibly go wrong. She placed her soft palm on yours and told you you looked very beautiful, but she wished you had chosen a white wedding dress. More virginal. And you are a virgin, are you not? You pretended not to hear her. You had had the color argument before, but you were happy she did not seem to be thinking of the rain anymore.

The church was full, and some guests had to stand outside, huddled under umbrellas to hear you tell Obi (in a voice thick with tears of joy) you would be his forever and forever and forever. His! His! His! It was an easy vow for you to make because you couldn't imagine ever wanting to be with anyone else. Obi was the zenith. Your soul mate. Your perfect fate. He was where you wanted to be. When you walked down the aisle, holding to the hem of your cream wedding dress, the flower girls sprayed you with confetti and rice. You do not mind that a grain of rice got into your left eye and that you had to rub and rub to get it out (which made your eye puffy and red as if you had *apollo*, conjuctivitis, in the wedding pictures).

The pregnancies came soon after. You had three healthy children in two years: twin beautiful girls with their father's smile and their mother's nose (the perfect nose, Obi called it) and a son who was the apple of your eye (he looked—looks—very much like Obi) and who, your mother delighted, secured your place in your husband's home. They were the kind of children who strangers liked to coo over, pinching their cheeks and rubbing their heads, saying how very healthy they looked:

Chei! These are very beautiful children.

They are as healthy as those plump chickens at *okuko* agriculture.

You must be proud of such children.

See how their skin glows with health and good living. *Ndi uwa oma!*

You had a house. A duplex in a quiet part of town. Your house was proof of the comfortable lives you lived inside: wall to wall carpeting with a rug so deep and so lush, your feet practically disappeared as soon as you stepped in; a huge color television (that guests admired and your neighbor jealously told you looked like a cinema screen—she did not know why you need such a huge screen anyway, looking so out of place in a sitting-room); and a Sony CD player, on which you and Obi played all your favorite tunes (you were both in love with Barry White, and when you heard he was dead, you actually cried). The children had a room each with air-conditioning to protect them from the temperature, and the guest room your mother used had air-conditioning, too, but she never turned it on, saying it made her feel as if she was in a mortuary and even though she was old, she was not dead yet, thank you very much!

But when Obi died at 36 (and you were 34), your life shattered like china. You could not even begin to pick up the pieces.

Obi was too young to die, and your mother-in-law wanted to know why his fate had been so cruel to him. She invited the prophet of her church to your house and demanded from him the answer to the question burning within her, threatening to consume her. Who was to blame for her healthy son's death? The wild-haired prophet burned incense in all the rooms, his white prophet's gown sweeping the rug that swallowed his bare feet. He rang his little bell and chanted incantations in a loud, strange voice that sounded like he was singing (but he was not singing). He swayed from side to side and pointed the finger of blame at you. It was his index finger on his right hand, the nail bandaged with a browning bandaid, and when he pointed it at you, it looked as if he was offering you a cigar. He told her you had a binding marriage in the ocean with a water spirit. A water spirit who was jealous of Obi. It was this spirit who afflicted him with an illness.

This marriage is news to you, but nobody believes you. You do not know whether to laugh or cry. How can anyone believe marriages are contracted between spirits and humans? Your mother-in-law clapped her hands in your face and almost spat at you for daring to cast aspersion on the prophet. The prophet shook his head, sending his locks gently flying from side to side, and accepted the glass of cola Obi's mother brought for him.

"A young man like that, he just died in his sleep. That's not normal," your mother-in-law proclaimed as she gathered support from relatives to turn you out of your home, the duplex on the quiet side of town with the air-conditioned rooms.

"The doctors say he had a heart attack. The autopsy concluded that," you protested, but nobody was listening to you.

Obi's incensed mother shouted above your voice, "You killed my son. Why did you not just stay with your water-spirit husband? Why? You may deceive everybody else, but you cannot deceive the prophet. He has seen you for what you are," she sobbed as Obi's uncle assured her you would pay for your evil. Evil of which you knew nothing. How could you begin to pay for the prophet's imagination, an imagination as wild as his over-grown hair?

You moved out with nothing but your clothes and your two wailing daughters. Obi's family kept your four year-old son. He was theirs. Heir to the family name. But your five year-old twin daughters were yours. They did not want the burden of raising the female children of an evil mother.

Obi's mother swaggered her way into the house with her two younger sons. From then on, your mother-in-law would hold court in your former house. You would no longer be welcome, not even to see your son, the perfect image of his father. You held onto that bit of Obi at his funeral, crying until your eyes swell like bunched-up fists.

Your father was dead, and your mother poor and depending on you for financial support. You had no family to ask for help, and you had mouths to feed. You swore your children must go to school. This had always been your dream, and one shared by Obi. You did not have to listen hard to hear him say, "*Uche,* our children must go to school until there is nothing more for them to learn. I want them to see the end of school."

You could not get a job because you had no qualifications. You did not have even a standard six certificate. Your mother always said that all a woman needed was a generous husband. She was wrong. A woman needs more. She needs generous in-laws, too. Above that, she needs an education, a job, independence. These were what you wanted for your daughters. Your dream for them.

It was this dream that pulled you into this blue-lit room you rent while your daughters sleep in your apartment on the other side of town. They think you have a job helping out at the university hospital.

You are lucky. Even after three pregnancies, your body is still as firm as a just-ripe tomato. Your stomach is taut and has just a little bulge right under the navel. People say you look like you did at 16 (and unlike many compliments, you know this is entirely true).

Your mother says you have a body like a rubber band. No matter how far it is stretched, it always snaps back. This body becomes your money-spinner.

The first night you worked, you were shy. You wanted to cover your eyes when the pot-bellied man took your nipples between his teeth. You kept your legs tight together, hardly daring to open them. He laughed and said it was just like being with a virgin. He liked it. He thought you were a tease, that the coyness was part of an act. He growled in pleasure, and when he got up to go, his eyes shone like a cat's in the dark. He reached into a black leather wallet with gold lettering at the side and pulled out a bunch of notes, suffocating the room with their smell of central bank. He was a big spender, and he was happy with you. He gave you enough money to pay your house-rent for two months. The money helped de-shy you, and soon you were able to chuck the shyness in a bin to mildew.

As the man with the sandpaper hands whispers in your ear, you close your nose to the stench of his breath (it smells like the raw fish stand at the Kenyatta market) and count your blessings: your daughters are in a private school, your mother is being taken good care of, and your retirement plans are already in motion. You will be the owner of the biggest bakery in Enugu. You can already see it, a white bungalow with a huge neon sign lighting it up, "Dream Bread" emblazoned in red, its fame spreading from Enugu to Onitsha.

ELENA TUPAREVSKA

Skopje 2011

From October/November 2015

I ONCE KNEW a Macedonian girl who had a long-distance relationship with a man working in Taiwan on the construction of a space craft that would save a chosen few from the end of the world. And standing here today I finally realize how she got herself in that mess. For you see from the perspective of a 1.65m-tall woman standing beneath a 25m statue, messes are very easy to get into. Effortlessly, thoughtlessly, and in 10cm stiletto heels, I got myself into this particular jam. Standing on my feet all day for a spectacle the like I have only seen in old black and white recordings from the times this country was part of a federation, witnessing a parade of what seems to be one of the world's smallest infantries and air forces followed by allegorical and not so allegorical performances of every artist and institution in the country who received an order to prepare something for the occasion, getting disorientated by tackily lit monuments, listening to speeches of soporific nature, wondering who are these people cheering enthusiastically.

If given a choice, I would be at home now. Yet I am in all the photos. Captured for history, for posterity. And in the company of such unfashionable people. I gaze around the sea of ill-fitting suits, polyester dresses, bad hairdos, wishing there was someone with whom I could share a laugh. Finding no such one, my eyes settle on the Minister.

Look at him. His counterfeit modesty. As he buys the most expensive apartment in town, as he refuses to stay in anything but the most luxurious hotels on his trips abroad.

His I-am-just-a-man-of-the-people pose. As two of his bodyguards run after him carrying his children's bicycles, while in his own words he tries hard to just be a normal dad, or as he rides in the backs of fancy black cars, his ear forever attached to BlackBerries and iPhones taken to meetings of imaginary urgency and importance.

The meekness in his eyes. As he calls his employees into his office to question them what the rest of his staff is saying about him.

All his prejudices. Those cocksucking Greeks, he yells as he drives to Thessaloniki for a weekend by the sea; those motherfucking Bulgarians, as he inquires about obtaining a Bulgarian passport; those dirty Albanians, as he finishes a statement on diversity and cohabitation; those stupid Americans, after he has his picture taken next to medical equipment donated by the US government.

I wince.

I resent him at receptions when Western diplomats smile at me with glacial politeness and remark how capable he must be to hold not one but two ministerial posts and at such young age, or when he gets this very proud and genuinely impressed look on his face while listening to his prime minister talking. I am ashamed of him in front of friends when he quotes Alexander the Great, or when he resembles a tom turkey doing a mating dance when he hears people call him minister. I hate him during interviews when he speaks with admiration of the Skopje 2014 project, or when he masterminds antiabortion campaigns. I swallow all of it with a smiling face, and more. But the jokes, his stupid jokes are my undoing.

He is not stupid himself. I wish he were; it would have made this easier. And he is not bad looking. In fact he is very handsome, and very tall. Ah. I used to think we made such a beautiful couple. People still tell me we do as if they intentionally want to wound me.

Of course I am his wife.

As the song comes to an end, the Minister looks at me. No doubt checking if I am smiling and applauding. Although I am doing both, he frowns, probably disapproving of my green dress. I should have worn black.

We need to talk, he says suddenly over the applause.

My heart stills for a second and then begins crushing against my rib cage. My hands grow cold and damp, and I realize he knows... He knows. The sarcasm, my secret tiny smirk, dissipates in an instant. Yes, I am afraid. Years ago when I dreamt and yearned about him finding out, I imagined standing in front of him full of defiance. Now I look at him out of the corner of my eye with a fearful heart and barely manage to mutter, What about?

Later, he says coldly, and the last hope I have of being wrong is gone.

I close my eyes. My temples tense in a forewarning of a headache, which makes it difficult to think of the ways he could have found out and how long he could have known, and the horrible music just won't stop. But I have to think. When did he find out? He didn't seem to know last night. He didn't complain about making him go to the theater. He loved what I wore. He let me choose the station on the car radio and didn't turn it off when I picked Classic FM. Beethoven's ninth symphony was playing in the background as we drove. He looked almost happy.

He couldn't have known last week when he came home all triumphant, could he? He said the statue and the rehearsal looked incredible. And you look incredible, he added drawing closer. He grabbed me off the floor and tossed me on the bed. Very uncharacteristic of him. And very torrid, I must admit. But then in a manner characteristic of me, I closed my eyes as he unzipped my dress and imagined another tall and handsome and a bit fairer-haired man in his place. And that made it better.

Tremulous I stand in the night. Ever since a date for that damn report was announced, I found myself restlessly anticipating something bad to happen. It has to be about the progress report. It seems to be the only thing the media writes about. And somebody was bound to read the name of the commissioner working on it and remember they had heard me mention it before. From the time when he was appointed to this post, I have been carefully erasing every trace of us having known each other, but I've always had a bad feeling about this that only worsens with every impending report.

The Commissioner didn't tell me about his new job. I learned of it from the news. I heard his name and felt in my liver the old illness. For some heartbreaks stay in you forever like a dormant hypnozoite.

I knew him before getting married, before even meeting the Minister. Our love was... like a dropped can of Coke suddenly opened, like a light bulb switched on too fast. That is how I remember the beginning of our love. I do not wish to remember the end, which was protracted and messy.

He said he didn't want a long-distance relationship. Then he called and said he missed me, still had feelings for me, wanted to come to Skopje to see me. Honestly, he wrote a week later, I am not sure if it is a good idea to come down after all. I don't want to lead you on. Please don't be mad at me, he begged four months later, I hope you can give me a second chance. After a second chance reunion in Paris, he emailed he should be honest with me, that he had wanted to meet me because he thought there might be something there. But he didn't feel anything, he didn't develop any feelings for me and didn't think he would. Sorry for being blunt, he said, and then took it all back six months later. He called it a terribly botched attempt of an email. He wished he had never sent it and blamed it on work pressure. He begged to see me again, and when I got tired of waiting for him to suggest a date, he said he didn't know what I expected him to say— that he'd meet me for a weekend somewhere, that we'd have a great time, that we'd move in together, get married and live happily ever after? After I didn't answer, he claimed he would totally devote himself to me and my needs and that I could totally do with him as I pleased. He would also love to have me stay with him in Stockholm for a week, he said. But then two days before I arrived, he wrote he had to say things as they were: he was not going to take days off work, and I couldn't really stay at his place after all. He knew he said he wouldn't change his mind when I asked, but he did in the end. He should have said right away he didn't think it was a good thing I was coming, it would only encourage me to think there was something there, which there was not, at least not on his part. I was free to pour scorn on him, but he didn't think he was going to reply to my emails anymore.

I met the Minister, and I never wanted to see the Commissioner, who wasn't yet a commissioner, again.

A year later I opened my inbox: *I am writing this now because I really can't stop thinking about you.*

I liked the sound of that sentence, and because things with the Minister were no longer great, I wrote back.

And so it began again. Registering for conferences and seminars around the world, seeking volunteering opportunities in countries where he was on diplomatic missions, making up excuses, sneaking around. There was nothing we couldn't pull off. We were too crafty for our own good. Nobody suspected anything, and we started becoming too reckless. I even began showing up in his office uninvited.

What the hell are you doing? He seemed very angry when he found me waiting there.

I stepped in front of the big oak desk with the blue flag hanging above it on the wall. I said, I've come to check how the report is coming along.

I told you that will depend on you, he said.

We had been fighting a lot in the last few weeks, and I could feel him slipping between my fingers. I asked for patience. I begged him to tell me how I could make it right.

He repeated he wanted me under his terms or he didn't want me at all, and he asked what I was willing to do for him.

I lifted myself onto the desk, his eyes watching me. He told me to stop, but he walked towards me. I placed the palm of my hand on his anatomically correct but strange heart. He said no, but he closed his eyes.

Oh, do it for peace, for your peace of mind and heart, I whispered, and he asked, Is this all I get?

For now, I answered, and he told me I better be fucking amazing if this was all I was ready to give him, and if I didn't want that report to be negative.

He took my ankles in his hands and pushed them gently apart. I lowered my back onto the table, shut my eyes, and started seeing stars.

And things were right back where they were.

Another conference in Rome. I smiled at the tall, handsome, and a bit fairer-haired man next to me. I linked my arm with his, and we walked down the street chatting about the exhibition we had just seen, trying to figure out what to have for lunch, engaged in a faultless simulation of love and life. Talking about pizza toppings, I walked beside him with my envy. Envious of the couples who passed us hand in hand, of the girl in the orange skirt waving at someone she knew, of the polite maître d' who showed us to our table. Envious even of the birds.

We almost never talk about the future. We never acknowledge this could never have a happy ending. He never mentions my children. And he rarely brings up the fact I am married.

Jasikovska, he calls me by my maiden name.

That is not my name, and you know that, I repeat for the 100th time.

That will always be your name, he smirks sarcastically.

On the occasions when he does mention my husband, it is always in some insulting way to belittle him or find out something he can use against him.

So what did that fool say, he asked after he heard the government was building a monument to Alexander the Great, and he looked at me keenly, hungrily, waiting for me to slip, to give something away.

I don't know. He doesn't confide in me anymore, I said, and I hated I was for once telling the truth.

He doesn't give up. Because this is me, the Minister's live-in traitor. And over the years I have fed him scraps he can use to ridicule my husband. His uncouth parents, his grammatical errors, his ambitions, his snobbery, his cousin he employed as a secretary at my faculty and who sleeps around with everyone.

I am careful not to reveal anything that could jeopardize the Minister's political career. And that's why the questions do not stop. What was his opinion about the new law? Did he know about the changes? Was he involved in the scandal? He asks innocently, and I know there is nothing innocent about this man. There was nothing innocent about him when we were very young and met for the first time, and there sure was nothing innocent when he only wanted me free from student loans and possibly with an apartment in the center of Stockholm. Today he wants to see my husband destroyed, his career in tatters, me and my children back in the ghetto of the Balkans where for most of my youth I couldn't leave without filling out a dozen forms, showing bank statements and my parents' salaries, queuing for hours outside embassies.

When I think of all that, I get very mean.

I tell him never to contact me again. I nag him to tell me about his dating life.

When he said he couldn't talk about that with me, I said he could tell me with the same mouth he used to tell me how he wanted to come in my mouth. I told him all our problems stemmed from the fact that half the time he thought I was crazy about him and half the time he thought I felt nothing for him, and I laughed that he was right half the time.

He slams the phone down in a rage, but strangely he always comes back.

Why is this man still contacting you, my mother who is unfamiliar with respecting her children's privacy lifted my cellphone in front of my face as I returned from the bathroom. What does he want? She looked at me suspiciously. But in an instant I was in her arms with her tears in my hair. Do you love the two of them?

Oh, mother, if it were so simple, so almost redeemable.

He wanted to know the same, why was I still answering his calls, why didn't I leave him alone, did I love him, did I love the Minister, did I love him?

Be honest with me, he said.

If I were to be honest, truthful, ah, darling... you wouldn't be able to get out of bed for a month, I thought, and I remembered how he never offered to pay for anything, not once. Not a single drink, not one dinner. Not even when I treated him to a meal. We would always split the bill. And how he refused to wear a condom, and how we had sex only once a week, how he always said FYROM instead of Macedonia, how many of his sentences addressed to me started with you Eastern Europeans, and how his idea of a joke was saying people call Macedonians primitive.

Oh, how I hate this man. This horrible, arrogant man. His games, his condescension, his discriminations, his selfishness, his touch. The way he rolls his eyes when I am talking. And the knowledge he wants to fuck the Minister's wife. He wants to do to her things the Minister would never dare ask her. That is what he wants, that is his ultimate, diabolical revenge.

I let him. And then I do what I always do when I am in bed, on tables, kitchen counters, public toilet doors, and every other surface with him. I close my eyes and think about the Minister.

But strangely I come back for more.

Sometimes even he can't believe I still haven't left.

Why are you here, he asked when he arrived in Skopje and I snuck into his hotel room.

I am here... because he betrayed me once.

And he quieted, waiting for the rest. This was the first time I gave him something more than my usual I miss you, I never should have let you leave me, or life would be too boring without you. For the first time, I think, He is starting to get it.

But I said nothing else. He sighed, probably preferring his version anyway.

Then he touched me. And I wondered what it was like as he traced his fingers down my clavicle, to know that this body, this skin, these bones were once his and that he decided to instead fill the rooms and the beds in his apartments with other bodies, other skins and bones.

Is that easy, is that insignificant to know?

I love you, he said, and he moved his fingers down.

I love you, I said. And it was not a lie. I was just repeating old truths.

Leave him, he whispered later as he lay short of breath next to me.

You know I can't, not now. In the words of the great Albanian poet Fatos Arapi, do not hate me, I said and gently stroked his face.

I don't, he shook his head, and I sadly thought, Look who's foolish now.

To think I would ever do anything to hurt my children. As terrible as the Minister is as a man, he is the twins' father, and no one could take his place. No one could love them more than him. And I could never trust any man with little girls that are not his. I would never let anything happen to them. Because they are my everything. Because yes, mother, I have two loves in my life and only two loves, I thought this afternoon as I put the twins in bed for their afternoon nap before starting to get ready for the Independence Day celebration.

I put on my green dress. In the mirror I saw the Minister walking slowly towards me with a jewelry box in his hand. He moved my hair over my left shoulder. I think he's been watching too many movies. He fastened the chain with the small diamond cross onto my unreligious chest. I wondered how I could have possibly fallen for this man.

How happy I had been when I met him and finally forgot about my ex. That first season passed in the rhythm of smiles, heartbeats, trodden autumn leaves, and occasionally very good sex. It was just so simple, the way I always imagined it would be. I love this man, I surprised myself thinking while stuffing cabbage leaves with minced meat. Six months later we were engaged. With kneeling, ring, and everything.

And then it all went to hell.

Tonight I flutter in the windless heat as I allow myself to ask the most important question: How powerful is he?

As many others have been sacked, replaced, or disgraced, the Minister has withstood several cabinet reshuffles, two failed multi-million euro projects, and perpetual budget constraints. Scandal-free and carefully uncharismatic so as not to eclipse his prime minister, he has managed to never fall out of favor. Whether opening hospitals, churches, or baroque buildings, he is always right behind with his patented meek and affable expression.

But I have heard the stories. How he owns every judge and policeman in the country, how he calls tv stations and threatens to fire journalists or shut down entire stations for reporting news that displeases him, how half of all project funds end up in his secret bank accounts, how he fires anyone unwilling to become a member of the ruling party, how he pressures his employees every election, how his brothers practically run their town, and how people don't even dare look them in the eye.

I have seen the ass-kissing dean at my faculty squirm as she asks, When are you going to finally complete that PhD so we can make you a professor, in an attempt to find out how far I am from the possibility of the Minister replacing her with me. I have found his list of ideas ranging from assigning six bodyguards to guard the prime minister for life, erecting a monument to every ancient king and queen, painting parking spaces on the sidewalks and charging for them, busting elevators in apartment buildings to prevent people from voting for the opposition... to fining people for hanging their undergarments on their balconies.

I have even witnessed him in action after receiving the news my sister had been fired. What happened, he asked and picked up the phone. Impressively, two calls later, my sister got her job back. Now could this same man who once had so readily protected my family turn against them? Could he leave me and my sister without a job, my mother without a pension? Oh, I know he can do this.

The question I guess is, would he do it to the mother of his children? The thought of my children suddenly snares my heart. In the still night air, I am wind-swept. Could he take them away from me? Is he that powerful?

Shit. How could I be so stupid as to let this happen? And with all my debts, maxed out credit cards, no savings, a closet full of clothes, no backup plans. Stuck like a doorstop.

The plan to gather evidence against him for a rainy day has so far amounted to a few useless shreds. He has become very cautious. Bringing home no documents from the office, leaving no incriminating texts on his phone. He no longer trusts me. And this is a man who had once claimed I was his soul mate. I had never gone as far as to say that, but I had been so happy with him. I used to love how ambitious he was. And how kind he was, and of course handsome. We used to have so much in common: listening to the same music, watching the same movies, both into cycling and skiing, sharing the same liberal views, not wanting to get married in church, resenting corrupt Macedonian politicians.

That is why this hurts so much more now.

Although I know all loves will eventually have to be betrayed, even the ones who stay together for the rest of their lives, I was hoping his betrayal would be of the kind that involves a mother-in-law and a husband who always takes her side, or a husband who hates my cooking. Instead, the Minister walked in the door one day with an expression like he had single-handedly solved all of Macedonia's economic problems and announced he had just helped arrange a €500m loan from the IMF. And that is why this provokes so much more sadness. I clutch my chest and think of my poor children and grandchildren.

The Minister reaches for my hand, and I hold onto it tightly as if it's hope. Maybe I am wrong. He knows nothing, and his angry expression is actually supposed to pass as dignified. I feel that if I believed in anything, this would be the moment I would turn to it and implore. Then he could go back to not knowing and we could start over. I have this fantasy, even after all this time. It usually torments me on beautiful, sunny weekend mornings, when watching sad movies, and on every Sunday of Forgiveness. He lays his head in my lap. He closes his eyes. Forgive me, he whispers, I don't mean any of it, none of it. It is all just an act.

Although he never says it, I will stay with the Minister. If he will have me after tonight. Please let him have me after tonight. I will renounce the other man in a second. I will never see him again. I will erase his phone number, block his email, unfriend him on Facebook. No more conferences around the world or pretending to use the John just to send him an SMS. I will be a better wife.

I will ask about my husband's day. I will buy the kind of bread he prefers, make sure we don't run out of his favorite coffee, start making the dishes he likes more often, care once again what's bothering him. I will do anything the Minister wants. The time taken up currently by the other will be dedicated solely to my children and the Minister. From this perspective and desperation, even loving him again seems possible, seems easy. Like a man drowning himself in a bucket of water. Well, perhaps I will also spend a bit of time ensuring nobody ever again makes me feel cornered like this. A PhD, a new nationality, and a joint savings account for a start. I make the list in my mind and almost miss the announcement of the last song for the evening.

The word "last" gets people restless, and the Minister leans over my ear.

I wanted to talk to you about your upcoming conference in the UK, he says. My mother won't be able to look after the twins, and I'll be stuck in meetings all week.

That is what he wanted to talk to me about. I am so relieved, I could kiss that ridiculous woman with teased hair who goes twice a month all the way to Stip to have her hairdresser increase three times the circumference of her head, and who probably can't look after her grandchildren while I am away because of a hair appointment.

I should have run the first time I saw her hair. Who are these people? my mother asked as she laid eyes on the famous bouffant. You deserve so much better than this, my father said. Don't forget you come from a family of doctors, engineers, businessmen, musicians. You are the fourth generation born in the capital, not some small provincial town. And one day we will come into our own again, they repeated lest I forgot, and referred to the Minister's family as a bunch of field hands and illiterate partisans. They never thought much of my previous boyfriend either, or "the little Scandinavian civil servant" as they used to call him.

Yet in the end they agreed I should marry the man I love.

And tonight as the music finally stops and I know he doesn't know, I smile at the man I used to love. He pulls me towards the person who has given him not one but two terms in office and says his servile goodbye. I look at him and feel the friability of my hope. But the fear is gone, replaced by a more recognizable feeling. Somewhere in the vicinity of my pancreas, I still feel the same rage I felt the first day I received an email that began with, "I think I should be honest with you." Undiminished, the sentiment remains in that exact spot, reassuring me everything I do is justified and well deserved. But on a day like today I have an unnerving suspicion I will wake up tomorrow to find our photo in the paper and think, Hey, there is the horrible minister and his horrible wife. That is not a very comforting thought. But I had been good once, quite good. Enough now.

I feel my cellphone vibrate in the clutch under my arm. I sneak a peek and see the long, familiar yet unmemorized number on the lit screen. And I know regretlessly what I want and what I will do.

I will take the call later.

I will retell all the colorful tidbits of today's event, and then I will tell him to meet me in London next month. Because you see, I want all his resources: his energy, his time, his youth. Only when I deplete them all will I leave him alone.

PAUL SILVERMAN

The Home Front

From January/February 2007

OUT OF THE corner of his eye, Harold watches his son build a sandwich, thrusting the tongs into the pastrami cauldron and fishing up a fat wad of brine-soaked, heat-curled slices and dumping the slippery mass onto the base of a roll. He possesses an eyeball that could have been engineered by the Toledo Scale Company, and this calibrated mechanism sends alarm signals to all parts of his brain. "Jack, you're killin' me," he says, his eyeball telling him Jack has dropped four ounces easy onto the roll, four ounces when the house rules, the margin requirements cast in stone for all time—no exceptions, even on the night the Korean War has ended—specifically call for three and a half ounces, three if you can get away with it with the Irish cab drivers.

"Concentrate, Jack," he says, "concentrate," watching out of his eye corner mournfully as Reggie Bondurant (stage name, Bond), jet hair ironed like Cab Calloway's and top-to-bottom zooted and spiffed in his weekend piano-playing tux, snatches the fiscally unsound mound

(Jack gave up extra pickles too) and scuttles away from the counter to a far corner table, holding the sandwich close to his chest the way a running back hugs the football. Saving the fissured formica table for him is Dixon James, the lanky old middleweight who once killed a Kid Something in a Scranton ring but now gives no physical sign of this whatsoever, as his wilting wino arms quake and spill coffee and his lips quiver around a wet, unfiltered Chesterfield snipe.

At least Reggie's a regular customer, thinks Harold, but he also thinks that now Reggie will want four-ounce sandwiches all the time, and so will every other pastrami fiend standing in the scowling mob who saw what a prize Jack handed Reggie.

But Jack will never be able to concentrate in this place, not with hookers offering hand jobs for meal plans, not with every tenth diner threatening to punch his white face black should he underweight the sandwich, not with razor-toting drunks lurching into the phone booth for an easy piss then hanging in the alley for a little slash n' stash, not when he knows the sickening truth that he'd be happier shooting spitballs at the rabbi's blackboard back in Hebrew school than slinging salami alongside his nocturnal old man, always surrounded, always outnumbered, always counting on food alone to calm the horde and ward off the slaughter. He's sick and woozy with the colonialist dread, worse than malaria: Some day, when will it be, they'll stampede, they'll come over the glass, and the few of us, we'll be trampled.

By three in the morning, it's grown from ten deep to 13 or 14 deep, the yells of hunger and anger have an edge sharp as the countermen's knives, sharp as jailhouse shanks; the drunkest and the baddest join the food fray in droves as the afterhours clubs shut down and dump the diehards into the streets, where the smells from the Blue Hill Deli stir them and pull them off the sidewalks the way the odor of passing antelopes stirs lions dozing in the African grass. Harold has never gripped a tennis racket but develops tennis elbow raking it in; he's nearing the Guinness record for cash register ka-chings. Jack is nursing two fingers he gashed from nerves, and sweet gospel Ollie, the choirboy dishwasher who never says a swear word, churns so hard at his tray-stacked machine he seems ready to melt and seep into the kitchen grease bucket they save for the hog farmer who in daylight will arrive in a stinking truck to carry off the swill.

Now that the Rupelman's bread man has come and taken Harold's signature on the post-midnight delivery bill for rolls, not another white face is expected until the first slices of light, pink as lox, begin to fall across the night sidewalk and mute the neon window script sizzling orange like the wires in a toaster. They will be shopkeepers and synagogue-goers, dour-faced, the prune juice customers who wear their felt hats indoors.

But the expected doesn't happen. And the white man who bursts in doesn't establish himself first off by race but rage. What turns everyone around to face the doorway he fills is the roar, the red-eyed, hopped-up, caveman war cry: Fock you niggas. I'm here to kill nigga. Kill fockin nigga. Fifty-two blacks, all but six of them men and some of these are men with Sonny Liston hands and cellblock scars. They all turn as one, this pastrami-hunting pack, and the four white Jews whipping them up grub for money, they turn and cease all sound and motion and sniff the wind, at that first instant not a mob or a solid human wall at all, just solo humans each in his own skin, stunned by the invasive brazenness, the raw demonic force of the threat, taking its measure, scoping where to duck when the barrel of the gun comes out.

None does, at least not yet. The intruder takes two lunging steps forward, and the crowd takes three steps back. He has that combat look, olive splotchy stuff and jungle boots, and he's big, thick, and dirty. In those first moments the least fearful are the four Jews, even Jack the simpering Hebrew School hipster. They have no concept of a posse, a lynch mob, even a one-man lynch mob, not in this country, never. But the deep Southerners, brawl-worthy as they may be, get stalled in the thicket of two entangling instincts: the urge to never lose a single hard-won inch in the food line, and the inbred, gone-but-not-forgotten dread of the raging negro-catcher, the plantation brute who could be packing a bullwhip and worse. Even way up in Boston, the fabled Underground Railroad town.

As for the four countermen, they all have carving knives in their hands. Any one of them except the student Jack could grab a chunk of meat and, in a blur rivaling a Hormel processing machine, hand-cut it into perfect paper-thin slices. But meat-slicing and man-slicing are worlds apart, so no one moves or even thinks of violence at such an extreme, and the only soul in the place who's not paralyzed and all frozen-eyed on the doorway monster is Ollie, oblivious and closed off by the kitchen door and the hissing, clanking, howling, deafening action of his infernal hydro-apparatus. This is the lull, the moment of surprise the intruder, whose old camouflage clothes are the genuine article—U.S issue, dispensed at the 38th Parallel—has been trained to take advantage of, and he cuts through the stalled mob like a bayonet, because he knows exactly where he's going. As he staggers for the kitchen, though, Harold notes from the shoulder carriage that this bull seems already at half-strength or worse, drained by whatever torrent of chemicals he's poured into himself and the marathon debilitations of his own uproar. His blood-hot eyes, his stench, say he hasn't slept for days; the dried blood on his lips and ears say he's been in battles all night or even all week.

Tha' moddafocka is mine. The mad soldier bellows this as he butts the kitchen door open, and something about his back and not his eyes being the new focal point for this crowd of threatened individuals releases the mass palsy, and every one of them, finally, each of the countermen and Jack, too, begin to stir and bond into an invaded, maligned collective (although they do this watchfully, more as a somber, violated citizenry than a screaming gang or war party) and mill and surge behind him. They see the soldier wrest the big foundry-cast handle out of the meat grinder; they see Ollie pull himself away from his tray-mopping and scouring and stacking; they see Ollie's stooped shoulders stiffen and turn, and his attention along with it, and they watch the horror pry open his eyes and bulge them like two poached eggs about to be impaled by a fork.

But a fork is nothing compared to the murderous weight of the meat-grinder handle whizzing through the steambath fog of the kitchen at Ollie's head. He bobs, and the steel hunk just misses and crashes into a freshly-scalded tray of dinner plates and saucers, shearing the restaurant china like a missile taking off the tops of buildings. Why him? Why Ollie? thinks Harold. But Harold's whole focus has always been the front of the place, the front door and who comes walking or waltzing or barging through it. He's the performer, the master of ceremonies—taste this potato salad, come on taste it, it's like ice cream—he only concerns himself with the spotlight and center stage, not the murk and backstage. So he's baffled.

Ollie, however, is anything but baffled. Even in the blood-draining instant when his head dodges the meat-grinder handle and he backs his haunches up for defense against his red-hot machine, the corner that blocks any chance of escape, even in the deadly blur of all this, his mind replays the weeks he and the grandfatherly Rufus, busboy since the Turn of the Century, have suffered the soldier's assaults on the bolted back door and grime-crusted bars of the dungeon-size kitchen window, the raving in the alley, the tossing and crashing of garbage cans, the soldier roaring through the window bars for a piece of food, for a piece of the job owed him that Ollie and all the motherfuckers like Ollie came north to steal while he, the soldier, was off across the ocean busting the Red chinks in Korea—yes he shouts to the sky above the alley—busting the Red chinks and saving Ollie's brown ass from the yellow A-bombs.

Now the crowd that had been knee-deep and swarming around the succulent meat vapors of the counter has bottled itself, the way pickles are bottled into a jar, between the jambs of one of the two entrances from the dining room to the kitchen. They've turned this doorway, the one Rufus pushes his Daddy LongLegs frame through when he's clearing tables, into an airtight impasse: dozens of sweating, muttering faces and craning necks behind it, dozens of mouths and stomachs that were oozing the juice of pastrami anticipation just moments ago now gape and curl and snarl, empty and unfed, their insides turned bilious by the flung weapon, the whizzing iron bludgeon that could have cracked the head of a brother.

But from where Ollie crouches, cornered by the soldier and the steel bulge of his own machine, the human sea jamming the doorway—as long as they only stand there and do nothing—is just one more blocked exit, a hole he cannot slip into, as is the other doorway as well, the one leading to the runway behind the counter. This portal is bottled up by white men, Harold, Jack and their two aproned comrades, Shivvie and Katz, the hired guns Harold won't permit even after eight years of faithful service to ring up a single, solitary sale because he wants their fingers busy with the pastrami and rolled beef and pickled tongue and nowhere near the sacred till.

To Jack, as usual, Ollie's imminent massacre is as much about himself as about the real victim. His mind is working rabbit-fast, and the sight of the soldier wading in on the slender, shuddering boy jerks his image-track back to the hour before midnight two weeks ago when he himself was in Ollie's shoes, challenged and bullied by a weightlifting behemoth on a dance floor, a hulk who snickered at Jack's pink hipster shirt, at his black shoes with the pink tassels and the dandyism of his dance moves as he boogied and swiveled with so much verve and polish, a better dancer than the girls—that was his talent, his curse. The weightlifter snorted and pawed, called Jack a fag, and the dance floor cleared, leaving just the two of them until Jack turned and ran. As he always ran.

However, when the soldier picks up a new weapon, a wooden kitchen mallet, and Ollie cringes and trembles, Jack feels something he never felt before. His heart bangs against the cage of his chest, and he has to fight against crying out, against sobbing like a child. He can't believe it, but he actually wants to jump in there—with Ollie—to stand at his side. But he can't budge, even when the mallet sails like a tomahawk, grazes Ollie's pate and clatters against a greasy girlie calendar pinned to the browning yellow wall. His feet feel glued to the spot on the floor where his shoes are planted. His arms feel weak as toothpicks, reduced from muscle to cartilage, his whole skeleton as insubstantial as a bird's. And this makes him want to sob all the more.

Out of all of them, the one who does step into the ring is the one who knows the ring, the way Harold knows the heel of a pumpernickel loaf. He's dipsy and twisty as a licorice stick, his blood is half Muscatel, and he jabs like a ghost of himself, but Dixon James is so nonchalant about trading punches, he weaves in with the Chesterfield snipe still tucked in his lips. And the geometry is written in his limbs, never to be erased: the jab is efficient and straight, and even though decrepitation and inebriation have shrunk the jab from an icepick to a toothpick, it still travels at professional speeds and stabs the crazed vet true in the right eyeball. The blow does its job, too, spinning the stung soldier towards his attacker and allowing Ollie to run into one of the two bottlenecked doorways, his instinct driving him like a paper clip to a magnet smack into the jampacked black gaggle as opposed to the four frowning whities who all have that storekeeper look.

Fock-in nigga. C'mon. C'mon you fock-a.

While the bout wrecks his kitchen, Harold curses the deductible and tries to strategize. He sorts the facts, of which three stand preeminent. First, all commerce has ceased, the cash register is still as death, and Harold feels this as he would feel his toenails being removed by pliers. Second, the prominence of the meat grinder handle and the wooden mallet suggests there is no gun and never was one. Meanwhile, Dixon the ancient wino middleweight-wasted-to-nothingweight has stuck the wild, wailing pig a half dozen more times, and the eyes, nose, and mouth are leaking blood like a lawn sprinkler. Harold has seen newsreels of bullfights, seen how the picadors stick and sap the monster until he bows his woozy head for the matador. But then there are the horns and the killer instinct and the chance, always the chance, for one last goring, killing swipe, and time and wine and Chesterfield smoke have taken enough away from Dixon, so when the swipe comes, he's an inch or two off his dance routine and the ganged-up faces, both white and black, wince for him and themselves as a thudding splat messes up Dixon's mouth, snuffs his stump of a cigarette and flattens his comeback, although his licorice legs manage to clamber back up and wobble on the once-natty, sole-flapping saddle shoes.

But the force of the roundhouse punch, just throwing it, has wounded the bull, too, commanding more energy than he can spare, and Dixon's last jab, which hit the Adam's Apple, has brought forth carmine-streaked vomit, and the soldier gags on this surging effluent as he tries to roar hate and suck oxygen into his smacked, suffocating windpipe, all at the same time. Harold watches him reel and falter, blood-blinded and gasping, and he makes a calculated estimation that now is matador time.

Unlike his babied son, Harold has been bounced around the schoolyard a few times, and his own father, Shmuel, was a blacksmith in the old country, and Harold retains, at least for one generation, a truncated version of the barrel back and smithy arms, arms bred for the Russian bearhug. This scenario, though, with the bull soldier lurching and bowing low, blinded by his own blood and choking on it, too, calls for a different hold, the old headlock-and-eye-gouge straight out of Boston Arena wrestling. As Dixon soft-shoes it for the sidelines, Harold charges out from the counter doorway, wades into the kitchen, and throws an arm-vice around the blood-soaked, exploding soldier-head, a head that surprises him for its sheer gorilla girth. Slapping open a canister he palms a fistful of black pepper, smears it across the eyes and kneads it with all the finger-force he can muster, and as the resulting scream hits the decibels of an air-raid siren, he locks the pepper hand on his other hand and constricts, grinding hardest against the gore-slick temples.

Fucked up my kitchen, fucked up a record night. This one thought—the irony of a packed house and a cold, silent cash register, a seeming impossibility—hops up Harold like a hypodermically needled race horse and makes him squeeze so hard the short-sleeve of his white deli shirt lifts, exposing the buttocks of the blue girlie tattoo. They inflate like twin blimps, then distend into disturbing shapelessness like conjoined amoebae or adjacent bodies of water on a map. He's so intent on squashing the gorilla melon he's holding, he doesn't hear the general muzz-muzz from the throng, now a somber Coliseum crowd chanting thumbs-down, demanding death to this gladiator motherfucker who burst in and shut things down when the pastrami was but inches from their lips. He also doesn't see beyond the blood-matted nest of hair in his arms—doesn't see the soldier's arm snaking out behind his back, fishing around like a tentacle, landing on a wooden case of empties and hoisting a root beer bottle out by the neck.

Harold doesn't see it, but Jack does, and for the first and maybe only time in all his life, the preconditions arise for Jack to act valorously as opposed to typically. It is a trifecta even he can't resist: filial yearnings stoked by crowd sentiment emboldened by the sight of the enemy captured and weakening. All at once, his veins gush the only solvent that can unglue his feet from the floor—courage—and he sprints from his haven in the doorway to the side of his grappling father, pounces behind the headlocked soldier, clamps a hammerlock on the free, mayhem-intent arm and pushes it up and up until the rising pain uncoils the soldier's fingers and the bottle, the cudgel of glass that was targeting Harold's skull, falls to the grimy concrete and shatters. I saved my father. I did. And in the very epicenter of the pandemonium, Jack feels calm, so at peace with himself that the blur of the two-on-one wrestling match appears to him as frames in slow-motion, each mote of time a still picture he can analyze and act on fearlessly. He of all men is the man in charge.

Harold, the matador, senses the change in the enemy, the deeper droop of the headlocked head, the sag of the entire torso, the moan of the depleted bull presenting his nape for the killing thrust. Harold nods to Jack and walks the spurting head forward two paces, and when he feels no resistance to speak of, he drags the head two paces more and employs it as a battering ram to part the doorway crowd, 52 partisans spitting with fury but nonetheless side-stepping the blood spray, not deeming it worth soiling their shiny weekend duds, not when the Jews are taking care of business themselves for a change.

Like a beast with three faces and six legs, Harold, Jack and the bent, pepper-blinded soldier they hold captive lumber through the gauntlet of blood-sniffers. Every couple of steps or so, Harold pulls his left fist out of the headlock, cocks it eight to ten inches and clubs and grinds the mass of raw, dissolving facial parts. He hits the mouth dead-center, but instead of stunning the groggy captive, it gives the demon inside the mouth new life. Fock-in nigga, it gasps blindly at the pale-faced Harold. I kill you fock-in nigga.

The words bring Reggie out of the crowd, in support of his friend Dixon. He takes a thick-glass sugar dispenser from a table and slams it home on the bridge of the soldier's gushing nose.

Yes, they shout. Yes, yeahh.

Fock-in nigga, comes the reply, automatic as a salute. But uttered rasping, as the soldier would utter it with his dying breath. And out the door to the cool rush of the sidewalk the three of them go. Harold stops the procession at the first lamppost, pounds the head into the post three times and releases it to the waiting curbstone and gutter. He and Jack jump back, the way you would if you had just shot a grizzly bear at close quarters. They scramble back into the deli just as a Boston Globe truck pulls up at the curbstone. Noticing only what appears to be a garden variety passed-out drunk, the driver tosses out the stack of morning papers, blaring stories of Truman, MacArthur, Inchon, The Yalu River, and another returning troop ship.

ANNA SIDAK

Myths of Minnesota

From October/November 2006

KATHLEEN, THE BABY'S mother, had moved a few feet away to window-shop the dime store. When she saw the Blackfoot couple reflected in the glass, she was afraid to turn, afraid to move.

The Blackfoot couple were tall and gaunt in denim, canvas, and elk-hide moccasins with the ways of their forefathers in their eyes— the forefathers who'd lived through the long battle for the hunting grounds, through the death of the buffalo—and through something new as well, for they'd left the slow starvation of the reservation to strike out on their own.

They took in the sights—the battered Fords, front wheels jammed against the sidewalk planks, listless horses shifting from foot to foot at the hitching rail, a barber's red-and-white spiraled pole—the forest primeval behind wooden storefronts—and were on their way out of town when they stopped beside the baby's carriage.

When their shadow fell on the baby, she smiled and opened her eyes.

"Papoose blue eyes!" they said, leaning over the carriage. "May not live through the winter."

They moved on down the street, the Blackfoot woman three paces to the rear, her thin shoulders dragged down by two ten-pound bags of potatoes.

When Kathleen saw they'd reached the end of the block and were crossing the street, she ran to the carriage and wheeled it in the opposite direction to the general store where JT was looking at hardware.

"They looked at her," she said.

"What if they did?"

"They could've kidnapped her. I'd never forgive myself—and all I did was look away for a moment."

"They can't feed their own. What would they want her for?"

"They just scare me."

"I need a new pickaxe," he said. "And a handsaw. Could use a cold-chisel." He bought ten pounds of potatoes and a pound of coffee.

JT Van Owen had no luck with his rented Idaho ranch—and after the misunderstanding with his landlord, verified by a two-year time-out in Walla Walla, he collected Kathleen and Daisy from Kathleen's family's farm in Missouri and took them to northern Minnesota, a land of enticing wilderness where he could try to live in the aftermath of his crime.

He doubled back on the trail of the Blackfoot, across the great plains and into the forest, the land of their cousins, the Ojibwa, from whom the Blackfoot had fled centuries before. There, he rented a tax-delinquent farm 12 miles from town with a lake and river outlet on the back forty, a pond in the pasture, and a stand of sugar maple.

He'd thought the Blackfoot of Idaho had once known how to live, before the Agency stepped in; he thought the Ojibwa of Minnesota, if he studied their ways, perhaps could show him a way to coexist with the known universe. He liked the way they could sleep in the woods—under a cedar to keep the rain off—make birch-bark baskets and draw pictures on them, or better yet—this was JT's spin—write a letter on one of the bark's thin layers and mail it to his sister in Omaha.

In Minnesota, the baby, now Daisy—short for Marguerite, her parents said—learned about crying: not to do it.

"Ojibwa put their bare-bottomed papooses in open-ended backpacks, and the babies never cry. Something to think about." But JT smiled when he said it—Daisy was well out of diapers—and showed her his footprints in the snow, straight as any Ojibwa, slightly pigeon-toed on the left.

"The Ojibwa work long hours in icy lakes to gather wild rice," he said. "They bend it over the gunwale and beat the grain into their canoes. They put it in brown paper bags that say Product of Minnesota, Harvested Wild. They tap maple trees and make syrup from the sap—sometimes sugar, too, although it takes forever—freezing their extremities in the process," just as he was to do that first early spring. "Why the Ojibwa Have No Tails," he called that story.

"There aren't any Ojibwa people around here now, are there?" Kathleen asked.

"Used to be some," JT said.

"They scalped people and stole their horses," Kathleen said to Daisy.

"Before the railroad, before game got so scarce," JT said.

"Good," Kathleen said, thinking, no doubt, of the Ojibwa who were gone now.

JT'd been hunting four days in a row with no luck. He was sore about it, but he told Kathleen and Daisy it was because Clote Scarpe, the Indian deity, had warned the animals.

"'When the hungry brother comes among you with the long stick from which fire strikes,' Clote Scarpe said to the deer, 'you must run.

You must hide,' he said to the snowshoe rabbit. He said nothing to the mink who had gone into disguise as ermine."

"Clote Scarpe is only who some Indians pray to," Kathleen said. "He's not real. There is only one real God."

"Clote Scarpe worked very well for the Ojibwa until the missionaries got here," JT said.

"When we lived in Idaho, the Blackfoot people came to look at you. Your eyes were bluer than anything. They'd never seen a blue-eyed baby," Kathleen said to Daisy. "They wanted to take you home with them, to keep you."

In Minnesota, land of the sky-blue water, Daisy's blue eyes were now seen to be brown. She quivered ever so slightly; she wanted her blue eyes back, wanted to be a marvel again to the Blackfoot.

"They didn't want anything of the kind," JT said. "And who can blame them?" He winked at Daisy. "We'll go and see the Ojibwa. We'll see how they live, now."

They drove many miles to the south, into the region of Mille Lacs. They drove slowly along beside the great water in JT's old Essex.

Across the highway from the lake were the wigwams of the Ojibwa. Racks of birch-bark baskets stood in front of the wigwams. Behind the wigwams were clotheslines. Alongside were the Ojibwa's Cadillacs and Chryslers.

"How they live!" Kathleen said.

"These people speak a language similar to that of the Blackfoot," JT said. He'd read up on the matter. "They are skillful at basket weaving and the making of birch-bark canoes."

The car lurched to one side. He turned off the engine and opened the car door.

Two braves came out of the wigwams and watched as he opened the trunk for the tools: the jack, the pump, the can of patches, the lug wrench.

"Need some help?" one asked.

"Thank you, but I'm in practice," JT said. "Second flat this week."

"Bad roads," said the other Ojibwa. "Bad weather too, but nice today."

Daisy looked at the Ojibwa through her fingers and made funny noises to show she was friendly. The Ojibwa paid no attention. She sulked.

"Daisy wants a drink of water," Kathleen said when JT got back in the car.

He recommended that Daisy "Shut up." They went home.

When Daisy was three, she went for a walk in the woods, moving silently, stealthily, like an Ojibwa. She had blue eyes again and wore the moccasins of Minnehaha, of Pocahantas, of Sacajawa. She wandered for many moons talking to the animals, sometimes listening to them. She stumbled and fell, tearing her dress, losing her shoes. The ground was cold. She was hungry. She went home.

"I thought maybe you hopped a freight for Chicago," JT said.

"I was afraid the Indians got you," Kathleen said.

Winter came. It grew cold and colder still.

"Just think," Kathleen said, "how those poor Indians down to Mille Lacs must suffer in weather like this."

"They don't live there in the winter," JT said. "They know better than to try to live through the winter in a summer wigwam."

"Where do they go, then?" Kathleen asked, already sorry she'd brought up the matter.

"They go south. They go to live in the city, probably. Minneapolis or St. Paul. Duluth."

Kathleen and Daisy gave him dark looks, as though wondering, Why don't we do that?

He went out to the woodpile and brought in more wood.

"Colder than blazes—" he began but thought better of it. "This would seem balmy to an Ojibwa."

Kathleen and Daisy put their hands over their ears.

It warmed up a little.

"Indian Summer," JT said.

He took Daisy for a walk in the woods. She saw partridge whirr into the blue sky from a thicket purple against melting snow. The white bark of birch tied the clouds of heaven to earth. They stopped to examine the tracks of rabbit and fox.

"This is God's country," JT said. "We'll plant potatoes in the spring.

The cold came back. The lake on the back forty froze over. JT went ice fishing and caught two small perch.

"Look at that!" he said. "Best fishing in the world, winter or summer."

He spent the rest of the day trying to warm up.

He went on snowshoes to Round Lake. There was a general store, a gasoline pump, and the post office where he picked up his WW1 disability check every month.

"I mean to plant potatoes in the spring," he said to Larson, the storekeeper.

Larson shook his head. "Too rocky for potatoes. You got the old Willows place—it was the rocks set Charlie Willows off that time, they say."

"Found out who used to live here," JT said to Kathleen at supper that night. "Fellow name of Willows—after they sent him away, he got loose, came back here and dispatched his wife and the other three kids. There'd been a four-year drought and all the game was gone. They were starving. He was half Indian, but his wife was from Armenia. They didn't take him alive."

"Oh, my," Kathleen said. "Right here?"

"Larson said an odd thing. He said, 'They don't come by and bother you folks none, do they?'"

When the potato planting began, JT said, "You plant them with the eyes up so they can see. Glaciers left the rocks." There were many rocks.

Kathleen thought there were too many rocks. She took time off from potato planting to plant the gladioli bulbs given her by their nearest neighbor, the old Armenian who lived alone a mile away in the log cabin he'd built soon after fleeing the massacres of his homeland. He'd had a wife and daughter years ago, he said, grandchildren, but they were gone now. Kathleen planted rhubarb, and strawberries to temper the rhubarb, while Daisy followed her father across the potato field with a pail of water, pouring a cupful into each hill.

Kathleen's gladioli reached six feet. Their funeral blooms swayed above the green leaves and red stems of rhubarb, above the white blossoms and green leaves of strawberries. She began to think about irises. Back home in Missouri, she'd have visited the Bethel graveyard, given those poor crowded rhizomes a fresh start by removing a few.

But when the time came to harvest JT's potatoes, half turned out to be rocks. When he was fooled that way, he thought of Charlie Willows. Sometimes he looked over his shoulder.

"No more than 12 bushel," he said to Kathleen at supper. "Please pass the potatoes."

"What else is there?"

He ignored her question and poured maple syrup over his hash-browned potatoes. He'd tapped 30 trees while three feet of snow remained on the ground, cutting a trail along the lake and into the woods. He'd boiled the sap down to syrup in a large sheet metal pan with wooden ends set over a fire-pit.

"There was an Ojibwa up near Kouderay," he said, for he was thinking of a story he'd heard as a boy from his father, who'd been a teacher and knew many stories.

"An Ojibwa medicine man. When this medicine man was told two braves were missing from the village, he asked that a special wigwam be built, just large enough to stand in."

Kathleen got up and began to clear the table.

"When it was finished," JT continued, addressing Daisy, "he went in and asked that it be set afire. It blazed up around him and he fell forward out of the flames onto the ground. In a little while, he came to, sat up, and said, 'You will find our brothers on the north shore of the small lake trapped beneath a pine that fell during the storm.' The villagers went to that place, which was six miles distant, and found the braves, still alive but unable to free themselves."

Daisy threw her plate on the floor and began to shriek.

"Now see what you've done," Kathleen said.

"I don't know why she's bawling," JT said, and felt the shiver he always felt when he thought of the burning wigwam.

NANCY SAUNDERS

Molding Reality

From January/February 2006

IT WAS A cold, January night. The trestle tables (kindly loaned to us by Mrs. Jean Webster) were set a-dazzling with every color and vintage of cheese imaginable, and the wine—well, there was the taste of something there to suit every gullet. The evening was set for a most enviable time, every vittle available to set the heart-a-fire and loosen the tongue to many a mushroom tale.

The hearty turnout soon plunged eagerly into the fray, and before too long, there was nothing left but a handful of discarded water biscuits and a green olive or two. Then it was time to get down to business. There was a slight delay when the lights needed to be turned down, and the pavilion manager (in charge of all the electric controls) could not be found for love nor cheese. Finally, he was located outside, ploughing his field of Turnips (rather late in the year, I felt, but I was not in the mood to quibble). The delay was no trouble—Mrs. Marie Arbutt came to the rescue with a delightful selection of homemade truffles. We were all... speechless.

Finally, the lights were dimmed and the show began. Those coming to the meeting expecting a lecture on gastronomic fungi (entitled "Introduction to the Gasteromycetes") were not disappointed. The slide show was a HUGE success. We were treated to a whirlwind tour of the fascinating (and sometimes mind-blowing) world of stomach fungi. We looked at the personality and behavior of this group (as well as the behavior of those who study them!). A heated discussion then followed as to whether *Suillus sphaerosporus* was beautiful or not, and most agreed that, if not beautiful, then at least it qualified as handsome.

It was only when our own photographer, Mr. Jack Bernard, brought out a box of slides that had been water damaged in a flood, that the evening turned. We were surprised to find that many of his slides had undergone a most incredible transformation. While they had been stored in a damp, dark basement, a fungus had chosen to colonize them! And after close inspection, we discovered the fungus to be *Aspergillus*, which seemed to have given a poignancy to the otherwise ordinariness of Mr. Jack Bernard's slides.

We were much impressed by the strange and wonderful swirls and mists created by the fungus throughout Mr. Jack Bernard's slides, and there were plenty of admiring Ooh's and Aah's lifting up in waves around the darkened room.

Then we came to one particular slide, and the room hushed to heavy silence. It was a picture of Jamie Bernard, Mr. Jack Bernard's son—then only a young boy of nine or ten. And this is what Mr. Bernard said to us, as he straightened his shoulders and lifted his gaze towards us:

"When people look at an original photograph of my son, they usually see a cute boy with a sad look in his eyes. What they don't experience is the range of emotions that the same image provokes in me. Now, because of the fungus, you see the same picture, but one which has taken on a new meaning, as if it touches a secret wound in your hearts, too."

We stood, then, and sang. I think it was Mrs. Vanderhilt who started us off with "I will never forget." We all joined in, each and every one of us, until our words lifted right up from the bottom of our hearts, rich, full and vibrant, floating Heavenwards, towards Mr. Jack Bernard's little boy.

ETHEL ROHAN

Saturday Girl

From April/May 2012

I AM 13-years-old and the summer Saturday girl at The Punnet, a mostly pensioners' hair salon located on the Old Circular Road, Manchester, England. I have no idea why the hair salon is named The Punnet. The salon owner, Teresa Murray, is nice enough, but not the type I feel I could ask such a question. My name's Viv, but the other kids mostly call me Tintin. I've a huge hooked nose, like some prehistoric bird's beak. The kids tease that my nose could open a tin of peas.

Mum says we have to know what's true. What's true is all that matters, Mum says.

"Could your nose open a can of peas?" Mum asked that afternoon after school when the nickname Tintin first took hold.

"No, of course not," Mum said. "See?"

I was seven and almost choked on my snot and the crash of my breath.

Saturday girl at the hair salon is my first ever job. I mostly shampoo the old dears, make them tea and biscuits, tidy the magazines, and sweep the floor bald. I also take out the pins and curlers for those getting sets and perms. Of all my tasks at the salon, I most like to brush Mrs. Dabney's tea-brown wig. The wig looks alive on my left hand, warm and moving and shining. I love that I don't have to worry about making small talk to the wig or causing the hairpiece harm or getting anything too much wrong. My least favorite task is when I have to rub wet cigarette ashes into the hairline of the women getting colors so the telltale dye won't bleed into their skin. I hate to touch the wet ashes and rub the foul black paste against the old women's papery skin. I worry I'll tear right through to blood and brain.

These past three weeks, every Monday morning, I take the Number Ten bus into town and visit the record shop. After I give two pounds to Mum toward housekeeping and one pound to Dad towards savings, I have two pounds left over from my Saturday wages to buy a 99-pence vinyl single, two magazines, and three bars of caramel chocolate. Last Monday, I bought Shakin' Stevens's "Green Door." Side B of the single is "Don't Turn Your Back." I've played both songs so often this past week, Mum and Dad say the record needle has gone through them, leaving grooves in their brains. While the songs float out like apparitions from the record player and into my bedroom, I dance in front of my wardrobe mirror. Sometimes, when I dance a certain way, I look almost lovely.

Last Saturday night, Mum and Dad finally allowed me to go to the youth club disco in the local school hall.

"If I'm old enough to work, I'm old enough to go to the kids' disco."

Of course Dad insisted on driving me to the hall and coming inside to check things out. He also shouted above the music before he left, telling what felt like everyone that he'd be back at ten sharp to take me home.

I joined my friends in the corner. I suppose, according to Mum's "what's true" tests, they're not really my friends. They didn't even pretend to care that I'd showed up. I just thought maybe, it being my first disco and all. Some of the older boys sniggered while I danced and teased me because I was out on the floor on my own. I wasn't alone, though, I was with the Beatles and the Stones and Madonna and Michael Jackson and Shakin' Stevens. When Spandau Ballet played "I'll Fly for You," I forgot anyone else was in the place. I think at one point in the chorus, I might have flapped my arms, and that's why Billy Barsden pointed and hooted.

Later, when I went into the girls' room, a boy hid in the last cubicle with Mary Martin. I recognized her red shoes with spiked heels. Mary and the boy grunted together like they were in pain. Then murmured like they were eating something delicious. In my head, I heard Mum's voice, "You don't drop your knickers for anyone, you hear me?"

First thing my fourth Saturday at The Punnet, Mrs. Dabney arrives to exchange her wigs. She has two wigs in constant rotation at the salon. The wig she drops off this morning is the older and sadder of the two, and it feels like a dog's coarse coat until I work my magic. While I brush the freshly shampooed hairpiece, I wonder what Mrs. Dabney's head looks like without her wigs. I see another flash of Granddad, that one time I had to help Mum lift him from the bathtub. My stomach sickens, thinking how Mrs. Dabney's bald head with stray hairs probably looks like Granddad's ball sack. Granddad's ball sack won't get out of my head, how it floated in soap scum on gray bathwater like something dead.

Mid-afternoon, Mrs. Roche appears for her weekly wash and dry. Mrs. Roche is the largest woman I've ever encountered, and she smells of vinegar. She likes to be shampooed hard and to have her scalp scrubbed. She likes to feel my fingernails.

Mrs. Roche moans while I wash her hair and massage her scalp.

"That's the girl," she says. "Get in there. Don't be afraid. I don't hurt too easy."

"That's it. Harder. Harder." She sounds like something gathering speed and about to take off.

Mrs. Roche also insists I towel-dry her hair with every last ounce of my strength. I go at her until my shoulders ache and arms feel like they're about to drop off.

"You've more in you than that," she says.

I feel all eyes in the salon on me. Teresa and the three other old dears shake their heads and hide smirks behind their hands and steaming cups of tea.

Mrs. Roche lets out a terrible roar. I pull the towel from her head.

"My ear," she shrieks.

Blood drops from her spilt earlobe and onto the shoulder of her ivory woolen cardigan. I've ripped out her earring. Teresa abandons her client and flaps and fusses over Mrs. Roche. She orders me onto all fours to find Mrs. Roche's gold stud earring and backing. I say sorry so many times I sound like one of my vinyl singles going round and round.

At the end of the workday, Teresa holds back three pounds from my wages, the amount of the discount she'd given to Mrs. Roche "on account of all the trouble." That leaves me with just two pounds for a nine-hour shift.

"I'm sorry," Teresa says, "but I think I have to let you go."

"I'm afraid you're just not as sharp as I'd like," she continues.

I drag myself toward home in the sunshine amidst the buttery rush of people and fumes of smoking cars. In the distance, St. George's church bells ring out six o'clock. I try to hear what Mum would say, what she'd try to get me to see as true and not true, but I can't lower the needle onto the right vinyl. All I hear are the echoes of the church bells, clinging to the afternoon air.

GOKUL RAJARAM

The Boy With The Hole In His Head

From January/February 2003

"HE HAS A hole in his head," Vivek's mother says, pointing at the boy. Her words startle Vivek out of his reverie. Groggy after the 20-hour SFO-DEL flight, he is ruminating moodily upon the capriciousness of Indian customs officials. Upon landing at Delhi airport three hours ago, he had endured an interminable wait at customs, culminating in a $50 payoff to the inspecting officer.

Fifty US dollars.

It still rankles him, especially because it was ten dollars just two years ago.

She calls out to the boy. "Raju, *idhar aao!* Come here!" The boy comes unresistingly. When he reaches them, he bends his head, as if on cue, and Vivek looks down in spite of himself.

Holy shit. There it is. But...

"There's a plastic strip covering it," he says.

His mother is miffed. What does he expect? The poor boy can't very well walk around with an open hole, can he? She pats the boy's head, asks him to run along home. The boy doesn't budge, instead stretching out his hand. "What? You want money?" she is incredulous. He nods. Vivek cuts her off before she can chastise the boy. "Ma, it's not his fault," Vivek says. "Here, *yeh lo,* take this." He hands the boy a 50-*rupee* note.

Thanks for the peep show, bud.

His mother flushes red at Vivek's intransigence, then swings around and angrily walks back into the house. Vivek turns back to the boy, who is staring thunderstruck at the note. The boy is wearing the universal uniform of street urchins: tattered undershirt, shorts, bare feet. He is 12 years old, 13 at most.

"Uh... Raju. Bye." Vivek says. He waves and picks up his suitcases. The boy waves back. As Vivek enters the house, he looks back. The boy is still waving.

That night, Vivek dreams he is watching *Tom and Jerry* on television, the episode in which Tom uses a band-aid to stanch a breach in the Hoover dam. Except that Tom is Vivek, and the Hoover dam is not a dam at all, it's Raju, his head bursting at the seams, as Vivek-Tom tries frantically to stem the flow of blood. It is of no avail, the tiny plastic strip is utterly ineffective, and the head-dam bursts completely, leaving Vivek-Tom awash in blood. It clogs his nostrils, gets in his eyes, fills his mouth so he can feel its tangy taste. He tries to scream but only swallows more blood.

Vivek wakes up sweating. He doesn't get much sleep after that.

Parvati watches Raju. How peaceful he looks asleep. He used to love reading. He would read English books, lots and lots of them. She would pick up books for him whenever one of the sahibs threw their children's books away. She was never prouder in her life than when Rawat-sahib called to tell her that her son was selected for the school's top scholarship; she promised to herself that day that Raju would not turn out a *dhobi* like her, would not spend his life washing and ironing and delivering other people's clothes.

But that was before Bhagwan entered Raju. Parvati refuses to believe Raju fell from his bicycle and pierced his head on an iron rod. Oh, no. She knows it's God. He has snuck into her child and struck him dumb. The hole in Raju's head is Bhagwan's point of entry, and when Bhagwan is done taking residence in her child, he will exit the same way he entered. One day, just like that, he will be gone, and her Raju will be all right, brilliant and bubbly and talkative as ever. He will.

"Raju!" The shout rouses her from her trance. She gathers herself and comes out of the *jhuggi*, or shanty, where she lives with Raju, the baby, and her husband. Her emaciated face breaks into a smile when she sees Vivek. Her family ate well for two whole days off the 50 *rupees* Vivek gave Raju. Last night, she even slipped in a little *kheer* as a treat. Sweet rice pudding was his favorite, and Raju-Bhagwan ate it happily.

Bhagwan, if I have appeased you, please leave my child. Please make him whole again.

Vivek asks her about Raju. How did he get the hole in his head? Of course she doesn't tell him the real story. He'd think she's crazy, just like her husband does. Why doesn't Raju go to school? The school thinks he can't learn any more, that nothing will penetrate his brain. She knows better, knows he can do it—how can he not, with Bhagwan inside him?—if they only give him a chance. What does she want for Raju? She wants him to go to school, of course. "I want him to escape this life, *sahib*," she says.

Vivek tells her he will try and talk to Rawat-sahib, the Principal, about a job for Raju. Maybe the job could morph into something more. She is absurdly grateful. As he leaves, he gives her another 50-*rupee* note. "For Raju," he says.

An hour later, Parvati goes shopping. She knows her husband will shout at her for missing the scheduled laundry pick-up at the Grewal residence, but she doesn't care. She comes back laden with vegetables, rice, flour for rotis and puris, and of course, milk for *kheer*. Her family will eat well tonight. Bhagwan is taking care of them through Vivek, his emissary. She is happier than she has been in years.

That night, Parvati dreams that Bhagwan is finally leaving Raju's head, leaving to reside elsewhere. She watches the plastic piece fly off his head as Bhagwan exits in an ectoplasmic shimmer. Raju smiles at her and his lips move. Is he speaking? But the dream remains maddeningly silent. Very slowly, she starts leaning forward to see if the hole is still there.

Please, bhagwan, let it be gone let it be gone let it be gone.

And then Raju is screaming uncontrollably.

She wakes up with a start. The baby is crying. She feeds it and does not go back to sleep.

Vijay Rawat is intrigued when Saini, his assistant, announces a visitor. Nobody comes to see Rawat at his office. Not parents, not teachers, not students. Not unless they are stupid or desperate. He sees people when he wants to see them, not the other way round.

He looks up at the framed school logo on his wall. English Convent School. An incongruous name, since the school is not Catholic, nor is English the primary medium of instruction—that honor goes to Hindi. He is passionately proud of everything about the school, including the name. Especially the name, which he chose himself. Where are all those naysayers who predicted ten years ago that the fledgling school, started by Vijay Rawat, high school dropout, would amount to nothing? Where are those doubters now that English Convent is the largest and most profitable private school in town?

He knows how to run a school, oh, yes, he does. Case in point: the teachers who tried to start a union two years ago. He had been a nice guy, had tried reasoning with them. They remained mule-headed. So he made a few phone calls, the erring educators were paid a visit, and there was no more talk of a union. Since then, fear has been an integral part of his administrative toolkit.

He knows of his visitor. Vivek Kapoor. Captain Kapoor's son. Army brat, lives in the States. He knows Kapoor's type only too well. The brat probably thinks he exists on a different plane from Rawat, probably has no respect for his elders, probably will call Rawat "Vijay," a moniker nobody but Rawat's mother uses. Well, Rawat will show him what.

"Mr. Rawat?" Vivek's hesitant question jolts him out of his musings. Vivek is apologetic. He explains he has disturbed Mr. Rawat's undoubtedly busy schedule to ask for a huge favor, namely, a job for Raju Kumar. Surely Mr. Rawat remembers Raju? He was a student at English Convent before his unfortunate accident. Raju is a good kid, a hard-working kid. He can do odds-and-ends tasks for Mr. Rawat, be useful around the school. He hopes Mr. Rawat will give Raju a chance.

Rawat seethes.

The brat's trying to feel me up for a job!

He's about to refuse curtly when he realizes Vivek has unknowingly touched upon his weak spot. Saini is a completely incompetent assistant, and Rawat suspects Saini might even be a little corrupt. If only he wasn't Rawat's wife's sister's husband. He remembers Raju. The boy has a hole in his head. His accident was a bad turn of events for the school; the boy had great potential and would undoubtedly have done well in the national boards. Hiring the boy might put some pressure on Saini, signal to him that he cannot take his job for granted.

So he asks Vivek to send Raju to meet with him tomorrow. He might have something for him. Vivek thanks him profusely. Rawat watches him leave with a certain satisfaction.

What do you think now, brat? Do you respect me now? Ever thought you'd have to call me Mr. Rawat, brat? I'm as good as you.

That night, Rawat dreams he is addressing students at the morning assembly, as he does each day. Out of the corner of his eyes, he sees Raju waiting in the wings. Before Rawat can react, Raju walks slowly to the center of the stage and turns around to face the audience. A gasp goes up. The entire top of his head is covered with a gigantic piece of plastic. He grabs one end of the strip and starts peeling it off. It makes a ripping sound as it comes off, taking with it slivers of skin, strands of hair, drops of blood. The plastic strip is almost off now, the hole is partly visible, there it is... and then Raju is screaming with horrible, mind-blowing pain.

Rawat wakes up drenched in sweat. He spends the rest of the night tossing and turning.

Saini is upset. He has a good thing going at English Convent, and this *saala,* this bastard, this idiot mute, is ruining it. Saini is the defacto gatekeeper for school admissions. Parents pay him to get admission interviews for their children. They also pay him to cover up their progeny's escapades, and on a couple of occasions, to convert a grade from "F" to "D." But Saini's bread-and-butter, the way he makes most of his money, is arranging admission interviews. Access to Rawat's ear, recommending who to interview and who not to, is worth a lot of money. Saini's three-story house is testament to that.

Of course, he takes extreme precautions to keep the payments on the down and low. Rawat demands absolute loyalty from everyone who works for him. Saini quails to think what might happen should Rawat get a whiff of how, he, Saini, is running the admissions process.

But now a few parents are discovering an alternate route to get to Rawat. Both Dr. Taneja and Mr. Makhija used Raju as their emissary to set up admission interviews for their children, slipping a letter in Raju's pocket to take to Rawat, thus bypassing Saini entirely. It is only a matter of time before word spreads around town, before prospective parents see Saini more as a hindrance than a resource and cut him out completely. Things are getting out of hand. And the urchin is at the epicenter of it.

Saini is too scared of Rawat to say anything to him directly. When he complains to his wife that Raju is slacking off on his job, asks her to convey it to Rawat through her sister, she comes back and relays to Saini that Rawat actually likes Raju, has taken a shine to his uncomplaining, quiet efficiency.

This is getting out of hand. I must...

"Saini!" Rawat's shout cuts short his ruminations. Rawat, as is his style, cuts to the chase, asks him what he thinks of Raju.

Sir, he is a lazy idiot. Sir, we should fire him immediately. I can find ten boys better than him.

Before Saini can articulate his thoughts, Rawat tells him he is considering getting Raju to enroll part-time in the school. There is a lot of good in the boy, Rawat says—that brat Vivek Kapoor, despite all his character flaws, seems to have been a good judge of character—and the boy will return loyalty with loyalty. He, Rawat, will think about it some more before making a decision. He then dismisses Saini peremptorily.

Saini is stunned. The boy is attacking his livelihood, is kicking him where it hurts. That this urchin off the street, this son of *dhobis*, this walking freak—the hole in Raju's head both fascinates and repulses Saini—can do this to him, Rakesh Saini, is unthinkable. He must act.

That night Saini dreams he is an announcer at a circus side-show with Raju the main attraction. "Come see the eighth wonder of the world! The boy with the hole in his head!" People are paying Saini money to gain admission to the cage where he has the *saala* locked up.

And then, somehow they switch places.

Saini suddenly finds himself locked in the cage, a large plastic strip attached to his head. He starts scratching at the strip, trying to rip it off. It seems welded to his scalp. He will surely die even if he manages to take it off. There, he has it partly off, he can feel the edges of the hole. But the pain is incredible, and even as he marvels at the hole in his head, he finds himself screaming in more pain than he has ever experienced in his life.

Saini wakes up abruptly. He knows what he must do.

Raju is bewildered. The last three weeks have been a blur. First he met Vivek-sahib, then his mother told him that Vivek-sahib had found him a job at English Convent. He has tried to make his mother happy, has tried to work hard and do his best.

Rawat-sahib is happy with him, he knows it by the way Rawat-sahib pats him on the head and says *Shabash,* well-done. But Saini-sahib is not pleased, Saini-sahib does not like him, he knows it by the way Saini-sahib constantly glowers at him. Why? Raju doesn't know.

Once upon a time, he was a student at this very school. He remembers people applauding him, remembers Rawat-sahib patting him for something other than bringing him lunch on time. But those details are as dim as a ray of light from the depths of a dark cave, and after some moments trying to recollect sharper images from his pre-blackness life, Raju gives up. He has internalized the fact that since the blackness, he is now a new person leading a new and different life.

He was cycling to school that day. His friend Bunty pointed to something, it might have been a shiny new car or a funny advertisement on the side of a bus, he can't remember now, and Raju turned his head for an instant, and then the blackness descended.

He woke up feeling as if a million hot needles were piercing his head. He cried continuously because of the pain, till it became a part of him and he stopped. He could feel an emptiness, a vacuum in his head, and then Doctor-sahib did something, and the emptiness was gone, replaced by the alien piece of plastic.

Initially he tried pulling at it, tried itching it, tried scratching it. It remained implacably attached to his scalp. Slowly, over a period of months, he made peace with it, with the sporadic bouts of blackness that descend on him, with the sudden shooting pains in his head, with the four tablets he swallows each day. Not so the neighborhood kids, who were his friends a lifetime ago. They taunt him. "Mute idiot! Mute idiot!" they shout. Raju avoids them. Eat-sleep. Eat-sleep. The routine was comforting, familiar, and he was content.

Until Vivek-sahib showed up.

"Raju!" he hears Rawat-sahib's voice, and obediently walks into the office. He is surprised to see Saini-sahib. They look at him strangely as he comes in, and he is suddenly scared.

Rawat-sahib asks Raju if he, Raju, has anything to tell him.

Raju shakes his head, puzzled.

Rawat-sahib asks him the same question repeatedly.

Raju shakes his head harder each time.

What is Rawat-sahib talking about?

Finally, when it appears they are at an impasse, Saini-sahib suggests that they search Raju's tiny cupboard in the school basement. Raju is puzzled but confident, confident because there is nothing in the cupboard worth taking, besides a few odds and ends—pencil sharpeners, empty water bottles, that kind of stuff—he has found lying around the school.

Saini and Joginder, Rawat's bodyguard, walk Raju between them, Rawat a few steps behind. They reach the tiny cupboard, Saini throws it open, and there it is: 2,000 *rupees* in plain view.

Saini turns triumphantly to Rawat. Rawat looks grim but peculiarly downcast.

"From my office?" Rawat asks Raju. Raju is suspended in fear; he is unable to nod or shake his head.

Rawat whispers something to Saini and Joginder, and they nod. Raju wants to speak more than anything he ever wanted. He wants to shout, Rawat-sahib, it wasn't me!, but no words come out, and he can only struggle futilely as Joginder slings him on his shoulder like a sack of grain and strides away.

Raju does not dream that night.

Vivek's phone rings at work. It is his mother. It must be midnight in India, he thinks, she will never call him unless there is something wrong. She seems to be struggling for words. "Vivek, Raju..."

"What about Raju? Ma, tell me!"

The words come tumbling out in a rush. Raju didn't come home yesterday afternoon. When Parvati went to English Convent to check on Raju, they told her he had left for home at the usual time. Vivek's mother helped Parvati file a police report yesterday evening. Today morning, the police called. They had found him. His body was completely unharmed.

"But his head—his head—Vivek, the plastic strip was ripped open," his mother says. "I can't even bear to think how painful it must have been for him. He must have died horribly."

Vivek's mouth has gone dry.

"I'm worried about Parvati," his mother continues. "She keeps repeating how happy she is that God has left Raju's body. She thinks he must have gotten into a fight, maybe with the boys who make fun of him."

Vivek doesn't say anything. He feels incapable of speech.

"Mr. Rawat has been very nice. He was really concerned about Raju's disappearance yesterday, and he came by the *jhuggi* this evening to offer his condolences," his mother says. "He offered Parvati's husband a janitor's job at the school. They could not thank him enough."

PADMA PRASAD

The Same Story

From July/August 2004

WHEN HE WAS 23 years old, Pandu went across the Godavari River to get his wife.

He was a quiet young man, this Pandu. And, he had not made any girl from anywhere pregnant.

He had a red complexion that came from his mother. He was a bit short. He had always eaten sour curd rice in his big, dented silver bowl, no matter what they were cooking in the house. When he smiled, it was as if all the happiness in this world began from his face. When he was angry, he went with a stick to the fields and found seven or eight snakes and killed them each with a blow. He had a good head for languages. Just once, he visited Madras and came back with a mouthful of Tamil words. Even English, he knew some of the words, enough to talk with, though he stopped school in the middle of the eighth grade. His father and his father's father could trust him to hold onto a harvest and bring the cattle home.

It was a huge journey, this crossing the river to an island village many miles away. But the wind from the water rose like an excitement in the brain, and the vermilion sky was bold with color. Inside the boat the bridegroom sat in ordinary clothes, his eyes a little red from looking at the glamour of the river.

Next to him sat Maya, his first cousin from Madras. She was fourteen. She wore a parrot green city shirt with a v-neck revealing the new shadows of her just grown chest. He was becoming irritated with her questions.

"So," she said as if she had lived with him all his life, "how do you feel now, to be getting married and all?"

His head moved slowly.

"Did you get to see her? If you want, I will go and see her and tell you what she's like as soon as we get there. Do you want me to do that or not?"

He slid the little window of the cabin so some wind would come in.

When she was small and came during the summer vacations, he had tied a rope swing for her from the roof, and then when she was tired of that, she trailed behind him in the fields and climbed the mango trees with a fervor he understood. But now the sweat poured from his forehead and wandered down his back, and his hands had to be still.

"What happens if you don't like her after you see her? Answer me, Pandu, you have to tell me the truth, what are you going to do then?"

"That will not happen."

"How will that not happen? It can happen as much as it can not happen."

"Here, it is like that. My mother has seen her. My father has also seen her."

"You cannot simply be happy with that."

"Here it is like that. You tell me now, when are you going to grow your hair? Last time you came, you promised you will not cut it."

She laughed. "It's too hot, you know. And the friends in my class all have bobbed hair."

"Who will marry you then, if you go about looking like a boy?"

"Stop that. All you people ever think of here is getting married."

She ran away to the top of the boat, where the rest of the wedding party talked, smoked, and joked, oblivious of the mighty sunset. The wind was moist and smelled of silk, fish, cigarettes, and women.

Back in Pandu's village, his grandfather sat beneath the hundreds-of-years-old *neem* tree. In its shadows were his deepest thoughts. He felt his age diminish when he breathed the wind filtered by its leaves.

For some time he watched the very pregnant goat tied to one of the pillars of the verandah. Then he called Maya's six-year-old sister, Sumi. She had refused to go on the boat, and her mother had stayed behind with her.

"Come here. Get that little stool and sit beside me," the grandfather said. "And tell me again that story of the President and you."

The child obeyed at once. She was a round, well-fed child, her face filled with such innocence, you could not resist pinching her cheeks.

"How many times you want to hear the same thing?" she said.

"Never mind, you tell me."

She adjusted her frock over her knees and began. "Once upon a time, when I went to Washington, I met President Kennedy. We both went for a walk. On the way, we saw Mrs. Indira Gandhi."

"Who's that?"

"Indira Gandhi, don't you know, our prime minister. The three of us went and got some ice cream. Just then, a man came with a gun and tried to shoot. But I threw my ice cream into his face, and he fell down. So the president said I should go to the White House. But we lost the way and went into a deep and dangerous forest." She broke off at this point, staring at the goat.

"Look, Thaatha, look, the goat, something terrible is happening to the goat."

Pandus' grandfather looked at the goat, who was now moaning and stamping about.

"She's going to have the baby, that's what the fuss is about. You continue your story now."

"No. She's crying so much. It's paining for her. Do something, no?"

"She'll be alright, that's how it is. Go on with the story, now."

"I want to go to my mother."

"Here, this is for you. Go to your mother, if you want." The grandfather plucked five seedless grapes from a bunch in the bowl near his chair and gave them to her. The goat continued to moan for half an hour. The grandfather shooed away the flies and stared down the dusty road, where an occasional farmer or laborer passed by, folding his hands respectfully as he went along. Crows were up in the *neem* tree, eating its bitter berries. They dropped the seeds and cawed till he almost dozed off.

There was a struggling sound. The mother had finally pushed out the sac with the baby goat. For a few minutes it hung from her and then reached the ground with a soft little thud, spattering some discolored blood and fluid. The tiny goat pushed suffocatingly against the sac and hurried to stand up. Again and again its knees buckled. When it finally stood, it was puzzled by its achievement; its legs splayed outward, and it tried out the capacity of its throat. It made a high *maeaeh* sound and swiveled its neck in many directions. Then it was back on the ground. The mother goat waited beside her effort.

It was almost lunchtime. The grandfather got up with great difficulty from his easy chair and stretched himself. He went into the house and into the back.

Sumi's mother was lounging on a camp cot with other female relatives. They were looking at wedding saris and each other's jewellery.

"See if there is a servant or laborer," the grandfather said. "Ask them to get some hay and wipe the new goat."

Everyone scattered before him.

Then he went to his bedroom safe. He took out the big key tied around his waist and opened the iron door. On the top shelf, amidst the neat piles of bank notes, there was a blue velvet case, which he opened. He carefully lifted the magnifying glass inside. This glass was made in France, and the grandfather had bought it from a man who smuggled French cigarettes from the neighboring French territory of Yanam. It had an ornate silver handle. He went through the house to the goat. On the way, he said, "Where is Sumi? Tell her the baby goat has come. Ask her to come and see the baby goat."

The goat mother was now sitting down, and her face looked different. The little baby was on its knees. Pandu's grandfather peered through the magnifying glass. He lifted the face and studied the nostrils, the ears, and the shape of the eyes. He lifted the tail and looked under.

Then he patted its head. For a moment his long graceful fingers stroked the neck. "You're a beautiful girl," he said.

Sumi crept forward to touch the back of the goat.

Weddings in that village usually took place at 12:59 AM.

Or such a time during the night, like 2:26 AM.

"I can't keep awake," Maya complained to her aunt. "Why do they do such things? How can anyone keep awake?"

"Don't worry, the drums will not let you sleep. What will you do when you get married, I don't know."

"My stomach is paining."

"Then go and lie down."

Earlier in the day, Maya was asked to see her cousin-to-be. The girl sat with her face down and would not say a word to Maya. She was very fair, and her hair reached below her waist.

Many thoughts jammed into Maya's head:

The mother is dark brown, the father is just a lighter shade of that.
The island is a hot island, but this girl is so white?
All the novels I have read tell me you are the ice maiden.
Pandu, poor cousin Pandu does not look like a great lover.
I can help you, you know, if only you will tell me something.
I can easily get a picture of my cousin for you.
But you look frozen beyond fear.
Pandu is not taller than you. If you stand up, I can be surer of that.
His mother is a little dangerous, even I get worried.
How you will manage with her?
My grandmother once told me, women are like flowers.
But you are a sad, drooping flower. Why?
You don't want this marriage, or not.
If I had lived here, I would be married by now.
No, no, no. I can't be older than you.
Plus, I have to finish school and go to college.
I'm thinking of journalism all the time.

It was silent in the room. Finally, Maya's aunt said, "You must be hungry, no?"

That was when Maya ate the shrimp cooked with cashew nuts and all those sweets and developed the stomach pain.

Which was good, because she didn't need the drums to keep her awake for the midnight wedding. She found a good corner to watch Pandu's face when his wife was shown to him. There was only one initial flash from his eyes.

There were no big flowers for this wedding. It was too hot on the island, and the boat that brought such things had not come that day. Only a few marigolds were strung up for the bride's long hair.

The ceremonies went on till the dawn. In the afternoon, the bride said goodbye to her relatives and was at the door. The husband and wife were ushered to the boat, and the whole crowd there was silent. The wife hesitated at the water's edge. Then her fingers closed around Pandu's brown and eager wrist. She hitched up her golden wedding sari and stepped into the boat.

When they were sitting inside, Maya said to Pandu, "Have you spoken to her?"

"There's a lot of time for that."

"You're not going to say anything to him?"

For the first time, the bride smiled.

"If you don't even talk to each other, what happens next then?"

"What happens next, Maya, is your marriage. I have already thought of a good man for you," said Pandu, pinching her nose. "I know the very man. A little old, only seventy-six. With a big house, though. He has three wives, Maya, but I don't think they'll mind. Just to have a city girl like you, with bobbed hair, wearing pants, English..."

"Shut up, you, shut up. Let go, you silly cousin, let me go!" Maya struggled as Pandu brought her over his lap. Her hands clawed over his mouth, her nostrils flared, her teeth clenched.

Stirred by this skirmish, Pandu's wife reached for Maya and tried to remove her from Pandu's clasp. He stared, weakening at the strength of her fingers. Safe at the cabin doorway, Maya said, "I'm going to tell Thaatha. Just wait and see."

It was evening when they reached Pandu's village. The carts with all the baggage were already ahead of them. There was a big crowd waiting to receive them. Pandu's grandfather sat in his easy chair in front of the crowd. He was wearing a long, white Khadhi silk shirt with gold cuff links. There was a golden shawl around his shoulders. His completely metal-white hair was freshly barbered, and the parting was perfect. His face had been seamlessly shaved, and his nails, too, had been trimmed by the barber. Beside him, Sumi sat on her stool. She wore a magenta sleeveless frock, and a rose was pinned on her hair. The goat and its baby were somewhere else. The crowd stayed still.

Pandu and his wife got down from the taxi. The grandfather made his preparations to get up. His hands cupped around his walking cane. Pandu's brother held his arm, and then he rose, a tall, proud man, his mouth neat and stern. He was the tallest man in that crowd. Pandu and his wife touched the grandfather's feet. When they stood up, the grandfather spoke to Pandu. Pandu nodded and ran into the house. He returned at once with the magnifying glass. A little hush developed in the crowd. He gave it to his grandfather and stood behind his wife.

The grandfather gestured, and Pandu's wife moved forward. He tipped her chin and studied her face through the magnifying glass. Her face said nothing. Sumi jumped off her stool. "Are you going to say, "You're a beautiful girl, Thaatha?" she said.

The stern mouth relaxed. The grandfather nodded twice. From the long pocket of his shirt, he took out some sugar candy. He put it in the bride's hand and spoke to Pandu's mother, "Let her go inside and rest."

ANNE LEIGH PARRISH

Loss of Balance

From October/November 2007

THE WOMAN IN green talks again about her boy, Joey. Her face bears all the pain he's put her through, the broken promises, the stolen money, the calls from the police. Joey can't stop shooting drugs into his arm, so he's in rehab again. Only on Thursday he gets out, and this woman, whose name you can't remember, is sure the cycle will start all over.

She doesn't know what to do with Joey, and you don't know what to do with your father. Your father is not a drug addict, only an old man who likes to give his money away. Joey has a problem with self-control, your father has a problem with self-control, so you, the woman in green, and five others who bear responsibility for a wayward soul, meet today with Dr. Schiff in a church basement—the best he could arrange after hearing his office had flooded overnight.

You don't want to be here, but your husband insisted. He says it's time to get at the root. When your father's retirement home called last month to say he'd written them a bad check, you paid the bill, then went into a bit of a tailspin, it's true. *What's pissing you off goes a lot deeper than money,* your husband said. Maybe yes, maybe no. The point is, you recovered. You always do.

Dr. Schiff—Leonard—moves on to Edmund. Edmund's wife is an alcoholic. She hides vodka everywhere, including the toilet tank where Edmund discovered two bottles when the plumber came to fix a leak. Edmund told the plumber the bottles were his.

"Did anything bother you about that?" asks Leonard.

Edmund seems to consider the empty space above Leonard's head. Finally he says, "Yeah. The look on his face."

"And what look was that?"

"Like he was sorry for me, like he knew I was lying."

Edmund's eyes are troublesome. One is blue, the other brown. Leonard's eyes are like dark honey. Their deep grief says how much the world has had its way with him, how much he's given up against his will.

Edmund says nothing. Leonard lets the silence continue. People stare at their own hands. Someone coughs. Your mind wanders. What are you going to make for dinner, you wonder. Is your husband going to be home before you? And what about the yard work you've been putting off—all those shrubs to be dug up and replaced with something more attractive?

Can't go wrong with a big, healthy rhododendron, your father said, looking with pity at the scrap of ground you call a yard. *Or a hedge. A nice azalea hedge. Something to balance out your fruit tree in back.* The tree being an apricot, of all things, and very old. It occupies most of the room behind the house. Your father doesn't understand why you bought a house with such a small yard. It is evidence of your poor character, somehow, your inability to do anything right.

"Ralph," says Leonard. "How's it going with Shauna?"

Ralph's daughter shoplifts. She's 13, and has been in and out of juvenile detention.

"Fine," says Ralph.

"Just fine?"

"Well, I had to tell the police she's getting counseling."

"I see."

"But she's not, is she?" says Miranda, whose sister steals, too, but only from family.

"No," says Ralph.

"Because she doesn't think she has a problem." Miranda's eyes burn with bitterness. Miranda's sister ran up her credit card in Vegas for over $10,000, then begged for a plane ticket home.

"Right," says Ralph.

"She probably thinks *you're* the one with the problem."

Ralph nods, his big eyes sad, like a spaniel's. He has big ears, from which tufts of hair reach out. His shoulders are huge, but his feet are small. You've never seen a man with such small feet, smaller even than Leonard's, which sit primly in their shiny brown wingtips.

The church basement is cold, and hard morning light breaks through high windows. The gray carpet is stained with coffee, and you imagine Styrofoam cups in the hands of pious people, deciding how best to raise money for that new steeple. You are not a churchgoer. You're not an atheist, exactly, but the idea of organized religion sits poorly with you. Your father was once a Quaker, a leaning he inherited from his mother, a woman you didn't know and of whom he said little, except that she never raised her voice. You cannot imagine this petite, quiet woman. You're neither petite nor quiet, facts your father seems to regret when he looks at you.

"Darlene," Leonard says. "Why don't you tell us how it's going?"

You shift on your metal chair. Your pantyhose make a rasping sound as you cross your legs. You can't think of anything to say.

"Have there been any more incidents?" Leonard asks, urging you with those anguished eyes.

"Well, yes. He wrote another check."

"A big one?"

"Two thousand dollars."

Ralph whistles. "That's not chump change," he says.

"Who'd he give it to?" asks the woman in green.

"An old student of his. Guy got a PhD, then some teaching job that fell through."

How can you ask me why, Dar? Because I know those clowns who denied him tenure. No job, and stuck at home now with a sick baby. Didn't know that, did you, about the sick baby?

A sick baby would be easier to handle than your father.

After the bounced check to the retirement home, he took cash advances on credit cards whose monthly payments he can't meet. It's less important to stay current with them, since there's nothing they can attach if he doesn't, but staying current with the retirement home is key. If he falls too far behind he'll be asked to leave, and his only option then will be a Medicare facility, which wouldn't have the wide green lawns, nice artwork, and afternoon teas he has now. *I don't care about any of that, Dar. I'd be happy in just a little room. As long as it's clean. And has the Golf Channel. I've come to enjoy the Golf Channel quite a bit.*

"What kind of loser asks an old man for money?" asks Miranda.

"He didn't ask. My father offered."

"I should get his number." This is from Janice, the group's most hardcore sufferer. Her husband sleeps with any woman who will have him, and apparently many will. He always returns, and she always takes him back.

"What does he say when you ask him to stop?" the woman in green wants to know.

"Nothing."

Because you never asked him to stop. You can't even bring yourself to remind him he owes you money for the retirement home bill.

"Sounds like my daughter," says Ralph. "Just looks away and pretends not to hear."

Nods of sympathy all around.

Janice's cell phone rings. She grabs it from her battered vinyl handbag, stares at the caller's number, then silences it. No one asks if it's her husband. Everyone knows it is. He calls with an excuse, a lie, a story, to say he's working late. All eyes are on her now. Everyone feels her pain. As she returns the phone to her bag, you see that laces of her athletic shoes are mismatched. One is silver, the other white.

Leonard concludes by asking everyone to reflect on the limited ability to control another person. Living with destructive behavior can turn us into control freaks, he says. To regain your balance, you'll have to find a way to accept what you can and cannot change.

This is where you're way ahead. You've known forever there's no changing your father. Who he is was determined years before you were even born.

Your mother always blamed him on the war. Your father was an ordinary person with an extraordinary ability to recognize complex patterns. This was not a skill he knew he possessed before a military analyst discovered it. How the discovery was made, you're not exactly sure. Some aptitude test, probably, which quickly eliminated the possibility of active combat and moved him right into code breaking. After the war, rather than make a full-time career in military intelligence, he became a professor of history. His time was divided between known events and secret ones. How he reconciled these two worlds, you don't know, except by what he said and what he didn't. He was open about his life in the university, winning grants, beating out colleagues for promotion, but on the military life he continued to lead when called upon, he was, by necessity, absolutely silent.

The balance he struck didn't work for your mother. She needed all of him, not part, and left after 20 years of marriage.

She was soon replaced with a second wife who had no interest at all in your father's secret world. You were replaced with a stepdaughter—Leslie. You grew up, got married, lived your life. You had regular contact with your father, cordial and impersonal correspondence, brief, well-managed visits. You always wanted more. There was never enough real interest in who you were, as if your father could have been sitting across from anyone, instead of his only child. How that hurt! How hard to keep that hurt secret—your own secret—your own dual life.

Not long ago the second wife died. Your father paid you another visit. Although it had only been about a year since you'd seen him, you thought how much older he'd become, how frail. For a moment your heart went out to him, the lonely widower. You prepared a nice dinner and got a bottle of Johnny Walker Red, his favorite. He was grateful. He enjoyed himself. He mentioned the sale of the house he and his second wife had long occupied. You said you were glad, because he'd have plenty now to meet the retirement home's steep entry fee.

Oh, I'll have to scramble a bit for that, he said. *I let Leslie have it all.*

You fell silent. It's possible you even made a face, because when your father looked at you, he said, *She needs it, Dar. She's had such a hard time.*

The hard time, you soon learned, consisted of not being able to find a job, not being able to make the rent on her small apartment every month, not being able to find a good man to spend time with, and so on. Then your father added he wouldn't need his car at the retirement home and would give that to Leslie, too, since her car was so old and undependable.

He went to bed early, not long after you cleared the table. You sat in the living room alone, drinking your own gift of Scotch, and drafted the letter you'd write the next day to Leslie about responsibility, trying harder to get a job, not taking money from your father who had reached the time in his life when he must survive on a fixed income.

Her return letter arrived quickly enough to make you certain she felt terribly guilty. She didn't feel guilty. She wrote:

It was weird to hear from you after all these years. You don't exactly stay in touch. Your father used to say he wished you'd pick up the phone or drop him a line once in a while. I hope you're not mad I said so. I'm very concerned for your father's welfare, as you know. I've made every effort to keep him company these last few months, and I don't mind telling you that your poor father is very grateful to me. The time I spend with him has made it hard to develop my pet sitting business. Your father is very supportive of my career. It gives him pleasure to extend his support and thanks to me. I know you understand that it would be unkind of me not to accept it.

You remember Leslie as a child when you were still one, too, and the visits to your father's new home on Sundays, the one day the divorce agreement allowed. Leslie's mother insisted on eating in the formal dining room, an ugly box with deep red wallpaper and dark, heavy furniture. Conversation centered on your father, his students, the papers he was grading. And then it always came, that moment when Leslie wouldn't eat her vegetables. Your father made her sit at table staring at her cold plate, while you waited tensely in the living room. You wonder how she has forgiven him, and think maybe she hasn't, that wanting his money lies behind her kindness. You're proven right, because with the house gone and the car in her hands, she's nowhere to be found.

You skip the next meeting of the group. Things have gotten crazy at work. You're facilitating the acquisition of a large electronics company by an even larger discount chain. The dreary time you spend negotiating the buyout ratio makes you regret majoring in economics. You would have preferred to study English literature, but your father discouraged you on the grounds that he wanted you to make a good living, not struggle for money the way he always had to.

Several days later a social worker from the retirement home tells you long distance that your father fell in his room and needed to be hospitalized. His condition isn't grave, but she thinks now would be a wise time for a visit.

During the three-hour drive northward from Virginia, you consider the information you received about the incident in question. Your father was standing on a chair he'd brought into his closet. There was something he wanted on the top shelf, what, you don't know. You don't know what things he brought with him from the old house. You don't even know what his room looks like. As to the fall itself, it was assumed fluid in the inner ear was to blame for the loss of balance, also the medications he took to control blood pressure and quantity of Scotch consumed against the advice of his doctors.

The hospital hall is quiet and the rubber soles of your shoes squeak on the flecked vinyl floor. The noise slows as you near his room. You're afraid to enter, afraid of your own thudding heart.

His eyes open at the light touch of your hand.

Dar, is that really you? Did you really come all this way?

With a little tease in your voice you say, *Come on now, don't sound so surprised,* then you look for evidence of Leslie, some gift she might have left, a bouquet of flowers or a box of his beloved chocolate cream. There's nothing.

You take a chair and draw it to the bed. You mention the weather there in Pennsylvania and remark that your spring at home is several weeks ahead. How silly you sound, because any fool knows spring travels from south to north.

The radiator bangs, then hisses. The ugly beige curtains don't quite close, allowing a column of glare to fall across the floor.

The nurse comes to take your father's temperature. She takes his blood pressure, too. She refills the pitcher of water, slides the thermometer from his lips, reads it, and drops it in the pocket of her bright, floral print smock. Then she's gone. You wish she were still there, occupying space between you and your father.

Guess they told you what your dopey ol' father did. Sailed right off that damn chair. The bruise on his cheek is florid and difficult to look at. There were no major injuries, otherwise. He's being kept for observation only, for an assessment of his mental state, and to determine if he's fit to return to independent living.

Suddenly his face tenses, and his eyes focus on you hard. You're reminded of a picture taken years before, a candid shot by a student wanting to capture your father in mid-lecture. The expression is the same: fierce, intent, totally absorbed.

Did I ever tell you about Stu Drake? he asks you from his narrow, steel bed.

You hear that Stu was another Illinois grad whose straight teeth and high grades put him in the cockpit by the summer of '42. Stu wrote often about training paratroopers, the wide billow of the silk growing smaller as they dropped away.

So, that's what your father thought of as he fell. About dead soldiers, their chutes become shrouds.

Your words, not his. The drive has made you punchy. And the call from your husband on your cell phone as you reached town, his voice full of remorse about last night's disagreement, which you can't at the moment remember.

Did I ever tell you how I wanted to be a pilot? Failed the physical. Know why? Your father taps his crooked front teeth. *Wouldn't fit inside an oxygen mask. Probably saved my damn life.* His voice becomes as thin as the late afternoon light. *I was lucky. Luck is a kind of responsibility, and I didn't know what to do with it.*

He wants something to drink, something alcoholic, which he's not allowed. You consider buying him a bottle, hiding it in your large, messy handbag, and sharing it as the night comes on. You won't, though, because he's still talking, and he needs your audience even more than he needs the alcohol.

She hated me for what I did. I suppose she told you all about that, though, didn't she? Sometimes I feel like picking up the phone and trying to set the record straight, but what's the use? Your father has forgotten that your mother's been dead for ten years. *She thought I was arrogant, do you know that? She accused me of thinking that ordinary people were too stupid to be trusted with the knowledge I had, but that wasn't it at all. I couldn't talk about my work because I took an oath of secrecy. An oath is supposed to mean something.*

Information has become declassified and television shows about the war years, specifically the code breaking efforts on the part of the United States and Great Britain, have aired, yet your father keeps quiet.

He's grown tired and closes his eyes. In a few minutes he's sound asleep. It's unnerving to sit there, with him so still and peaceful. You feel as if death could enter at any moment without your knowing. But he's not close to dying. He won't die for another four years, by which time you will have given him a very late arriving grandson whose creation took faith and artificial means.

Later you stretch across the orange bedspread in your motel room and think of your father trying to make up for being lucky, for not talking, for wanting Leslie to eat her vegetables, but not for you, never for you. Maybe in his eyes you just weren't weak enough.

How well you've turned out, Dar. You've got such character. Don't need a thing from anyone. You're one independent gal.

His words, not yours, whenever the conversation failed, as it always did, because you didn't want him to call. Didn't want to tumble into something you couldn't control, where the weight was all on his side.

In the morning you find you've slept in your clothes, and the bed is as rumpled as you, but only on your half. You call your husband.

He's glad you did. He wants to know how your father is. *Out of it, really out of it,* you say. You say you'll be home tomorrow, and remember to say that you love him.

I love you, too, Dar.

Your father is awake and has had his breakfast. Egg has spilled on his front. He's fretful, his bent hands plucking at the bed sheets.

I don't know if I can go on helping my friends, Dar. I think I've run through all my money.

You nod.

I hate letting them down, but I don't know what else to do.

You're at a loss now, in the face of this candor, this worry. Your father never showed worry before. Only steely calm, even when his second wife berated him, or Leslie said she hated him, or when you accused him of arrogance that day on campus.

You make people into puppets! Sitting there in the dark, pulling strings! You'd learned that he had put in a good word at a college you'd applied to, just as a way of helping things along. You didn't want help. You had faith in your own merits, or at least you argued you did. In truth you had no faith at all.

For a moment your waving arms and loud voice had seemed to throw him off balance. His face opened, then closed right away because someone walked by and called his name, a colleague with a briefcase and expensive shoes. As your father called back, you walked off, perhaps not having the will to try to get his attention a second time.

You didn't go to the college he talked to. You went somewhere else, far away out west. The desert air was good for you. You put down roots in the dry ground, yet you returned, not to your hometown, but further south. Why did you come back east at all?

"Can you help me, Dar?" Your father's voice is quiet. He doesn't look at you. "I think I may need help."

"You mean pay another bill?" This would be as easy as the last, because you and your husband are frugal, even cheap, and you've got a lot put by. The balance in your money market account alone is over $60,000.

"No, no, I couldn't take a penny from you. Just help me manage what I've got. I can't seem to keep track of it these days," he says.

You agree to take a look at his checkbook and see if you can make sense of it.

He directs you to his rooms, his "cottage," he calls it, at the retirement home. The receptionist in the main hall opens the door for you but doesn't leave you the key. The front room is larger than you expected, with a sliding glass door. Outside the door is a small, concrete slab meant to serve as a patio. There's a single folding chair there and an empty glass someone overlooked. You lift the glass and smell it. You bring it inside and rinse it in the small, stainless steel kitchen sink.

The bedroom is much smaller. Cardboard boxes line one wall, stacked three high. The dresser is low, one you remember from childhood. A bright red drop of nail polish like plastic blood remains in the corner where you spilled it over 30 years before. The checkbook is there in the top right hand drawer, just as your father specified. You toss it on the carefully made single bed. The closet is almost too small to get the chair into, but you manage. On the shelf are boxes with letters inside. None from you, because you never wrote. There are sweaters, shoes, a curled up belt, a hat your father must have held onto from the 50s, the last time anyone wore such a thing. There is also a framed photograph of you. You're not smiling. The background color is too brightly blue, and you remember it as your class picture from the fifth or sixth grade. Unlike everything else on that shelf, it's been dusted, kept clean.

Was he getting it down, or putting it back? Or just taking a moment to look at it, wipe it off, then return it to the dark? There are no other photographs visible in the tiny apartment, or in any of the drawers you go through, even those in the kitchen—only yours.

You take the glass you just rinsed and fill it with a little Scotch from the bottle by the toaster. On the small sofa you drink some, then drink some more. The lake can't be seen from where you sit, but it's there for sure, long and deep, only a few miles away. On its shore there's a park where you went in summers before your parents split up. You'd fill a blue plastic bucket with pebbly sand and take it to where they lay on wide, striped towels. *What a pretty bucket,* your father would say, rising up to see better. Then, *I have a secret to tell you! The secret is I love you! Now off you go, find me some more sand for your bucket.*

Years after the bucket was lost, you were eating a T.V. dinner in your father's dark apartment. There was a game on the black and white set, the antenna off kilter, the picture in and out.

Who scored? he called.

Pittsburg, you were happy to say, knowing the teams at last.

He stood in the low kitchen doorway, a can of beer in his hand. He says, *I'm getting married again soon.*

You nodded. *Mom told me,* you said.

The final quarter was underway, Pittsburg reached Miami's ten yard line, and still in the doorway, your father said, *I want you to know that I won't have any more children. You're the only child I have, the only one I want to have.*

Years later you called up to say you just got married. A silence fell on the line. In the background there was a game playing, and you had to wonder if it was football. *I wish you'd told me, Dar. I would have liked to give you away.*

You finish your drink. Something within you shifts, then drops like a single flake of snow. You put the glass down and sit a little longer in the quiet of your father's empty house.

You find the checkbook in the bedroom. Inside bears your father's neat, square hand.

You'll take it away and go through it later. It will show only an old man who can no longer add or subtract. It won't be hard to put his affairs to right. The offer you make his creditors to settle for less will be accepted in time. The letters you send his acquaintances—including Leslie—will thank them for their friendship and give your father's new address in the nursing home where it's decided he should go. His boxes and books, the sofa and bed, the sweaters and shoes will all be sent along, sorted, or stored. The picture of you will take up residence on the television he watches day in and out. While the child you were frowns into space, the woman you've become will visit more often, refill a cup, open the blind, and gently restore the balance between his heart and yours.

RAUL PALMA

American Leather

From October/November 2014

I.

AT SALVATORE'S, spring arrives on January 15th. Collette, our
visual designer, flies in from Milan to reset our collection. Orange-
glazed porcelain vases, set with violet and pearl hyacinths, displace
wreaths and acorns. The display wall, a partition of restored French
oak, blossoms with new calfskin handbags—powder yellow, Egyptian
blue, Lolita pink. Each bag is accessorized: a pleated silk scarf tied
around a handle, black bachelite sunglasses tucked into a pocket.
Passersby ducking their heads from snow showers often revel at our
store windows, but they seldom step in. Even a Salvatore's leather key
chain can set a layperson back a month's rent.

The replacement, a 20-something-year-old kid recruited from
The Gap, follows Donald along the display wall. He's being trained,
but it's clear the kid's no Earnest. He's cute, for starters, clientless,
unshaven, wearing dark-framed glasses and a linen suit, looking like he
rolled out of a trendy fashion magazine, not a boutique. His youth is

probably why he was hired in the first place, to make Salvatore's appeal to an emerging audience: college kids and teens, penniless play plays, notorious for wasting our ups. Maybe he'd be better off working on 5th Avenue, selling to 20-year-old execs. He should be playing beer pong, waking up next to strange women, getting by in his classes, not slopping leather alongside little old me. I could be his mother, his silver-haired cougar; I could sour his taste for prudish tarts.

Look at him caressing those handbags, squeezing them like they're breasts. How generously he handles the satchels, slings, wristlets. How respectful he is with the totes, hobos. I'll bet he's the kind of kid who doesn't rush to take off a women's bra. Take it easy there, boy. He could tease a girl, let her get all worked up, his fingernails drawing circles along her skin. After undoing the clasp, he'd slip her arm through, one strap at a time, the warmth of his lips against her neck and ear, the coarseness of his chest brushing up against the tips of her nipples. I could watch him descend into my bust this way, feel his tongue explore the scars and creases tucked below my aesthetic alterations.

I'll have to show him that they're handbags, not purses. A Salvatore's bag ages gracefully, its leather forming natural stains and creases through the years. Our European artisans acquire the best skins from privileged calves. These calves never know fences; they have names; they graze freely, receive daily massages, drink watered down wine.

Truth is, the problem with American leather is that we rely too much on barbed wire fencing, which leaves its mark. Salvatore's would never truly use American cattle for product. In America, cattle are injected with hormones, herded in closed quarters, fattened with chemically engineered feed. When cattle are slaughtered, they are blindfolded and led into gas chambers. Carbon dioxide acts like an anesthetic, minimizing stress. Cattle are placed on a conveyer belt, blindly led through a processing plant where a technician uses a stun gun—a pneumatic penetrating rod—to pierce the cortex, making the cattle mostly brain dead. Still breathing, cattle are piled on top of each other for processing. Their brain stems remain active, which allows their hearts to continue pumping.

We were always pumped when Earnest was around. Though I find the replacement cute, Earnest was cuter, flamboyant at times, always ready to shake his firm tush to whichever song played over the sound system. God bless his queer little soul.

Manny and Earnest were casual lovers, often dedicating Tuesday afternoons to furniture shopping and champagne by Manny's fireplace. Earnest might have been my lover, too, if he were into that kind of thing. We'd kissed about a dozen times, but it was only because we'd been drinking. The first time I kissed him, he was so tickled by my inappropriate advance, he grabbed my breasts and declared, "Honey, you trying to make me straight? What is that you're wearing? Cocoa-kiss chapstick? Give me some more."

Often, Earnest and I would hang out at Manny's condo—a 1920s vintage high rise overlooking Belmont Harbor. Wednesday nights, after work, we'd dim the lights, snack on pistachios and prunes, watch films—classics by Kubrick, Hitchcock, Coppola, Tornatore, and Almadóvar. We'd unwind, rewind, fastforward, and occasionally pause if we felt like it. Earnest would lay his head on a pillow on my lap and rest his bare feet on Manny's lap. How easy it was for the three of us to drink and smoke and become passive observers.

At Salvatore's, observing is built into the job description. Inside, instrumental Bee Gees might play "Stayin' Alive," while on the other side of that windowpane, on-screen drama flourishes. One spring, police canvassed the avenue, handing out missing children flyers. Months later, an older gentleman was run down by a taxicab. There was that block of ice that fell off the Tiffany's building, crushing a pair of identical twin boys. Then even further along, gay rights protestors marched down the avenue. Mounted police officers kept the peace, trampling innocent bystanders. Then the traditions—men and women dressed in their best Irish, drunkenly marching towards the green river—and the once-in-a-lifetime occurrences, like Obama's motorcade leaving Grant Park after his 2008 victory, and like when a giant, 40,000 pound replica of Marilyn Monroe was dismantled in 2012, hoisted onto the bed of a few trucks, and driven off a section at a time. Too often, a man down on his luck sits against our windows when he begs. Passersby stand over him, ignoring his signage, admiring the exuberance of Salvatore's display windows, wishing they could reach through the glass and take a piece of our leather.

And although Salvatore's may be a beacon of fashion and wealth, it is not immune to this drama. While carrying six shoeboxes up the stairs, Earnest's heart stopped. He was at the bottom of the staircase when I found him, covered in women's shoes. Paramedics tried to resuscitate him. They placed him on a stretcher, rolled him onto the sales floor, and cut his clothing off. I'd never seen how smooth and unblemished Earnest's chest was; he was practically hairless. Beneath his handsome complexion and designer drab, he was all baby. Even his breasts seemed smooth as calfskin.

Paramedics asked us to stand back. Passersby stopped at our windows and observed, watching them prepare the defibrillator, clear, and administer the first shock. Afterwards paramedics formed a line and took turns performing CPR—25 minutes worth. I watched Earnest's chest bruise and redden, too, while consoling Manny. It was unreal and haunting. I'll never forget that one customer, wrapped in her black chinchilla fur coat, still shopping even while paramedics followed the defibrillator's directions, counting off chest compressions and breaths.

At the funeral Donald, Manny, and I dressed in Salvatore's very best. I can only speak for myself, but looking at Earnest on that day, all made-up and glamorous and also dressed in his best, reminded me of that time in the year when we'd pack up the old season and ship it off to the outlet stores. I stood over Earnest, admiring his still pronounced jaw line, and applied my Cocoa-Kiss chap stick over his thin cracked lips for the last time. "Goodbye, my friend."

Earnest was literally the (EA) in (TEAM), the buffer that made it possible for me, (T) Tess, to withstand (M) moody Manny. All together we were fantastic, top in the company, just as clever and corny as the acronym. We'd worked with each other for 20 years, so the replacement shouldn't expect this kind of camaraderie to come naturally. We're older, and Earnest's death weighs heavily on us. The replacement needs to be patient, especially with Manny, who is particularly offended by the hasty hiring.

The replacement shouldn't be threatened by our chiding. At Salvatore's, sometimes the only way to stay sane is to poke fun at customers (the customers hardly notice). Earnest used to gather us by the storefront window so we'd knock passersby—senile ladies with dogs in strollers and that kind of crazy. For years, passing judgment was simply a form of play, a secret communion we participated in, protected by the large storefront windows.

Now that Earnest is gone, we really don't play games anymore. Everything has become deathly serious. Corporate's goals are more aggressive, less realistic. Manny and I wait for our ups or argue over Earnest's clientele. Now, we have to keep records, stay within the top 50% of the company's sales average, justify our salaries. Nowadays, we don't talk about it, but we're both afraid of losing our jobs.

If the replacement wants to keep the peace, he should learn and honor the up system and stick to it. He will already make us uncomfortable; he is young, energetic, while we are old and tired. When we walk up and down the stairs to retrieve product from storage, the replacement will pass us, two steps at a time, and he should avoid doing this.

The up system is simple. The first person to arrive in the morning gets the first customer, the first up. We then alternate ups based on arrival. Ups can be wasted. A person asking for directions is a wasted up. A customer returning product is a wasted up. A visit from a girlfriend is a wasted up. The replacement should keep his eye on Manny, who likes to take other people's ups when they're not paying attention.

During down time Manny likes to lean against the leather goods case, reading and rereading *House and Garden* magazine. I like to organize and reorganize the women's ready-to-wear display, my pumps ready at my side. The replacement will need to find his place in the store, too.

Occasionally, one of Earnest's old clients visits, unaware. At Salvatore's, HR doesn't allow us to tell customers where he's gone, even though he's dead, so one of us will hand the client a little prayer card with Earnest's name on it. In time, I will show the replacement where the cards are.

Donald takes the replacement over to the shoe lounge—a series of ivory-colored shelves, teaming with display shoes: ballet flats, mules, stilettos, kitten heels, wedges. Most of the shoes are constructed from a single piece of leather, dyed in our season's signature colors, but there are also the exotics: python, pony, crocodile.

Even if Donald spent a week teaching the replacement the history of Salvatore's shoe line—the difference between suede and nubuck, the proper way to treat leather, or the various methods of coordinating shoes with an outfit—this would not prepare the replacement for the way in which women shop for shoes. These are seldom practical purchases.

More often than not, a woman is empowered by her footwear. She might not even wear the shoes she buys. Just as Dorothy's ruby red slippers whisked her home, and just as Cinderella's glass slippers paved the way for a happily ever after ending, the clack clack of suede purple heels can give a woman the confidence she needs to win a job interview. Yellow ballet flats can influence a woman's lifestyle, inspire her to purchase a vintage bicycle, dump that old boyfriend, get an abortion. A woman timid in the sack can become a raging nymphet in chocolate knee-high leather boots. So when a woman is surveying Salvatore's shoe lounge, it is important the replacement understand she is likely considering the various ways in which she will reinvent herself. That's why I take my shoes off whenever I can. The replacement will need to watch where he walks, so he doesn't crush my little toes.

When the replacement steps away for a moment, I approach Donald. He's pulling some handbags and pairing them with display shoes when I ask, "You plan on introducing us to him?"

Donald doesn't look at me.

"Hey, Donald. If you want me to help out. Mentor the replacement or something. Just let me know."

Donald smiles. "Tess, thank you. I appreciate it—you know that, but don't take this the wrong way. I'll handle the training. Here. Hold this." He hands me four display shoes, and he walks away. I follow him to the women's ready-to-wear line where he stands the shoes up on the couch, places the leather bomber jacket against the couch's back, and drapes the pants over the jacket. "What do you think?" he asks. "Tess? Focus for a moment."

"This," I say. "Is this what you're teaching him? I wouldn't wear it."

"Ok," Donald says, smiling. "Great. Thanks."

II.

In the afternoon, Donald calls an impromptu store meeting so he may formally introduce the replacement. The replacement doesn't wait to be introduced; he's shifting his weight from one leg to the next, moving about to the sound of the in-store soundtrack. He extends his hand to Manny and then to me. His hands smell like incense, and he says things with his eyes: "Pleasure to meet you. Lovely necklace. Nice rack," but he really doesn't say anything.

We give him our names, but he doesn't share his. "You know," Manny says, "usually when people introduce themselves, they also share their names. It's kind of the purpose of an introduction. So you want to try this again?"

The replacement forms a C with his hand, presses it to his eye, and then slowly moves it up and towards the ceiling. He repeats the signal, smiles.

"Kid. What's wrong with you?" Manny asks.

"Play along," Donald says.

The replacement draws an imaginary circle in the air with his finger. He brings his hands together, as in a prayer, and proceeds to separate his palms while keeping his fingertips touching. Soon, even his fingertips pull apart, and his hands break their connection. I picture them drifting this way, never touching.

"Are you talking about...?" I say.

The replacement snaps his fingers, points at me and winks; his excitement is infectious, which makes me laugh. He performs the sign again, hands like a prayer drifting apart. Then he touches my arm, inviting me to guess again.

Manny turns his back to the kid. "Boss, what are you trying to do to us?"

"I think I see what he's saying," I say.

"Yeah. Me, too. He's a mute kid from The Gap."

"Manny. Don't call him that. How would you like it if he called you a fag?" I asked.

"Let's avoid name calling, please," Donald says, fixing his lapels.

"So tell me, then. What's he trying to say?" Manny asks.

"'Sun.' Like the sunrise, the way it radiates. His name's Sun," I say.

The replacement smiles, shakes my hand again, and brings it to his lips.

Manny swings the magazine into his palm. "Explain me this, Boss. How's Sunny supposed to sell if he can't talk? I mean, we sell, so we have to talk, right?"

Sun responds by touching his ear and bringing his hand forward while rubbing his fingers together. Manny avoids eye contact with him, so Sun stands in front of Manny and performs the gesture again, following Manny's eyes.

"No offense, Sunny. I was asking my boss." Turning to Donald, Manny says, "So in addition to selling, we'll be playing charades?"

"He's trying to tell you," Donald says. "Good sales people are good listeners. Good sales people make more money."

"So now you're training us, too. I thought he was the new guy."

Sun cleans his eyeglasses with his dress shirt and walks away. As Donald and Manny bicker, Sun returns to the handbag wall, poking around, caressing the women's display shoes. He's holding the Middleton, a women's woven leather sandal, and reading it as if it were a book or magazine. I wonder what he's getting from it. How I wish I could look at something as simple as a sandal and still be fascinated by it.

When the store opens on Saturday morning, Sun claims the scarf display case by the front door. He's equipped with an iPad, which makes my pink pocket notebook seem pubescent. Manny is reading and rereading the same old *Home and Garden* magazine. I'm barefoot at the back of the store, checking inventory on the women's ready-to-wear. Donald's in the basement writing reports and watching us on the monitors.

It's a freakishly warm winter day—upper 40s. Through the wrap-around windows, we can see that snow has become slush. Orange cones warn pedestrians of falling ice. Though the streets are filled, it is likely we will have few walk-ins. Holiday sales quenched shoppers. January is generally a time to regret debt.

At 10:00 AM, a woman walks into the store, our first walk-in. Though its warm out and warmer inside, she's still wearing a shearling coat and rubber soled boots—a good practice when dealing with Chicago winters.

"It's your up," Manny says. "Looks like a crazy."

He's right. She has the look: CVS bag filled with meds, sloppily applied lipstick, and clunky men's boots. Even when she walks by Sun, she completely ignores him.

I approach her. "Welcome to Salvatore's," I say, eyes smiling.

"Yes. Yes. I'm not going to buy anything. I'm just looking," she says, walking past me and into the women's shoe lounge. "So darn bright out there. I just want to look."

Manny sings, "I'm just looking. Just looking. Not buying. Just looking."

The woman enters the shoe salon and kicks off her left boot.

"Would you like some champagne or Pellegrino?" I ask.

Ignoring me, she grabs display shoes, favoring dark, closed toed kitten heels over flats or higher heels. When she's found one that interests her, she drops it on the floor. She smooths the folds of her nude-colored nylons and pokes her foot into the sole. "Oh lordy lordy," she says. "Feel that insole." She models the shoe in a ceiling-high mirror, the variation in height between her boot and the display shoe makes her balance staggered. "Lucky me," she says. "My left foot is always the display size." After a few poses, she tosses her handbag and shearling on the sofa.

"Do you need help?" I ask.

"Lady, do I look like I'm crazy?"

"You look very glamorous today."

Underneath that coat the woman's wearing jeans and a black glittery t-shirt, tucked in, emblazoned with the head of a horse, hair flowing in the wind. The price tag is dangling beneath her hair. "The problem with Salvatore's," she says. "It's that you people don't fit shoes right."

"The Catalina seems to fit you just fine," I say.

"Yes, Honey. Of course it does. On my left foot it does. My left foot's normal. If you would look at my right foot... There's no Salvatore's shoe that could ever fit my right foot." Using the Catalina as leverage, the woman kicks off her boot. It scuffs the base of the sofa. "Do you see the problem, now?" She asks. "Looks like a bunion, right? Nope. It was my Papa's horse, Chap Stick, stepped on my foot when I was just a little girl, ruined me. I was seeing horse shoes for weeks."

"That's terrible," I say.

The woman grabs my wrist. "Never. Never. Never. In all my life. Have I walked into a store. And purchased a pair of shoes. All because of that damned horse. You know how I get my shoes?" she asks, kicking off the Catalina, using my wrist to balance herself, and trying on a black patent pump, "I have to buy them in outdoorsman shops. Men's shoes. They're the only shoes wide enough. Isn't that just a bunch of cheese fluff?"

"I'll bet you're not very fond of that horse," I say, squirming out of her grip.

"Chap Stick?" she asks. She lets me go.

Manny is smiling, just about to start laughing. He's hiding his face in the magazine. Sun listens intently. The woman grabs four different shoe models, some from our new spring collection, and drops them on the floor. After slipping her foot into each of them, she kicks them over to the couch and sits.

"Did you want to try the right shoe? Maybe you get lucky?"

"It wasn't Chap Stick's fault," she says. "That's what you asked me right? I just wanted to play with him. Papa had told me to stay away, but he was such a pretty horse, so black. They made everything but chap stick out of him."

Sun approaches me, shows me his iPad. He has an app open that looks like a loose sheet of paper. On it, he's written "Sun Glasses!" in thick letters. He points at the black bachelite glasses tucked into the Lolita Pink handbag. "A moment, Sunny. How about the shoes, Ma'am?"

"I have a belt made of him, you know? Isn't that just the neatest thing you've ever heard?" she asks.

"Ma'am, did you want to try any of these on?"

The woman rubs her nose clean. "Didn't you hear me? They're not going to fit," she says. "Gee whiz! You sales people."

I walk away. Watching this woman sit, her deformed foot surrounded by so many dainty shoes, makes me wonder what inspires her to get out of bed each day, let alone walk into a shoe store. I picture her sliding that frayed old horse belt around her waist each day, too attached to the thing to ever buy another one. She seems like the kind of woman who has pictures of horses hanging on all her walls, maybe even one of those cloth toilet covers in some horse theme. I wish she'd hop on some imaginary horse, ride out of the store, and burn up in the sunset.

"High ho silver," Manny says, his mouth concealed by the magazine.

"Cut that out," I say. "She'll complain."

Manny holds the magazine over his mouth and mimics a horse's neigh. I shove him. "Don't look now," Manny says, "but it seems like she'll be here for a while. The replacement's getting ready to break her in."

"What's he doing?" I ask.

"Bringing her a bucket of apples and carrots," Manny says.

We laugh hysterically, which overpowers the store's soundtrack. Sun ignores us, sits beside the woman and organizes the display shoes.

I shoot him a look, enunciating "Stop it." He shakes his head, returning to his work with her.

"This kid is making you waste your time," Manny says. "You're going to have to tell him something; he needs to learn the way things are done in this business."

"How about I just make it his up," I say. "Teach him a lesson."

"You should do that," Manny says. "Show him how valuable our time is."

But there is no lesson to teach Sun here. As we continue to observe, we see that the woman isn't bothered by Sun. In fact, she's calm and silent and watching Sun arrange the display shoes on the sofa cushion beside her. Without saying a word, Sun hands her the black sunglasses on his open palm—the ones he'd asked me to fetch her. They look like a little black spider all folded up. In her nude-colored nylons, she walks to the ceiling-high mirror and tries them on. "Isn't that something?"

"Yeah," Manny whispers. "Now send her back to the stables."

"Really," I say. "Keep it down. She'll complain."

"And so she'll complain," Manny says. "What difference will it make?"

"Maybe our job," I say.

"Shut up."

The woman turns towards us. She says, "What do you think?"

We nod in approval, holding back our laughter (what else are we going to tell her?). The customer turns to Sun, glasses hanging off her nose, and tells him, "You're so thoughtful and cute. I'll take them."

For a moment, I wonder whether Sun is going to steal my commission, but he doesn't. Instead, he invites me over and allows me to complete the transaction: $1,175. "She wants to wear them out," he writes on his iPad.

"What a sweet boy you have working here. How long has he been here?" She asks, as I hand her the receipt.

"Brand-new," I say.

"Not much of a talker," she says.

"Nope. He doesn't talk at all, actually."

"He's what Salvatore's needs. You should tell him I said that. He could be my grandson, you know? That's what Salvatore's needs. Grandsons working here. Tell him that."

"I will."

"Tell Salvatore, too. Maybe Salvatore's doesn't have a problem like people are saying, not with fresh young people like him. So nice, so thoughtful, so quiet. Maybe this store won't turn into an Argo Tea after all."

Manny's up.

By noon, the Saturday street drummers arrive—a gang of four shirtless kids with skeleton tattoos on their backs (I wonder how they manage not to freeze to death). Sun stands by the window, his palm against the glass; he is mesmerized by the performance. Two drummers sit against the store's embankment, surrounded by upside plastic buckets and iron-clad ovenware. The other kids dance, swing cartwheels, somersaults. Occasionally, the performers break-dance on the salted sidewalk, or freestyle, or invite passersby to partake and tip.

Manny hates street performers: "They better not come in here and waste our ups," he says. It used to be that these street artists would take refuge from the elements by entering Salvatore's. Shirtless school boys would drag slushy buckets and drum gear into the store. They could get away with warming themselves up for three to five minutes, before the police would arrive and kick them out. I mean, we certainly weren't going to kick them out ourselves. But this practice ended; police actually started arresting them.

Though Salvatore's windows are plenty thick, the sound of their drumming penetrates the sales floor. I think it gives the store's soundtrack an added flair, but Manny disagrees. He says, "There's nothing charming about the street." Obviously, Manny is bitter. Even if there *were* nothing charming about the street, there is certainly something to be said about Chicago's Magnificent Mile—the very nature of the avenue, lined by storefronts, perfectly manicured gardens, and sky scrapers, informs the notion of the great American city. Even in the winter, when we're walking down Michigan Avenue, passing Tribune Tower and the Wrigley Building—a lone saxophone warming the night—we are amidst the great engines of the last century. It's hard to associate such a marvel with killings and gang violence, but Chicago is violent. It is a segregated city, always has been.

The second walk-in of the day is a youngish-looking black guy, looking like he could be the street performer's manager. He's a preppy thug, wearing a black leather hat backwards, which shows off a red and green Gucci logo, and he's sporting a knee-length coat with Burberry's signature pattern.

Manny approaches the guy but doesn't greet him (this is Manny's style: he finds it offensive when he's greeted in a store, so he returns the favor). The guy lingers around the Men's Small Leather Goods case, eyeing some of our wallets, then backs away from the display case and browses through his smart phone. "Pretty dope," he says, to no one in particular. A duffel bag catches his eye. "How much?" he asks, indifferently motioning towards the bag with his head.

"Depends on the size. Six to ten-thousand dollars," Manny says, bringing down a full-grain brown leather duffel bag. Manny unzips the bag, removes its stuffing and show's off its crimson interior.

"It's sweet, swag. Pretty nice stuff for a store I've never heard of."

"Stuff? Well, we've been here for over 60 years."

"Is that right?"

"We're only the premier leather goods seller in the world. I mean, Ferrari commissions our artisans for the leather detailing in their cabins. American presidents walk around in our shoes."

"That's really dope," the guy says.

"It's more than dope," Manny says.

"Hold that duffel for me. I'll keep it in mind."

"Sure you will."

"Excuse me."

"I'm sure you will."

"Oh, I will. Hold it for Plush," he says, all matter-of-fact, like he's made of gold. Then he turns, full swagger on, shuffling out of the store to the sound of the drums outside. On his way out, he throws Sun the sideways peace sign. Sun returns the gesture. Manny stuffs the duffel, zips it back up, and sets it back on the display wall. I come up beside him.

"You're not going to put it on hold?" I ask.

"For that clown?" Manny asks.

"Maybe he's got money," I say.

"When guys named Plush start buying our premium product, I'll happily resign."

Chicago's winters bring about an early night. By 5:00 PM, the temperature has dropped into the teens—a 30 degree difference from earlier in the day—and the slush on the sidewalk has frozen. The white Christmas lights on the Mile's bare trees come on, swaying back and forth in the evening's gusts. Slowly the foot traffic thins, and the homeless, preparing for another freezing night, set up their down sleeping bags on the side streets against the stores. An hour from closing, I'm not surprised no one else has walked in. Business can be dreadful this time of the year. Understandably, customers would rather be sitting by their fireplaces or snowbirding in Florida, not braving the Mile's chill.

It's Sun's up, has been for a while.

In his boredom, he's succumbed to sorting and organizing the woman's silk squares. He's making a real mess, taking the silk squares by their ends and tossing them open on the glass display. Each square depicts a safari animal: a silver cheetah on a cold blue backdrop, a yellow elephant against a pink safariscape. This is not the bread and butter of our business—merely $410 per square—but in temperate weather women do love tying these around their necks. It makes them look real sophisticated, real European. Some women go for that bohemian look, wearing the squares out like a bandana, and then there are those real fashionable types, the kind who go braless, using two or three squares and tying them together to wear as a halter top— a look I could never master. I'd like to tell Sun to quit making a mess, that we'll be cleaning up soon.

"Are we just supposed to ignore him the whole time?" I ask.

"Ignore who? What?" Manny asks.

"Nothing," I say. I'm sitting on the couch in the women's shoe lounge. It's tiring to stand all day. Manny's going through his client book, likely trying to figure out how he will drum up business next week. Plush walks back into the store, too cold to swag. In fact, he's practically shivering, stomping and rubbing his gloves together.

"You gonna take this one," I say. "You were working with him earlier."

Manny closes his client book, rolls his eyes. "I'd rather be home. Give it to the replacement," he says and walks off the floor.

Sun greets Plush with a sideways peace sign.

"Yo," Plush says. "How is it? Let me see that set again?"

Sun nods his head, smiles. He sets his iPad down and retrieves the entire luggage set from the storage room. In addition to the luggage, Sun provides Plush with a glass of champagne and invites him to sit with a hand gesture.

"Wining and dining me," Plush says. "I just came to gander."

Sun shrugs. As he removes the luggage set from its packing, Plush drinks champagne and browses through the men's shoe wall. "Tell me, what else should I know about Salvatore's before I spend my fortune here?" he asks.

Sun stops unpacking the luggage set for a moment, takes his iPad, writes something and shows it to Plush. "You can't talk." Plush says. "What kind of bogus sales rep are you?"

Sun makes some signs with his hands.

"I don't have time for this," Plush says, and he looks at me. "Lady, can you speak? Can't you help me out?"

Sun shakes his head and hands the iPad to Plush. He's uploaded a documentary produced by BBC, recounting the life of Salvatore. The documentary eases Plush's original dissatisfaction. "I can respect this," Plush says. "Just the facts. Maybe it's a good thing you can't talk. I always says that, yo. Some people probably shouldn't be saying nothing in the first place."

This seems to entertain Plush until the iPad runs out of battery. With no scraps of paper to write on, Sun runs off to the cashier room. He emerges with a stack of Earnest's prayer cards.

"Sun," I say. "What do you think you're doing?" I ask in passing.

"So what was that last bit about Salvatore's custom shoe program? How much will that set me back?" Plush asks.

On a prayer card Sun had obtained, he takes a black permanent marker, strikes out the memorial we'd written for Earnest, and writes, "$4,200." Then he hands it to Plush, who responds: "Jesus Christ, kid. Your leather is rich."

At closing time, I take the remainder of the prayer cards and hide them in my locker. Sun pours Plush another glass of champagne. Manny and I are sitting around waiting for Sun to finish up with Plush, until Donald finally decides to check our bags by the back door and excuse us early. It's cold and snowing outside, so Manny and I huddle together under a warm bus stop.

"This kid isn't going to last a week," I say, slapping the cold out of my legs. "You should have seen him, Manny. His iPad ran out of battery during the sale. And that thug, he was getting all worked up because Sun couldn't speak to him. You know the way our customers are. They're never going to buy this mute thing."

"He wasn't so bad," Manny says. "I mean he didn't say anything, but he wasn't so bad. He wasn't great, either. But he wasn't annoying."

"He took one of Earnest's prayer cards, you know?"

"How so?"

"He took it, and scratched out the memorial. He used it like scrap paper."

"Asshole," Manny says. "Who does something like that?"

"The replacement," I say. "Do you think we're going to get replaced, too?"

Manny chuckles. "I'd like to see corporate try."

"All I'm saying is that if they try, I'm leaving. I won't be fired."

"Tess. We've been there for 20 years."

"I hate this feeling, Manny. I feel so unwanted."

"Come on. Who could they replace us with? A blind monkey and a deaf monkey?"

"Shut up," I say, shoving Manny.

"See no evil. Hear no evil. Speak no evil."

"Sounds like a recipe for sell no leather," I say.

"Look at you, Tess. Being funny. I'm curious. What do you think of the replacement?"

"He's a bit standoffish."

"So you're not going to try and screw him then?"

I punch Manny. He chuckles and hugs me.

"Tess, I can hardly feel my nose." Manny hails a cab. "You should do the same. Want to share a ride?" he asks.

"No."

Manny holds the door open for me. "Come on, Tess. Don't be hard headed."

"I'll be fine."

"All right then. Get home. It's no night to be out."

"Okay."

"And one more thing, Tess. I love you."

When I'm finally alone at the bus stop, I can hear the snow falling. Michigan Avenue is quiet except for an occasional taxi or the steps of a passerby. It's been some time since I've seen the store all illuminated from the outside. I'd forgotten how platinum it looks from the street. The aluminum window frames reflect the iridescence of the indoor lights, making the windows shimmer.

Sun runs around the store; his shadow falls onto the avenue, extending halfway across the street. I see Donald sitting next to Plush, animated in conversation. Things seem to be going well for them, and yet something about looking in from the outside makes me feel unwelcome and numb all over, like I'm not wearing a coat or a suit or anything at all.

III.

On Sunday morning, Donald's in his office talking on the phone. The music is still playing, and it's evident the lights were left on. In the spot where Plush sat, a champagne bottle lays oozing into the couch. Some more of Earnest's prayer cards lay folded and scattered about, used and wasted like scraps of paper. Beside the cards, there are Salvatore's dress shirts, pants, jackets, plastic sleeves ripped open, the ready-to-wear folded in a pile beside the hangers. There's that luggage piece that Plush was looking at, but there's also the entire set. And I can see through the opening in the upright set that it's filled with Salvatore's Men's shoeboxes. Ties hang from the display cases. Belts lie in a jumble, tangled on the women's shoe lounge area rug. A mannequin from the window has been disfigured; his upper body is lying flat on the Small Leather Good's display, while the lower portion of his body is standing beside the sunglasses case. I'm about to start picking this up when the phone rings. It's Donald. "Don't touch the merchandise," he says.

"What happened here last night?"

"We sold a whole lot of leather."

"Well, I hope you don't expect me to pick this up by myself," I say.

"No. No, Tess. Sun will be in earlier than scheduled. He will pick it up."

"So he'll be working through my shift."

"You'll share the floor," Donald says. "The more people on the floor, the better."

"Not better for my commissions," I say.

"Well, it's better for the store," Donald says and hangs up.

I find Donald in his office. He's in a navy suit, legs crossed, talking on the phone. In front of him are the security monitors. He lifts his finger at me when I step in. When he's done talking, he turns to me, smiles, and says, "You look lovely today. How can I help you, Tess?"

"You going to replace us?" I ask.

"What?"

"Me and Manny. Are you going to replace us?"

Donald sits back, plays with his cuffs. "Why would you say that? Here. Sit," he says, kicking out a chair for me, but I don't sit. I lean against the wall, fold my arms. "I don't know why you would say that," Donald says. "Who told you that?"

"Who told me?"

"Yeah. Who told you?"

I back off the wall and head to the break room.

Donald follows me. "What happened?"

"You just said it. 'Who' told me. 'Who.'"

Sun walks in, fresh, sporting new glasses. He waves "hello." I turn my back to him, facing my open locker. There are things I will need to take, so I unload my locker, letting all the things I've hoarded through the years pour into my handbag. There are pens and awards I've won—certificates, pins. Taped to the inside of my locker are photos—the original team. We were so young, then. I have old sets of clothing, old shoes, things I must have forgotten to change into after work. Within minutes, my locker is an empty shell.

Sun touches my shoulder. He sincerely looks concerned for me, but I walk out of the break room. Upstairs there are a few more things I keep by the register: my pink measuring tape and matching pink notepad. There's my silver shoehorn, which I won for leading the company in women's shoe sales, and there's a small stuffed bunny Earnest gave me, which I keep behind my register—the bunny was an inside joke about my sex life, but in the last few months, it had been a source of companionship.

I should call Manny, I realize. He'd walk me off the ledge, but it would only be prolonging the inevitable. I'm at the back door, holding it halfway open when Donald comes running up behind me. Now he's muted by the situation, a look of guilt and embarrassment on his face. I look at him, and then I look at Michigan Avenue sprawling out before me, stores stacked on top of stores. I wonder, how will I get by? The chill wind is channeling past me and into the store, making my eyes water. With a heavy Salvatore's bag over my shoulder, I walk out onto that street, into the crowd.

A. RAY NORSWORTHY

All the Way to Grangeville

From January/February 2006

IT WAS CLOSE to dusk when Reckless pulled into the gravel parking lot of Wilma's Diner. Trish, the young Reno hooker who'd hitched a ride, stirred awake and sat up, looking dazed. She stared at him as if she'd forgotten who he was. "Oh, yeah," she said, yawning. "Winnemucca." He could tell she was used to being disappointed when she woke up. He'd seen that look many times; he would have seen it on his own face if he'd woke up looking in a mirror. He asked her if she was hungry. She said she could use some orange juice, maybe a muffin.

He picked one of the worn red vinyl booths where he had a view of the highway. There was a Thanksgiving candle burning on the table, and the jukebox was playing redneck Christmas music. While she was on the phone calling for a tow truck, he ordered the miner's special for him and a wheat-berry muffin for her. She came back with a look of disgust on her face. "I'm in the wrong business," she said. "They want me to pay them to fuck me!" The background voices quieted. "Scuse me," she said, smoothing down her black leather miniskirt as she swiveled around. A teenage boy at the counter laughed out loud, and his girlfriend elbowed him. Trish cleared her throat and sat down, blushing like the sweet, innocent Mormon girl she must have been, or maybe still was underneath her whore crust.

"How much?" he asked.

"More than I can afford." She took a big, toothy bite of the muffin.

"I'll cover it." He reached in his pocket and pulled a few 100s out of his wallet.

"Oh, wow. You're feeling generous," she said. "No wonder your nickname is Reckless. So like, what do you expect in return?" Her brown eyes had gotten bigger, but they weren't giving anything away.

"I want you to pledge your eternal, undying love."

She rolled her eyes. "Too late. I already did that in the second grade. All he did was steal my candy. Come on, I'm not in the mood."

"No strings. I'm so loaded, I burn money for pleasure. Here, I'll show you." He took one of the 100s and lit it with the Thanksgiving candle.

"Hey, don't do that!" She grabbed the flaming bill and dunked it in her water glass. "This isn't counterfeit, is it?"

He grinned. "No, it's a real Benjamin, Trish. You're a Mormon girl aren't you?"

She made a face and stuck the wet, partly-burned bill in her pocket. "Sure, I'm Marie Osmond's little sister. Why?"

He shrugged and took a sip of bad coffee. "I have a habit of trying to figure people out. It's saved my life a few times."

"You'd be dead if you'd bet on me."

"You have nice teeth. You remind me of Molly Ringwald. You even got the freckles."

She rolled her eyes. "I get that a lot. I paid enough for 'em."

"You paid for freckles?"

"No, goofball, these." She tapped her top front teeth with her pinkie.

"A girl your age with fake choppers?"

"Half and half." She ran her tongue along the inside of her lip. "If you were any good at figuring people out, you'd already know I used to be a tweaker."

"Meth?"

She made a sour face and nodded.

"That's a very unhealthy habit, I hear."

"It's suicide is what it is. I damaged my heart, the doctor said. I haven't been home since I been clean. Six months now. Three years I rode the rollercoaster." She rolled her eyes. "Anyway, who cares?"

"You never know."

"Are you married? I don't see a ring."

"I don't wear rings. I was married. To a Mormon girl."

"What happened? You fuck around?"

"Not exactly. My wife had serious mental problems. She tried to kill me a couple of times. The last time she almost succeeded."

"You're kidding?"

"I never kid, kid. I got a knife scar on my shoulder that says I love you."

"In cursive, right? So, no kids, right?"

He smiled and shook his head.

"Where is she... your wife?"

"She's dead. As of two weeks ago Thursday. Car wreck on the way to Lake Tahoe." He didn't mention she was drunk out of her mind and smashed head-on into a minivan with a family of six, all but the mother killed instantly. He had been to the hospital to visit the mother, but she couldn't have visits except for family and there was no family to visit. So he left the flowers and went to the morgue to visit his wife for the first time in two years. Half her head was cut off. The part that wasn't was still beautiful.

"I'm sorry, you know? I mean, fuck."

"Thanks."

He looked away from the girl's voluminous gaze, out into the shadowy desert and up to where the spectral moon had peeked out from between a ragged wave of clouds. A chance of rain, the radio said.

The coughing, middle-aged waitress brought his miner's special. On the large plate decorated with gobbling turkeys, there was a dark rubbery slab of something that was supposed to be steak, some make-believe mashed potatoes, and green beans that looked regurgitated. He took a single bite of each and then set down his fork. "I think I've lost my appetite."

"I can make better muffins than this. The secret is to use real butter, not cheap shit margarine. My mom used to buy homemade butter from a woman in the country. God, that was so good."

"I bet it was good. I'm definitely a butter man."

"So where are you, like, headed, butter man?"

"Like I told you, darlin', when I picked you up looking so broke down and forlorn. North."

"Stop being cute. I hate cute. Where north?"

"My cuteness is purely unintentional. Coeur d'Alene. Promised my wife a long time ago I'd dump her ashes in the lake if I outlived her—I think she knew that was almost a certainty. We went there on our honeymoon and on our tenth anniversary."

"Sweet," she said. "It's beautiful up there. I never been, though." Then she lit up. "Hey, you're probably goin' right through Grangeville."

"Don't you want to wait for your car to be towed in?"

"Why? I can't afford to get it fixed."

"I'll cover that, too. It's just a water pump." He only had $600 left in his wallet, enough to make it to Coeur d'Alene. After that, who knew?

"Well, that's great, mister Reckless, but I have to be home tomorrow, you know? I promised. I can't break my promise. Not this time. What is it you want from me, anyway? As if I didn't know. I've heard that no strings shit a hundred times before."

"Not from me you haven't."

Her gaze narrowed. "I don't work on holidays," she said. "I'm already in holiday mode. Time to hug the family. Look at old pictures when life was good. Stuff myself with turkey and dressing. Family crap. Giving thanks and shit."

"I'm a day early, I guess," he said. "I'm a natural thanks and shit giver."

"Hmph. What have you got to be thankful for?"

"Peace, love, and understanding, I guess."

"And I'm thankful for your charitable contribution to my favorite cause."

"Right," he said, rubbing his tired eyes. "As far as I'm concerned, you could be one of Jerry's Kids."

She giggled with delight. "Maybe I'll have a miraculous recovery and rock your world." She tried to read his reaction. He didn't even blink. "Anyway, I was thinking, I could ride with you all the way to Grangeville. Show my gratitude."

"To a fellow pilgrim?"

For some reason she thought that was hilarious. She cackled and had to cover her mouth to keep from spitting out the last crumbs of the muffin. Then, still grinning, she took a drink from her water, made murky by the burnt edges of the hundred.

When he paid the bill, he told the dour looking man at the cash register it was the worst food he'd ever tasted. "Aw, hell, you ain't supposed to taste it," the man said, giving him a nasty smirk. "You're just supposed to eat it."

"Why don't you eat this?" Reckless said, quietly. He leaned forward and let go a violent punch that stopped with his closed fist within an inch of the man's face. The man flinched and went pale, staring at his oversized and scarred knuckles. With a grin, Reckless opened his hand and lightly slapped him.

The girl calmly picked up a pack of Juicy Fruit gum and winked at the stunned cashier. When they were in the car, the girl giggled and said, "Are you some kind of tough guy or somethin'?"

He put on his driving glasses. "Do I look like a tough guy?"

"Hell, yeah. Even Superman wore glasses."

"Uh, huh, but I'm not in disguise. I used to box, that's all. And I don't appreciate that kind of disrespectful treatment."

"Ever fight Muhammad Ali?"

He grunted. "Hell, no, thank you, Jesus. I sparred a few rounds with the Bayonne Bleeder one time, though. Chuck Wepner. Fucking madman. I would have beat him on points if they would have kept score. Ali fought the guy one time, turned his face to hamburger, and the guy still didn't quit. He was the inspiration for the Rocky movies that little hump Stallone made. Me, I was strictly in it for the ride. I had potential, but I was undisciplined and wild."

"My life story."

"That was a long time ago. I still go to the gym sometimes. Nowadays I'm mostly civilized."

"Old, in other words."

"Yeah. Old."

Temporarily revived by the five cups of 30 weight coffee, Reckless held up his end of a conversation until after they crossed the Idaho border, when he started seeing stars blazing not in the sky but on the highway and realized it was time to find a place to stretch out and snuff out all the lights that sought to blind him. They found a seedy motel in Homedale, the only one in town with a vacancy. "I'll get you to Grangeville tomorrow in time to peel potatoes," he said to her when he pulled into the Saddleback Inn. She didn't seem disappointed at all. She looked as exhausted as he was.

The next morning he awoke to the beep alarm on his watch. Outside it was spitting rain again. The motel room was dank and dingy, smelling of long-ago smoked cigarettes, sour linen, and bad dreams. The heater rattled and blew out air rank enough to have come from deep underground. Trish had said her whole family would be there, except for her dad who had died of a heart attack, and maybe he would show up, too. She was going to help her mama and little sister cook their feast. She seemed genuinely excited about it.

He glanced at his watch. Another hour or so until the levee broke and sunlight flooded the Idaho sagebrush. He threw the thin covers off and sat up on the side of the twin bed. His stiff joints ached, especially his right shoulder. Fucking arthritis. He wondered how many punches he had left in it. Better not waste any more just to freak out some small-time grease pimp.

Through isolated smears in the window grime, he had a good view of the almost empty parking lot. The motel's Vacancy sign flashed on and off. The girl was still asleep. She was asleep last night when he got out of the shower, curled in a ball with the covers pulled up over her eyes like she was scared of the boogeyman. He was no boogeyman, although Laurie had thought so during many of her alcohol-induced psychotic episodes. He watched her sleep for a while. He wondered what it would be like to have a daughter.

"Wake up, sleepyhead," he said, yawning. "Time to go to Disneyland." His voice was full of phlegm. He cleared his throat and tried again. She didn't stir. "Jesus," he said. He got up and gently shook her shoulder. "Hey, kid!"

He turned on the bedside lamp. He reached over and touched her cheek with his rough knuckles. He sat back down. He turned off the lamp. Then he turned it on again. He held his head in his hands. TKO.

There was thunder in the distance. He thought about Laurie, his love, his life. Once upon a time she was a lot like this young hooker had been once upon a time: sassy, naïve, fearless, flush and fettled with the vigor of unconditional love from a good home, ready to set forth with him as her companion on an expedition to wherever fate and fancy led them. She hadn't realized you could fall off the edge of the world. Neither had he.

Now Laurie and Trish were exactly alike. The way everyone was alike at the end. He didn't need his world rocked; it had been rocked enough. He had wanted to deliver her to her family's doorstep. He had wanted to see the smiling faces of her family as they came out to greet her. He had wanted to be a part of it though he knew he could not.

He had slept well. The best sleep in ages. No dreams. Now it was almost dawn, and he welcomed the coming of the light. Even the barren desert looked good in the morning, whether it be rain spattered or sun beaten.

"Don't worry, little darlin'," he said. "One way or another, we'll be home soon."

ROGER MENSINK

Lone Pine Says Howdy

From October/November 2015

THE CLOUDS ROLLED in from the west. They broke over the mountains and scattered over the desert, over the giant valley through which we drove. The road was in good shape—straight, no potholes, predictable. The sun was placed about a hand's width over the mountains, on the driver's side window. Ahead of us rose a mound of sorts. This is when Dolores asked, "When you painted, did you prefer to wear cowboy boots or slippers?"

Dolores turned her head to look at me. She had blond hair piled on top of blond hair, Bridget Bardot style, and she was sporting brand new eyelash extensions (because that is what most of the women in her gym wore, and they were her girlfriends). But Dolores, being Dolores, also wore Columbia snow boots—the kind guys who are paid to put on snow chains by the side of the road wear. In between the eyelashes and the snow boots she wore a Patagonia down sweater, light blue, with just the right amount of duct tape holding it together. And she wore jeans. And underneath her jeans Dolores had a tattoo across the small of her back that read "Ski Tart," a present from me to her on her 34th birthday.

Earlier that day, we had stopped in Mojave, at a Shell station across the main road from the parallel railroad tracks, where big yellow and black locomotives sit and wait for who knows what. I took some photos of Dolores hanging onto one of those locomotives. She had one leg on the first step leading to the cab. The other leg swung out over the tracks. *Whoohoo!* she seemed to be saying. *Coming at ya!* But what you can really see in those photos, as you can see in most of the photos I've ever taken of Dolores, are her enormous thighs, bulging through her jeans, thighs made of steel.

Afterwards we filled up the tank, used the restroom, and bought a bag of Funyuns. Dolores ate the entire bag almost right away, and for a couple of hours we drove along without saying much. Dolores had her earphones in. I preferred to listen to the steady sound of the car as it parted the desert air—the mufflered engine, the tires as they hummed over the pavement. At some point I made the decision to pull over so we could check out a cluster of abandoned buildings. A bit of desert exploration. One of the abandoned buildings had a For Sale sign on it, and next to it stood the remainder of what had once been a diner. Dolores walked around the building with the For Sale sign—I saw her peeking into one of its large grimy windows—while I went to inspect the diner. It must have been out of commission for decades. I stepped cautiously inside through what used to be a front door. Holes in the walls and roof let in slanting rays of sunlight. Boards and sheets of old plywood lay scattered across the bar and barstools. Real ghost town stuff. When I came back out, I could see Dolores walking backwards and holding out her hands at some lanky dude with a ponytail and a dog beside him. She was saying something to him, but I couldn't quite understand it.

When the guy saw me, he pointed his finger at our car. "You both need to get back on the road and get out of here," he said.

"Whoa," I said. I looked at Dolores and asked, "Are you all right?"

She didn't seem too rattled, just careful. "I'm fine," she said.

I asked the man if he was the owner of the building for sale.

He ignored my question. "How would you feel if I came snooping around your place? You'd probably shoot me," he said.

"No, I probably wouldn't," I said. "Besides, there's not a For Sale sign on my house. *For Sale.* People are going to check it out."

Dolores said, "Let's go." And just as we turned our backs and began to walk toward the car, the man's dog came sniffing up behind us. "Goddamnit, Bo. Get back here!" the man hollered at the dog.

I almost jumped. But I didn't.

After Dolores asked her question, I thought about it a little, then said, "It's actually not a bad question. I think what you're asking is, was I a predator, an insouciant raptor, who paints in his slippers and robe, or did I appear on the stage as someone more action oriented, someone willing to express himself, and who, although he might not have worn cowboy boots, certainly wore some kind of paint-splattered boots? Is that what you're asking, sweetie?"

She answered, "No. That's not what I'm asking at all."

I groaned in my seat. Umpteen times is how many times we had driven this road we were on. Looking back now, I can postulate it might have become the thin thread that bound us to each other. And now this. I was tired of the jive, tired of Dolores. Hence, when I saw the welcome outlines through the windshield of the mound—red, cylindrical, and almost perfectly symmetrical—I said, with a gusto not entirely feigned, "There it is. The mound."

The *mound* is in actual fact a cinder cone. A few winters ago we had climbed it, slipping one step down for every two steps up until we got to the bigger rocks near the top, where it was far steeper and higher than I had anticipated. But Dolores showed the way, and we scrambled hand over hand. Finally we stood on the summit. From up there the highway appeared as a slender pencil line, thinning and disappearing to the north and south. Before us to the west began the step-up to the Sierra Crest, and when we turned around, we could see all the way across the bare, stippled valley—at that time of day it was the color of an unripe guava—to the Coso Mountains to the east. I took loads of photos, and in the ones I took of Dolores, her sportswoman's thighs once again dominated.

But Dolores was not finished with her question. She asked again, "Slippers or cowboy boots?"

I answered, "Neither." And I left it at that.

Dolores snorted and shifted her focus from me to the mound. Its growing presence was not just a beacon of adventures past, it also signaled our turnoff to the place where we planned to have a late lunch. I looked in the rearview mirror. With no one behind me, I took my time turning off the highway. We rolled over some cattle guards and onto a dirt road, dusty and dry and ribbed like corduroy (or like a washboard) by some concealed process of physics. I put on the gas, and right away the car began to rattle and shake.

"Slow down please," Dolores said. "You're going to ruin the car."

I held onto the steering wheel with both hands and extended arms, and with a firm set to my jaw, sped up some more. I wanted to try something new. "It's the only way to even out the ruts," I said. Still, the faster I drove, the more the car complained. It sounded as if the whole thing was going to come apart. I must not be going fast enough, I thought. There has to be a point at which the car begins to glide over the ridges in the road. To reach that magic moment, I sped up even more, but then, well, I didn't want to ruin the car either, so I slowed down, almost to a walking pace. And things quieted down.

Dolores said, not very loudly, "Fuck you."

I said, "It's okay, no harm done."

Around us, piles of black volcanic rock, rough and serrated, reared up from the flinty valley floor. The road took its time winding its way through these dark, Godzilla-like formations, then abruptly straightened for the last mile or so to end in a flattened cul-de-sac occupied by a handful of empty camping spots, a couple of picnic tables, and a little cinderblock house sheltering a pit toilet. There was no one else around.

While Dolores visited the toilet, I fetched the provisions out of the back of the car. I also checked the box that carried our skis, clamped onto the top of the car. I thought the vibrations might have loosened it, but it turned out to be fine. Dolores must have thought the same thing because the first thing she asked after coming out of the little cinder block house was if I had checked the *boite*. Dolores had recently toyed with the idea of learning French, and that was one of the first words she had learned. She had learned other words as well, but *boite* in reference to the box on top of the car stuck around. That, and an expression, *Voila, bon appetit!*, which she sometimes said after doing something simple like taking out the garbage or putting the laundry in the dryer.

Dolores next asked for the keys to the car. She wanted to retrieve her climbing shoes, shoes as delicate as ballet slippers. "Are you going to climb a boulder?" I asked. Dolores had been climbing boulders since forever. She had tried to interest me, but I have pretensions to playing the classical guitar and so I have to be careful with my fingers, especially my fingernails. Dolores doesn't have those limitations. I remember very well the first time I shook hands with her. This was in a cable car filled with ski instructors. I had been taken aback by how rough and hard those hands were. Her grip was at least as strong as mine. Not that it mattered. I was already smitten. She could have been born with flippers instead of hands (as some people are), and it wouldn't have made a difference.

With climbing shoes in hand, Dolores pointed behind me to an imposing stack of volcanic rocks, just behind the picnic tables. "Those boulders," she answered.

I began to grope around for my favorite bottle of alcetto balsamico. "Do you want me to spot you?" I asked. I did that sometimes, stand under Dolores' butt with my hands in the air, as if I could somehow *catch* her. But Dolores was already gone, tromping her way through the creosote and manzanita to find the leeward approach to the challenge. I took out an awesome loaf of bread I had scored at the farmer's market and a plastic container of homemade mozzarella. The tomatoes I'd picked the day before, and the bag of organically grown spinach I had gotten at Whole Foods on the way out. I had also brought along a case of ale from one of my brewing homies, and I thought it might be nice to open one now so I could drink it with my sandwich.

The sandwich was good, as was the beer, but the beer chilled me. Trying to keep warm, I crossed my arms and folded over myself. A small bug, smaller in length than a dime, half black, half orange, crawled between my feet. I wondered where it might be headed, so far out in the open. I moved one foot, and it stopped, hesitated, then kept going. I moved the other foot, same thing. I whispered something to it, then looked up when I heard a scream. Overhead, Dolores stood on the last of the pile of rocks in a typical mountaineer's pose, legs wide and arms outstretched.

"*Arrghh!* Yeah!"

I leaned back to better behold her triumph. Dolores was breathing in great gulps of air. She made a fist pump, then fearlessly toed the edge, from where she pretended to clear her throat as if to spit on me. I didn't react, so instead she closed her eyes and arched her back to receive upon her bosom the last of the golden light. Replete, she spun around and made a little jump. Another, one more, and she was gone, to reappear shortly thereafter from around the pile of rocks, still breathing hard. She sat down across from me at the picnic table. "Fuck, I banged up my finger." She held it out to me. Her hands were as grubby as could be, her fingers stained from dirt and rock. One of them bled slightly. I could see it was a scratch, just a little deeper than the rest. "Lick it," she said.

I slid her sandwich forward on its paper plate and looked at her, bemused.

"You're not going to lick it?" Dolores kept her finger poised in front of my face.

"I can pee on it if you like. To disinfect it."

"That's disgusting." Dolores retracted her finger. "But thanks for making my sandwich." She bit into it and said, "*Hmmm.* Delicious. I love this place."

I noted then the way she looked around as she wiped her mouth with the back of her sleeve—that look of innocent satisfaction, plain *belief,* the same look she beamed when for instance describing her faith in interplanetary travel—and no matter how I would have liked to join her, in truth I was somewhat blinded by familiarity and incomprehension. I was aware this place had something to do with water flowing out of the giant dried lake a little to the north, eons ago, and volcanic eruptions, and lava cooled by the water. Even so, I couldn't care enough about what I was seeing. Geology is not my strong suit. Besides, we had eaten lunch on this very picnic table so many times before. The years were flitting by, that's all I knew.

Dolores took a swig of what was left of my beer, then partially unzipped the front of her down sweater. A moment later, the sun dipped behind the mountains and put us into shadow. I said, "That's it. I'm going to switch out my shorts." I had put my cargo shorts on that morning on account of my contacts. When I'm wearing contacts, I need reading glasses for seeing up close, and suddenly shorts with lots of pockets become eminently practical. I'm able to put my reading glasses in the pocket by the side and whip them out whenever I need them. In the other pockets I put my sunglasses, my smart phone, the lens hood for my camera, my wallet, keys, and whatever else I need to carry.

I walked to the car and took off my shorts, and before I put on my pants I did a little jig in my underwear, daring the cold, and yelled to Dolores, "Hey, do you think I have old man's legs?"

To my surprise she said, "No, you look good." She meant it, I think, at least by the way she was watching me—legs crossed, leaning back, elbows on the table. I guess it's something I worry about, even though I make light of it: the eventual degradation of the body, loss of muscle mass, bone density—this whole issue of aging, though I'm not that old. On the other hand, I'm a decade older than Dolores, who furthermore works as a trainer and yoga instructor. And before that she worked in the upper echelons of California ski instruction. Hence the handshake in the cable car. Dolores had been the testing clinician for a group of part-time ski instructors whose aim was to attain a higher certification. I was among the instructors. Call it a mid-life crisis. Others have, but it matters not at all to me; as far as I'm concerned, it was fun being a ski instructor for a while.

The first ride up the gondola we had huddled together, our goggles and gloves loose on our laps. To loosen us up and perhaps take our minds off the blizzard conditions and the way the wind whipped the car back and forth, Dolores had each of us tell a joke. *How many ski instructors does it take to change a light bulb? Three. One to turn the bulb and two to criticize the turn. How can you tell who's the ski instructor in the room? Don't worry, he'll let you know.* Stuff like that, but when it came my turn to tell a joke, I couldn't think of one. I was too distracted by Dolores' prominently displayed nametag. It read, after her name, *Western Division Tech Team.* I glanced at the Subaru patch on her official tech team jacket and let my eyes wander, discretely, over the thighs that stretched the fabric of her ski pants. Frozen tresses of blond hair, woven into icicles, poked out from beneath her white, stickered helmet. She was, all of her, jaw-droppingly wonderful.

With the long pants on, I set about getting everything back into the car. Dolores remained sitting idly, as if to stress we were in no hurry. And it was true, the bulk of the drive was behind us. Before us, we only needed to drive to the town of Lone Pine. There, we had friends—Dolores' friends, really—who ran a motel. These two, a full-time climbing and hiking couple, tattooed and pierced, had put whatever money their parents left them into the motel, which they had bought from an old Mormon woman whose husband had died the year before. It lay on a side street and had a sloping lawn out front, between the parking lot and the street, over which were scattered a mismatched assortment of deck chairs. A huge stone barbeque pit was sunk into the middle of the lawn, around which we routinely ate, smoked, and drank beer and talked about what conditions on the mountain would be like the next day. It could tire me out. The last time we came up, I had excused myself. I said I had felt something like a cold coming on and that maybe I should go inside and stay warm. I had returned to the little wood-paneled room with the queen-sized bed in the middle and watched three back-to-back episodes of *Fat Guys in the Woods* before Dolores came back in, glossy eyed and a little drunk and angry with me for having opted out.

After I finished putting everything away, I sat down beside Dolores. "So, are we ready to take off?"

"I've been ready," she said. "You know, maybe we can camp here next time. It's an awesome spot."

"Not going to happen."

"Really?"

"Too close to the highway," I explained. "People around here, those who live outside of the towns, are most likely feral. Even now, a truck with pipe stacks belching diesel smoke could come skidding in, and we would be in a world of trouble." I asked her to remember what had happened earlier that day. In my opinion, it had been a potentially serious situation.

But Dolores merely placed her hands on her knees, yawned, and stood up. "I'll drive."

"Yeah, you drive," I said. "The fucking oddballs that live out here. People like us, we drive up and down this highway, and we're just a tremendous source of anxiety for them."

Dolores stopped halfway to the car. She shuffled her feet in the dirt, sending up little plumes of it. "You don't even like carpet," she said.

I had to laugh. Carpet. To wit: Dolores, after we married, had moved into my house. I live in one of the oldest neighborhoods in Los Angeles. My house has original hardwood floors, put down in 1914. Rare, good housing stock. But Dolores thought the flooring was cold and wanted to put in carpet, at least in the bedroom. The first times she mentioned this, I remained calm. I explained that the people who had lived in the house before had for decades covered the hardwood floors with carpet, which is why the floors were in such good shape. But later, after Dolores brought it up a few more times, I lost some of my patience. One night I yelled at her. "Are you fucking kidding me? This is not a fucking ski condo. This is my house!" I corrected, "Our house."

But what did Dolores want, really? When she was not wearing ski boots or hiking boots or climbing shoes? What was wrong with her wanting nothing more than to spread out on a nice, soft carpet, on her tummy, and watch big screen TV? I regret to say there were times when I thought Dolores incompatible with my Mission style oak chairs, when the thighs that had so predisposed me to her seemed to have become too big for my fully restored Craftsman bungalow. That night, after I lost my patience, she cried for the first time, and I knew I had effected an unforgivable sin. I had taken a ski goddess down from her throne—never mind that at the time she was wearing slippers with bunny ears—and watched, numbly, as she wept in frustration.

Once back on the highway, back on a level asphalt surface, the car rolled smoothly forward. From the beating of the washboard road to this, barely a ripple. It resembled a miracle. Most of the valley was already dimmed. Only a third of it to the east was still lit by the sun, a stretch of land turned garish orange against the sky's deep blue. Meanwhile, the scattered clouds overhead had turned into long, lenticular waves, painted pink. Next to me, Dolores sat in silence, dreamily driving. Half an hour or so later, I yelled, "Emergency!"

Dolores' hand jumped on the wheel, and the car lurched. Dolores corrected, and it lurched in the other direction. We both held our breath; it could have gone either way, but the car straightened. Flushed red, Dolores turned to me and asked, "What the fuck is wrong with you now?"

I said, "I don't have my wallet." I had become aware of it in the last few minutes. I had checked to make sure my wallet was not in my back pocket where it could pinch a nerve and make my left leg go numb, and it wasn't—but it wasn't in my front pocket, either. After some further checking, I found my wallet wasn't anywhere on me at all, and that's when I had that awful feeling.

"You must have left it in your shorts. Check them," Dolores said.

I reached into the back seat, but I could tell just by picking up the shorts that they were empty. I untwisted myself and tried to reach under the seat. We had just passed the turnoff to Death Valley and were slowing down as we approached Lone Pine. I felt something wet or melted. "The hell with it," I said. "Maybe you could pull over, and I can have a look around."

Dolores steered the car onto the shoulder and flicked on the hazards. I opened the door and stepped out. There was little traffic.

Along the shoulder was strung the usual fence of barbed wire, and on the other side two thick poles supported a wood sign across the top that read "Lone Pine Says Howdy!" In the failing light I knelt down to look under the seats. Nothing. I checked the backseat, under the clothes, in the food bags, the glove compartment. Still nothing. Beaten, I scrunched back into the front seat. I said, "I need to think about this." I ran my hands through my hair, scratched my head. Could the wallet really be gone? It hardly seemed conceivable. How could I acknowledge such a thing? Then, in a flash of memory, I grasped just how gone it really was. I slapped my forehead. But of course! It had happened when I switched out my shorts. I had put the wallet on the roof of the car by the driver's side and then promptly forgotten about it. I leaned forward in my seat. I beseeched Dolores for forgiveness. I explained everything to her. I confessed my stupidity. But I had to ask: "Did you not see the wallet on the roof of the car before we drove off?"

Dolores said, "Let's just go back and look for it."

"Look for it?"

"Why not? Think about it. The wallet would have bounced off long before we got to the highway." With the back of her hand she somewhat uncharacteristically smacked me on the chest. "It's somewhere on the dirt road. We can backtrack and find it."

I saw her point. It would take some time, but it was worth the try. I sighed deeply. "Turn it around," I said. "And let's give this a shot."

The entire way back Dolores drove ten to fifteen miles over the speed limit. I sat hunched forward in my seat and wrung my hands. All my attention was focused on the small chance of finding the wallet. It was unbearable to imagine it lying in the dirt, alone and forgotten. All because of a stupid mistake. "How could we have been so stupid?" I asked again and again. Dolores for her part said very little. She seemed barely concerned. We drove into the night, and by the time we turned once more onto the dirt road, the mound no longer seemed to welcome us. It was now a somber silhouette, a mere shape, uncaring and aloof. But that's how all things appear to me, once the sun has gone down.

The plan was for me to walk before the car and scan the ground by the light of the headlamps. At first I walked slowly, deliberately, looking left to right. Five, ten minutes later I began a light jog. I ran to part the darkness. For once Dolores and I were concurrent. As I ran, she kept pace with me perfectly, and the washboard road opened up before us. I scanned it back and forth, from one side to the other, determined nothing would escape my scrutiny. If the wallet were anywhere on this road, I would find it. That's all that mattered now, more than carpet or hardwood floors, more than my "artsy fartsy" background—which would never be entirely knowable to Dolores anyway—more than Dolores' frustration at having been reduced from ski goddess to weekend warrior—though, as I often told her, her life had considerably expanded—more than the distrust and disappointment we sometimes directed at each other, more than the distress I had felt when Dolores hung up not one but three hummingbird feeders and the slight embarrassment I suffered when she held my hand at social gatherings. The hell with all that, I thought, as I trotted along. Look at us now—we're a machine, a wallet-sweeping machine tunneling through the darkness of the valley. What could be better than this?

My breath soon stabilized. There was not another light to be seen, and nothing to be heard but the tires as they rolled over the ribbed dirt road and my own two feet as they pounded the dusty surface. It made for a steady and comforting rhythm. As long as we continued to advance through the darkness like this, hope could not be extinguished. Indeed, I might have liked for it to go on forever, and it was not until we had very nearly reached the end of the road, within sight of where it opened into the little campground, that I saw something. At first it looked like just another rock, but as I got closer, it began to take on the quality of an object, of a thing that didn't belong there. This thing, which turned out to be a small and leathery triptych, lay supine in the middle of the road, open to the sky. I ran toward it. I crouched before it, and I wanted to say, "I'm here. I've come back." But instead I snatched it up and held it aloft, and now it was my turn to scream, "Whoohoo!" I ran to the passenger side window, which I had left open, and leaned in to show Dolores. "We actually found it!" I cried.

Dolores smiled and said, "I told you so." She instructed me to back up a little. She wanted to turn the car around. I put the wallet in my left front pocket and watched, content, as she made a U-turn in the cul-de-sac. Then, quickly, I skipped across the road and reached out my hand as if I were hailing a cab—over here!—with my head tucked into my shoulder to escape the glare of the headlamps.

But Dolores drove right by me. And I laughed. On our way to the movies, to buy groceries, drive to the gym, whatever, I sometimes opened the door with the remote and got in and drove off as if I had forgotten all about Dolores. Then of course I would stop, back up, and Dolores would get in the car with a wry look on her face, and I would say, "Oh, my God. I knew I had forgotten something."

I could easily have caught up to her of course, on account of how slowly she drove over the washboard road. But I chose to remain rooted to the spot. I thought, Dolores will just have to back up. Funny girl. But Dolores didn't stop, didn't back up, didn't open the door and tell me, "Stupid. Get in!" Dolores kept driving. The car must have dipped down because the red glow of the tail lamps suddenly disappeared, then popped back up. I began to think: Not funny. The taillights blinked out and reappeared again. "Hey!" I shouted, in spite of myself. The little lights were already far too small. When they disappeared a third time, they stayed gone for good.

For a few moments I stared, motionless, at the exact point where total darkness had taken over. My eyes adjusted to the void. I said,

"This is not cool." Alone in a vast emptiness, I decided to make myself smaller by squatting down on my heels. I rested my forearms on the top of my thighs. I looked at my phone. No reception. Minutes went by. Actual minutes. And as these long minutes accrued, a terrifying possibility began to fill my chest, to which I somehow wanted to sketch and give shape in the sand before me. But all I could do was sit still and repeat to myself the word, *Seriously*. Could Dolores *seriously* have left me in the most literal fucking way possible?

I began to shiver from the cold, or tremble from the sudden excitement of the moment—a bit of both perhaps. I played back in my mind the events of the day. It's true I had to be talked into going on the trip in the first place. Dolores requires a minimum number of snow days. For me, they are too many—almost 30 days out of the year spent skiing—but we've talked about it. I've reminded Dolores that it had been her decision to go back to school and leave the mountain life style behind, if only for a few years. At a certain point in time, of course, there had been no question of returning. We have a substantial life together. And though the long drives over the desert and through the valley, from late November to May, are beginning to make me physically ill, it wasn't that long ago we were perfectly happy. It wasn't that long ago we went to the tattoo parlor together (upscale; more than a three-month waiting list) and I held Dolores' hand while the needle etched into her skin.

When I finally looked up out there—a strange effort—I was immediately overwhelmed, maybe appalled, at the number of stars I could see. Enormous clumps and giant swaths of them were thrown across the night sky. It was hard to make out even one simple constellation. In the face of this perfect disorder, I couldn't even begin to think about what I might do next. I was loath to do anything, really. Why should I disturb the crystalline purity of this brand new reality? I wondered if things had already gone past the point of no return.

Straight ahead, the ridge of mountains to the east rose up to begin the shape of the earth. Once I focused on the outline of those mountains, as flat against the firmament as if cut from cardboard, I had a most unusual feeling. For a moment, I felt the entire earth tilt forward and the stars stand still. And I was on the earth, balanced, riding it through space, with one hand resting lightly in the dirt before me.

It all ended with a slight scintillation to my left, a flickering aura. At first I thought I had imagined it. But when I stood up to see better, I could tell that, yes, the night had been compromised, and more or less from where Dolores had earlier dropped out of sight. A rock formation, still very far away, glowed faintly, then dropped back into darkness. Another did the same, and pretty soon I was able to follow the strange bouncing light, from one pile of rocks to another, until eventually it lost its borealis-like quality and became centered into two blazing beams of white light headed my way, first swinging about a little, then focused, on the final stretch.

A part of me wanted to laugh, but another part of me was too angry to laugh. So Dolores was coming back for me after all. And look at how she was driving. It could be panic. It could be she had become afraid of what she had done and was making up for lost time. But then again, knowing Dolores as I do, she might just have been showing off. Because Dolores was simply flying over the washboard road. She was ripping it up. Go Dolores! But then a little later I could see it was not Dolores. It was not our car. The headlamps on this car were spaced differently, lower and wider, and it was missing a *boite*.

That's when I started to picture how I might have looked out there, in the beams of those headlamps. Perhaps I looked frightened, or perhaps I looked frightening. Perhaps I looked like an insect, pale and upright. Or like an apparition. Or perhaps I looked like myself. Regardless, and for the second time that night, I half turned away from bright, blinding lights.

But this time the car did not drive by. It stopped. About 30 feet before me, engine running, a well-tuned low rumble. I then had a choice: I could either run like a rabbit, zigzagging through the shrubs and rocks, or I could walk forward and hope for the best—say, a couple of teenagers with a six pack of beer in the backseat, their faces caught between fear and indecision. At that point I felt like I had nothing to lose. And so this is what I did. I walked up to the passenger side of the car. I bent down, peered through the dark-tinted window, and bravely waved hello to whomever was inside.

ERIC MARONEY

The Incorrupt Body of Carlo Busso

From July/August 2010

We always carry around in our body the death of Jesus, so that the life of Jesus may also be revealed in our body. —2 Corinthians 4:10

I.

CARLO BUSSO STEERED his cousin's old Vespa up the via Latina and around the corner of the via Vesuvio.

"Carlo, be careful," his girlfriend Mariaflavia yelled, but it was too late. All she saw was a flash of raven long hair and a wake of exhaust, and Carlo Busso was gone from sight. She sighed and walked into the pizzeria, tamping out her cigarette on the sidewalk with a heel. So she was spared the squeal of breaks, the screams of bystanders, and the wail of the ambulance with its two notes, one high and one low, seeming to grow larger in space as they approached the scene, like two scissors slicing the air as each heavy, profound moment passed on the corner of vias Latina and Vesuvio.

II.

The impulse to beatify Carlo Busso was there long before that early spring day when he steered his cousin's Vespa up the wrong way on the via Latina and was killed by a bus. Carlo was an elegant, dark young man with graceful, arching eyebrows, long, curly black hair, and a face of symmetry, proportion, and simple economy. He was raised by his Nonna and mother, his father having died when he was an infant, so his natural predilections were allowed to grow under the careful governance of the women, who pruned his personality here, nipped his psyche there, and watered his pristine roots just so, developing the full flower of the masculine ideal that had been uprooted from their lives.

Even with the attention, all that praiseful "Carlo is this" and "Carlo is that" gave him no more than the essential allotment of self-love. Why force the issue with other people, why demand and require, if it would come naturally? Why worry about getting this or that when the circumstances of his fate, his position in life, his soft good looks and firm posture worked to bring the coveted goods of life into his hands?

When he was 13, Carlo's grandmother called him over:

"You've been confirmed, Carlo," she said, squinting through a veil of cigarette smoke. "Now always wear this." She hung a small red bead suspended from a black thread around his neck. Carlo fingered the bead.

"What is it?" he asked. He knew full well; he just realized there was a ritual to enact here, that his Nonna demanded this question.

"Put it under your shirt," she clucked. "Don't let the world see it. It's so people won't give you the evil eye. They will resent you. Your beauty and your brain. They will wish you harm. This will protect you, my boy." And she patted Carlo on the head and told him to go outside and play.

III.

Carlo's mother worked, so on holidays Nonna Busso watched the boy. She attended Mass every day. She had been widowed for two decades—Busso men were never long in years—and she still felt she should be wearing black.

"I should be wearing black," she would tell Carlo on the way to Mass, clucking her tongue. "But it is so old-fashioned." Instead she wore pleated gold polyester pantsuits with bright green buttons, or jumpsuits of primary colors with knee-high boots. Her golden loop earrings elongated her lobes. False eyelashes fluttered beneath her well-defined brow. The boy and his grandmother walked down the via Latina to the little church. Scooters and cars sped by, ignoring stop signs and traffic lights. Nonna Busso wagged her finger in disapproval.

She prayed, she sang, she stood, she sat, she kneeled. She took communion, thrusting her tongue out at the priest—none of this new fangled cupping the Host in her own hand for her—and went to confession. After Mass the local priest always shook Nonna Busso's hand and tussled Carlo's hair. The church was nearly empty. Only the very young and the very old attended.

So it was particularly painful to Nonna Busso that right after his confirmation, Carlo announced to both his Nonna and his mother he would no longer be attending Mass. He was a man now, he explained with dignity. It was his choice. The women exchanged glances. They disapproved but let him travel along his own benighted way. They allowed him to reflect the image of men they had known and loved who had died and inhabited the world of memory, repeated, urgent prayers, and a thread of long trailing regret.

IV.

Mariaflavia held Carlo's hand. They sat on a bench on the via Latina in front of a wall scrawled with a generation's worth of graffiti. A bus drove by, enveloping them in acrid exhaust.

"Phew," Mariaflavia waved a hand. "What a disgusting city."

"It's not that bad, baby," Carlo leaned into her, resting his head in the lap of her faded denim jeans. The warmth of her legs was soothing, even on this scalding summer day. She played with a lock of his hair. She looked down at him as if from far away.

"Is your Nonna home?"

"Where else?" Carlo scoffed. "She is always at home. No job. No husband. Just Mass and TV."

"I hate to do it in my apartment," Mariaflavia mused. "It doesn't feel right."

"Oh, no," Carlo purred, running a hand up her thigh. "There you are wrong. It always feels so right..."

And they pulled each other down the via Latina, past a shrine to Mary in a niche along a pitted, graffiti-laced wall. All around the little statue were placards of supplication and thanks: *GRAZIA PER GIULA* and *PER GRAZIE RICEVUTA* or simply *GRAZIE MARIA*. Once in bed Carlo and Mariaflavia made very quiet love, for in the living room just feet away her young brother was studiously watching cartoons.

V.

"Go with her," Carlo's mother pleaded. "I know you don't go to Mass anymore. But your grandma doesn't remember how to get around Rome. She'll get lost on the Metro." Carlo was 14 and reluctant to go. He had no wish to see the exhumed remains of Padre Zisa's incorrupt body.

"It's disgusting, Ma... a dead body."

"It's only an afternoon. If you do it, you can stay out until ten tonight," his mother waved a pleading hand at her son. Carlo hung tough, so she said, "I'll give you 20,000 lire. You can stay out till ten and play video games as much as your heart desires."

"Fork it over," Carlo held out his hand. His mother rummaged through her purse. She placed a folded lire note in his palm. They looked at one another without apparent emotion. Then Carlo smiled, revealing his glimmering white teeth, and his mother patted his head and kissed his brow, depositing a layer of scarlet on his smooth brown skin.

VI.

Padre Zisa was laid out in a brass coffin covered by a glass case. Tapers burned from high candlesticks. Flowers draped the coffin and festooned the low arches of the ceiling. *Carabinieri* stood at the entrance and the exit. When supplicants in line would dawdle, cry, pray, fall to their knees and begin the rosary, the *carabinieri* at the exit would lazily step forward and move them along. Thousands lined up to see the incorrupt remains of Padre Zisa. On the Metro ride Nonna had regaled Carlo with stories he had already heard about the miraculous powers of the famous Padre Zisa. The poor parish priest ran an orphanage and soup kitchen. He was crushed by his worldly duties in one of Rome's most squalid neighborhoods. His back was hunched, and he was blind in one eye. It was said he suffered from painful stigmata, although the Church did not officially endorse this rumor. When he died 20 years ago, nearly 40,000 people accompanied his remains to the grave. And now the Vatican had exhumed his body to beatify Padre Zisa, and not surprisingly they found his flesh had not decayed. It was as if, as Nonna Busso explained, the soul of the man had been so pure, it had stamped an imprint of sanctity on his poor departed flesh.

After two hours in line, they reached the vestige of Padre Zisa on this earth. After all this time, even Carlo's interest was stirred. He peered through the glass: a waxy, shiny skin and a thin, yellowing beard. A tuft of frizzy hair ringing the head. Hands folded in prayer and a rosary intertwined between each finger. Nonna Busso told Carlo that the bodies of the saints did not emit any odor but sweetness, but Carlo could not smell a thing besides the overwhelming odor of a dozen varieties of flowers, and before he could take another whiff, the *carabinieri* had whisked him and Nonna away from Padre Zisa and out into the bright street of an unfamiliar Roman neighborhood.

VII.

"Here it is," his cousin Fabio said, holding out the little banged up Vespa. "It's a little dinged up, but it's fucking free, you know? So don't bitch, Carlo."

"Jesus, thanks, Fabio," Carlo said as he sat on the scooter. He grasped the handlebars and turned the front wheel. Mariaflavia stood there, her arms crossed, chewing the end of a strand of hair.

"You bet," Fabio drawled. His hair was slicked back. From the top of his jumpsuit a plume of black chest hair erupted like a geyser. "You got a hot girlfriend, so now all you need is a hot ride."

"Shut up, Fabio," Mariaflavia snapped. "Where is the helmet?" she continued. Fabio shrugged.

"A waste of money," Fabio chuckled. "If you are gonna die on one of these things, there is nothing that is gonna stop it. And if you do live because of a Goddamned helmet, you are gonna wish you were dead."

"That's a stupid thing to say." Mariaflavia turned to look at Carlo, who was sitting on the Vespa, rocking back and forth like a little boy on a hobbyhorse. "Give it back to him, Carlo."

"Come on, Mariaflavia, don't be a pain in the ass," Carlo answered, laughing gently.

"Give it back, Carlo," Mariaflavia said again, more sternly. Both boys looked at her uneasily, ready to cede to her feminine authority. Carlo was the one to laugh first and break the spell.

"Get off it, Flavia," Carlo chided. "You're not my mother."

And Mariaflavia watched as both boys sped away on their Vespas, Carlo unsteady and following his cousin down the via Latina like a child's wayward top.

VIII.

Carlo fell once and broke a finger. Then he fell a second time and cracked a rib. He stayed off the Vespa for a month, but when the rib healed, he was back again, riding the squealing bike around the neighborhood and in the *campagna*—the rolling, open fields just beyond the highrise apartments. They passed an old Roman ruin. A partially detached marker explained that Emperor Ve-something—part of the name was illegible—had built this temple in honor of his lover, a boy who had drowned in the Tiber. This emperor had him declared a god, and this was his shrine. Fabio and Carlo raced round the circular foundation, trying to catch each other, like a dog chasing his own tail. Carlo skidded on some gravel and fell. He cursed. He dusted off his coat and hopped on again.

IX.

The police report dryly stated that Carlo Busso, 18, of 525 via Latina, apartment 7B, had been disoriented by the afternoon light, had swerved out onto the via Latina in the wrong direction, and had been hit by a bus. He had died immediately. He was thrown from the Vespa and flew 30 feet to the sidewalk near the retaining wall of a hill overgrown with scraggly trees.

After the funeral Mass, the priest and Carlo Busso's women and friends accompanied the body to the Church of Santa Adenzia, where there was much wailing, crying, and raising of hands and arms to the sky.

A month later, the neighborhood association approved Carlo's mother's petition: a plaque was placed on the pitted concrete retaining wall where Carlo died. "IN MEMORY OF CARLO BUSSO," it read. "1972-1990. ALWAYS REMEMBERED." There was a niche for fresh flowers and a clear plastic plate affixed to the top of the plaque. Carlo's Nonna inserted his photo under the plastic. Mariaflavia replaced the flowers every three days. Senora Busso was too distraught to even look out the window at the spot where her beloved son had given up his sweet and gentle soul.

A year later Mariaflavia married a man and moved to another part of Rome. Nonna Busso replaced the flowers, but in another year she died. Six months later Senora Busso took a job in Milan and never returned to Rome again.

The little monument to Carlo Busso appeared to sink into the concrete wall. The etched letters bearing his name and the brief spell of his life—a crack of light between two walls of darkness—became chipped and splintered. One day the faded photo was gone and the plastic plate broken. The graffiti, which had been encroaching upon the memorial for years, was now profanely scrawled across it; the busy neighborhood swirled indifferently around the marker where Carlo Busso had stepped out of this life and into shadows.

Fifteen years later the Church of Santa Adenzia was forced by the diocese to sell its property, including the cemetery. The clerk sent letters to various Francesca Bussos in Milan but never received an answer. So the body of Carlo Busso was to be exhumed and reinterred at the Roman municipal cemetery.

Three workers dug the coffin out with a backhoe and shovels. In the fading winter light, the men were aghast when they unevenly raised the coffin and the lid slid away, revealing the body within. Carlo Busso's long hair, left perched on his shoulders in the coffin, remained a lustrous black. His face was smooth and the color of cocoa. His eyebrows were arched and full. His lips were red and slightly parted, revealing the gleaming teeth within.

"Holy Christ," the first worker said. "It's just like he is asleep!"

"Jesus, Mary, and Joseph," the second worked cried. "It's like they buried him yesterday." Then he sniffed. "He smells like chocolate."

The third worker was silent. He simply peered at the body and made the sign of the Cross. All three quickly resealed the coffin.

"What do you make of that?" the first worker asked.

"How the hell should I know?" the second answered. "But we keep quiet. Agreed? We don't need the trouble."

But as the driver came out of the truck to help haul the coffin into the back, the third worker got on his knees and said an Our Father and three Hail Marys, and the others watched in respectful silence. When the truck pulled away, they all collected their tools and silently went toward home down the via Latina. A scooter swerved to miss them on the via Vesuvio, and the first worker raised his fist, ready to curse the rider and his mother. Then he thought better and quickly lowered his arm.

LOUIS MALLOY

Jailhouse, Jailhouse

From July/August 2004

THE PRISON WAS ready for a riot, and by dinnertime everyone knew it. They were just waiting for George Cannon to get it going. By half-past six the noise was rising in the canteen, and no one was caving in. The prisoners got braver, and the more threats the warders made, the less they mattered. It was so loud now, they couldn't talk to each other, and George watched them check for their whistles and truncheons.

Then he jumped up onto a table, stretched his arms out wide, and shouted:

"Riot!"

George stood there for a second, his face looking up at the lights, his eyes closed, a joyous smile on his face. Then, as a ferocious chorus of cheers answered him, he skipped heavily down the long table, punching the air. He jumped and turned in mid flight. He listened for the laughter and the rumble of boots on the floor. He kicked up his legs like a can-can dancer and knew that he could have been one. If he'd been a woman with the right legs, he would have loved that, lifting up his skirts for a flash, turning 'round to see the raging delight on the men's faces.

Then the riot started. George had no idea what it was about.

He usually liked prison, sometimes loved it, and only hated it when there was nothing to do. An empty cell was fine, because he could do press-ups and sit-ups and hold his breath and wear himself out till he could sleep. That wasn't having nothing to do. What he hated was sitting down for dinner and having to remain sitting, long after he'd finished his food. He hated the TV room because watching TV was doing nothing. Sitting down was doing nothing. George's body needed to move all the time, even if it was just walking around the prison hundreds of times while the others had a smoke or played cards.

The other thing he needed was noise, just to check that the world was still working and there were more things out there for him to do. So he ran his plate against the bars of the cells, grinning in delight at the awful rattle. The warders and the other prisoners shouted at him to stop, but he loved the shouting, too. The prison was full of echoes and reverberation, so George went into the showers and howled like a jackal, and everyone hated that as well. He got into fights, of course, usually because someone was furious at the noise, but sometimes because there was nothing else going on. There was no softness on George's body, so he won most of his fights, but even the ones he lost he enjoyed. It didn't mean he wouldn't be coming back for more.

"You're not at it again, Georgie? I told you to stop, didn't I? You can't say I didn't tell you."

Another fight. If he won this time, there would definitely be yet another, what the other man would think was a decider; if he lost, he might still come back another 100 times. Mr. Perry, the chief warder, had tried to talk to him about it, but now he seemed to have given up. Mr. Perry always looked tired, because he had cancer, or his wife did, or maybe they both did. George had seen them once when he was working in the garden. They were walking across the open fields, dressed up against the cold. They looked gray and weak, and George didn't know why they wanted to go on living like that. He wanted Mr. Perry to forget about his wife—he thought it probably was her who had the cancer—and run like George would have done, run across the miles of flat fields until his whole body thumped with exhaustion. Then get up and run again, into the blank gray sky and to the North Sea where he could swim in the cold, rolling water. Mr. Perry told him not to fight, but he must have been wrong. In fact, Mr. Perry needed to fight as much as George did.

The only other person who tried talking to him was Rob. He was up for the riot as much as George, though he would never have got up onto the table. Most of the time George liked to go around with Rob because they both wanted action and a load of things to do. What he didn't like was when Rob got miserable and wouldn't get off his bed. He'd just sit there, usually with an old letter in his hand, staring at the floor.

"What's the point? Jesus."

"Come on, let's wreck the showers." George thought Rob would need something special to get him up and running again.

"Fuck's sake man."

"Come on. Let's move. Move." George tried to pull him off the bed, but Rob shook him off.

"Leave me, will you?"

"Come on." It was urgent now. George was desperate to get out, get moving.

Rob lay down on the bed and put his forearm across his eyes. He was nearly crying.

"It's my mum."

"Come on!" George knew when Rob talked about his mum, he could go on forever. Was his mum dying or something? George didn't know; he'd never listened.

"Didn't you ever have a mum?" said Rob. "What's wrong with you?"

Then Rob pushed him out of the door and slammed it shut. George ran for the showers, banging into the walls and shouting, "Jailhouse, jailhouse!" He laughed at the echo and shouted again and laughed again and kept going until two prisoners dragged him away. There was no fight, and George was disappointed because he needed to do much more before he could get to sleep. He looked in on Rob again, but he was still lying there, not promising any fun at all.

Rob was right. George never had a mum, nor a dad. He had no idea where or when they had gone. He'd had a lot of foster mums and dads, and they all hated him. Not cruel hate, just natural, ordinary hate for a boy so full of dangerous stunts. He broke everything and terrorized the other children, and he never stopped.

"Stop it!"

He heard that a lot, and he loved it. When they said it, he stood on his tiptoes, looked up at the ceiling, and laughed in triumph. He hadn't needed anyone else. He was a riot all by himself.

But he ate his food, so the foster mums were really pleased for the first ten minutes that they met him. He ate whatever they gave him and asked for more. Then, as soon as he had finished, he was bored and started to kick the table and then kick the other kids and within half an hour, everybody hated him. So he left. The last family was no different to any of the others, and he knew that the next wouldn't be, either, so he left when he was just into his teens and lived anywhere. He liked the cold, he liked breaking into houses, he liked fights and stealing food. It was a grand life for a boy like George, who looked like he was 18 and was free of everything.

George leapt off the table when the riot began and started to destroy the canteen. The warders were overpowered for now, so it was rapid, easy work. The tables, chairs, and windows all went first, then it was into the kitchens. George hadn't been allowed to work in the kitchens, but Rob did, and he usually made sure the food was salty or sweet, how George liked it. Salty stew and potatoes so he could taste it properly and sweet pink custard. When Rob made the custard extra sweet, George would have three big platefuls, and then he'd be good to Rob. Take him outside and have a two-man scrum down, pushing each other all over the yard for hours. Or they'd find some of the others and get a gang together, or else they'd fight. George almost wanted to look for the custard now and make sure it stayed safe, but there was no time. They had to rip the cooker out, that was the hardest job, then they could smash up everything. It would mean more months inside, but George liked it here, so that was all right, more than all right. He'd get solitary, but that was fine. He was happy to be here for more than a year.

He had got the year for assault. It wasn't assault—it was a fair fight and a good one too in his opinion—but he didn't care because he was happy to go to prison again. It happened in an Indian restaurant. He didn't usually go into restaurants or cafes because it meant he had to sit more or less still while he waited for his food. But he was just walking by when the smell hit him. He liked Indian because he could taste it properly and it always came quickly and was easy to eat. So he went in and ordered and sat there drumming his hands on the table and breathing in and out very heavily. At the next table there were three men and a woman. They looked smooth and soft, all of them. The men were trying to flirt a little with the woman, looking at her with their pleasant smiles and talking like they wanted to be younger than they were.

"The guy from London from the meeting this morning saw you in the canteen. Said you were a babe, a real babe."

"Well, we all know that, look at her. We don't need someone from London to tell us that."

"Well, you're lucky to have me then, aren't you?"

"To have you? Now, is that an offer?"

"No. You're getting cheeky, you boys."

"Do you want a fuck?"

The last one was George, and it was a question he used a lot. Not because he wanted to offend, but because he hated hanging around, especially if it was hanging around for nothing like these soft guys were. It had got him into a lot of trouble. It had got him a lot of fucks as well.

"Do you? Do you want a fuck?"

They were all scared, though George was asking the question without too much malice. They would have sat there for hours in silence, but luckily for them the waiter had heard him.

"What's happening?"

He was big for an Indian and looked like he could be in a film waving a cutlass around or cracking open skulls with a club. George had never fought an Indian before.

"She doesn't want a fuck. She won't get one off these lot. Is my Madras ready?"

Before George had finished the sentence, he was being dragged out by the Indian, who was clearly up for a fight. Why wouldn't he be? Going back and forth with dishes of food all night, it would have driven George crazy, too. So he felt some friendliness towards the Indian as they started to punch each other around the head. Good heavy punches, no holding back. George was impressed. For a second he could look through the window and see the sad cases on the other table looking down at their plates. The woman was crying, and the men looked like they might be about to as well. He held onto the

Indian, rubbed his cheek against the thick, soft beard, and pulled at the turban, wondering what was really underneath.

The Indian was good, too good in the end, because he would have won if he'd fought as dirty as George. When George rammed his thumb into his eye, the Indian stepped back, howling, and then it was easy for George to take his time, to choose a position and punch the Indian through the restaurant window. The big man in his lovely coloured turban fell back, and the glass shattered and fell down over him. It looked spectacular, and George leaned back and laughed at the wonder of it all. He laughed for so long that he'd only just opened his eyes when the Indian heaved himself back up like he was rising from the dead, and with a final surge of energy, smashed his lacerated fist into George's mouth. So when the police came, George was still semi-conscious, and the Indian was bleeding everywhere and gasping desperately. A perforated lung and some other nasty business, which kept him in hospital for six months and sent George to prison. It had been a fair fight though, or nearly fair. But prison was all right, definitely all right when there was a riot on and George was the star turn.

When everything had been smashed up, George went up on the roof. This was what happened in riots. He didn't know why, any more than he knew what the riot was for, but he was sure this was what happened. So he scrambled up and danced like an idiot and courted the crowd down below. Hundreds of police had arrived by now, and the other prisoners were split up but not yet locked away. They cheered as he threw down slates, took off his shirt, and conducted the shouts of "Georgie, Georgie!"

Mr. Perry had a megaphone and gave out warnings to come down, but he didn't even sound convinced by himself. Then the fire engine came and the ladder went up. No one came up to get George because they knew he might do anything, like kick a man off a ladder just for the thrill and the cheers he would get. When George had run out of things to do on the roof, he got onto the ladder, pulled and pushed at it for a while to make it swing dangerously over the crowd, and then came down. They jumped him immediately, Mr. Perry taking the lead. With five men on top of him, George was beaten for the moment, but he really needed to keep moving, so he embraced Mr Perry more tightly and kissed his neck. For a moment Mr Perry seemed to just let him, but then he shouted, "No!" So George laughed his screaming laugh and bit his neck. It was a deep bite, a mouthful of flesh, and there was warm blood in his mouth. Mr. Perry howled. George had made him come alive. Now maybe he could run across the fields, away from this wife and the cancer, to the sea. The screaming of the gulls and the cold, dark water.

They got George to stop biting by banging away at his head with their truncheons. He laughed as he was escorted away—threw back his head and laughed. The warders and the police and most of the prisoners were looking at him with a kind of horror. Not Rob—he was grinning, and George knew he'd keep the food salty for him while he was in solitary. George kept dribbling blood and laughing with such delight. He looked at the faces, the grimaces and the shaking heads. What was wrong with them? He laughed all the way. What was wrong with them?

PD MALLAMO

Heralds of a Fallen World

From October/November 2012

1

SPOKANE, PULLMAN, Lewiston, then south on 95 to Grangeville and narrow, deserted Idaho 14, which he hopes will take him smoothly across the Bitterroot Range. Then, if he's lucky, 93 to Blackfoot by noon. But foul weather and poor road have slowed him, and by Elk City he knows he's blown it.

Now rain crashes against the windshield. He flips the wipers to high and slows enough to make out the pavement. He sees a woman running on the road ahead. When he reaches her, he sees another farther on. They look like they're running as fast as they can. Since he's come up behind them and has passed nothing chasing, he assumes they are moving toward, rather than from. Beyond the second woman he sees two figures, dark shapes laboring against the heavy gray weather.

He accelerates and in 20 seconds finds himself behind a man pursuing a woman. The man is tall and carries what appears to be a large piece of firewood; in a moment he raises and heaves it, striking her neck just below the skull. She falls and the man is upon her, kicking her head and her back. When the man stoops to pick up the log, the driver nudges the car forward and bumps him away like he's cutting a calf from a herd. The man turns, and he sees his face, water streaming from long dark hair and long black beard, his mouth forming an O as if coming up for air. The man lifts the wood again and with both hands hurls it at the windshield, cracking it right down the middle. The driver touches the gas and the man goes down. Another little tap and he's all the way under the car.

2

By now the two women behind have caught up. The injured woman sits on the road, holding her neck, bleeding through her fingers. One of the women goes to her, pulls her trembling hand away and examines the wound. The other drops to her knees and hands and peers beneath his car.

He's not moving, she yells over the storm. Back up.

The driver slowly reverses direction. When he's gone ten feet, he steps out and looks at the man, who lies on his back with arms stretched past his head. His face has been torn entirely away. A thick tributary of blood mixes with rainwater flowing off the shoulder of the road.

Anna! the woman shouts. Hurry!

The two yank the man by the legs and drag him 30 feet up the road to where a torrent spills through a culvert and throw him in. The body tumbles over and over, arms akimbo and legs aloft as the flood carries it rapidly downstream, around smooth boulders and into deep woods.

The first woman races back to the car and reaches beneath it. In a moment she pulls from the undercarriage what's left of the man's face.

She runs to the surge and flings it in. Then she bends to the flow and washes her hands.

She walks slowly back through the downpour, rubbing her palms on her saturated skirt.

Who was he? the driver asks.

James Livermore, she says. Our husband.

3

The two help up their injured sister and stand starkly before the driver like heralds of a fallen world. The one with whom he has spoken looks to be about thirty-seven. She wears a long pioneer dress, and her hair is braided and golden; the others, in their mid-20s, wear haltertops, hotpants and black fishnet stockings broken at the bottom and gathered about their ankles. Their hair is cut short and colored black; makeup drools over their eyes and cheeks. All are barefoot. They are attractive women with the saddest faces he has ever seen. Thank you, the older woman says. He would have killed her. He's better off dead anyway. You've done the Lord's work. Go home.

The three link arms and walk past his car, toward whatever place they'd left in such a hurry. There is no trace whatsoever of the affair: blood, body, and face all now wholly absorbed into the pouring wilderness.

He walks to the culvert and considers for a moment the furious waters. He starts the car and u-turns in their direction. Get in, he says when he reaches them. Where do you live?

4

It is an awful, rambling shack pounded together by a madman. There are hexsigns and warnings both affixed and freestanding, and haystacks of firewood scattered randomly. Six vehicles stand elevated on bricks and stumps. Oil-slicked rainwater trickles downhill from the open door of a shed. Inside he sees a white van with sections of blue and red obviously scavenged from similar vehicles. He looks for an entrance to the house, something to pull up before, but sees nothing.

The door's in the back, the older woman says. That's so he has time to shoot before you get in the house.

He shakes his head. What are you doing out here?

The blond sighs and folds her hands in her lap and doesn't speak for a long moment. It started as a church, she says. It became a poodle service. Then a sex club. He sold drugs. He went crazy. I believe this is the end.

5

They walk around the structure, and she opens the only door, cut so low they have to bend almost double to get in. The interior is dim, cold, and deathly quiet, although children's toys and dolls lay all about. In the kitchen a flame still burns on the stovetop, pots and broken dishes litter the floor, soup and jelly run from the walls and down cabinet doors. In the middle of a room adjoining, he sees a large motorcycle with flesh-colored tank and fenders resting on its side as if it were sick livestock or a shot-up elk.

You want to know what happened? she asks. Well, I'll tell you. There was going to be a wedding: my 15-year old to his brother Posy. The Lord told him to, or so he says. I said I'll see you dead first, and he takes a knife. Pink hits him in the eye with a can of peaches, and the race is on.

She rights a chair and sits down. The other women move deliberately through the debris, shifting this and that with their bare feet, touching nothing with their hands as if everything is contaminated.

Where are the children? he asks.

Over the gulch in the mobile home. They go there after breakfast. They didn't see nothing.

From across the room Anna says, He never hurt them. We made sure of that.

What will you do now? he asks.

Get ready for Posy, I guess, says the woman on the chair. He's coming at five for the girl.

Then what?

I don't know. I don't know how I'll deal with that.

She pushes her wet, dirty blond behind her head and wearily rubs her face. Nothing's going to work for a while. The Lord told me, just do your best and keep your eyes open. I told James—she rubs her face again and sighs—James, I say, Why can't we just be simple farmers like the Saints of old? You know what he said?—Honey, only one crop pay for this farm, and it ain't tomatoes.

How many children? he asks.

Six.

Go get them, he says.

6

She's a waitress for the Electric Cowboy west of Grangeville. She works the Mango Room. The younger ones are telephone actresses— among other things, she says.

Telephone actresses?

Phone porn. They don't leave the compound. Hook up a headset and cook or walk around with the kids. All day, all night. Any time the men want it. It was James' idea. They may as well be prostitutes. Jezebels.

She lifts herself off the chair, walks to the stove and takes a frying pan by the handle. She works her way through the litter to the door, and when she is almost there, turns quickly to where he stands and swings at his head, connecting with a glancing blow as he tries to duck. Then she is upon him, screaming horribly and lunging for his eyes. He kicks her back a pace, swiftly aims his left, and bangs her on the forehead. She staggers sideways and sits suddenly down. He catches his breath and checks his head for blood. Go get the kids, he says evenly to the others. Grab what you need. It's time to go.

7

The children are all girls, six in number, ages two through 15, subdued as if mute. He fits the five smallest into the back of the sleek wagon and tells the teenager to sit in the rear seat behind the driver. The two younger women rush through the house, grabbing photo albums, purses, a few clothes. The blond one leans against the car, pressing with both hands a towel to her bloody nose and weeping eyes.

She kept this mess together too long, says Anna, motioning outside with an armful of children's clothes. By herself.

He helps her back inside, supporting her as one would a wounded child, and bathes her damaged face in the kitchen sink. Anna comes in and says, There's both of them bleeding. We need to bring the paper towels.

Get her another shirt, he says, and Anna runs into the room with the motorcycle. She helps her change into a t-shirt that says in large blue letters, "The Hamptons," then takes one last look around.

Lock the door, he says. Like you've gone somewhere.

As they load, he sees the van in the shed with the door standing open. Can you close that up, too?

There's a padlock, says Anna, and runs to the shed. She finds it just inside, swings the heavy doors bangshut against each other, and snaps it in place.

He puts the blond in the middle of the seat behind him so she won't jump out of the car, but far enough he can slip a punch if he has to. The sky still drenches Idaho as he pulls out of the compound and kicks the turbocharger. All three women look back as home disappears like earth from a rocket, becoming finally nothing more than the horizon itself.

8

Her name is Chloe, says Anna. She reaches behind to touch the blond's leg and whispers, It's okay if I tell him, isn't it honey?

The other is Pink, she says. In case you're wondering, she's called that because James had a revelation. He said that's her name in heaven, so it might as well be her name on earth. Then it kind of stuck. Her real name is Harmony, but we just call her Pink. Now it's Peaches, she says, and all three women laugh.

What about your name? he asks. And Chloe's? Are those real or heavenly?

Both, I guess. He never said. She leans across and looks at the teenager sitting behind him: Her heavenly name is Bathsheba, so we call her Bath. The rest are just numbers, one through five, oldest to youngest. He hadn't figured those out yet. Too late now. We'll have to name them ourselves.

9

Explosions of sunlight flash through cracks in the overcast, rain-filled bursts striking the forests in dancing shafts. They have driven 100 miles in silence. The children in back seem to sleep. Beside him Anna stares out the side glass as if she is stone. Then she turns toward him, moves her mouth to his ear and whispers, She loved him. No matter what she says.

He sees that she is crying. And you? he asks.

She shakes her head. Hell, no. God told us to marry him. There wasn't any love at all. Good thing, too. He was a bastard.

10

Another 100 miles and they reach Hagerman, where he fills his tank. A Sonic drive-in is perched on a little hill at the other end of town, and without saying a word, he pulls in. Use the bathroom, he says. Get something to eat.

Pink and Chloe walk together into the sagebrush beyond the drive-in, conferring as they go. Anna leads the children one by one to the restroom. After she returns them to the car, she joins the others, three women standing anxiously beneath a broken sky, two of them bleeding. Ten minutes later Anna walks back and says, We don't know if we should get out or go on. We don't know what to do. Chloe is the oldest. She has to say.

Why don't you vote?

We did, but her vote counts two, so we're even. She wants to go back and bury James. We want to go on.

He's already buried, he says. You'll never find him. Nobody else will, either. He's ten miles downstream, covered in drift somewhere.

She's crying out there. She's so confused. Her eyes are getting black.

Jesus, he says. He hikes out to the women and takes Chloe by the elbow. He turns her toward the car, then wraps his arm around her shoulders and hugs her tight. She collapses against him, and he half-carries her back. There is no god but God, she says. If this ain't the end, I guess nothing is.

He fits her gently into the front seat and hands Anna a credit card. Get some food, he says. Enough for everybody.

11

What are you doing up there? she asks, jerking her thumb backwards to indicate that part of Idaho now behind them. After some effort she locates the window button on the door and surrenders her bloody nose rag to the slipstream.

I flew to Spokane, he says. My brother died in Pullman.

She considers this for a moment. What did he do in Pullman?

He taught at Washington State. He purses his mouth and exhales in a little puff. And he drank.

Did he have one of these? She waves her hand to indicate the car.

He laughs and says, This is his. He wanted me to have it. I'm taking it home for my wife.

What caused him to drink?

A bad fit with life, I guess. I never asked.

Why not?

It wasn't my business.

But he was your brother.

Doesn't matter, he said. Not in my family.

She sits quietly for a moment, then asks, What did he teach?

Spanish.

Spanish?

That's right. He loved Cervantes. He looks over at her. Spanish writer. Way back.

Spanish, she says. Imagine that. My mother got so fat, we put her in a wheelchair. Then we rolled her to the store. One day she tipped over a sidewalk and got hit by a car. The doctor said she weighed 409 pounds. We buried her in a crate.

Have you ever been to Kansas City? she asks? Jazz, so many churches, banks. Subway Sandwiches.

I have. Many times.

I thought Mr. Livermore was the Savior Returned. Yes I did. How can a person be so wrong? I have lost all faith in myself. I'm afraid to do anything. Now the animals have got him, or he's dead in the mud with no face. She laughs and says, Not even God will recognize him anymore. You may have done him a service. He can slip through the Pearly Gates with the war dead and plane wrecks.

12

When day turns to night, they do not stop except once for gas and restroom. He buys the biggest cup of coffee and finds something on the radio, an intellectual line-up discussing America's diplomacy gap and what to do about it. The highway is almost empty, the storm long cleared.

What time is it? she asks.

He checks the clock near the tachometer. 1:52 AM, he says and smiles at her. Late or early, depending how you look at it.

Where are you going?

Indiana.

Is that where you live?

Yes.

Is that where you're taking us?

Yes.

Are we prisoners?

No.

Then why did you take us?

He smiles at her again. Because I had room.

I'm sorry he hurt your car, she says. Such a pretty car.

The car can be fixed.

Twenty-seven, in case you're wondering, she says, pointing to herself. But you're never too old for love.

13

You've not seen anything until you've seen an African war, he says—The human race revealed at last.

You?

Three.

What do you do?

I work for a company.

Is it a good company?

No.

Then why do you work for it?

It's what I do.

She considers this for a moment, then says, You don't understand. We're no better than him. Who did you save us from, ourselves? Then she wags her finger in his face and says slowly, One day he told us to throw the girl children in the river. You can't consecrate females to the Lord, he said, it just don't take. He wanted to start over and have nothing but boys. We wouldn't do it. He walked around naked in front of everybody, even the kids. He hit every one of us—babies, too. We should have gotten rid of him a long time ago. We didn't. Then you came along. The Lord took mercy because we were weak. It makes me ashamed.

14

Orilla, he says at 4:00 AM. Do you know what it means?

No sir, I do not.

The bank of a river, or a shore. Reeds and grasses. Small silver fish. He sighs and looks out the window. Blackbirds.

15

Fire in the bones. That's what James had. He was irresistible. I couldn't see the Mark for all that fire. Nobody could. She laughs to herself and says, Holy men. There is no end of them.

On her forehead half an inch above the center of her eyes, he sees the indentation of his wedding ring. Her eyes are black and green, her nose is swollen, and when she talks, her voice is of one who suffers allergy or virus.

She rests her head against the back of the seat for a few minutes, then says, Cars are like buffalo. Soon there won't be any more. Someday people won't believe the mess we've made. I like this one, though. What is it?

A Volvo.

Far to the north, mile-long trains full of low-sulfur coal from Montana creep over the Great Plains, locomotive headlamps briefly and without intention divulging the dark world. His eyes search automatically and in vain for the thinnest sliver of dawn.

There's nothing to eat in a first-aid kit, she says dreamily. That much I know. He pulls her to him and tenderly kisses the top of her head.

16

By 3:00 PM west of Cheyenne, he can't drive anymore. He takes the second exit to a Motel 8 and rents three rooms, then buys dinner at a

Denny's next door. He tells them he'll knock when it's time to go, that it may be a little early but they'll be able to sleep in the car.

Across the table Pink waves at him and asks, Do you want to see something? She pulls a CD out of her purse and holds it up: *The Essential Molly Hatchet*. It's how we roll, she says, nodding her head for emphasis. She fishes around in her purse and comes up with an envelope. She leans over the fries and hamburgers and hands it to him. It's what we do, she says simply.

There are seven digital images, each of Pink and Anna in oral coitus. They are explicit and of startling resolution. He returns these to the envelope and passes them back over the table. I'm sorry, he says.

She fits them carefully into her purse. It's just a job, you know, so what? We don't hurt nobody.

17

At 4:15 AM. he knocks on the door next to his, and Chloe quickly opens it.

Load 'em up, he says.

They're gone. I didn't want to wake you.

Who?

Pink and Anna.

He steps back a yard. Where did they go?

Nevada. They caught a ride. They're going to Las Vegas. They have an act.

The kids?

Still here.

My god, he says—Just like that?

She shrugs her shoulders. A lamp behind haloes her hair and throws her neck and shoulders into sharp silhouette. I couldn't stop them. What was I going to do, call the cops?

Now what?

You tell me. But I'll be damned if I do this all by myself.

He returns to his room and sits on the side of the bed. He rubs his neck with both hands, then gets up and splashes cold water over his face. He takes a good long look at himself in the mirror, then gathers his things, turns out the light, and loads everybody into the car. Sunrise is still two hours away. He fills his tank with premium gas at a station by the on-ramp, buys coffee, and heads east.

18

He tried everything to make money, she says. He was a clown at parties, and once he rented a hall for Christian dance classes, as if he knew anything about Christian dance. I don't know anything about Christian dance, how would he? Then he was going to make a space movie...

She holds up her hands to count on her fingers. He had this idea for a faithfulness clinic where couples learn not to cheat, if you can believe that or not; porn for non-smokers, whatever that is; truck driving school for retarded people since they work for less money; spray on shirts; animal training, even for wild ones; spray on colors for animals; animal psychic. Nothing worked, of course, and that's when he had Pink and Anna do their little dance. That always works, doesn't it? They didn't mind a bit. I think they were doing it between themselves already. He wouldn't let them off the farm for fear they'd give themselves to men. He had a big thing about disease. Wouldn't touch me after the Mango Room, figured I was doing what I wanted out there. Long as I brought home the check, it was okay.

They trust you, she said, motioning to the kids in back. That's why they sleep. No rest in that house, James always upset about one thing or another, middle of the night, didn't matter. He'd get us up and read the Bible, or get his belt and beat hell out of somebody, usually me. You think this looks bad?—she points to her eyes—you could never tell. One moment he'd be fine, the next, Bam! One time out of the blue he beat Pink and Anna. Used his belt buckle. He said men like naked women with bruises on their legs, so shut the hell up, it's your job.

On the eastern horizon, clouds big as whole worlds mount and billow against the rising orb. Sunlight volleys through vapors and the crystalline void, splashing beam and shadow joyously about them.

19

They stop for lunch in Colby, Kansas, right off the Interstate. She and Bathsheba herd the children in and out of the women's room, then crowd into a booth he's taken by the window. They eat Subway sandwiches among families of Mennonite farmers, the women in lace bonnets and long dresses. She asks him if they might be polygamists.

I don't think so, he replies. These are German Baptists.

They look just like our neighbors, she whispers, peering over the tops of her sunglasses. Old-timey Mormons up the mountain. I think they gave James the idea in the first place. They wouldn't let him join because he was crazy. What's the sense of having more than one wife if you can't deal with the first? I have a question: What are Lutherans?

Bathsheba reaches across the table and touches his arm. We're good kids, she says. We won't make no trouble.

Chloe says, When Pink showed you those pictures, she was saying, Take what you want, Mister, you can have it all. If you did, they'd still be here.

I like the lowdown life, he replies. We all do. I just don't live it, that's all. He looks around the table at the children and shakes his head. Christ Jesus, he says. What they have seen.

In Topeka he takes two rooms, a large one for Chloe and the children, and a bed for himself next door. He asks after dinner, What should I expect tonight?

Nothing, I don't think. Everybody's real tired.

20

Then the pageant of America, glowing and uncontaminated, reels past in the early sun, vast and portentous as if of a dream—cheap blandishments and every variety of abomination masquerading as Christian church, fat easy food, Buicks for the aged, plasma centers with drunks, addicts and prostitutes already stampeding for the door, answers, cures, electric energies, spirits, Nirvana, exhaustion, promise, relief. The Burger King with crazy eyes. A bloody fetus on an enormous billboard that makes Chloe shield her eyes. Housing developments named after the various kings of France. Recruitment billboards for government killers. Diet Coke. Diet Coke. Diet Coke. Discount Tires. God. Diet Coke. Diet Coke. Diet Coke. Diet Coke. Diet Coke. Discount Tires. Walmart. Diet Coke. God.

Topeka recedes, and they are almost alone on the highway. The air is cool and moist.

Goodbye Oz, he says as he closes his window. God Almighty. He turns toward her: Smells like Japan—sweet. Like cooking.

Do you know what day this is? she asks.

Sunday.

Besides that. It's Mother's Day. I wonder if I'll get a present.

He searches the mirror for Bathsheba, but she is curled out of sight on the backseat.

What would you like? he asks.

Something from James, she says. He owes me big.

He takes an avenue off the Interstate into the heart of Kansas City and cruises slowly through downtown until he sees a Starbucks.

Ever been to one of these?

No, sir, I have not.

Get what you want, he says. Happy Mother's Day.

They sit behind a bar facing a window. He orders hot chocolate for the children, for himself simple coffee. A black woman wearing a high blond wig strolls by on the sidewalk outside. She seems to be examining her fingernails. She is followed by a large black man holding a wad of cash, walking with his mouth open. Chloe watches them through the glass and leans over hard to track their progress, removing her sunglasses and pressing her face to the pane.

His Strong Hand on Everything, she says wonderingly. Even here. Even in Gomorrah.

She takes his own hand in hers, then brings it to her lips and kisses it.

I'm white trash, aren't I? she asks. There's part of my brain doesn't listen to me.

I wouldn't say that.

Yes, we are, we're all white trash. Up until I met James, I thought I was raised with a little dignity. But normal people don't do what we do, walk around with a headset talking filth, all married to the same lunatic. It isn't normal.

She reaches gently to the dashboard and brushes the dials and instruments with her fingertips. I've never even seen one of these, much less sat in one. This thing isn't on the radar where I come from.

Just a car, he says.

That's what you think. You just don't know.

21

So one day James tears the van apart and puts in a big sink. This was between his new church and Christian dance. He nails together some damn kind of dog washer and paints a sign on the side: Poodle

Polisher. Can you imagine? After a month of no business, he makes Anna and Pink go with him. He sits in the front, and there's a hole behind the seat so he can watch. He dresses them up like whores, and after a while makes them take their shirts off. This is how they wash the dogs. The phone's ringing off the hook—but it's all these rich old women in Missoula. I almost fell off the stump! Well, they're the only ones with poodles, he says. Besides, they don't touch nothing, they just look. Sometimes they invite them over and so what, what harm can the old women do, they don't have diseases or nothing. That lasts about a year, and he's got this idea for bikini wax back there, too, the same old gals—wash the dog and pluck the cat he liked to say, ha ha. Then the sheriff comes out. They had his trial in Pocatello. Such a collection of mental defectives and backwoods lawyers you never saw, feeding off each other like roaches. James does four months on pandering and makes Posy, who is married with five kids, keep us on the farm, even me. He never brought us any food, and we almost starved to death. We lived on cans and garden, what plot James didn't use for his goddamn weed.

She points to a button over her head. What's this?

Sunroof.

He touches the switch, and the cover moves slowly backwards. She reclines her seat and regards the heavens for several minutes. Again she points upwards. He looks and sees an airliner trace a vapor trail miles above. She says, That thing catch fire and roll up there, you'll Believe in a hurry, that's for sure.

That's for sure, he repeats. But is it real? The Belief—would it be genuine?

Of course, she says. Genuine as the fire. You can't deny one and then the other, can you?

I suppose you can't.

James had another five or six spiritual wives, she says. He never had sex because he was afraid of disease. But they all sent him money. Did I tell you about the Pumped Up Party Place?

Don't think so.

All these things you fill with air and jump on. Where you take kids on their birthdays. Then you have cake.

How did that work out?

Same as the rest. Because we didn't take our shirts off. Too bad, she laughed. We should have.

22

We're married about eight years, and James has a dream. The Lord tells him go Old Testament all the way, so he sends me out to find him some wives. I was stupid enough to do it. I hung around the Mormon college in Rexburg so I could peel off some Mormon girls, but they told the elders and I got chased. One day I was at Denny's in Cour d'Alene and saw these two in a booth smoking and laughing by themselves. I knew right away. When I brought them back, James almost died for joy. Told me I was the greatest wife ever. That very night he slept with them both. Didn't leave that room till afternoon next day, happiest man you ever saw. James didn't teach them nothing new, believe me, but he did get them pregnant. They had beautiful babies. I'll say that much.

She reaches a hand through the open sunroof and catches the cool slipstream with her fingers, then reaches the other hand up, too. She laughs and rubs them together; then, withdrawing her hands and folding them primly in her lap, she turns to face him. Have you ever heard of quarks?

Parts of an atom, I think. Subatomic particles.

God's little angels, she said. That's what they are. We finally found them.

23

James made good money off those girls, she said. The dirty movie in the trailer and the phone bit. He sent a good bunch of it up to British Columbia, to invest in a big marijuana operation his brother heard about. Posy takes it and comes back a month later, said he got robbed and doesn't have a thing left. James beat him almost to death, laid him up six weeks his wife said, and I believe it. One time I took some money, too, but James never found out. I was scared half out of my head. Figured he'd kill me. He liked that Mango Room money too much, though. You don't kill the prize chicken.

She turns in her seat and regards the children behind her, two now sitting upright in the back and looking through the windows. This is not the life I wanted, she says. You take what comes your way, but this is not what I wanted. This is a nightmare.

24

Jesus is who you love when there's no one else to love, she says. I wanted to open a bridal shop. Pretty young things. I made wedding gowns for Pink and Anna. James said keep the front open so their bare bosoms stick out, but I said, You want me to make the dress, you do it my way. We had a double wedding out there. I made a pie, and his brother came, that's all. Right before the ceremony Posy says he wants one, James doesn't need them both, and James says, Just read the damn Bible where I tell you and shut the hell up. That's how it went, the wedding. That was pretty much the whole thing.

25

You have your rights, now, she says. You saved us, we're yours. She shrugs her shoulders. What else would we do anyway? Where would we go? Posy's looking right now, believe me. Soon as he figures James is out of the picture, he'll swoop right in for all of us, even me. Nothing's safe from that thing, even the kids.

Does he have a phone?

No.

What does he do?

Firewood. Says he prays in the forest, which is bullshit I think. His wife works. School lunch lady.

Bad family, he says.

He blew off two fingers Fourth of July, she says. Blasting cap. We had ourselves a laugh. I've never thrown myself at a man before. Never had to. I could throw myself at you and not feel bad about it. Until recent I was fairly good-looking. A little rest and good food gets me my looks back.

I'm sure it will.

Will you help me?

Of course.

Are you married?

I am.

I need some vitamins and vegetables, she says. I need to get sane. At least I know I'm crazy. She places a hand on his arm. Give me that.

That and more, he says.

I'm ashamed. You would be, too.

She points above her, through the sunroof and atmosphere and airliners, all the way through blue sky and space to something she imagines clearly and cleanly, as if she has left behind for good the infinite politics of evil. He can make you new from anything, she says, even shit. He can start with that and change it all in a heartbeat. She motions behind her to the children. You can't leave these in the bulrushes. It worked okay for Moses, but this is a different world.

26

They enter Indiana late evening, and when they reach Kokamo, he rents two rooms at the first place with a vacancy, a run-down Best Western next to Liquor World at the south end of town. Midnight comes a soft knock, and when he opens the door, Bathsheba steps through. She pulls her long t-shirt over her head and stands naked before him, well-developed, fifteen. Don't worry, she says, I'm not a virgin.

Where is she?

Gone.

Where?

I don't know. She took the photo albums and left.

He grabs his keys, runs down the balcony, and quietly enters the sleeping room. He checks the bathroom and closet, then runs down the stairs and looks through the deserted lobby. He runs out to his car, rips from the parking lot and for the better part of an hour patrols the blocks around the hotel. By the time he returns, Bathsheba has gone back to the children. She has wrapped and draped herself with white bathtowels and sits on the only chair in the room. On a side table under a low dim lamp, he sees a note Chloe has scrawled across a motel tablet: Pray Pray Pray Always. For We Are Creatures of the Sun and Not Gone Yet! The room exhales the ghastly sweet dead breath of cheap rooms, and he wants to spill himself through the door and vomit.

Am I your wife now?

God, no. No. No.

What am I then, Mister? Will we be okay?

Get dressed, he says. We're going home.

When he brings them mostly still sleeping down from the room, he finds Chloe standing next to the Volvo, clutching the albums to her chest. I'll come back, she says. Will you take the children?

I'll take the children.

Because I can't do it anymore. Nothing happens when time don't move. We'll lose every one if I'm still here, every one. She points to Bathsheba. She's about lost now, my little girl.

He takes his wallet from his pocket and finds a business card. The bottom number's my cell phone, he says. Call me someday.

He pulls out several large bills and hands them to her. Listen to me: Steer clear of Idaho.

When they roll out, she's standing beneath a streetlamp, still hugging the photographs. Bathsheba looks briefly behind her, then reclines the passenger seat and sets a hand over her eyes. I'm hungry, she says. When can we stop for breakfast?

RACHEL MAIZES

Retardo

From January/February 2008

THEY TOUCH ME sometimes, pat my arm, smooth my hair. "Don't mind them," my mother says. It's all fine for her. They don't touch her. Maybe it's because she spends all day waving needles around or sticking thermometers in unpleasant places, or maybe it's because she's angry all the time, but they keep their distance. But I'm like a magnet.

I wonder if what they have is catchy and if one morning I'll wake up not knowing how to tie my shoes or how many quarters are in a dollar. I'm no genius, but when I buy an *Archie* comic, I know how to count my change.

"Yaw a good gurl," Lisa will say, sitting down next to me in the enormous dining room. When she speaks, the words come out so slowly it hurts to listen, and I want to grab the words and pull them out faster. Her mouth is full of crooked, yellow teeth, and she's always smiling. She has a boyfriend, if you can believe that. Robert spends half the meal rocking back and forth in his seat like a wooden rocking horse I once got for Christmas. The same thread of saliva is always hanging from the corner of his mouth. I keep waiting for it to break, but it's as strong as Superglue. Lisa and Robert hold hands under the table, and even if it is spaghetti night, I lose my appetite. I think someone should stop them, but when I tell my mother, all she says is, "You mind your manners." I know better than to talk back because the last time I tried it, she slapped me so hard the mark left by her wedding ring didn't fade for a week.

I wish we didn't have to eat with them, but when I tell my mother, she just says, "This is our home now." Some home. Me and my mother and 300 retardos living together at the Freemont Residence for Retarded Adults.

It wasn't always like this. We used to live in a real house with my mother's Plymouth and my father's Cavalier parked in the driveway. We had a chain link fence around the front yard so that Buster, our fat English bulldog, could bark at the neighbors and could leave his large piles where no one would step on them. But one day my father loaded Buster and two suitcases into the Cavalier and was gone.

After my father moved out, it took my mother a month to stop setting a plate for him at dinner. Before she would serve the food, she would stare out of the kitchen window and down the block as if she expected him to drive up any minute, as if he had just gone on a business trip and forgot to tell us. When it finally sunk in he wasn't coming back, she gave up on dinner altogether and stayed in her bedroom with the TV blaring. One night I heard Sue Ellen say good night to John Boy just as my mother started crying.

That's when I started worrying that she would leave, too. In the middle of the night, I would hear a car door slam and think she was going. I would lie in bed wondering what it would be like living in the big house all alone and who would take care of me. I'd worry until my heart was beating out of my mouth. Then I would get up and look in their bedroom. She would be there, curled up like a baby on her half of the bed, his side strangely flat, like a balloon with the air gone out of it.

One day I came home from school and she was packing, and I thought, *it is finally happening,* that I would be on my own. But it turned out we were moving to Freemont. We got there in the middle of the school year.

"What are you, retarded?" a dark-haired boy shot at me the first time I got on the bus next to the sign for the home. I found out later his name was James. He had turned around in his seat and was staring at me. So were the rest of the kids on the bus.

"No, I'm not retarded." I made my way to the last row so I wouldn't have to sit next to anyone. The seatback in front of me wasn't tall enough to hide behind.

"The sign says retarded," he said. "Oh, that's right. Retarded people can't read." That gave everyone a good laugh. Everyone except me, that is. All I could do was sit there while my face turned red and wish I had some snappy answer. The truth was I did live with the retardos, and for all I knew, it was rubbing off.

I had begged my mother to drive me to school or at least to arrange for the school bus to pick me up in front of a regular house. "I'm sure the kids will be very nice," she had said, staring over my head at some other life she wished she was living.

At school that first day, I had to get up and introduce myself. "I'm Ellen. I just moved to Freemont," I said and started back to my seat.

"Tell us a little more, dear," Mrs. Baxter urged. "What do your parents do?"

"My father's dead, and my mother is a nurse." The part about my father took Mrs. Baxter by surprise, and she didn't object when I sat down. And he might as well have been dead. There was no telling when I might see him again.

At recess, a group of girls came up to me. "We're sorry about your dad," they said.

"Yeah, me, too," I said, not knowing what else to say.

"When did he die?"

"I was just a baby. I hardly remember him."

"Wow, that must have made your mother really sad."

"Nah, she likes it just being the two of us."

They invited me to join a game of truth or dare, and that is how I learned the boy Nancy Jenkins most wanted to kiss was Simon Dane and that Laura's earrings weren't real pearls. When it was my turn, I chose dare because I was afraid of having to tell the truth about my father. They dared me to sit next to James on the school bus on the way home, and so I did it, and James said, "You can't sit next to me," and I said, "I think I already did," and got up and went to another seat.

When I got home, I went straight to the clinic to check on my mother. In her white uniform she looked even more pale than usual, like she could disappear or maybe already had. She had gray circles under her eyes like smudges of ash, and the rims of her eyes were red.

I wanted to ask her if my father had called, but the way she was tearing the wrapper off of a gauze pad—like she was trying to strangle it—made me change my mind, and I went back to my room and thought about Buster and wondered whether his life had changed as much as mine.

When my father lived with us, my mother would put on a dress just before he got home for dinner, a dress covered with flowers or bright, wavy designs. They would have a drink together, a drink that smelled like cherry soda and made my mother's cheeks pink and her voice high. She would ask my father how his day was, and he would tell her, but I can't tell you what he said because that's when I would stop listening.

He had to travel sometimes, and then it was just me and my mother, but not like it is now. Then it was an adventure, and she would make a tent in the living room, and we would sleep in it on piles of blankets and roast marshmallows over the gas burners in the kitchen. She would put a flashlight under a sheet and pretend it was a campfire and tell ghost stories until I was so scared I begged her to stop. Then I would fall asleep in her arms, and she would still be there when I woke up, her hair all soft and messy.

In a corner of the room where my mother and I now sleep, there are boxes piled as high as the ceiling, and I wonder if that is where all of her colorful dresses are and the crystal glasses that held the cherry drinks and Buster's food bowl.

Above the fireplace in our old house, there was a framed picture of my father holding me when I was two or three. In the picture I am wearing a green velvet dress and white tights and black patent leather shoes, and everyone is smiling. Even my mother, who is not in the picture, is smiling; I am sure of it. In another picture my mother and father are with their friends at the beach. My mother is wearing an old-fashioned bathing suit with a little skirt at the bottom, and her head is thrown back, and she is laughing, and my father is looking at her like she is the only other person in the picture, maybe the whole beach, maybe even the world. I guess those pictures are in the boxes, too. At least I hope so.

My second day at school, the girls spent part of recess hovering around Mrs. Baxter's desk and then brought me a card they had made. The cover said, "We're Sorry," and inside, "ABOUT YOUR DAD." I thanked them and stuck the card in my book bag, but believe me, I was sorrier than they were, but there was no going back. Everyone was extra nice to me, and at lunch Tanya offered me her cupcake, and I ate it, but it tasted like the sand that gets between your teeth at the beach.

Mrs. Baxter had decided to have a class about families. She explained to the class that some families have mothers and fathers, and some only have one, which you would have to be a complete idiot not to know. She made Nicole talk about what it was like having parents who were divorced. Nicole said that at first she thought it was her fault that her parents got divorced and that it was a tragedy, but then she realized divorce wasn't so bad because you got a present from each parent on your birthday and the same thing at Christmas, and if her mother didn't want her to do something like go to a certain movie, she could just ask her dad, and if her dad said she had enough clothes, she could always get her mother to buy her more, and now her father had this pretty new girlfriend who gave her presents, too, and the girlfriend was always kissing her father, but then Mrs. Baxter said, "That's enough, Nicole, thank you."

Then I was supposed to talk about what it felt like to have a parent die. But I didn't. Instead, I told the class that there was something much worse than having only one parent, and that was having *no parents at all.* I said that if you lost one parent, you had to be very careful not to lose the other one, or to do something that would make the other one leave you, only you couldn't be sure what that something was. You had to worry about your mother dying, but you couldn't do much about that except to remind her to wear her seatbelt and to tell her to please slow down when she was passing all the other cars and cutting some of them off and the other drivers were waving their hands and saying words I'm not allowed to repeat. I said that losing both of your parents would be like the dream where you can't stop falling, and that was when Jennifer began to cry and Mrs. Baxter told me to sit down.

When I'm home, I am surrounded by retardos, or as my mother insists I call them, *residents.* I hide in our room most of the time so I don't have to see them, and so I can keep an eye on my mother. But I don't have a TV in my room. When I want to watch TV, I have to go to the TV room and watch with the retardos, which is annoying because they talk during the show and walk in front of the set and laugh too loud at the sitcom jokes, which aren't that funny. Robert is there rocking, and you get dizzy if you look at him for too long, but sometimes it's hard not to stare. They pick their noses and fart and burp and aren't the least bit embarrassed.

I hate to look at them. Their clothing never seems to fit. They are too wide in the chest. Their bottoms, which should be tidy circles, are like pumpkins. It is no wonder their buttons pop off and their zippers break.

Lisa is so skinny, her clothes look empty, like no one is wearing them. Her hair is full of knots and shoots out in all directions just like the hedges in front of my old house before my father trimmed them. She carries a little green purse close to her body and sometimes pulls a red lipstick out and puts some on, staring in a compact as if she is a normal person putting on lipstick. She thinks she looks beautiful, but I know better. I know that beautiful is the way people look on TV: tall, with perfect teeth and silky hair, smiling—a clever smile, not some retardo grin. I want to be around people like that, not a bunch of drooling idiots.

Sometimes Lisa and Robert sit next to each other on the couch and hold hands and even kiss, and then I have to leave the room, TV or no TV. It is too weird. I tell their counselors what Lisa and Robert are doing and wait for them to put a stop to it, but they just laugh. I don't know what kind of a world this is where my parents can't stay together and a pair of retardos can.

I visit other kids after school, and my mother picks me up when she finishes working, but I can never, ever, invite anyone to where I live. I would die first.

We have been at the home for two months, and my father hasn't visited or called. Maybe he really is dead. I wonder if by saying it, I have made it true. Maybe *I killed him.* One night I repeat 500 times, "My father is alive," to undo what I have done, but I don't know if it is too late and he is already dead and it is my fault. Worrying about it keeps me awake, and my mother says, "What's bothering you?" but of course I can't tell her. So that's when she says, "You know your father loves you," which is the first time she has ever lied to me. I am surprised she doesn't say, "To hell with that sonofabitch," which I heard her say to my grandmother on the phone just last week.

That weekend I go to the mall with my friends and we eat hot pretzels and pizza and drink cokes and hang out in front of stores and go into the music store where we listen to top 40 songs through headphones and pass the headphones back and forth at the best parts and look at magazines and shriek when we find pictures of our favorite bands. We go into department stores and try on clothes and pose behind lingerie saying, "Dahling, you look gorgeous," until the clerk chases us out and we end up back in front of the pizza store, laughing so hard we can hardly stand and imitating the clerk, hands on hips, saying in low, serious voice, "This is not a toy store, girls. Where are your parents? We don't allow children in here without their parents."

We are looking at the wedding rings in a jewelry store window when I hear Lisa shouting across the mall, "Eh-len? Is thaaat yuh-oo?" She is charging toward me, her counselor a few steps behind. "Eh-len, hiii." Her pink pants come up to her chest. As she comes closer, my friends look at one another. "You know her?" Melissa asks.

"Kind of," I say.

But there is no pretending, because she has reached me and is all over me like a long lost sister.

"Luhuck whaaat I bouuuugt," she says, holding up a flowery blouse even my grandmother wouldn't wear.

The next thing I know, a whole group of them have reached me and they are pulling purchases out of bags, saying, "Luhuck," and "Seeeee." My friends have edged away, but I am trapped in the middle of the shouting, arm-waving mass. I am telling them how beautiful their hideous purchases are when I see a chance to escape. I run without looking back.

I find my friends in front of the music store.

"Eh-len, looook whaaat I bouuuugt," Jennifer says.

"Eh-len, Eh-len, loooook," they all begin to chant, and for good measure they pat me on the arms and hair.

"Cut it out!"

"We didn't know you had so many friends," Melissa says.

"They're not my friends. They live at the center where my mother is a nurse."

"Don't you live there, too, Eh-len?" Melissa says.

"I don't have a choice."

"They're creepy," Melissa says. "I would take ten showers if they touched me."

"Too bad your father's not around," Chris says. "You could live with him."

"Yeah, too bad," I say.

"We shouldn't have to look at them," Melissa says.

"They shouldn't let them out," Chris says.

"Yeah, they should lock them up," Jennifer says.

"I don't know about locking them up," I say, because even though I don't like the residents, I figure even they deserve to get out of the home every now and then.

"I forgot, they're your best friends," Jennifer says. "Maybe you want to hang out with them."

"Don't let us keep you," Chris says.

"All I'm saying is they're not dangerous."

"She likes them. I can't believe it," Chris says.

"I don't like them. They give me the creeps. But they're harmless, that's all."

"I still say she likes them," Chris says.

When my mother picks me up from the mall, I get in the car and pull the door shut harder than I have to. She's listening to a news program on the radio, and even though I know it will make her mad, I turn the dial to a rock 'n' roll station and turn the volume up loud so I can pretend not to hear her when she says, "You know I don't like that kind of music."

She snaps off the radio, and I shout at her, "Why did you bring us here? I hate it here! I hate the retardos, and I hate the home! Why can't we live in a normal house like normal people?" Then it's quiet, and I wonder if she's looking for a place to pull over and let me out, and if she'll drive away and I'll never see her again.

But she keeps on driving, and after a while she says quietly, "I'm saving money so we can buy our own house."

"The girls all made fun of me," I say, although I don't know if she hears me because I'm crying pretty hard. I wipe my eyes with the back of my hands, but that just makes my hands cold. The seat of the car suddenly feels too big for me, and when I try to hold on, my hands are slippery on the vinyl.

Later that night my mother takes me on her lap, and even though I am too old for that, I let her, and that's when I notice she's not wearing her wedding ring anymore. "I know it's been hard on you coming to live here. I know you want things to be like they were," she says. "Sometimes we don't get what we want," she adds, but I think she is talking to herself.

On Monday from across the room, I see Melissa and Chris talking to James, and I think I hear Melissa say "Eh-len," and then they all laugh, but when I reach them, they stop talking. When it is time to go home, I see someone has written RETARDO on my book bag in red marker, and I have to think of my favorite food—seven layer cake—to keep from crying. When I pass James on the school bus, he is smirking, and that gets me thinking he has done it.

My mother tries washing it out, but no matter how many times she runs it through the washing machine, a red shadow of the word remains, and I make her take me to Kmart to get a new bag that night, and she doesn't argue with me. The next day at school, I look around to see if anyone's fingers are red, but I can't turn anything up. I don't tell Mrs. Baxter because I know that would just make things worse. "Nice book bag," James says to me on the bus that night. "What happened to your old one?"

I take my seat in the back of the bus and stare out of the window and imagine the bus rolling down a rocky embankment and me jumping out of the window in time and James getting crushed against the rocks and his parents crying at his funeral.

On Saturday I see my father's car climb the steep driveway to the home. I run to meet him in the parking lot, but even after he pulls into a spot, he doesn't get out right away. He just sits in the car with the engine running and me outside his rolled-up window shouting, "Hi, Daddy," and hoping he can hear me above the engine and whatever he is thinking. He stays that way for a few minutes, and I wonder if he has changed his mind about coming and if he is going to leave without ever getting out of the car, but just then he shuts off the engine. He is barely out of the car when I wrap my arms around his waist and bury my head in his side. I hold on tighter than I have ever held on to anything, tighter than I held on to the side of the ice rink when I was first learning to skate, tighter even than I held on to the safety bar on the Magic Mountain roller coaster last summer, but he peels me off anyway.

I look in the car, hoping to see Buster, but he tells me he has left Buster home, and I realize I don't know where home is. I wait for him to notice I have started wearing glasses, but if he does notice, he doesn't say anything. He is wearing wrinkled jeans and an old Coca Cola sweatshirt. The letters are peeling off the logo so that it reads,

Co Cola, like someone with a stutter is trying to order a soda. But I know better than to make a joke about that. When he lived with us, my father wore buttondown shirts and khaki pants my mother ironed in the basement. As I lead him to our room, I reach for his hand and squeeze, but he doesn't squeeze back. His hand feels cold and rubbery, like a toy snake I once hid in my mother's bed. When we get to the room, my mother says they need some privacy, which means I'm not wanted.

I have nowhere to go except the TV room. I am hoping it will be empty, because I don't feel like hanging around retardos. But when I get there, it is as busy as ever. I settle on the couch, and when Lisa tries to touch me, I tell her to get the hell away, and when Robert laughs too loud, I call him a retardo, which I have never said to his face, and he starts to cry. I stare out of the window and try to ignore his uneven sobbing and Lisa patting his hand and saying, "Dohhhnt cryyy Rohbert ihhhts awl riiight."

I wonder if my father has come to get my mother, and if they are planning to leave me behind. I stand outside our door for a while making sure I can hear their voices, making sure they have not left me.

When my father finally emerges, he takes me to a diner and orders steaks for both of us, but from the way he is looking at me, I don't think we have anything to celebrate. He tells me he and my mother are getting divorced and that I will live with my mother except for two weeks in the summer when I will stay with him. I am glad he isn't dead but happy I will be staying with my mother, even if it means living at the home. He says he will call me every week, but I know it is a lie from the way he doesn't look at me when he says it.

When I get back to our room that night, my mother has begun to unpack some of the boxes, and she has put the picture of me and my father on the nightstand, but the picture on the beach is nowhere to be found. Through the open door to the closet, I see she has hung some of her dresses. I realize she must have just hung them, because they are swinging back and forth on their hangers like they are keeping time to a song.

On parent teacher night, Mrs. Baxter finds out my father isn't really dead. She never says anything to me about it, and it wouldn't really matter if she did. By now I have made friends, and even though they occasionally make fun of me for living at the home, it isn't really that different from the way we make fun of Melissa because her mother sometimes picks her up from school in a bathrobe, or how we tease Chris because her father works as a garbage man. My friends and I hang out at the mall every weekend, and every now and then we run into a group of residents, but it is never as bad as that first time, and besides, I have bought a black book bag so that even if someone gets it into their head to write on it, it won't show.

I am even getting used to the residents. When Lisa reaches out to touch me in the dining room, I tell her, "I don't like that," and she says, "Whyyy di-dn't youuuu saaay sooo," and pulls her hand back and doesn't try to touch me again. Even Robert sits down in the TV room when I tell him he is blocking the set, although by the next day he has forgotten and I have to tell him again. When I catch the two of them holding hands or kissing, I still feel sick and have to leave the room, but I have given up trying to stop them. I figure the chances are pretty good they'll break up soon, anyway, without any help from me.

SVETLANA LAVOCHKINA

Semolinian Equinox

From January/February 2009

AT DONETSK UNIVERSITY, talking about money reveals bad manners—there has been no sight of salary for six months. Students and professors go to the marketplace after classes. They stand at the stalls side by side, their ankles equally soaked in April sleet. They sell groceries, poultry, hosiery—whatever the dealers supply them.

"French socks latest cut, sexy stockings for your butt!" student Andrey recites into the drizzle, helping Professor Nikolai Vassilievich arrange listless bunches of carrots for display on the stone counter. Nikolai Vassilievich guards Andrey's wallet while Andrey heads for an inconspicuous place at the market fringes to relieve himself. Drinking moonshine to get warm, they count their gain in inflated millions, munch the carrots, shoo mongrels from under the stalls, and never talk about the University.

At summer solstice, however, the learner and the learned meet in a short circuit at the State Examination. Andrey feigns due awe of Nikolai Vassilievich of course, but, mumbling unintelligibly as he does,

Andrey still knows for sure his mark will not quite exactly mirror the fact that he has neither opened any book on the course programme nor seen the professor doing his main job at the pulpit, his silver tongue pouring out undiluted Middle English to the drowsing audience, too recently weaned from Mother Goose to be able to partake of *swiche licour.*

Sighing, Nikolai Vassilievich scribbles "satisfactory" into Andrey's record book. After all, in the domain of cutting edge Ukrainian market folklore, Andrey is far more proficient than Nikolai Vassilievich will ever be. If Andrey, in his turn, were ever to examine Nikolai Vassilievich in retail practice, the professor's mark would inevitably be "poor." In Donetsk, the ability to tell Pushkin from Gogol, Shakespeare from Chaucer, or sinus from logarithm is rather a handicap than a privilege. Such details put one at a tangent to the central focus of survival.

At a tangent I may be, but I am truly privileged today. Andrey has given me a million to get a good chicken at the market. He wishes me to make a three-course dinner out of one bird corpse. He says I must make a broth, then peel off the chicken's skin, stuff it with schmaltz and onions, and serve the filet separately, with mashed potatoes. We will feast in his locked room in the United Hostels, no hungry guests to diminish our delight.

Dizzy in the sweet, festering air of the poultry row, I am glad to see many chubby chickens displayed. I slap them on their thighs and breasts and finally choose the one that resonates most. My mouth is watering at the promise of a golden treat.

"What do you study, lass?" the vendress asks me, wrapping the chicken into a newspaper.

"English," I reply.

Her greasy fingers fumble under the counter to produce a blue hardcover book. She points at the title, "The ABC of Dirty English." I run the pages between my fingers, incredulously: "Abishag, Able

Grable, Abyssinian medal..." The brazen beads descend the page in neat strings, all provided with matter-of-fact Russian translations. Dirty English is not in the curriculum. We learn it combed, buttoned-up, and gelded.

"It's yours for a million," the woman says, knowing she has already won. Chubby chickens are much easier to sell than barmy books in alien tongues. So much for tonight's dinner.

It takes the tram two hours to cross the city of Donetsk. It is warm in the tram, good for the first date. The workers, going home, already Brahms and Liszt with moonshine, wink at me, but then they see at once I am already promised.

"Taboo words are inseparable from the language," the dictionary preface says. "Their artificial banning leads to the language's impoverishment. It is widely believed that Anglo-Saxon vulgarisms denoting male and female genitals are the true aristocracy of the language."

I don't notice that the tram has traversed the city of Donetsk twice and it has grown dark.

When I come back, Andrey is not asleep yet. His hand is still able to reach his mouth with a cigarette, his elbow resting in a dirty plate.

"Where is my dinner?" He is drilling holes in me with his stare.

My only problem with Andrey is that he is allergic to English for its sheer impracticality. He doesn't see any opportunity for himself ever to live in England or the States, so why bother at all? Andrey tells me off for a long time, hauling objects about the room to give his words more weight. He is very eloquent, and I very ashamed. Yes, he is quite right in calling me a selfish bitch. Andrey is right in saying I don't respect hard-earned money. He is right in saying I always do what my left foot desires. Right or left, around midnight I am being routinely forgiven—let the iron bed bear the brunt of my guilt.

Loud singing wakes us up before dawn. We cannot recognize the male voice whose pitch ranges amply from peacock to goat, but we know the female one by heart and to the marrow of our bones. The walls of the hostel rooms as thin as a calico curtain are being dissolved by the sulphuric acid of voices. Thank God we woke up to the *allegro vivace* part, which usually precedes the *presto* culmination with a final *fortissimo* out of the full breast of the diva and the breathless tenor losing its virility in falsetto heights.

The singers harvest their storm of applause from the listeners in adjacent rooms along with a loud account of their performance.

"Six times!" heralds the neighbor downstairs.

"No, seven!" argues the neighbor upstairs.

Andrey addresses me meaningfully, pointing in the direction the singing has been coming from. "Learn, Semolina, learn!"

The diva so praised is notoriously famous in the labyrinths of the United Hostels of Donetsk University. Nourished on raisin buns and peasant butter, now almost in possession of an intellectually unobliging diploma in English philology, Tanya spends her nights in cockroach-teeming cells not out of bitter necessity. Her parents are, for Donetsk standards, well-off. They live in a high-ceilinged flat in Artem Main Avenue, where Tanya disposes of a whole room. If Tanya were asked to explain her behavior, she would say she is just enjoying her student life before stepping into all too early adulthood, skimming cream from the thin milk of the toppled times. She would also imply she is escaping the pressure of her philistine family and gaining invaluable experience for life.

Our parents and teachers told us God was invented to stupefy and poison people. It is only upon ourselves, the summits of creation, that we are to rely to thrive and multiply. But then Donetsk's embrace has become too sultry, too tight, so we have had to find some more ethereal air to breathe.

When the sky is as starry as it can ever get in Donetsk, I wriggle out from under sleeping Andrey's biceps and sneak upstairs to the 12th floor, through a narrow door to the roof of the United Hostels. I cuddle up against the belly of Ursa Major because she is my only friend up there to listen to my complaints. I tell her I am in love—impossible, unrequited, shameful, carnal love. I follow him, I covet him and yet cannot possess—he is made of the green sea, of the chalk curve, of flowing ink, of topaz breath, my Angle, my Saxon, my Jute.

"You will soon have him," Ursa says to me. "Fill your limbs with his tide, your head with his mind, your heart with his beat—and then your loins—fill them with his final spice. He will then take you in his arms and carry you far away from the United Hostels, up into the vernal equinox." The only thing Ursa Major does not say is when.

Tanya is awake in small hours to lay an offering of flesh and voice on the altar of a Ukrainian goddess, moon-faced and arch-browed, full-bosomed and heavy-hipped. It is this goddess who will protect our faithful Tanya, under the condition she learns the art of lovemaking in all diligence and devotion, because in Donetsk it is through men that all women's dreams come true. The goddess will care for Tatyana's steeply rising career in Kiev, the capital on seven hills, marry her to a rich, dignified Englishman, or American, Tanya doesn't mind, and bring her several meridians west. The way is long but well lit, and it is not only at night that Tanya toils. To facilitate Venus' tutelage, she studies English in a shrewd, practical way, to be able to compete at the markets of business and love. How I wish I were her.

Tanya and I spend lecture breaks together smoking American cigarettes we buy for 10,000 apiece, for none of us can afford the luxury of a whole pack. We share her cigarette today because I am too broke for even one snout.

"Was I too loud this night?"

"Not louder than usual."

Tanya informs me abundantly, as she always will, of Alyosha's codpiece characteristics. Alyosha is her latest infatuation whom we had the boon of perceiving. The last inhalation of Pall Mall is hers. In a bluish, bridal veil of smoke, she confides in me the latest Secret of Secrets.

"This night Alyosha said he wants a baby by me."

In Donetsk, as everybody knows, children are rather aborted than born.

"Lucky you," I say. "No one has ever wanted children by me. But you can give it a try."

"God forbid," Tanya says. "I'm waiting for the reply from the Kiev Travel Star. I wish they would take me!"

The bell to the next lecture rings, and we go to listen to the Truth of the Truths of Theoretical Phonetics of the English Language delivered by Lubov Gavrilovna, a fierce spinster. Tanya is sitting next to me, looking directly into Lubov Gavrilovna's mouth and zealously copying transcription signs from the blackboard, begging her goddess to forgive her premature thoughts of progeny: "/θ/ as in 'thick': voiceless, dental, fricative. /ð/ as in 'then': voiced, dental, fricative. /æ/ as in 'bag': front, open, short."

The blue book under my desk is revealing different truths to me. I am copying them, pretending to be in a theoretical-phonetic trance.

"A Bag of snakes in Birthday clothes is in Bad shape."

"The Calf's lesson in Curve is well-learnt."

Andrey has just performed what he sardonically calls his marital duty. He is lying on his back, his head resting on my forearm, seeing the evening off with his last cigarette.

"Have you ever wanted children?" I ask.

Andrey turns his head to me.

"By whom? You? No, thanks. You're too inept to wipe your own ass."

He raises his head, propping it on his own elbow.

"Don't take it personally," he says. There are basically no women in Donetsk to have children by. They're all either sluts or fools, and you're the latter."

I know that Andrey is right about me, but I want to redeem the female gender of Donetsk—I know an example.

"Alyosha does want a baby by Tanya," I say.

"Really? What a hoot! He was thinking with his other head when he said that."

I shouldn't have aired Tanya's secret, but it is too late.

"A baby by a slut! That's a good one!" Andrey grins, his teeth glaring in the fag light.

Alyosha has left for his native village for the weekend. He needs a rest from incessant performances. He badly needs a substantial meal of mama's purple borsch, with a hunk of generously larded rye bread. Tanya is at home. Yawning, she puts on a flowered nightgown, which has no idea of its mistress' nightlife in foreign quarters. She has taken up a deadly boring textbook with which she has never progressed beyond Page 14 when the phone in the hallway rings. She hastens barefoot to be the first to pick up the receiver and make her nosy mother retreat into the kitchen.

"Hellooo," Tatyana says in the deepest of her bosom tones.

"Oh, Andrey, it's you." She switches into standby mode, knowing why he usually calls.

"I would like you to help me, Tanya."

"I know you want my lecture notes again. Listen, can't you try and do your homework yourself for a change?"

"Tanya, it's not your notes I want."

"Be quick, I'm falling asleep."

"Tanya... I would like you to give me a gift."

"Your birthday was two months ago, dear, and you got a whole pack of Marlboro from me!"

"Tatyana, it's a different gift I am asking you for. I would like you to give me a baby."

"Have you lost your wits? Have Semolina give you a baby."

Deeply, though, Tanya is flattered by the request. Even Andrey the market champion... She is half-wondering if she could secretly refit her duet score for his bass.

"Let me think," she says. "Call me tomorrow."

In the morning before classes Tanya runs into Dmitri the baritone at the cigarette kiosk. He leaves his entourage of two blonds and takes her by the hand to the side.

"May I ask you a question?"

"I didn't sleep with anyone yesterday. This is why it was so quiet in the hostel at night," Tatyana snaps.

"It would never occur to me to doubt your innocence, dear. It is a different question I have."

Tanya understands she has been betrayed. A deaf-mute janitor publicly inserts a note into Tanya's curvaceous décolleté. A joint choir of male students chants on her entering the lecture hall, "We want a baby by Tanya!"

Tonight the diva is not up to singing. Neither is she up to it the next day or the day after. At college she bears a stern face and moves like an icebreaker. She refuses to visit Alyosha in the hostel. She is not on speaking terms with me. I miss her cigarettes, and even more, her detailed lecture notes.

In Donetsk, the air temperature at summer solstice does not differ much from that of a furnace. The weather enhances the Great Account feeling for the examinees. Fifty heads in a single long row, sweat in rivulets streaming down their foreheads, recline, yielding to the fate and the heat against the hallway wall, waiting for their names to be called to enter purgatory. Every quarter of an hour a victim is thrown out of the examination room, squeezed, bedraggled, sucked dry. The examination board is presided over by Lubov Gavrilovna, a spinster *sans merci*, an expert in torture. Lubov Gavrilovna is sometimes known to favor assiduous, simple, healthy-looking girls of peasant descent, but pale decadent species with long noses stand no chance with Lubov Gavrilovna, this is well known.

Tanya has just been resurrected from the dead. Her hair is combed into a tight ponytail, her blouse buttoned to the top, her dark skirt sweeping the floor. Sweat must be trickling all the way down her legs, but she emerges nonchalant. "Excellent," Tatyana pronounces to those of us who are still in the anguish of waiting.

The secretary calls my name.

I am ushered into the place of execution. The table is covered with a once white tablecloth, now stained, creased by the racked martyrs' fingers. Nikolai Vassilievich is placed next to Lubov Gavrilovna but seems to be blissfully away in vibrant April, seeping ale at the Tabard Inn. A withered bunch of carrots is peeking out of his string bag on the floor, for summer solstice makes no exception from his market chore, to be performed after the examination is over. With a climacteric rustle of fingernails, Lubov Gavrilovna opens my record book. Her toad eyes rise at me without expression.

"Semolina. Absent for seven lectures. Covert reading of extraneous sources in class. We look forward to hear what you have learnt about the phonemic system of English."

I take a communal water glass from the table, half empty, its rim scalloped with lipstick of various shades—scarlet, pink, orange—a token of mercy, a last gulp from the executioner. My hand remains suspended in the air as if in a toast to Lubov Gavrilovna and summer solstice.

"The phonemic system of English is very beautiful," I start. "The sounds are of many colors and shapes. They purr, they moan, they bark, puke, squeak, and sometimes spit. They live in people and animals and leave them only with their last 'h.'"

Lubov Gavrilovna parts her lips to pronounce my verdict, but then, upon a second thought, tightens them up again to hear what comes next.

"For example, /θ/ as in 'thunder thighs,'" I continue. "It looks like the Wife of Bath's leg in a red stocking. /ð/ as in 'tether one's nag' is Chanticleer about to love his Pertelote. And here is the /æ/ as in 'abishag'—it's made of rough leather, broad and bawdy—like Absalom's kiss. Then there is O, as in..."

Nikolai Vassilievich awakens from his slumber at the mention of the creatures he knew so well. But Lubov Gavrilovna has had enough of my phonemic system.

"Out! Out with her!" she yells. "Expel her from the university!"

Nikolai Vassilievich's string bag tilts on the side, and the carrots all tumble down in a fan of "i's, /i:/" as in "shit Street."

"Come on, let's buy the little fool some chocolate," Andrey says. He is not upset. So much the better. Didn't he tell me 1,000 times honest studying is not worth the hassle? At last I can do something useful. Now that he has become a market dealer himself, I can take his place at the counter beside Nikolai Vassilievich. There is so much to sell, so many millions to earn. Andrey himself has not needed to come to the State Examination. He sent the rector 100 pairs of socks, which are enough for a "satisfactory," and not even Lubov Gavrilovna could do anything about it.

With no haste, already in possession of the intellectually unobliging diploma in English Phililogy with honors, Tanya picks up the receiver. She hears an unfamiliar male voice on the line. "Could I speak to Miss Tatyana Prokopenko, please? There is a matter of some importance that I would like to discuss with her."

The humiliating events of the recent past surge into Tatyana's head.

"You fucking bastard, go to hell, you hear me? You go to hell with your fucking offers, and I don't want anything. Fuck you!"

She hangs up with a bang, and, when the telephone rings again, lets her eager mother answer the call.

"Tanya, a nice gentleman has just told me he was sorry you don't want to work in Kiev, for the *Travel Star*. He said you must be snowed up with job offers to curse him as you did."

Tanya picks up the telephone and throws it against the wall. The machine is smashed to smithereens. Tanya utters The Cry of Cries, louder than any of her final duet chords. The cry is drowned in the Whirlpool of Tears. She leaves the house in her nightgown and slippers. She runs to the United Hostels. Alyosha can't believe his fortune. He jumps to his feet, throws a half-finished cigarette out of the window, lifts her solid weight as if it were a feather, and hauls her onto the iron bed.

"Not before we marry," Tanya says, pushing him away with a firm hand.

If her goddess dumped her, she has now to take the remnants of her once-promising fate by the horns.

In Donetsk United Hospitals, men are neither allowed into the delivery room, nor can they visit the mother at the Obstetrics, so the babies are shown to fathers through ward windows. Alyosha, like every young father, appears daily for a two-minute display of the son. It is, however, difficult to define Tanya as an ordinary mother, at least as seen from the point of view of the hospital staff. No less than 20 times in five days Tanya spent in hospital, the perplexed nurses have been accepting flowers and cards from sundry men. The contents of the cards stuck in the bouquets does not vary in a single word. Each of them says, "*Tanya—Thank you for the son!*"

I am at the United Hospitals, too—nothing serious, just family planning. Andrey says they will serve me a chicken wing when I wake up. He has paid for that. I am sprawled like a starfish, and there is a needle in my arm bend. One doctor is behind my head, and one is between my knees.

"Why is she still twitching? That dose should have put her under by now!"

"Ah, what the hell. Just get on with it."

My limbs are washed by the green tide, my mind crumbles like stardust and flows down into my stomach. *Zazzy, zaftig, zing, zigzag.* The alphabet is over now. My loins are full of the final spice. "Well-done," says Ursa Major. "You have deserved your prize."

I hear his topaz breath, I feel the swing of his cloak. He wraps me into its folds, and off we start, away from Donetsk, away from everything united, up into the vernal equinox. He is holding me tight, my Angle, my Saxon, my Jute.

WILL LASKY

An Ugly Man's Guide to Self Improvement

From January/Febrary 2014

1.

THE MOMENT of recognition came one evening at De Luca's. He was having drinks with his friend Mike, who was kind of a good time Charlie, but whom he had never recognized as his quintessential opposite. He had gone to the bathroom, a Roman type space with water trickling, opera playing, mirrors everywhere. In an instant, he caught a glimpse of himself from all angles: his stooped posture, his frizzy red hair, his reddish fat-yet-narrow face, blond eyebrows set low over close-set, tiny blue eyes.

"Shit, I'm ugly," he thought. "This is why I've been unsuccessful as both an actor and a waiter."

"I'm an ugly man," he said, his voice echoing off the tiles of the bathroom. Even his voice sounded ugly. "Why didn't anyone tell me? Why didn't I realize?"

Back in the restaurant proper, he approached Mike apprehensively, shell-shocked beneath the weight of his revelation.

Why did he spend so much time with Mike? Often when he was with Mike, they met women. The women were of course totally consumed by Mike. Mike Blake, actor, author. Was that why he and Mike Blake hung out so much? Was there the germ of some sort of reasonableness there?

Mike was intelligent, talented. He wrote a screenplay that he sold for $250,000. The name of the screenplay was *Proteus Nine.* It was science fiction, incredibly creative, engaging. They inked Steven Seagal, which kind of doomed the whole thing from the start. Still, Mike made a bunch of money, enough to buy the vintage Jeep Wrangler he had long coveted, and to not really work.

On the other hand, the ugly man had never managed to complete one of his screenplays. Since moving to LA, he had only been an extra. They used the ugly man to pad crowds, busy city sequences, concerts... He wasn't one of those extras you wanted walking across the street, oblivious to the lead role passing in the opposite direction. He was less an extra and more human bulk.

As thoughts regarding work ran through his head, he realized he was still listening to Mike talk.

"I'm just an ugly guy," he blurted.

"Like Paul Giamatti."

"Paul Giamatti's not ugly," the ugly man said. "Paul Giamatti has a frail beauty."

"Come on, you aren't ugly. There are a lot of guys who look like you. Just look around."

They looked around. He was the ugliest man in the room.

2.

He slid down off his bar stool, all five feet, seven inches of him, seeming to take an inordinate amount of time, almost as if he was oozing off his stool.

That was the end of his friendship with Mike. Sometimes certain relationships don't survive transitions. It was as if a spell had been broken, the spell of his own self-illusion. He would no longer let himself be the sore thumb at De Luca's.

It was night. He walked down Sunset Blvd, past the huge Hustler shop. He went back and went in. He browsed the pornos, looking at the other men browsing the pornos, strung out on vicious forms of internal and external ugliness.

Jesus! What it means to be an ugly man! He thought. Your entire destiny is governed by the fact that people make excuses for not looking at you. He left the Hustler shop, a shiver running down his spine. He stopped in at a liquor store and bought a fifth of Bim Black.

He made the turn onto his own street, walking up the silent little block toward the hills.

3.

He entered the little door embedded at ground level in the bottom of the triplex. His flat was little more than a kitchenette, smaller than a studio. Everything was in one room. "Okay, I get it," he thought. "Ugly man, ugly living space."

He poured some whiskey into a coffee mug and sat at the rickety little plywood table.

"I have to get out of show business. What the fuck am I doing?"

The whole point of show business was that you had to be appealing. Even your archetypal ugly men—Woody Allen, George Costanza—these were deeply appealing men. Yet, there was nothing appealing about him. He was neither pleasantly plump nor downright silly, nor funny or pathetic looking. He got up, went over to the kitchen sink, looked in the mirror. His face held a disturbing, warped quality, as if it had been pushed a little to the left.

Often over the course of his life, people read in him some emotional disturbance that wasn't there. The emotional disturbance of course was their own disturbance at having their perceptions of harmony shaken. His face was troublesomely, challengingly ugly. It got to people on a level, made them feel like something was wrong. It exposed them. No one wants that sort of thing. Ugliness should be opaque, like a brick wall. You can hammer on that ugliness all day long, and it will take your blows because it's a strong, supportive kind of ugliness. His own ugliness was brittle, threatening to splinter at the touch.

4.

He got out pen and paper and began to make a list of jobs.

Janitor. Janitors were notoriously repulsive. Not just ugly, but creepy ugly, in-hiding ugly. Computer programmers had a kind of geek chic: neither attractive nor ugly, but syndromatic. Air conditioning repairman was more like it. Cable guy. All these jobs were in reach. Ugly men all over the country made a living at these jobs. They made a living enough to afford a ticket to where they could find a bride who would accept them because of their money. They could go and find women totally worn out by poverty, willing to accept ugliness as an occupational, gold-digging hazard.

All these years he had tried to force himself into the life of a handsome, talented man from a good family. He shuddered at the thought of Mike. What had Mike wanted out of their relationship? Maybe out of some deep-seated, incomprehensible insecurity, Mike needed an ugly foil to go around with as a constant reminder of his own beauty.

5.

"Ever think of settling down and having children?" his mother asked him the following day from over the telephone.

This seemed like a good moment to break the news. "Yeah, I guess I've thought about it. Of course I've thought about it."

"I guess someday you'll decide that you might like to have children," his mother said, oblivious to realities.

The big difference between his experience and his mother's was that companionship was not a choice for him. His mother was not ugly, not even a Plain Jane. She didn't understand companionship was not something offered to him from out of a range of choices. It was not within his life's lexicon of trajectories, which primarily consisted of toward, and away from, homelessness.

"I guess so," he said, not knowing what to say.

His parents and much of his family were handsome drifters. He often observed that handsome people produced ugly children, as if life were trying to right a ship, to teach a lesson.

Working on the margins of the celebrity world, he had seen how beautiful celebrity parents often gave birth to ugly children. Take Jake and Deborah Osbeck. Their kids Tyler and Jessica were downright beasts, like inbred Central European royals. They were the children of beautiful celebrities. They had boyfriends and girlfriends. The boyfriends and girlfriends were unsuccessful musicians or unknown models. They came to visit on the set.

When you were the children of celebrities, you married better looking but poor wanna-be celebrities or celebrity bartenders.

6.

The ugly 32-year-old continued to work as an extra, although he stopped trying to stand out. He graciously accepted his role as human background bulk. He managed to hang onto just enough day shifts at The Grill to make rent. He quieted within himself. His coworkers troubled him by what he now perceived as their cloying, frustrating fantasies. They weren't ugly but were for the most part confused plain Janes. The troubled plain Janes weren't really speaking with him: they were simply speaking—to the air, to the room at large. They lectured no one in particular on fame, fortune, despair, and confusion. Had it always been like this? He had never noticed their monologues when he had been among them, entrenched in a lie.

In the evening he rode the bus down to the community college. The bus: now that was the ugly man's natural environment! Everyone on the bus was either seriously ugly or born in a way that made total assimilation impossible. There was something angelic about the men and women who rode the city bus in LA. It was as if God had spared them from the burden of differentiating themselves from society and coming to grips with their own oddity. They seemed brimming over with acceptance, like saints. Riding the bus, he felt his troubles lesson, felt himself in a humble world where even the most brutally ignored people had a place.

Sometimes, you couldn't quite peg the mental capacity of the bus riders. It was occasionally hard for him to delineate between the insane or the lucid yet wall-eyed ugly. Being cross-eyed did not necessarily indicate a lack of capacity, nor did Tourette's syndrome make for a totally unpleasant riding companion. In fact, some of the most delightful passengers were those who rattled off lists at random, did intricate, unbidden calculations, or announced out loud the objects of their interest. "There's a Maxima. Another Maxima. Another Maxima..."

Riding the bus in LA was an experience reserved for society's forgotten men and women, as was standing around for hours on desolate, scorched strips waiting for the bus to arrive. There was no point of real contact. The only speech came in the form of unbidden, random babble, as if dialed in from *Proteus Nine.*

Before bed at night, he wrote in his journal: "It's not that people don't reach out to other people. It's that people don't reach out to me." He couldn't help but giggle. Another grim epiphany, but he felt comforted by it all the same. It meant things were out of his control, that control itself was an illusion.

Then he wrote, "In this society, it matters less who you are and more what you look like."

He shed a tear and then fell into an unruffled sleep.

Since his epiphany in the De Luca's restroom, his sleep had improved.

7.

He rode the bus down to Contra Costa Community College, which was planted like an alien colonizer on a strip of blasted earth. The landscaping consisted of dirt and ripped, plastic garbage bag material anchored in the dirt, come loose in areas, flapping in the wind. The skeletons of shrubs scraped up against stucco walls. Inside the building, he saw many ugly people like himself with that brittle, critical-mass kind of untouchable ugliness. Big glasses, narrow shoulders, heads too tiny, too big, frail, obese, pasty, hairy, squat, gangling, blank, transparent, mottled, dripping. His people. Not only that: *the* people. The ones who toiled beneath the gloss of the lie.

Contra Costa Community College was only for the ugly and those cloistered entirely within the Spanish speaking community struggling to acclimate to an alien society. The two groups didn't mix, as he learned over the six months of his air conditioning repairman training.

That's where he met Daniel and Maria, an ugly couple from Orange County who had moved to the city because they wanted to be stage actors.

"We really feel like we have something to offer, but we discovered it's impossible to break into the L.A. market!" said Maria.

"Impossible," affirmed Daniel. "What were we thinking?"

They were at Daniel and Maria's place. Like him, they lived in the lower, sunken level of a duplex, although they had the run of the entire dank lower floor. All their furniture was old and worn. Although they were large, their clothing was larger. Daniel's hemispheral jeans continually slid down, revealing his buttcrack. Maria's tremendous blouse hung low, displaying her pendulous breasts. They were eating some kind of repulsive barley stir fry. Barley: the ugliest grain.

"So, when did you realize it?"

Daniel and Maria looked at each other. "Realize what?"

"That, you, you know, I mean, that you don't really look... like... show business people."

"You mean that we're ugly?" Daniel began to laugh, loud and uncouth, barking, throwing back his head, revealing his dark brown nasal bushes.

"We've always known," said Daniel.

"How do you cope with it? I mean, doesn't it bother you?"

"We see each other's inner beauty," said Maria, who was in every way Daniel's equal in terms of ugliness. She looked god awful.

He sat clutching his mug of Jagermeister, the ugliest of alcohols. He wondered if he would someday learn to see inner beauty.

"When did you realize?" Maria asked.

"About four months ago."

"That's interesting, isn't it? Some people always know, while others find out," said Maria.

"Not everyone knows!" said Daniel. "It's easier if you always know, don't you think?"

"Definitely," said Maria. "If we have ugly children, we're just going to tell them."

"You're going to tell your kids they're ugly?"

"Definitely," said Maria. "I mean, we won't put it like that. And after they reach a certain age. But I don't think they will be ugly," she said, smiling at Daniel, who raised her hand to his lips and bit it tenderly.

The ugly man wanted to parse the interstices of their love, to chart its course, to trace it back and understand where it came from.

8.

Everyday he got out of bed, looked himself in the mirror, and thought, "Everywhere people are falling in love with each other, reaching out to each other."

This somehow made everything easier to bear. It made life seem sane and comprehensible, softened the impact. Everywhere people are falling in love...

He was approaching the end of his air conditioning repair course. Through Daniel and Maria, he met others like him who possessed a fragile, threatening ugliness. Like Erik, the comic book artist from Vermont, who was training to supplement his income as a night bookkeeper.

"I just don't make personal appearances," said Erik. "It's bad for sales."

They sat around his table, drinking Bim Black, watching the light fade. They had no desire to go anywhere because they knew that doing so would be absolutely pointless.

"They often want to meet me," said Eric, his voice partially lost within his sinuses. "They send me letters, even with photographs.

Sometimes bikini shots, really actually quite attractive women. Before I realized what the problem was, I used to send autographed headshots in return. I'd send out the headshot, and then I'd never hear back. Once this girl who had sent me dozens of photos and letters felt so bad when she got my headshot, she wrote back telling me she was planning to move to New Zealand. It was hilarious. You could tell she was disappointed but wanted to preserve my feelings, and so she came up with this weird story. Totally crazy shit. All I wrote was my number and look me up next time you're in LA. I knew I probably shouldn't have sent it, but I wanted to see what would happen. You could tell she had constructed some elaborate fantasy around me."

Erik suddenly began to laugh, a kind of spastic convulsion beginning at his diaphragm, rolling up through his esophagus, releasing a hollow, machine gun, *ehehehehehehe.*

"Now, I just have fun with it, send them random clippings from *National Geographic,* pictures of lions and stuff, with a note, like 'What do you think of this?' just to see what their response will be. This one writes, 'Ooh, I like animals, too!' It really gives you a weird glimpse of what life must be like for attractive people, like it doesn't matter what you say, like you could just say, *'duh, blu blu blu,'* and people would be like, 'Oh, that's so fascinating! You're so interesting!'"

The ugly man thought of the Nissan Maxima guy on the bus. "There's a Maxima! There's a Maxima!"

He met Dwight Bode, one of the first people he had seen at Contra Costa Community. How could you miss him? Dwight Bode was seven feet tall. He was a giant with long, noodle arms, ginger hair neatly parted on the side, incredibly thick glasses. His most repulsive feature was the overwhelming smallness of his face planted right in the middle of his head. The eyes, the nose, the mouth: it was as if you could cover them all beneath a coffee mug. It was like he didn't have a face, only glasses.

Dwight Bode was a really nice guy, but really, really gloomy. When he drank Bim Black, he wasn't funny and chatty like Erik, or cheerfully odoriferous like Daniel and Maria. He became reckless in his despair, looming, hunched beneath the ceiling, breathing hard, fogging up his glasses. "I just don't know what to do anymore," he said, looking at his hands, his voice incongruously high pitched. "It's so... crippling." He fell to his knees.

Some of his finest memories from his student days came from his walks with a sober Dwight Bode in the hills around LA. They sat watching the stars come out, each beyond the need to try to summit the indescribable with paltry language.

9.

He let his extra jobs dry up. Without hustling, his day shifts at The Grill were slowly granted to other actor-waiters. This allowed for a smooth transition into the life of an air-conditioning repairman.

He kind of let himself go physically, filling out his ugliness, becoming less like Erik and more like Daniel. Being 30 pounds overweight made sense. His hair fell out over a month span. He shaved his head. Since becoming fat and bald, he noticed that on occasion total strangers had a word or two for him. They didn't say a whole lot, just commented on the weather, on current events. It was kind of nice. He was morphing from a state of fragile ugliness to durable ugliness: transforming from something disruptive and hard to something intelligible and commonplace.

He began to save money. He found himself making $60,000 a year, which for him was an absolute fortune.

Since he never went out in the evening and didn't need to think about renting a nice place, he saved approximately $20,000 the first year after taxes. He had a bankroll now, and he felt like the world was his oyster.

Since that moment of epiphany in the De Luca's toilets, he had learned and accepted the world's terms and conditions. He had learned about his limitations. Most importantly, he had learned that everywhere, people were falling in love, just not with him. Despite his own singularity, the world revolved on the axis of love. This awareness liberated him from the false assumption that he was always to blame for something.

10.

Three years later, having saved up $62,000, he bought a ticket to Japan. He just didn't know what to do with himself and thought in Asia things were more possible and that he might as well go there if only to binge on his favorite foods.

He spent several weeks in Tokyo, going out in the evening, talking to no one, reading a Japanese novel written in the 1960s about the ghost of a traveling salesman who comes back to live with his widowed wife who, having remarried, doesn't want anything to do with the pesky ghost. And yet the ghost remains. The novel reminded him of Japan in general.

From Japan he traveled to Korea, and from Korea he flew to Thailand. The Thai expatriate scene repulsed him. Ugly men from around the world traveled there to inflict themselves on beautiful young girls who, out of sheer poverty, were ready to embrace any form of ugliness, be it disruptive or immovable, creepy or hilarious, radioactive or inert. They would accept anyone as long as he had money.

Although he had engrossed himself in work and had for several years set aside the need to solve the human puzzle, in Thailand old thoughts reemerged. He felt blocked from the possibility of connection, like he was being trailed by inhibiting ghosts. Walking Bangkok's lurid streets, he began to think the problem was really beneath the surface. There was something beyond gross looks that kept him from contact. It was something that made him turn one way and the world another, shrouding him, preserving him from entering the common flow of events. At times like these, his ugliness felt magical.

11.

Several weeks later, his rusty, iron junk bound for the Andaman Islands sprung a leak. He had been told this kind of thing happens all the time in those waters. When he heard the crewmen shouting, he could hardly believe it had happened to him. But it had. His ship was sinking.

"They go straight to the bottom," some ugly white guy had said the night before. In a Hawaiian shirt, a beautiful girl on his lap, the ugly white guy seemed to know everything about the area. "Plish, glug, glug, glug," he blithely mimed the act of a ship sinking. The mostly naked teen laughed.

The encounter made him desire all the more a long trip on a Thai rustbucket. Anything to escape the freakshow of ugly Americans and their child concubines. So, the following morning he paid the 60 or so dollars and gathered his stray belongings.

He sprang out of his cabin and into the light. The water was already frothing over the edges. The captain chattered frantically over radio, but it was happening so quickly, and they were miles from land. Now they were bobbing in the blue-green sea. There were eight of them but only four life jackets, which the senior crew had quickly snatched up. A shark attacked the captain, who had been one of the first to grab a life jacket and leap overboard straight from the bridge. They all watched the attack. The ugly man felt no fear as the captain's eyes closed and blood bubbled from his lips.

Another member of the crew, one without a life jacket, suddenly began to struggle. He went under. He came back up. He tried to cling to one of his crewmates, who pushed him away. He tried to cling to the ugly 35-year-old. They went under together. Beneath the waves in full view of the sharks, he struggled to free himself from the sinking Thai sailor. Finally, with his last breath, he kicked away, rising slowly, barely reaching the surface without passing out. The remaining six were in hysterics as the hammerheads circled. Sharks picked off two more during the night. Another sank.

He was amazingly calm. He floated on his back beneath the starlight. His fat belly kept him well above the waves, and his lanky arms and legs tirelessly treaded the salty sea. The sharks were on his mind all the time, but he learned to compartmentalize that anxiety and to live with it as he lived with his own repulsive exterior. He never knew that outside of being ugly, he was also surprisingly courageous. After being rescued 27 hours later, sitting on the edge of the bunk, he said the words that brought him full circle from his epiphany three years previous: "I'm an ugly, courageous son of a bitch."

Then, in a moment of celebration, he walked over to the sink and smashed the mirror with his fist. Later that week in Saigon, he got a hammerhead shark tattoo on the inside of his right forearm.

When he returned to Los Angeles several months later, he discovered his old notebook. Reading the epiphanies contained therein, he realized how much he had changed. For one thing, he was no longer the sort of person who tries to understand why life is as it is. At least he thought so. At least he wanted it to be so.

CAROLINE KEPNES

This Is a Jellyfish Eating a Barracuda

From January/February 2011

WHEN ALBIE'S MOTHER went on an okay date, the man would come home with her, at least for a little while. He would sit on the green velour couch with her, laughing at things she said, letting her tell her stories. She told Albie the hardest thing about being alone was not getting to tell her stories. "All women, we have so much to say, Albie, and when there is no one to say it to, you start to fade."

"Like the kid in *Back to the Future*?"

She sighed and put more sugar in her coffee, and he knew he'd said something wrong.

"Don't always make everything about a movie."

"Okay. I won't."

"It's the worst thing men do. Just listen to what I'm saying. Don't make it sound like everything I think, all my thoughts and feelings and things, that they're all like some movie somebody else made."

"I'm sorry."

He grew to think of her stories as another person who lived with them, like a wheezing grandma or a baby brother, someone who couldn't take care of himself. The stories needed to be told the way old people couldn't take baths on their own, the way babies needed to be fed. And it wasn't just about listening. The way a baby would die if you fed it fried chili peppers and whisky, a story would die if you didn't feed it the right questions. The right questions: *Did you work at Friendly's or Dairy Queen? Did you really just jump up on the stage and grab the mic from the singer? How old were you when that happened? Wow, have you ever thought about writing all this down? Why didn't you try out to be a Rockette a second time?* But since Albie knew the stories, he couldn't ask those questions.

Albie didn't have any stories of his own yet, but maybe that was because he was a boy. It seemed to him that only girls had stories. The men his mother dated never told stories. Maybe men listened because they wanted what they couldn't have, or maybe they just wanted to touch his mother.

If the date had been more than okay, good actually—if the man paid for dinner, wore a necktie, and didn't talk with his mouth full of mashed potatoes—Albie's mother would come home alone, thrilled. She would turn on her computer and blast music, *Whoa whoa you got the best of my love*, singing along so loudly he almost couldn't hear the real music. Albie would get out of bed and go into the living room. She would always dance for him a minute, pretending she didn't see him standing there in his long pants and t-shirt. And then she'd gasp and put her hands to her mouth and say she had no idea he was up and that he was supposed to be in bed. He knew she was lying. He knew she always saw him come into the room. But she would pretend to get over her embarrassment and then try and get him to dance with her, which he would, and then she would squeal "Max!" or "Doug!" and spin him around.

(The ones with potential tended to be named Max and Doug. Or maybe those were just Albie's favorite names. He wasn't sure. Albie's favorite girls' name was Jessica because it was too pretty for words like the Allman Brothers song. He also liked Rose because once he danced with a girl named Rose. She said he didn't do things right, didn't put his arms in the right places, and then she walked away, but he still liked the name.)

On these occasions Albie's mother would say she might be married someday, and that she and Albie would have the second dance at the wedding, that they were practicing. He didn't understand the logic, that she didn't let the ones who might be good sit on the couch with her, only opened the door for the ones who were bad. But it would have been impossible to ask her a question like that when she was bouncing and singing at the top of her lungs, *Doesn't take much to make me happy and make me smile with glee.* What a nice way to think of your mom, easily made to smile and dance. Besides, good or bad, they all went away after a date or two, so maybe it didn't even matter.

If the date went badly, which they usually did—one named Paul paid for dinner and tapped the credit card on the table and looked at his mother sternly and said, "This is me being a gentleman. So I'll expect you to be a lady and reciprocate"—then she would enter the house slowly, slam the door shut, and Neil Young would soon be in there with her, whimpering from the computer that housed all the singers and all the songs. She would cry as Neil whinnied about how he never saw a woman look finer and how he used to order just to watch her walk across the room. The sound of his mother's heartache was wild and scary, and it made sense that a noise like that needed to be sheltered in harmonicas and bass.

Music gave Albie hints about his own future. He was a kid, no car, no bike (not anymore, anyway) and his morning was a direct result of his mother's evening, of whether she'd been kissed or not, of whether she'd been jumping up and down with Rihanna *ella ella ella* or weeping alongside Damien Rice, on and on about the colder water, the blower's daughter, the pupil in denial, over and over, a reverse lullaby. Albie listened to all the songs, though. He had to. Without them he wouldn't know what the next day would bring. He planned on learning to play an instrument, but every day had a way of not seeming like the day he would learn to make music for his mother, the day he would become special, able to contribute something new to their family.

It was raining the night of her first date with Max Wenner. This had been a very important night for her. She said Max Wenner was a friend of her sister's, "One of the good ones: employed, decent, normal for once. Pearl even says he's cute." She'd taken a lot longer getting ready, changing her outfits, doing what girls do. But when she got home that night, it was still raining. The rain hadn't stopped for his mother and Max Wenner, and now she was alone for a long time in the quiet, and this was very unusual. There was no music. He was just about to walk out there when Ryan Adams joined her all sprung and country about *Oh the days the rain will fall your way*, and within seconds he could hear her crying. It wasn't like she hadn't cried before. But usually when she cried, it was with the old hippy saps like Eric Clapton or Joni Mitchell. She'd never cried with Ryan Adams. Ryan Adams was supposed to be for dancing.

Like when she started going out with Horrible Don. The first night he was there, Ryan Adams was there, too. Albie had not walked out to join the dance party, knowing he wasn't wanted. The song had ended quickly, and then, being the dumb adults they were, they made a giggling festival out of the trip to her bedroom, as if now they had to worry about waking him, as if *When you're young you get sad* at high decibel hadn't startled him out of bed.

(Don was the worst boyfriend, ever. He drank full-fat milk and ate all the bacon and told Albie that trying to learn guitar was a waste of time and that Albie would be better off focusing on science. Don was gone after three weeks, but they were very long weeks.)

When Ryan Adams finally shut up, there was a brief silence, and then some '80s guy was mewing *She's just 16 years old, leave her alone, they said.* The song was very melodramatic, and his mother was crying very hard. She always said people who laugh at songs like this one, songs that are all crashing drama, those people have no heart, and you have to watch out for them.

Albie worried Max Wenner had done something bad. Maybe he had told her she was ugly. Maybe he had squeezed her titties too hard. He felt gross for trying to figure out what had happened and wanted to think about something else, but her crying was animal-like and *Separated by fools who don't know what love is yet* was getting louder by the second.

One thing was in his head that would not go away: the way she'd spun around before leaving earlier. He went to his door and sat against it. There was probably something very wrong with him, and he shamed to think of it, but the loud beats coming into the room made his body tighten, and soon his pants were off and he was stroking himself the way some kids said he would one day. When it was done, he could hear her crying again. It was as if he'd gone deaf and gotten his hearing back, only now his ears were buzzing, and he wondered if he might ever hear anything clearly again. The music was off, and she must have gone to bed, and he hoped she hadn't heard him doing what he'd been doing, but he had no way of knowing if she had as he couldn't recall if he'd made any noise.

In the morning there were scrambled eggs and microwave bacon, and she was at the table all dressed and smiling. He couldn't think of anything to say. This wasn't a day after crying over Max Wenner (or any Max) kind of breakfast. This was a spread. He looked at the fridge where a picture he drew once when he was a dumb kid was still stuck there, taped on with masking tape. At the bottom, his teacher had written what he had told her to write: "This is a jellyfish eating a barracuda." His mother didn't save much, but she said that particular drawing had touched her because it was dreamy.

He had asked what she meant, and she had said a jellyfish couldn't eat a barracuda. "Well, jellyfish don't eat. They just sting," she'd told him, in a tone that instructed him not to ask any more questions—even though it didn't make sense, that something could stay alive and move through the water without any food at all.

"You're not hungry?" She felt his forehead the way she always did when he did something wrong. He thought of what he'd done to his body and worried he might have a fever. But she took her hand away. "Eat up. None of it's any good once it's cold."

He started to eat, and she put her bare feet up on the table and stretched her arms high over her head. "You know," she said. "That's why breakfast is for lovers. Lunch is just the middle of the day. Dinner you can heat up the next day. But breakfast is only good right in the moment. Remember that someday when you're dating girls. Best thing you can ever do if you really like a girl is take her to breakfast. She'll know she's special. It's the love time of the date. Night is for people you know really well who already know you love them."

Albie promised he would remember. He wanted to ask why all her dates were at night, but he knew better. That would be a cruel question. His mother was not a loved woman, and it wouldn't be nice of her son to say so. "You're quiet today," he said instead.

"I'm just tired."

"Couldn't sleep, babe?"

She scooped eggs onto her plate, set the spatula on the platter, and reached for the bacon with her hands. She was always taking things she didn't want and hoarding them and then picking up what she really wanted. Why didn't she just grab the bacon if she wanted the bacon?

"I slept."

"If you say so, kiddo."

She kissed him on the forehead, the signal it was time for him to stop eating and go out and get the bus. He complied, got his backpack and his lunch money, and walked out the front door. When he turned back, she was standing there waving, and he waved and walked to the bus, wondering if she would eat all the eggs now that he was gone, wondering why he wondered about such stupid things, like the jellyfish and the barracuda.

The next night he made macaroni and cheese and stroked himself three times. After all, his hearing had returned to normal, so there was reason to celebrate. Really, it was the greatest thing he'd ever done. He thought of his bicycle that got stolen, but it didn't compare. He thought of Doug #2 taking him to the dog track where greyhounds ran wild and controlled in synchronized circles, but that didn't compare, either. Thankfully, he was all done when his mother got home. She wasn't alone this time, and the Beatles were there. Max Wenner, too, and there was more crying, and Paul McCartney was promising *The wild and windy night that the rain washed away has left a pool of tears crying for today*. It was pretty scary stuff. Max saying words he couldn't make out, Max being there while she cried underneath Paul's wailing, Paul a guy she only sat with when she was alone.

Somehow, he forced himself to sleep. It was easier to nod off after stroking, so there was that. In the morning, he was surprised to find his mother was again dressed and smiling, with just as many eggs as yesterday, and bacon, too. There was no Max in sight.

"Well, you look like you got some *z*'s, yeah?"

"Yeah," he said, hoping she was not onto his new hobby. "Are you okay?"

"What kind of a question is that? Of course I'm okay, honey."

He was torn. He was being lied to, made a fool of. Of course she wasn't okay. Was he deaf or something? No, he was not. Yes, he had heard her crying, and he had heard Max saying things. But at the same time, there was nothing more beautiful than his mother in a cheery mood in the morning, again forking eggs onto her plate, again picking at bacon. He wished he were younger, maybe five, because if so he'd be able to feel only what he was feeling based on his current surroundings. It was hell knowing when the pieces didn't go together. It was hell wondering why a person would lie to you.

When he got home after school, she wasn't there. His Aunt Pearl was in the living room, smoking a cigarette. Her legs were two snakes wrapped around each other, tightly knotted at the ankles. She was very skinny and very made up around her eyes. His mom said the lines around her eyes had been tattooed on, but that couldn't be possible. She had very small tits, and her arms were always crossed, and she made him nervous because she was his aunt and there he always was, thinking about her small tits.

"Albie, you're home."

"Where's Mom?"

She put the cigarette out and patted the sofa. He knew what she wanted, but it felt good to not give it to her. He remained standing at the front door, so he could flee if he want to.

"Fine," she said. "Stand."

She hung her head and rubbed her hands in her hair. The house was very quiet without music, and he wanted nothing more than for his mom to walk in and kill the suffocating silence with something, anything, even one of the whiny dirges would do right now because it would mean she was here.

"Albie, do you know what mental illness is?"

"What do you mean?"

"Do you know what it is?"

"Yes." He thought of the guy at the donut shop nearby who was always there, always clapping over a chocolate frosted donut, never eating it, just looking at it and clapping.

"No, wait. That's not what I meant. She's not mentally ill."

Good. He didn't want his mother clapping over donuts. His bag was heavy on his back, but he would not put it down.

"Sometimes ladies need a rest."

"Uh, huh."

"Your mom is gonna rest for a while."

"Is she in bed?"

"No, Albie."

"Where is she?"

She looked at him in a way she hadn't ever before, like she was a teacher and he was, too, and they were talking about a student. He felt old and took off his backpack because suddenly it really was too much.

"What?" he said.

"Let's get your things together."

His aunt Pearl's house was nothing short of a nightmare. His cousin Angela was in high school and always talking, and his aunt Pearl was always listening and always talking back. His uncle Richard sat in a chair and watched horses run around in circles, an activity Albie couldn't imagine doing. Why would you want to watch them on TV when they were mere miles away, in the flesh? There was never any music, and nobody said much to him all week, and he didn't ask many questions. He didn't know if he lived there now, and the worst part was that he couldn't stroke himself, not there, and worse than the worst part was he actually considered the inability to do that worse than the fact his mother was "resting" somewhere. His head swam, and he slept very little and ate a lot.

Eight treacherous days passed until his aunt told him to pack up his things. Instantly, he felt sad, as if he had done something wrong. He kind of liked the way Pearl and Angela were always talking. It was a sound different than music. The stories being told, long as they were, sometimes actually went somewhere. Now he would never know if Angela would go to the homecoming dance with Bryan or Nick. Now he would never know if Aunt Pearl was going to get beige lipstick or stay with red. He didn't know what channel the dogs ran on, and he knew he wouldn't find them. He and his mom didn't have a TV. His mom said TVs were poison.

In the car Pearl turned the music on, and Bruce Springsteen joined them, again not knowing *what a woman like you is doing with me.* Some of Bruce's ones always hit Albie hard, especially this one, one of his mom's main ones, and he hadn't stroked himself in days, and he didn't know if he was getting dropped off at a bus station or his house, and *You better think hard or think twice*, and he started to cry. Aunt Pearl put on her blinker and pulled into a parking lot. His mom never used the blinker, and the gesture stung, like the other drivers mattered—mattered more than his damn tears. Then she silenced Bruce and turned off the car and looked at him like at any moment he might start clapping over a chocolate frosted donut. His mother was right. Pearl could be a real bitch when she wanted to.

"I'm fine. I just got sad for a second."

"You can talk to me. I know you can't talk to her, but you can talk to me."

"We talk just fine."

"Why are you crying, Albie?"

"I was, but I'm not now. Can we go?"

She sighed. She looked like she wanted to cross her legs up all tight but couldn't. It was an awful thing, knowing an adult would much rather be somewhere else, with someone else.

"Albie, she can't help the way she is. The doctors can't help her."

"The doctors?"

"The resting doctors. I don't know. They don't know. They've never known."

Aunt Pearl itched her nose and shook her head, and it was funny, the way she said so many words to Angela all week long. When it was the two of them talking, there was never a break in voices. They talked over and under each other, and they talked in the morning when most people didn't have much to say because the day was starting, and they talked in the evening when most people didn't have much to say because the day was ending, and most days didn't involve all that much activity. But here now, there really was something to talk about, something that didn't involve diet foods or boys or dresses, and his aunt had no interest in talking about it. His love for his mother rose in his chest and threatened to come out in the form of a punch. He breathed, "Where is my mom now?"

"She's home now. I'm taking you home."

"Well, can we go?"

"Well, can you talk a minute? All week you don't say anything and I, I have no idea how to talk to you, damn it. You're just..."

She shook her head and started to cry, but then she stopped, and he noticed that none of the black stuff around her eyes had moved. His mother was right. It must have been tattooed there. She started the car and backed out and headed out to the road. Again, she used her blinker.

When they pulled into the driveway, his mother was standing on the front porch. She wasn't cheery like she'd been last week, but she did wave. He didn't even say goodbye to Aunt Pearl, sensing this was one of those lucky moments in life, where the rules don't apply and you don't have to be nice, where you can just run.

He flung himself at his mother as if he was a kid and waited until Pearl's car was gone to break away.

"Hey, you," she said as she scruffed his hair.

"Hey."

The house smelled different, or maybe his senses were off because of the week at Aunt Pearl's. Her computer with all the music was in its usual spot on the table.

"So!"

"So," he said.

"I'm sorry I had to go away. It was a business trip."

"Was it fun?"

"It was a lot of work, but it was okay. How was school? How did that math test turn out?"

Albie nodded, unable to look at her, feeling like it wouldn't be of any use to look at her until many years had passed and he knew how to ask questions. "Can I put music on?"

She nodded and started biting her nails, and he was trying to picture her in a suit with a briefcase, resting alongside all the other business people, and he wanted the music now, loud. "What do you want to hear?"

"Oh, anything," she said.

He wanted her to talk to him so badly, to tell him where she had been and why. And this was the way she talked to him, through all her songs inside the computer. She only needed to pick one. She could do that for him. She had to. *Business trip.*

"Mom, what?"

"I really don't care, Albie. Whatever you want."

"You always care."

"Oh, honey, I just let the music do what it wants. You know, what's it called? Shuffle."

He didn't know what his face looked like then, but it must not have looked good because she pulled her robe tighter and kept talking, as if there was someone else seated across from her. "Yes, see, we didn't have that when I was your age, you know. You had to go and get the record out of the sleeve and put it on the recorder, or wait, tapes. Yeah, I mean I guess I didn't do much with records but tapes, CDs. You had to *pick* them. It's magic, the way the future is. The songs pick you, and I think that's just magic."

"You don't pick them?"

She just raised her eyebrows and kept talking. "You know if someone told me when I was your age that there would be a magic box that chose the music for you, that just knew what was inside of you even if you didn't know, oh, man, I would never. I would have lost every last penny on that bet, oh, yes, I would."

She reached over and hit the mute button, and Led Zeppelin was there instantly, a minute into it, telling about the *Many times been bitten, many times I've gazed along the open road.* And now his mother was up and grooving and reaching for his hands. The music told her she felt like jumping.

"Albie come on! This is one of the best!"

She was pumping the volume as high as it would go, grabbing at his arms, beckoning, sweating already. He felt dense all over, thick like Aunt Pearl's shrubs in the front yard. His mother was crazy. Nobody said so, but if the random songs coming out of the computer made your moods, well, the guy clapping over the donut, at least he'd asked for that donut, at least he'd walked down to the store, sat down at the counter and asked the old man behind the counter to give him one with chocolate on top. He couldn't look at her for a minute, couldn't even feel her hands grabbing at his.

"Albie, come on."

He danced. And when Led Zeppelin finished, Van Morrison started in about *When all the dark clouds roll away and the sun begins to shine.* She sat down at the table and started to cry very hard. She didn't seem all that rested for someone who had been resting for a week. Max and Doug had left for a reason. He wrapped his arms around her. He moved forward to press the button that would make another song come on, but she grabbed his arm, hard.

"No," she said. "It doesn't work like that. Life throws you lemons, Albie."

There were ways to save her. He could throw the computer out the window, but no. She would get another. He could delete all the sad songs in the middle of the night, but no, she would notice if they were all gone at once. She wouldn't *Jump for my love* and *celebrate* and *ella ella ella* without getting very tired or suspicious. God, if he took away all the slow ones in one fell swoop, she might even have a heart attack or ground him. She wasn't stupid, and she knew more about music than anyone he knew. But what he could do was take one song away every day. He would start with this whiny bitch Morrison dragging his nice mom down, going on about a *brand new day* but not acting like it was one. Albie would eliminate that one first, tonight, right after he had his alone time. He would wait to do it until she was asleep in her room.

He set his alarm, but when it sounded, he must have been overtired because he just rolled over and shut it off and fell back to sleep. In the morning she was already awake and doing things in the kitchen. He had failed. He felt dense again, as if his body was a bad place to be, bad almost as his home. He lugged himself out of bed. He was the man of the house. He had to be. He ate eggs and bacon and focused on the night ahead. He would eliminate two sad songs to make up for his failure the night before. He ate his bacon and looked at the jellyfish eating the barracuda, the proportions all wrong, as stupid as a mouse grabbing his mother's titties or a Max moving his things in and paying half the rent.

When he got home from school that day, he tore the picture of the jellyfish and the barracuda off the refrigerator and ripped it into pieces and threw it in the dumpster outside. His mother never asked where it went. She might not have noticed, but she *had* to have noticed. The refrigerator was barren now. Every time she opened her mouth in that kitchen, he expected her to ask what happened to it, but she always said something else, something about needing to buy bacon or paper towels, or something about a man she was talking to in the grocery store. He wondered when she would ask him about it. Maybe it would be years from now, when she was old and unable to give herself a bath. He could picture himself a man, grown up, maybe even a wife in the kitchen, and he'd be lifting her saggy, naked body into a warm tub, and she'd cling to the hairs on the back of his neck and ask why he'd thrown away the jellyfish and the barracuda all those years ago.

THOMAS KEARNES

Fast, Cheap, and Out of Control

From January/February 2013

WHEN CORBIN RETURNED to Austin, navigating the dark acres between shame and freedom, he promised himself he wouldn't go back to rehab. Before his aborted stint, he often saw a sweaty black troll named Jermaine. The big man worked at the bathhouse and possessed an endless supply of crystal meth.

The building crept into Corbin's view like the moon, large and full, ascending from the skyline. He pulled into the parking lot, surprised to discover so many cars. It was a weekday, not long before midnight. He missed the erotic charge of the hunt, missed the men, missed the oblivion. He was forty-two. Two weeks ago, Lex forgot his birthday. No calls, no text. As Corbin crossed the lot, gazing at the few stars, he called Lex—sweet, sensible Lex. Lex didn't answer, and Corbin felt the flutter in his stomach that overwhelmed him each time he heard Lex's voice asking callers to leave a message despite the fact Lex rarely checked it.

There was always Alvy. Corbin didn't think of him until he pushed open the glass door, nearly colliding with a short, thin man. The moment Corbin sent a text or returned his call, Alvy would emerge from the night-drenched city. This fact comforted Corbin. He'd compromised himself. The man he truly wanted, truly loved, would never travel the 200 miles south to rescue him, making Corbin question whether he deserved redemption.

Wearing only a white towel around his waist, Corbin examined himself in the mirror, content with his face and body. He towered over most men, his eyes shimmered, his torso was long and lean, taut as a trampoline spring. He enjoyed the unending desires of men. The slender man he had encountered at the entrance slipped out from a stall and joined Corbin at the mirror. He beckoned Corbin closer as if to share a secret. Instead, he told Corbin his room number and stroked his chest. The man left, and Corbin hesitated to follow; the man was too bold, too brazen, too much like Alvy. Corbin tried to calm himself with a trick from rehab. He mouthed "I love you" into the mirror. He kept doing this until a voice on the loudspeaker advised the man in room 210 to check out or renew. Corbin left the bathroom.

Most days Alvy left Corbin a message on voicemail or sent a text. He'd followed Corbin to Austin, but Lex had not. Despite Corbin's numerous hints and outright pleas, Lex refused to budge—he returned to Dallas after graduating the rehab. Alvy offered convenience, devotion, and wit. Corbin had no qualms about stringing him along until more acceptable offers cleared the horizon.

Jermaine clucked in surprise when Corbin stepped into his lair of pungent odors, dark corners, and whispered negotiations. He teased Corbin about his long absence. Ducking his head to avoid the doorframe, Corbin muttered some nonsense about an ailing mother. In truth, his mother died five years ago in a room with white lace curtains and bed able to fit three. This shit will knock you on your white ass, Jermaine said. Corbin forced a laugh and knotted his hands behind his back, unsure what to do. Jermaine shook a clear, tiny bag of crystals high above his head as if Corbin were about to swing at a piñata. With his other hand, he undid his fly and beamed at Corbin with a certainty that made Corbin sick yet grateful. Corbin fell to his knees, but it wasn't enough. He has too tall, so he leaned forward, Jermaine's pimply, swollen cock awaiting his lips.

Barry was not the first man Corbin brought to his rented room. He was not the second, nor the third. As Corbin led him to room 325, he schemed for a way to check his voicemail without offending Barry. Three hours had passed. Corbin doubted Lex was awake. Barry stumbled behind Corbin, his flat feet smacking against the concrete floor. While plotting a way to detect whether Lex thought of him tonight, Corbin recalled the first voicemail he left after Corbin's sudden exit: Call whenever you can. I don't care whether you're high or sober. Alvy and I miss you.

Alvy and I—Corbin's only regret about leaving. The thought of Alvy and Lex alone together terrified him. Corbin stopped abruptly at the door of 325, and Barry crashed into him. Barry laughed and dropped his head upon Corbin's shoulder. He looks a bit like Lex, Corbin thought. Thinner, younger. He kissed Barry, but Barry backed away, eyes wild and dimming.

Corbin trotted across the parking lot, clothes foreign against his damp skin. Lex hadn't called. The crystal meth, however, provided Corbin a safe harbor, his doubts and suspicions whimpering in a far corner of his psyche. Once behind the wheel of his dented, vintage Camaro, Corbin struggled to recall the men he'd taken to his room: Eddie, Bruce, Steve, Barry—nothing. He remembered the flecks of the amber in the fifth man's green eyes, the downward curve of his cock. He tried but failed to forget the fact each man left room 325 disappointed.

Alvy had left a message, sometime between Eddie and Bruce. It was half past three in the morning. Corbin pictured Alvy waiting by his phone, thoughts bopping like bumper cars. Once Alvy arrived in Austin, he and Corbin relapsed together, Alvy commenting on the perverse romanticism of the moment. You and me, Alvy said, high and naked like we fantasized. Corbin didn't respond except to take another hit.

Eve refused to sell street drugs, offering only medications a doctor might prescribe: uppers, downers, painkillers. She welcomed her customers with arms wide across the doorway, hand gripping the frame, an easy smile and high, scratchy voice. Hey there, lovely. What took you so long? Corbin shed his wool pea coat as he stepped inside. The stagnant heat in Eve's apartment seeped underneath his skin. He collapsed onto the sofa, offered her a tight smile. He wanted to be done, to drive home. Alvy belonged to him, he knew this. Eve returned Corbin's smile. You're goddamn high, handsome. She winked, her eyeliner caked and thick. I know what you need. She swished out of the room, allowing Corbin to collect himself.

During their rehab days, Corbin enjoyed torturing Alvy with stories of his trysts with Lex. Alvy never questioned the veracity of Corbin's lurid tales. In truth, Corbin and Lex achieved an odd intimacy only once. It rained that day, and Corbin appreciated the company. Thunder still scared him.

Crossing the rehab courtyard, Lex's stroll resembled back tires on an unpaved road. His laughter belched forth like fumes from an exhaust pipe. He rubbed his belly when digesting new information or speculating about the future. When still, Lex blossomed—his translucent eyes, two days of stubble and lips so full and inviting, one hardly noticed the thin, white scar intersecting his upper lip, vanishing just below his nostril.

Corbin knew his sexual prowess was poor at best. No matter how intensely he focused, semen shot forth moments after the start of each encounter. He'd been desperate to please Lex on that afternoon months ago, to prove the risk Lex had taken by joining him wasn't foolish. Lex waited on the twin bed, unable to respond to Corbin's request: stay there, just watch. Through the fabric of his cargo shorts, Corbin rubbed his crotch. Soon after, his erection appeared. Lex watched, his face betraying his bewilderment. Corbin studied this excellent man, wondered how many hearts he'd broken with a quick laugh or easy flirtation. The nervous host's orgasm arrived and ended so suddenly, he didn't have time to alert Lex, who then asked Corbin what happened. After sliding down the wall until he hit the floor, Corbin bunched his knees underneath his chin. He asked Lex to join him in Austin. We could be neighbors, he said. We'll have a wonderful life.

Eve returned, face flushed. She held a pill bottle, Xanax rattling like metal balls on a roulette wheel. Corbin reached for his wallet, but Eve shook her head, dirty blond hair spilling onto her shoulders. Gesturing toward the bedroom, she bore her teeth. Corbin knew her tactics. After college, he survived a year-long marriage to a woman by routinely fucking her up the ass. Show me how your hair does that, he said. It's sexy.

Five minutes later, Corbin stood before the bathroom mirror. The bottle of Xanax fit snugly against his thigh in his pocket. Perhaps it would work now. "I love you," he said, breath shallow. I'm so lost without him, he thought. "I love you." Eve called out from the bedroom, said another customer was due. Gorgeous like you, she said.

Headlights filed past Corbin on the Interstate, bleary soldiers drifting toward unknown fates. Alvy answered on the third ring. He often answered sooner. Corbin didn't ask if it was too late to call. He knew Alvy would drive directly to his place and wait in the raw November wind. Hands moist and cramping around the steering wheel, Corbin worried he might not have enough dope for both of them. Fortunately, Alvy's rapid speech and dropped consonants indicated he'd started without Corbin.

When he moved to Austin, Alvy wasted no time contacting Corbin. Alvy crossed the welcome mat with his resentments and delusions, his frayed denim and soiled Converses. He greeted Corbin by leaping into his arms and wrapping his legs around Corbin's waist. Alvy was small and bony like a starved dog. Even as his number of conquests ticked higher, Alvy possessed no faith in his charisma. At rehab, Corbin often praised Alvy's charms, both physical and otherwise. Eventually, however, Alvy's epic neediness swallowed Corbin's benevolence. It was no coincidence this shift in their dynamic occurred mere days after Lex's arrival.

Alvy paced the lot where Corbin always parked. He didn't trust Corbin, and Corbin knew this. Alvy waved as if signaling for help, his smile eager as he hopped in place. After Corbin rolled down his window, he flashed Alvy the same smile that triggered all those men, all those women to concede defeat. Alvy leaned over and announced he was nowhere near high enough. Corbin chuckled and shushed him. We live in low-income housing, Alvy said. Everyone is fucking high.

Despite the late hour, Alvy wanted to dance. Corbin declined his invitation to join, but he searched his music collection until he found a Donna Summer CD, over one hour of remixes. He wore his boxers, having slipped into them the moment after he came inside Alvy. The dope shot through his veins, sweet and ruthless. Alvy spoke softly but his voice betrayed a hard edge: Move with me, handsome. His feet remained rooted in place, but his hips swayed like the needle of a metronome as he ran his hand through his dark hair. He asked about Lex. When Corbin pretended he hadn't heard, Alvy asked again. It's been over a month, Corbin said. Have you spoken to him? Nope, Alvy said. Not recently. He caught Corbin by surprise, gazing directly at him. I can't believe we shit on each other over a fat man who will die in five years, Alvy said with a laugh, one Corbin felt was forced. He wasn't that fat, Corbin said. He wasn't that thin, Alvy replied.

Alvy's stepfather had died two weeks ago. Had he told Corbin? Perhaps he hadn't been listening, or perhaps it had slipped Alvy's mind. Covering this variable, Corbin said no. Three husbands in a row, Alvy said. Can you imagine? Mom went insane from grief. Corbin cranked up the volume. A stomping bass, the trickle of a mandolin, the blast of a clarinet—Corbin lost himself in the music. He hardly remembered fucking Alvy a half-hour ago but shuddered to recall the silence that bloomed among the cries and moans of both. Corbin didn't love Alvy and never would, but he cherished whatever hours he wasn't alone in the apartment. The idea of spending his life enveloped by quiet chilled him. I wanna get higher, Alvy called, breaking Corbin's reverie. I'm not sure we have enough shit, Corbin replied. Liar, his guest said, laughing again.

Corbin passed through the kitchen, his leg grazing a cloth carrier stuffed with white plastic bags from Wal-Mart. In the bedroom, he spied his large mattress draped in the patchwork quilt his grandmother made. Like his mother, she'd died from cancer. Donna Summer's wail filled the apartment: Corbin almost missed the ringtone—a flaccid Maroon 5 number—from Alvy's phone. When he arrived, Alvy had laid both his cell phone and his wallet on the nightstand. The familiar gesture irked Corbin. Five months ago, he'd invited Lex to his room for the first and only time. Four weeks before that, Alvy had crossed his threshold. The tiny bag of dope lay innocently on the bureau. There was plenty; Corbin had misjudged his supply. The phone kept ringing.

Corbin answered Alvy's phone with a lukewarm greeting. The caller sounded younger than either Alvy or himself. He asked for Alvy, and Corbin offered to take a message. The line went dead. Corbin glanced over his shoulder only to discover himself in the mirror. Mouthing "I love you" would only delay what he needed to do.

He accessed Alvy's voicemail with little fuss, guessing Alvy's password on the first try. It was the same one Alvy used for his email account. After his sudden exit from rehab, Corbin sent Alvy's mother a series of vile messages, each loaded with profanity and condemnation. Alvy forgave him. I had no choice, he told Corbin after descending on his doorstep.

There were three messages. Alvy didn't vanish after their encounters, Corbin knew. He had dreams and ambitions. Corbin fondly recalled their impassioned discussions while lying in the courtyard at rehab—before matters grew complicated, before Lex arrived, before Corbin fled in a flurry of apologies and regrets.

The first message came from Alvy's mother, her accent thick and soothing like honey. He hadn't called in four days. Was he safe? Did he receive the money she sent? Corbin wished she were his mother. The mysterious caller from moments before left the second message. He cooed about how much he enjoyed last night. When might he see Alvy again? The Rainbow Room planned a special on dirty martinis that weekend. Corbin's mouth grew dry, his pulse quickened. He was always distressed to learn a lover conducted a life outside of him. And then Lex spoke.

Corbin's eyes widened. The sinister heat from his vent bore down upon him. The message had arrived at four that morning. Alvy, sorry to call so late. It happened, it finally happened. Sean wants me to move in. Finally, I'm out of this shitty boarding house. Be happy for me. Be careful with Corbin, little brother. I miss you. The beep roused Corbin, and he finally comprehended the allegedly happy news. An automated voice inquired whether he wished to save or delete the message; he chose the latter option.

Corbin again noticed the carrier full of white plastic bags, but the silence distressed him more. It had bloomed in an instant, as silence always does. From the living room, Alvy announced he was starting a new CD. I can't believe I know a guy who remembers Nine Inch Nails, he said. You brought the dope, right? A bass beat, rich and tense, preceded the chaotic notes of a synthesizer. Corbin removed a plastic bag from the carrier. In the next room, Alvy danced in his briefs, his movements grand and erratic. The open bag between his fists, Corbin entered the room. Alvy danced and danced, ignorant of his fate.

Corbin wrapped the bag over Alvy's head. It covered his head completely, its edge collected around his neck; Corbin began to squeeze. The Nine Inch Nails song mocked him: I wanna fuck you like an animal. Alvy's knees gave way. Only Corbin's grip kept him upright. The bag clung to Alvy's face like wet grass to shoes. Alvy gasped and choked, anything he might be trying to say forever lost. Instead, Corbin heard only the song: I wanna feel you from the inside. After Alvy stopped struggling, Corbin eased him to the floor. He retreated to the doorway and observed the small, fragile corpse. He knew Alvy once loved him, perhaps still did. He had lied, however, about Lex contacting him. The most dangerous man in the world is the one sleeping next to you.

Be happy for me!

After snorting the rest of the dope in the bathroom, he stumbled toward his full-length mirror. Several weeks ago, he'd bent Alvy over and fucked him while gazing at his own reflection. Alvy took the assault with enthusiasm but fretted when Corbin didn't climax with his usual speed. After two minutes, Alvy lifted his head. Corbin saw the same confusion on Lex's face during their strange sexual encounter. Only one thing would calm the velvet hysteria of the dope, he thought.

"I love you," he whispered into the mirror. I wanna fuck you like an animal. "I love you," he repeated. Be happy for me! He said it louder. "I love you." It didn't work. It would never work. Corbin left the bedroom. He left the apartment. He left the city. He drove to Dallas, faster and faster, the sun rising to his right.

TIM KEANE

Greta Garbo's Hair Was Made in *Egypt*

From October/November 2004

ROBERT WATCHES Mr. Clancy, who's like an animal, walking on his knees in the kitchen.

Robert likes to watch. Life is a zoo with animals free. Mr. Clancy's arms are hairy and pink-red, and blue veins show in the bald patches of his skin. Veins like blue rivers.

Veins are rivers. And blood is red water.

Rolling up his sleeves, Mr. Clancy kneels, searching the bottom cabinets, his white hair messed like a hurricane made it that way. With his body half inside the cabinet, he shouts words Robert can barely hear.

"Where's your Dad hide the Jamesons?"

"Only Ma knows," Robert says.

Mr. Clancy slides backward out from under the cabinet like a turtle going back under a second shell. "Well, 'Only Ma knows' doesn't help me much, little demon."

Robert asks Mr. Clancy if there could ever be a drink-potion that would give supernatural powers, like grace gives supernatural powers. "And what powers would you try to get, if you could, Mr. Clancy?"

"Patience," Mr. Clancy says. "I'm out on that." Lifting a green bottle out of the top cabinet, he sings in a hillbilly voice, "Praise the Lord, I say, praise the good Lord Jesus."

Pouring a drink, Mr. Clancy tells how driving down there through Tennessee when he was working for the mines, that the Dixies had white crosses stuck in their hills. "Crosses, big as estates. Enormous, ominous-like crosses, just planted down there in a field in the middle of nowhere." He pours another half a glass, sniffing it before gulping it down, then pats his hair, as if patting your hair is proper manners after you drink a glass that quickly.

Robert shows Mr. Clancy the drawing of the green boat with Pepi sleeping off the side. "That's me. That's my bed. And that's my cat."

"How's this vessel a bed?" Mr. Clancy asks, pouring another drink. "A bed in the water is it? How's a man manage such a trick?"

"My bed is a bed and a boat," Robert says. "That's how I have a dream. Beds turn into boats after you fall asleep. You don't know that?"

"No, I don't know. A bed is one thing; a boat is another."

"I make different rules about that," Robert says. "Things are both."

Mr. Clancy nods and smiles. "I take you on your word 'cause I like your Ma a lot, and plus I think you've some clever quirks, really. Odd, but you're an honest kid. Am I wrong? Honest?"

Robert hardly knows what all that asking about honest means, so he asks Mr. Clancy, "You know my father's gone, for good, right?"

Mr. Clancy frowns, licking red-orange drops off the edge of his glass. "Don't talk. Draw. Draw some men where this bed-boat vessel of yours goes." Mr. Clancy turns the radio knob on, and voices and songs crack and fizzle until a serious voice comes in, clear, as if the man in the radio might be talking from the wall over Mr Clancy's head, a slow voice in the radio talking about a rocket test. Not a spelling test or a math test. A rocket test, in the desert. A rocket launched with white mice. Who gets to take that kind of wild test? Experiments in gravity, the radio says. "Effects of gravity."

"My father's gone for good," Robert says over the voice from the radio. "You know that, Mr. Clancy?"

"Gone. Is that the case? And gone where to?"

"My mother told him to go to his hussies."

"She said that, did she?"

"She told him Brooklyn hussies."

"Oh Jesus, Robert, don't be literal. She didn't mean for him to truly go there."

"That's not where he is, anyway."

"Well, why don't you enlighten an old man and tell me where your dear father is gone to, then?"

"I'll draw the place for you."

Robert uses the yellow pencil, sketching a line fast, tracing out a thick triangle with a shaded line at the side. He draws a black door in the corner of the pyramid and rounds out a depiction of the Bast God with the cat head. Bast, guarding the pyramid door, with black human arms with big, flowing muscles—black, wavy—and then the long, strong legs and feet so flat on the ground you could never knock Bast down, never, no matter how hard you shoved. Using the yellow pencil, he colors in the pyramid till it's brighter than a flower.

"He's in this, a pyramid jail," Robert says. "I put him there. He's punished for life."

"Your father's in this triangle here, is he?"

"Yes. But my mother doesn't know. Keep it our secret. She thinks he's with Brooklyn hussies. What's hussies?"

"A hussy's a woman. A woman who knows what she wants," Mr. Clancy says, shaking his glass, the water in his glass swirling gold and red. "A woman who knows what she wants and takes it, as opposed to a tight woman, like my old lady. Sealed tight as Fort Knox. So what did they, or was it you, or whoever, the powers that be, your cat-man there, what did this whoever put your Dad in the slammer for?"

"I put him there."

"What did you put him there for?"

"For being who he is," Robert says. "Because I wish he wasn't alive, really. You don't need fathers. Just like you don't need schools and rules. So, he's trapped in this pyramid jail for life."

Mr. Clancy leans back in his chair, his hands behind his head, his elbows sticking out, pointy, like wings for his head. "You don't mean that. But I know the sentiment. My old man was... Well, let's leave it at that. I'm happy my old man was and now isn't. It was no bee-glad glade, I tell you that. I took blows from an old school Navy-man, my pops. But you'll take them, too. This is the lot we've as sons. So you dream up and draw a few fancies like this pyramid jail thing of yours to get yourself through the rough road, but you know, you grow up, you grow out of that sort of madness about no fathers and all that. You take the good and the bad; this is the hard truth of life." He runs his finger along the edge of the glass and then plays with the bottle cap, moving it around his glass like he's thinking about something that happened so long ago, he has to make circles here on the table to get the memories back.

"I don't take the bad," Robert says. "That's my own private rule. If you could draw as good as I can, you could make rules, too."

"Well the rule is, it's time you be gone to bed. Your mother gave me the strict marching order, nine o'clock sharp now. Look at the hour." Mr. Clancy shifts to get up, pushing the bottle cap away, and Robert takes the drawing back and tells him don't worry, he can tuck himself into bed alone.

"Sure?"

"Sure, yes, Mr. Clancy."

"Well, it's no engineering marvel, tucking in. Knock yourself out then. Not literally, though."

Robert closes the door, slipping into bed without saying prayers, taking his shirt off to feel the cold of the sheets. He can see Dad chained to a wall inside that pyramid jail.

But he'd rather think of something that glows, or tickles, soft, like a girl. Something white.

Like the spinning girl's white legs in the store. Her white tights. He can see himself help the girl sneak to the emergency door in the back of the store, an escape—every single building except pyramids has an escape door, even a clothing store. It's a rule—for fires, for quick escape—which is where he and the spinning girl can sneak out, through that door and go two doors down into Woolworth's, go in by the back door, sneaking up to the birdcages and that fat salesman in the pet section with the toothpick, the man who looks like a boar. The man can lift the girl up so she can see the parrot, and the girl will laugh because the man's so ugly, but he's tall enough for her to reach the cage, where she lets the gray African parrot named King Kong out. And King Kong, with those long, white-gray wings, flies out, flying toward the front of the store, and perches on top of a display case as if it's a tree, and the bird waits till the morning when the men with guns bring the money into the store, opening the glass door too fast so that like a crazy surprise, King Kong escapes, flying right out of Woolworth over the heads of the men with the money bags, gliding into that park, the one with the huge overweight bees, where he can bring the girl, where he sat with Ma eating ice cream cones today. And not making a mess except for the river of chocolate ice cream that ran down Ma's fingers, and she licked the ice cream off her own hand and giggled as if they were in school together. Playing hooky, is what Ma said. Above their heads was the mimosa tree. And when that tree gets too boring for the King Kong parrot, he'll fly over to the school that looks like a church, where older kids go, the genius college, and he can even fly farther than that. There's just no rules for birds. They're ready every second to fly from here to anywhere, and you couldn't follow if you tried.

When he wakes up, he hears whistling and quick laughing. Peeking out in the hard light, he sees Mr. Clancy dancing with an invisible lady. Mr. Clancy kisses the air as his arms sway to the music from the radio, horns and drums turned loose in the air, a slow lady singing through the horns, deep, and Mr. Clancy mumbles to the lady he's dancing with and lets her fall far in his arms, bending forward and holding her, almost touching the kitchen floor as he kisses her face and brings her up again, laughs at himself, or her, again, whistling. "Whatever you desire, my dear. I can turn water into champagne for you." The green bottle on the table is half empty, and it reminds Robert of the story about the bottle neck that got dropped from a balloon and ended up as only a piece of itself, a water jar in the bird cage. On the kitchen table there are torn bits of gold paper and an ashtray and a loaf of bread with a big knife sticking out one end like a tail. The horns and drums from the radio are loud.

He asks Mr. Clancy, could he lower the radio?

Mr. Clancy stares back at him like he forgot he wasn't alone. "Sure, go on back," he says. "My mistake. Got caught up in the party here."

Robert thanks him and hurries back into bed as the music in the kitchen goes quiet. He wonders will Mr. Clancy still dance with the lady even with the music low?

Mr. Clancy knocks on the door and creeps in, a shadow almost, tiptoeing, his boots squeaking. "I am awful sorry about the radio waking you, Robert." As he talks, he smells like medicine, like Dad, but he's shorter and his voice is calm. "Sorry I woke you, really. But keep it between you and I, hey? Or your mother will tell my old lady, and you can predict how that will go. Our secret, then?"

Robert says, "Yes, secret," and they shake hands. The hand feels slippery and thick, like Ma's hands after cooking eggs.

Standing in the doorway with Pepi rubbing against his legs, Mr. Clancy looks like he might cry. His shoulders are low, like hunching, as if being in the dark makes him stoop. Bad posture.

He tells Mr. Clancy that lady in the kitchen, the one he was dancing with, was pretty.

"You liked her, too?" Mr Clancy asks. "What did you like most?"

"She fit in your arms, perfect."

"She did at that, didn't she? Greta Garbo that was. Great dancer. Legs made in heaven, eyes made in hell. And that blond hair of hers. God only knows where that was made."

"In Egypt," Robert says. "Where that yellow pyramid is that I drew. Yellow is their favorite color, for Egyptians. I saw it in the E Book." Robert climbs out of bed and pulls the E Book out from under the bed, and passing Mr. Clancy, he reaches up and turns the light switch on. Mr. Clancy squints hard and pretends to care as Robert flips the pages to show the Bast God, the other Egyptian gods, too, in green and yellow, and the black and white pictures of the pyramids.

Mr. Clancy nods. "Egypt it is. I'll make a note. Greta Garbo's hair was made in Egypt. Gold, I'd say it is they fancied, not yellow."

"So is Greta Garbo still out in the kitchen?" Robert asks. "Is she going to dance with you even though the radio music is on low?"

"She is, Robert. But you know she's flirting with every man in the room. What's a man to do?" Mr. Clancy laughs at himself and says he should go attend to her. "She's waiting for me to buy her another drink. So I must go. Can't leave a leading lady waiting. Sweet dreaming, Robert. And thanks."

Robert pulls the sheet up, setting the E Book on its side like a doll. He asks Mr. Clancy, "Thanks for what?"

"For seeing what I see," Mr. Clancy says, switching off the light. "Greta Garbo. Our little talk here made my night." Without closing the door, he leaves, swaying slightly, snapping his fingers, and Robert can hear him asking, does she want the next round on the rocks?

Greta Garbo. She must be sitting with her legs crossed, like Ma does when there's company, so comfortable that her shoe hangs off her foot. She must have a glass half-full just like Mr. Clancy's. His voice is strong over the light music from the radio. "Toast? Can you take it without ice? Great, let's have a kiss, then," Mr. Clancy says.

From the kitchen Robert hears a sloppy kissing noise. Peeking, he sees Mr. Clancy making fish lips to the air as he raises his glass. "Nice, that. Now raise your glass, love. That's it. Here's to one last glass, to the good life, to the straight-up way it is."

JOAN SHADDOX ISOM

Remade Tobacco

From July/August 2004

"SEE TO YOUR papa, Josie Blackbull."

My grandmother tells me that at least five times a day, especially when I'm doing my homework.

Question # 3: What is the number one cash crop in Oklahoma?

I wonder what my geography teacher would do if I wrote the truth. Everyone knows what the main crop is in Keetoowah County. The sheriff and his men cut and burn it every month or so.

I get up and go to my father's bedroom. He has a football game on TV, but he's not watching it. His striped flannel bathrobe he wears every day is open, and his belly bulges out over his blue jeans. He's barefoot and pacing the floor, smoking the last of his ration of cigarettes. Any minute now he could start badgering me to go to the store and get him another pack of Camels. My mother stopped that a long time ago, so I'll explain it to him one more time, and he'll get mad and throw things against the wall. His shoes, the pillows, his *Field and Stream* magazines he never reads. His wall is a dirty yellow with scratches and scars. Once, my father traced his finger on the wall and tried to show me what he called a secret map. When I told him I couldn't see any map, he said I was as stupid as the old lady.

My mother works at the Indian hospital. Its real name is C.C. Hendricks Medical Center, but nobody calls it that. She's a practical nurse, a fancy name for piss pot carrier, my father says. She says he ought to be glad someone's making the living. He hasn't worked since he came home from Desert Storm. My mother tries to get him to go for counseling or at least to a veterans' group in town, but he won't. Once a month he goes to a doctor where my mother works and gets some kind of pills.

He tells me about the war. Not hero stories, but how he was scared out of his gourd and hid in supply closets and smoked pot. At the pot point in the story, he always stops and lectures me about how I shouldn't do drugs. My father used to play football in high school. He was all-state one year, but he doesn't care about that anymore. He gave me his football with all the players' names on it.

But this evening, before my father starts throwing things, my mother comes home. I go into the kitchen to help her with supper. She's banging pans around. "Have to get back and work E.R. tonight. Full moon, a weekend, and a payday to boot. It'll all break loose about midnight," she says as she rummages around in the fridge and pulls out four pork chops. "Peel some potatoes, Josie." I start peeling while she clangs the iron skillet onto a burner and lights it with a match. Our pilot light went out a few months ago, and we can't get it started. That's why the kitchen smells like gas all the time.

My mother is still talking about her job. "That George Birdtail— you know, he played ball with Jackson in high school—got in another fight. His pals threw him in the back of their pickup and drove him to the hospital." She scoops a big blob of Crisco out of the can and drops it into the cast iron skillet. "They called for me to come out and see to him, but when I climbed up into the truck, I seen he was already dead. Someone beaned him with a bottle out at the Steal-In."

Grandmother leans on the doorframe, listening. "Don't tell Jackson," she whispers. I don't know why she bothers to warn us. My father can't hold a thought for ten seconds unless it's about cigarettes. He's bellowing for more now. I guess my mother's too tired to argue. She gets a pack of Camels out of her purse and throws it into the bedroom. She ties a denim apron over her white uniform and starts to dredge the pork chops in flour. The grease is getting hot, and the potatoes are bubbling on the back burner.

"Set the table, Josie."

I get out the plates and the knives and forks and put them around the kitchen table. Grandmother is at the back door scolding the cat. "He's lapped up the milk I set outside," she mutters.

"What does she expect?" I whisper.

"Shhhhh." My mother puts her finger over her lips. Grandmother puts out saucers of milk near the vents in the foundation. Sometimes she gets down and peers under the house, making a funny little whistling noise.

"Who is it comes into my room at night and tucks the blankets around me?" I ask my Grandmother. She wags a finger at me and shakes her head.

I pour myself a glass of milk. I know Grandmother is watching me, so I leave a little in the bottom of the bottle and hold it up and shake it. Grandmother grunts and smiles.

"Shhhhhh." My mother warns us again. Grandmother waves her wrinkled hand as if to say, "Mind your business," and turns away to stare out into the backyard. She always wants us to take her to the stomps and the pork fries. My mother glares at her when she mentions these things. "Josie's going to Tulsa after she finishes school. She'll get a good job, maybe be a secretary with a computer and a fine office," my mother says.

At supper, my mother and grandmother talk about the tough new manager out at the Cherokee Living Museum where the next-door neighbor kids work in the summer. Boise, the one in my grade, gets paid for wearing a breech-clap and playing stickball all day. His sister wore a deerskin costume and showed the tourists how to grind corn the old way—before she got fired.

"Was Boise's sister really talking on the phone in front of the tourists?" my grandmother asks.

"Yeah, her cell phone," my mother says. "Holding it with her chin while she ground corn with that wooden mallet thing."

"That girl's crazy. They didn't have none of them phones back then." My grandmother takes a hunk of bread and sops up some grease from her pork chop and plops it into her mouth.

My father doesn't seem to hear the supper talk. He's busy tearing strips off his bread and making little partitions between his food, not letting the potatoes touch the meat.

After midnight I go into his room. I know he won't be sleeping. There's no light on, and he's crouched by the window, looking out.

"Duck down! Duck down, Josie!" he whispers. I get down on the floor beside him. He's smoking a cigarette, and he holds it below the window, bending down to take a puff.

"Them Bastards behind the well. Think I can't see 'em. Look!" He points. "Look hard!" I study the dark. The wind is blowing the trees around, making the shadows move. I guess they look like the enemy to my father. Somewhere a dog howls, and the cottonwood leaves rattle.

"Go to bed, Jackson. There's nobody out there," I say. But he shakes his head and lights another cigarette.

"I have to pull guard. Someone has to. Your mama, she thinks I'm good for nothing. I seen Loney Lynch bring her home from work more than one time. And she took my .22 away..." His voice trails off. He's still peering at the dark outside the window.

I sit there and wonder what Mr. Aimens would say if he met my family. Last week he called me to his office. He's the school counselor when he's not teaching Oklahoma history. He wanted to know how I was getting along in math. I made a "D" last semester, but I'm beginning to figure out fractions. Mr. Amiens is from New Jersey, and he's always badgering me to tell him about what he calls "my cultural legacy." Once he asked me about Jack Hummingbird. Jack's my uncle, and he works medicine. People call him when they want favors. If you have a mean boss on your back, you can ask my uncle for help—like Mickey Thompson did. Jack went out to the river right at sunup and remade some tobacco. I didn't see him, but he does this by facing east and singing the remaking song over a handful of Bull Durham. Then he rolled cigarettes and gave one to Mickey, and Mickey smoked it in front of his boss, and the boss got real afraid of him and let him alone after that. I don't tell Mr. Aimens about these things, but everyone in town knows what Jack does.

Mr. Aimens doesn't give up easily. "Now these Little People, Josie, that some of your old ones claim to see, does your uncle know anything about them?" Marie Blackfox, the librarian, says Mr. Amiens wants all us Cherokees for his exotic artifact collection. During Territory Days, Mr. Amiens divided us into groups. Melissa Sillbury's was the white settlers and mine was the Native Americans. Mr. Amiens lumps all the tribes together and calls them that. We were supposed to present our side of whether the West should have been settled by the whites. No one would argue for their side, and Mr. Amiens got so mad I guess he forgot about being politically correct. He yelled at me, "Josie! You're an Indian! Why don't you present your side!" When I wouldn't talk, he said I was "reverting to type," which made all us kids laugh.

On Tuesday, my father is not at home when I get there. Grandmother says Sheriff Blount came for him. Some neighbors had complained he kept coming to their houses to mooch cigarettes, that they were afraid of him. "What will happen to him?" I ask.

"Mebbe send him to Vinita," Grandmother says. Vinita is where the State sends people they don't know what to do with.

"What will Mother say?" I ask.

Grandmother cocks her head to one side like a chicken. Then she snaps her fingers. "That one—she'll say 'good riddance!'"

I go into my father's room. His bed is unmade, his shoes on the floor. I wonder if they took him away barefooted. There's a crumpled pack of Camels lying on the bed. I take the pack to my room and hide it under my pillow. I stretch out on my bed and think about how my mother's always saying she can't sleep with my father prowling all night long. She shares a room with Grandmother, and they keep their door closed. I always leave my door open in case my father gets really scared. When that happens, he cries. Then I go in and give him another one of his pills. They make him rest a little easier. I wonder if anyone will give him his medicine at Vinita.

I throw my history book against the wall. It makes a good thud. I lock my door, pull the shades down, and get into bed, even though it's just six o'clock. The tobacco scent from under my pillow fills the room. I shut my eyes and watch for the pictures that sometimes show up underneath my eyelids. When I'm lucky, I can see faces, all different, changing one into the other. Only this time, there's just a flat, plum-colored darkness. I guess I fall asleep, but the sound of my mother's car wakes me up. I hear her come inside, and pretty soon the house is quiet again.

I take the pack of cigarettes and slip into my father's room. I leave the light off and sit on the floor by the window. I light a cigarette and smoke it while I stare out at the dark for a long time. The wind has stopped blowing, but the tree shadows are still moving. The longer I study them, the more they look like squat little shapes beginning to circle our house.

I crush out the cigarette, kick off my shoes, and get into my father's bed. It's so quiet. Not even the cottonwood leaves are stirring. As I pull the tobacco-scented sheet up under my chin, I think about the gentleness of the small hands that tuck the blankets around me sometimes at night.

I wish I'd thought to ask my father if they ever did the same for him.

THOMAS J. HUBSCHMAN

I Am So Loving the Cello

ARTHUR ARANOFF and his wife lived in 6E, over Israel Bernstein's family. We—my mother and father and myself and sometimes Mary Henderson our housekeeper when she slept over—lived in 5C. Mr. Aranoff was our building's resident celebrity. He played the cello, mostly for Mutual or one of the other house orchestras radio networks maintained in those days, but occasionally he sat in with the New York Philharmonic or the Metropolitan Opera when one of their regular cellists fell ill.

We had other professionals living in the building, a six-storey affair with an elevator and dumbwaiter just off Tremont Avenue in the Bronx. Mitchell Papov, a retired oral surgeon, lived in 1D, and Bernice Kauffman's father was a certified public accountant. But Arthur Aranoff was our star, a man who had played, however briefly, under the batons of both Bruno Walter and Arturo Toscanini. When he tipped his floppy dark fedora to one of the building's housewives, she flushed with pleasure. "Good morning, Mr. Aranoff," she replied with a little bow as if he were nobility. Sometimes he wore a cape instead of an overcoat like other men. My mother said the cape made it easier for him to carry his instrument to a performance, but my father, a jobber in the fur trade who had worked his way up from cutter's helper, insisted the cape was an affectation, just a means for Aranoff to call attention to himself.

Mr. Aranoff practiced five or six hours a day, including Saturdays and Sundays. We couldn't hear him, but Izzy Bernstein said the noise drove his parents crazy and that they were always banging on the ceiling with a broom handle. They complained to the landlord, and there was even a court case, but the judge ruled that since the cello was Mr. Aranoff's livelihood, he had a right to practice "during regular business hours." My father said that if Aranoff lived over our own apartment he would know how to fix Aranoff's wagon, and he wouldn't need any judge to help him, either. Sometimes he cursed Aranoff in Yiddish, to which my mother, the daughter of a prosperous Upper West Side factors man and herself an amateur pianist, would respond by asking if he wouldn't like another slice of honey cake.

One evening when my father was only halfway through his baked chicken, she told him Arthur Aranoff was going to play the Haydn cello concerto on the radio that Saturday. My father immediately lost his appetite.

"But David, you always love my baked chicken."

"Sorry," he said, looking confused by his loss of interest in his food. He considered his wife's cooking on a par with his mother's, though Grandma's was a very different kind of cuisine, heavy middle-European stuff that would constipate an elephant.

"Why should you begrudge the man his moment of triumph? It's only with a radio orchestra."

"Aranoff is a *shnorer*. Never done an honest day's work in his life."

My mother replied with what I had come to think of as her stage laugh, a sound that reminded me of the celeste in Tchaikovsky's

Nutcracker, which she took me to see at City Center every December. We also had a subscription to the Philharmonic's children's concerts.

"Art is his work, dear," she said, clearing away his plate and trotting out a flan she had whipped up that afternoon. I saw him hesitate as she put the glass dessert dish down and pour some béchemal sauce on top. It didn't take him long to choose between the flan and his principles. "Just as fur coats are your work," she continued. "You both create things of beauty. Your own creations we can see and feel. Arthur Aranoff's are less tangible, something experienced only in the heart."

I doubt my father even knew what "tangible" meant. And he had no illusions about what he did for a living: he sold animal skins to fat rich women. But my mother always talked like that whenever the subject was remotely connected with art. My father probably didn't even feel offended. He readily acknowledged his wife was better educated and more cultivated than he was. He was not ashamed but proud of it, like a man who owned a work by a great master. The work of art did not diminish its owner simply because he was not himself capable of creating such beauty. Quite the contrary.

But he still hated Arthur Aranoff, and one way or the other he was going to settle the man's hash.

All week the building was in a buzz about the concert. The broadcast was scheduled for 8:00 PM, so even Mrs. Gottlieb who kept a strictly kosher house would be able to tune in. In the evenings my mother behaved as if the event were to be no big deal and scarcely mentioned it. But during the day she spoke about little else with the other women in the building. The performer himself was said to be rehearsing constantly, eight, even ten hours a day. The Bernsteins were furious.

I, too, was excited, though my loyalties were divided between my mother's love for music, which I shared, and my father's injured pride. His brother Michael was an orthopedic surgeon, and his sister had married a bigtime lawyer. All his family's resources, including those that should have been put toward my father's own education, had gone toward seeing his brother through medical school. From a very early age, I was familiar with how everyone had chipped in to make sure Michael got his M.D., only to see the new doctor turn his back on his uncouth relations the minute he started dating an OB-GYN's daughter from Forest Hills. Aunt Miriam, as I knew her, had a twitch I learned to imitate. "How lovely to see you, my child!" I would mimic in her quasi-gentile accent and then blink my left eye hard as if something had just flown into it. My father would rock with delight. "That's good! That's good! Esther, come see Annie's imitation of that stuck-up *shmalts*-ball Michael married."

When Saturday finally rolled around, my mother could no longer hide her excitement. We were not friends with the Aranoffs—as a couple my parents hardly ever socialized—but I had been with my mother any number of times when Mr. Aranoff doffed his big hat and stopped to chat with her on the sidewalk. I could see there was some kind of mutual admiration going on there. Aranoff didn't speak as well as my mother. Few people did. But his way of expressing himself was a long way from father's harsh *Bronxsprech,* and neither Aranoff nor my mother ever used any Yiddish during these conversational impromptus. Sometimes as I listened to them exchange opinions about Casals or Heifitz, I would think, What if Mr. Aranoff were my father instead of the coarse man fate had assigned me?

When my mother returned to our apartment after one of these chance meetings, she seemed intoxicated, the same way she looked after she had had a Sunday afternoon "highball" or a second glass of Manischewitz during a seder. Sometimes she even sang—gay little tunes with French lyrics about shepherds and long summer nights.

Father worked most Saturdays, and this was to be no exception. In the afternoon mother baked a cake and listened to a live broadcast of *La Boheme* on the same station that was going to air Mr. Aranoff's performance that night. She sometimes asked father if he wouldn't like to go to an opera with her, and he always managed to put her off without outright refusing: his schedule was too unpredictable; you never knew when a buyer would have to be taken to dinner; his hemorrhoids. She wouldn't dream of going to an opera or even a movie without her husband accompanying her. No matter how much French she spoke or how progressive her political and moral ideas, the loyal Jewish wife was still very strong in her. All afternoon we sang along with the music coming out of the RCA portable she kept on top of the refrigerator, and when poor tubercular Mimi was breathing her last, I saw two tears trickle down my mother's pale cheeks in perfect unison.

By seven o'clock the dishes were done and my mother had changed into the dress she wore when she took me shopping on Fordham Road. She rearranged some figurines in the big hutch that dominated half a wall of our living room. Then she flipped through old issues of *The Ladies Home Journal*. Father was reading a copy of the *Post* and almost visibly digesting the veal cutlet she had made for supper.

"How about taking a walk up to Cushman's for cheesecake?" he said, abruptly closing the paper. They frequently strolled along the Grand Concourse on a Saturday evening, weather permitting, a habit left over from my father's Orthodox youth.

She reminded him the concert would be starting in half an hour. "*That* shmuck. For him I have to give up my evening?"

"He's our neighbor, David. It isn't every day someone you know gets to play on the radio. Besides, I made a cake this afternoon. Your favorite. Annie helped."

My father grunted and regarded me as if I were part of the conspiracy against him. But he allowed my mother to cut him a generous slice and sat down at the kitchen table while she fiddled with the knobs on the RCA. "Why can't we get a real radio," she said, voicing one of her rare complaints, "like other people?"

"You don't need a radio to hear Aranoff," he replied, his mouth full of devil's food. "All you have to do is step out in the hall."

We listened to a long newscast, then a commentary by Gabriel Heeter or someone very like him, accompanied by snide comments from my father who looked as if he would very much like to leave my mother to her arty nonsense but was afraid what might happen if he did.

Finally we heard the theme music for the concert. Then the announcer came on, a deep, self-confident voice speaking in a kind of Anglo-American accent no one I knew spoke. When he introduced the soloist for the Haydn concerto, he called him "our own virtuoso, Arthur Aranoff," at which point my father made a vulgar sound. Mother shushed him.

Impressed though I was by Arthur Aranoff's being chosen as soloist for a radio performance, I really had no idea how good—or not—he actually was. Nor had I ever heard the Haydn cello concerto before. But I figured if I listened closely I would be able to tell if he really was a "virtuoso." So that was what I did, sitting quietly beside my parents at the kitchen table, which still contained a few dark crumbs from my father's dessert.

But father was fidgeting like a schoolboy being kept after class. He would stand up as if he suddenly remembered he had something to do, then abruptly sit down again. During the slow movement he went into the living room and rustled the pages of the *Post* until my mother asked him to please stop. By the time the final movement was under way, he was back standing in the kitchen doorway. But his restlessness seemed to have disappeared. He even seemed to be enjoying the bouncy closing theme, patting the doorjamb in time with the music. My mother smiled up at him. He smiled back.

"Need anything from the corner?" he asked after the concert was over. "I thought I'd pick up a copy of the *News.*"

"You don't want to take a walk up the Concourse?"

"After I get back. Annie," he said, "care to come along?"

"Do I have to?"

I suspected right away he was up to something my mother would not approve of, and I wanted to find out what it was. But I had to at least make a pretense of not being a willing party to it.

He took my hand as soon as we were out of the apartment and held onto it as we waited for the elevator and then during the ride down to the building's lobby, where we ran into the Leibermans.

"You heard the concert?" Mrs. Leiberman said, all a-dither.

"I heard, Mrs. Leiberman. A virtuoso performance!" father said, though I knew he was only using that phrase because he had heard the radio announcer use it. But Mrs. Leiberman nodded her head in approval, and then, noticing me, said, "What a big girl!" and patted my shoulder with her bony fingers.

Walking down Tremont Avenue he whistled one of the themes from the Haydn concerto, or at least his own version of it, introducing klezmer-like trills and Pop Goes the Weasel endings at the end of every eighth bar. I giggled at his interpolations but was impressed by his musical invention, something I never would have thought him capable of. I returned the pressure of his hand, and we began to swing our arms up and down rhythmically. When he came to the end of the next eight bars, I anticipated the twist he would give to the phrase and joined in. The next time, he let me fill in the phrase by myself, and I gave it such a wild turn, we both laughed till we were out of breath.

When we reached the corner newsstand, instead of buying a newspaper, he raised his thick index finger and nodded toward the telephone booth nearby. It was clear he had mischief in mind, so I followed him in. He closed the door, forcing me to stand very close, something I hadn't done since I was a young child. In the cramped, airless quarters, I became aware for the first time of his masculine smell, an odor of old sweat and some sort of solvent. To my surprise, I found I liked it.

He dropped a coin in the box and carefully dialed a number. I heard the ringing in the receiver he held, as he did all telephones, half an inch from his ear, as if wary of what might come out of it. Then I heard someone pick up.

"Please may I speak," my father began in the voice of a middle-age Polish Jewish woman, "with the great voytchuoso Arthur Aranoff."

I started to giggle. He glanced down and nodded as if to confirm my part in the ruse. At that point I didn't really expect Arthur Aranoff to come to the phone. You couldn't just call up a radio station and get to speak to one of the performers, whether it was just our neighbor from 6E or Jack Benny himself. And yet my father seemed so confident-I had heard him do a Yiddish accent before but never a full-blown impersonation, and certainly not that of a woman-that I was beginning to believe he could bring it off.

"That's you, Meester Aranoff?" he said in a voice that sounded like claw-handed Mrs. Leiberman and all the other superannuated immigrant Jewish women I had ever known, with a touch of Milton Berle thrown in. (How had he got the voice down so pat? Did he practice in the freight elevators at Feinman & Sons?) I could see great jiggly bosoms that had nothing to do with my own hard chest. I could smell *latkes* frying in grease so thick my mother would flee retching in disgust. I could hear all the raucous noises and uncouth smells of a Jewish ancestry I had till that moment tried so hard to disdain. And I was amazed at how much fun it all seemed to be.

"Meester Aranoff, I am so lovink the cello! For years I am leestening the Haydn concerto. Such beauty, Meester Aranoff. Such feelink! But never do I hear playink like yours. A voytchuoso, Meester Aranoff. That's what I'm callink you. A voytchuoso!"

He paused to give Aranoff a chance to respond and gave me a wink, part co-conspirator, part caution not to give the game away.

"No, no, Meester Aranoff. No false modesty. *Tsu fil anivez iz a halber shtoltz.* I'm sayink to my Moishe here, 'Dahlink, I must tell in person this man how much I am lovink his cello.'"

I was gagging with laughter. This was better than a Marx Brothers comedy. Better than Steven Rabinowitz's imitation of Mrs. Froelich.

"Not at all, Meester Aranoff. Every void you desoyve. Every. Single. Void."

The next morning we ran into the Aranoffs in the lobby. Mr. Aranoff was wearing his black cape and had set his floppy hat at a rakish angle. His wife had on a frilly print dress. Aranoff doffed his hat to my mother, and she immediately complimented him on the concert the night before. He flushed with pleasure.

"A virtuoso performance," my father said, surprising everyone, since nobody, the Aranoffs included, had any illusions about my father's interest in music. He once signed a petition for the Bernsteins even though we ourselves never heard anything from the Aranoffs' apartment. "Well, thank you, David," Aranoff replied, obviously moved by this compliment from an unexpected source. "Thank you very much indeed."

"It was very well received," Mrs. Aranoff put in. "Tell them, Arthur, about the woman who called in to the radio station."

Aranoff feigned modesty, but it was obvious he had been telling the story to everyone.

"Just some aficionado," he said. "An educated woman. European accent. Probably a musician herself. It was very gratifying."

"Isn't that marvelous," my mother said. "Well, we all know how good you are, Arthur, and we're very proud of you."

"Very," father said, giving my hand a squeeze.

My father never repeated his performance in that telephone booth. But those few minutes convinced me of something about him I would never forget and doubly cherished for being kept a secret from everyone but the two of us. It was like having a world-class gunslinger for a father, a Wyatt Earp who had come out of retirement just that one time to rid the town of bad guys before sinking back into anonymity. It was like having a father who was every bit as much a virtuoso as Arthur Aranoff, even if he didn't get to perform for millions of people and no one but myself knew how good he was.

Of course, we never told my mother, and even between us we scarcely ever recalled that evening—a couple exceptions being: when he took me in his arms at my wedding reception for the traditional father-daughter dance and, in response to an overzealous violinist in the trio he had hired for the occasion, whispered, "I am so lovink the cello!"; the other time was when I visited him in the hospital shortly before his death.

He was barely able to speak. He gestured for me to come closer. I did, until our heads were just a few inches from each other. His eyes were glazed from painkillers, and there were tubes in his nostrils. I thought what he wanted was a kiss, so I kissed him on his pink stubbly cheek. But then he parted his lips, and I turned my head sideways to catch what he was going to say.

Despite the grim circumstances I broke into a wide grin. Pleased with his success, he smiled as well.

Afterward, my mother asked what he had said.

"Just," I replied, "that he loves me very much."

STEPHEN HEALEY

The Resurrection of Lucille Posh

From January/February 2007

A SWEET SMELLING rain drizzled on the Holy Ghost Tabernacle's metal roof, leading Sister Millie to whisper to Sister Claudette, "Sho' a good sign for Lucille's buryin' day. A good rain likely to bring a Holy Ghost blessin'."

"Bless God," Claudette replied, adding, "but poor Reverend Posh. Imagine being a minister at your wife's funeral. Just look at him," she sighed.

Before Millie could reply, lightning struck a tree outside. Smoldering bark flew against the tabernacle's windows.

"Sister Millie, is that a sign?" Claudette trembled.

"It sho' is."

Trying to maintain a tenuous momentum, Reverend Jeremiah Posh sobbed, "Lucille, you dear to these sheep, but you gone now... gone. You too good for this world, too good for us, so God took you back."

But the ladies heard none of this, because Millie whispered, "Satan be stirrin' up an ill wind, and God is allowin' it." She was voicing what many others were thinking. "We got to stand in prayer behind Reverend Posh, else Satan—" ending her worry mid-sentence for fear it might be true.

Even Posh, whom the Holy Ghost had never failed, suspected pagan forces were conspiring to ruin the encomium. And so they were. Jupiter Pluvius pummeled the Tabernacle's metal roof with July rain, Thor rattled its windows with deafening thunder, and Sister Emmy's six-month old son Elijah wailed in aggrieved protest. Posh often invoked I Kings 19 to show that the Holy Ghost spoke in a still, small voice. Now, that soft voice proved to be a liability, because Pluvius was playing the metal roof like a snare drum and the sons of Odin and Emmy were shouting at one another. Each bout of deafening clangor preceded silence that quickened the people's hearing. Posh hopscotched between unheard shouts and piercing *sotto voce*.

Eulogy fit poorly with Posh's "all are sinners through and through" theology, so he had started with a confession on Lucille's behalf. How she was unworthy. How she liked the drink. How she liked the men who bought her drinks. How—

The storm became ominous just as Reverend Posh came to a rhetorical sleight that would transform Lucille's shortcomings into works of glory. The trinity of pagans drummed, thundered, and screamed, and Lucille's redemption was lost in the din.

Even at wakes, Posh incited the passions of his flock through dance, song, and acclamation in hopes of invoking the Holy Ghost. Today, he had begun in a muted tone, Lucille's sins having left him feeling ill. He was unprepared to battle the pagans. His arms felt leaden, his legs had lost their dance, and his face contorted with grief. More and more of the people regarded him with sadness, void of expectation.

Brother James sighed and looked at his wife Fanny, who did little to hide her smile. Lucille had seduced James when they both had been inebriated. "Just one little time," she had said, not much to Fanny's liking. Reverend Posh had presided over their public confession and reconciliation, "as demanded by the Holy Ghost," but Fanny still hated Lucille. "I hope that bitch burns in hell," she snarled, when news of Lucille's death made its way to her through the Tabernacle's prayer chain.

The storm continued, and Posh looked drained. He mustered the strength to say, "Lucille, there was no one like you," but again, his voice was drowned out.

Billy Edwards, a nine-year old sinner too young to be baptized and too big to be nine, shouted amen and chuckled to himself. Billy hated Lucille for too often calling him a hooligan and a cretin. Billy was no saint, but Lucille's judgment of character was fueled by the spirits, most especially Jim Beam. But as soon as she died, the people, save Fanny and Billy, forgot her love of drink.

When Sister Winnie heard of Lucille's death, she cried, "Sister Lucille a saint, a saint o' the lamb." That became the canonical thumbnail of Lucille's alcohol-drenched life. Hoping to buoy Posh, the people shouted, "Lord, you have taken a great saint from us. Help us, Lord."

Bitch ain't no saint, thought Billy. For fun, the young hooligan shouted, "Amen, she a great aint."

Oblivious to Billy's dropped "s," every quarter of the congregation responded with shouted amens and hosannas. Sister Mary Lou began speaking in tongues.

In the noisy ruckus, the combined chatter of Christians and pagans, Billy reached over the painted wooden pew and pinched his sister Sally May smartly on the rear end, just as lightning flashed. She shrieked. Sally May ain't no saint, either, Billy thought.

The saints surmised a Holy Ghost blessing was falling. The congregation shouted amen, amen, amen, nearly in unison. The sisters jumped to their feet; the brothers clapped their hands. Elder Bones, as the arthritic Edward Lasher was called, jumped to the top of a pew and danced in the spirit, hopping back and forth, sending shards of chipped paint fluttering to the floor. He shouted, "I in the Holy Ghost. The Holy Ghost is good. Amen, amen!"

These silly sheep, Posh thought. Do they have to amen everything? Here Lucille dead, and they amen like a blessin' fall. They probably amen and dance in the Holy Ghost when I dead, too.

Lighting flashed. The thunder sounded like it was tearing the sky's fabric. Wind raged. But Elijah remained silent, having discovered his mom's purse handle made for good gumming. Posh raised his hands in a sweeping gesture and jumped from the floor. Thunder and wind raged again, but Elijah cooed calmly. The effect was so dramatic that it overcame Posh's grief. He shouted, "Amen, amen, amen, amen, amen, amen, amen. Bless you, Lord of the Sabaoth, you lion of Zion, maker of men, dasher of fools, and foe of sinners. You blessed One. Amen. Who on earth here below? Who? Who? Who can question thy mighty will, thy inscrutable intelligence, thy bountiful mercy?" Posh's cheeks glowed with refreshed zeal. The black-dressed sisters started swaying back and forth, back and forth, back and forth. "Amen, Lord. Amen, Lord. Amen, Lord," they shouted like holy chorus girls. A heaven blessing, a season of halleluiahs, was under way.

Posh danced down the aisle away from the casket, kicking his heels in the air, tapping them together every third or fourth hop. He paused to kiss Sister Beadle, whom he recently healed of blindness. She asked, "Is it you, Reverend Posh?" Casting a furtive glance to the nearby saints, he chuckled uneasily, "Is it me! You like to kid, Sister." He hugged Elders Jones and Fletcher. As he approached the former Firebottom, Lucy Kilroy, he hesitated. Then he drew her close, held her snugly around the waist and pressed himself against her. He kissed her on the mouth, bent her back, and kissed her again. Lucy looked shocked but pleased. Several of the people grumbled. Memories of Lucy's demon possession, Posh's exorcism that left her naked and him hiding in the prayer closet when the deacons came calling to find out what the hell was going on, his unction-inspired command that she marry John Kilroy, and her miraculous fecundation by the cursedly sterile Kilroy—healed, just in the nick of time—had provoked the saints, even though the Holy Ghost condoned the entire affair in a word of prophecy.

Regarding the people severely, Posh stepped back and swept his hands around the congregation, to the North, South, East, and West—to the four corners of the earth as he would say in commentary on the hand gestures employed in his sermons. "Can I hear an Amen? Can the Holy Ghost hear an amen?"

The people shouted amen. "Now that, that," Posh declared, using the self-authorizing elliptical phrase he favored most. "What the Lord say, the Lord say," he concluded with theological tautology that rendered logical parsing blasphemous.

Sitting to Lucy's right, John Kilroy looked to the wide board pine floor, his gaze falling on a punched out tree knot, the home of a dark spider, eerily illuminated by a light inadvertently left on in the crawlspace under the sanctuary. The spider was wrapping a doomed insect in a silk coffin. John shivered. "John, raise your eyes, son," Posh demanded. Uncharacteristically, Kilroy looked Posh in the eyes. Posh said, "The Lord acts in strange ways, but none stranger than creating women, by whom even the best of us are ensnared. Is that so?"

"Yes, Reverend."

"And did not our great Lord raise you up? Has he not blessed your sorry loins, perhaps to make you a new Abraham? Might not your seed be like the stars in the sky and the sand on the shore?"

Blushing, Kilroy replied, "As the Lord will."

"Now that, people, is faith. This withered tree has already sired one child o' promise. He a promising man, if you follow me. I raise my voice in prophecy: John Kilroy will be blessed with many children."

"You hear that, Lucy?" he added, returning her admiring gaze.

"I do," she replied, demurely rubbing her expansive belly.

"John, you ready to be blessed like Abraham?"

Kilroy blinked hard and said amen. Lucy mouthed words to Posh indicating that the Little Kilroy—as Posh called "the baby" from the pulpit—also was saying amen. "Little Kilroy sayin' amen, too!" Posh announced to the congregation. "Give the Lord a hand, people."

A few saints clapped. Posh decided it unwise to seek more than tepid affirmation.

Posh hugged Kilroy and whispered in his ear, "The Lord giveth and the Lord can take away." He whispered, "You follow me?"

Kilroy kissed Posh on the cheek. "You a man o' God, Reverend. I follow the Lord."

Posh turned and strode the aisle, stopping at the open casket. Lucille's body was dressed in a yellowed muslin dress. Gaudy white ruffles encircled her motionless hands. Posh bowed his head and wept again. "She didn't make 50, but God is good," he offered. The people shouted amen. Brother Rupert Jones joined Posh, and the two knelt to pray. As they knelt, Jones' knees cracked.

Six-year old Sally Jones started to sing. In contradiction to Posh's all-are-sinners theology and his oft-repeated claim that children are "begat in sin and sin at the breast," he often insisted children are innocent. Sally's sweet, clear voice sounded angelic. She sang, "Up from the grave he arose; with a mighty triumph o'er his foes; he arose a victor from the dark domain, and he lives forever, with his saints to reign. He arose! He arose! Hallelujah! Christ arose!"

"From the mouth of babes," Posh intoned, directing Brother Jones back to his pew, "comes a wisdom that touches God, that feels no sting o' death. Sally Jones, I raise my voice to prophesy that you will be a great saint." Sally curtsied.

Posh approached the casket, his shabby funeral suit marked with sweat under the arms. He regarded Lucille's lifeless face. He kissed his hands and gently touched her cheeks. "You can't be dead, Lucille." Fighting back tears, he called out, "Lucille, I command thee, come forth. Like Lazarus, who answered our Lord's death-defying call, I command thee, come forth."

One-armed Sister Emily Feltzer shouted, "Amen, you a man o' God. The Lord is mighty on you. Mighty enough to do all things," adding in an unlikely coda, "I gonna clap down a blessin'."

Jack White, sitting in the back, whispered to his half-brother Paul, "What this damn fool up to now?"

Billy Edwards overheard and giggled.

Posh heard Billy's giggle and ran the aisle to him. "Billy Edwards? Billy, why have you delighted the Evil One, that dark destroyer, Satan, master of this world?"

Billy looked nervously to his feet.

"Billy? I don't think you want me to get Holy Ghost on you, do you, boy?"

Billy muttered, "Jack White call you a—."

Posh flashed his eyes to White. "Brother White, has God called you to prophesy? Are you a man o' God? Do you have the gift? Have you exorcised devils, healed the blind, and raised the dead?"

White, who was an unbeliever, a drunk, and drunk, said, "Reverend Posh, You a man o' God. No one doubt that. Even I don't doubt that. But you ain't able to raise Lucille from the dead."

Posh was outraged, "Get thee behind me, Satan. You foe, you beguiler, you enemy in a dress of wisdom."

White said, "Posh, she dead. Lucille gone to be with the saints. I a sinner, and I know that. She dead. I sorry, because I know she loved you. She never stopped loving you, even when..." As if putting himself back on track, White continued, "True, she loved booze, like me, but she loved you more."

Startled by White's honesty, Posh bowed his head, then whispered, "The Holy Ghost say to be silent. White, you give up that booze. The Holy Ghost say that, too. But the Holy Ghost also say, my Lucille gonna rise up."

Posh ran back the aisle, ugly snot swinging from his nose. "Lucille, I command thee. In the name of Jehovah, in the name of Jesus, our crucified Lord, stand up. Shake off the clothes of death."

Shocked, the people fell silent. Posh stared at Lucille, looking for signs of life. "I command thee. I command thee."

Sally resumed singing. "Up from the grave he arose—"

Arms raised, Posh began praying. "O Lord, you stronger than death. You create life. You the Lord of life. You raised Jesus from the dead, and he raised Lazarus. O Lord, this people, your people, need to see your power today. Our faith is falterin', Lord. Today, we need you to act. We need it today, like never before."

Sister Mary Perkins, whose husband Filmore died the previous month, cried softly. Her sister Eleanor murmured, "Reverend Posh, God tellin' me, he don't play favorites. Your Lucille, she no better than Mary's Filmore. Both them dead, both gonna stay dead."

Posh's authority on such matters was not subject to question. Furthermore, women were to be silent in the Church, unless Posh called on them to speak. He faced Sister Eleanor. "Eleanor, did not our Lord heal you of diabetes?"

"He did."

"Then say amen."

"Amen."

"Now say, God raise up Lucille."

"God ain't sayin' that. He sayin', some curses stay. After you healed me o' diabetes, even you say the Lord allowed a thorn to stay in my flesh. I pee every half hour. My cuts don't heal. I black out. Them thorns. Sho' I healed, but them thorns stay. God sayin' Lucille's thorn is death."

"Sister Eleanor, were you healed of diabetes?"

"I was. Bless God, bless God, O my soul."

"By whose prayer? By whose prophesy?"

"By yours, Reverend. I bless you for that."

"Then, why, why, you fu-, why you fightin' me now? What wrong with you? You want the devil to bring diabetes back?"

"I speakin' for God. He don't play favorites. I ain't sayin'. He sayin' that Lucille dead. She gonna stay dead."

Posh breathed deeply and choked on phlegm. He kneeled to catch his breath. Sister Baldwin helped him stand. "Thank you, Sister."

"Sister Eleanor, I got a word from God for you. This harsh word is not mine. I utter it in fear, fear for your soul. This week, we will bury you in this Church. Devil diabetes has destroyed your kidneys. Satan has been prowling, waiting for you to rebuke God's stayin' power. I'm sorry, Sister. God has spoken."

Eleanor sat, defeated, and began weeping.

Posh looked at the people. "Anyone else here ready to join Satan? Anyone else here want to rumble with Posh and the Holy Ghost?"

Brother Black raised his hands, and shouted, "Bless you, Jehovah, bless you. A word on me, Reverend."

"Then speak," said Posh. "God ain't used to waitin'."

Black looked somberly at the people. He shouted, parroting Posh's prophetic style, "You wretched, filthy, sinful, perverted, fallen, adulterous, licentious, drunk, whore-mongering people. You blight. You unworthy, backbiting, gossipin', Holy Ghost denying idolaters. God say, 'Get thee out o' my house. I gonna do a miracle. I gonna raise this bitch... uh, I gonna raise this saint... and I raisin' her now. But I ain't raisin' her to impress this house o' sin, this people like unto Ichabod.' God say, 'Get thee out. Go wander through the desert.' God say, 'Let the rain be a baptizin'.'"

Posh's voice boomed, "People o' God. You heard Jehovah's voice. Now out, out to the land of sin."

The people rushed from the sanctuary into the rain. Jehovah sent them to the wilderness once before, but that was on a rainless afternoon. Not as remote as it seemed, the wilderness was the parking lot. The people were to mill around the lot until the Lord and Posh called them back.

As the people rushed out, Brother Black stayed behind. When the people, including the 350-pound, wheelchair-confined Mrs. Jacobs, were outside, Posh took Black's hand. "Thank you, Brother Black," Posh said.

Black responded, "You a real man o' God, Reverend. None like you anywhere else."

Posh moved to hug him, but Black stopped him short. "But you listen to me, you stupid fool. The people gone now, and you need to hear this. Lucille dead. She gonna stay dead. Eleanor right about that."

Posh punched Black square on the lips, sending blood flying against the wall. Black dropped to the floor. Posh yelled, "Jesus, why have you forsaken me? Here I am, Lord. I ready to do your will, but my Lucille dead. How can I carry on, Lord?"

Black said, "Posh, I give you that one. You needed it, but if there another one, I will break you in half. You doubt it, run a line up to the Holy Gho' and see whose ass get kicked. Lucille dead. She gonna stay dead. You really wanna bring the people in here and let 'em watch you pray for her to be raised from the dead? What wrong with you? Even the prophets of Baal ain't that stupid."

Posh mumbled, "Lucille can't be gone. I can't live without my Lucille. True, I sinned against her night and day. True, I was sinning against her the night she... but I just a man."

"Posh, I know you hurtin'. But you listen. I ain't a man o' God, but I know she dead. Time for being sorry is gone."

"You right, she gone. My Lucille dead. True, she was a drunk, and she was a bitch, but she was my drunk bitch. Now she gone," Posh sobbed.

"Give me a hand, Black. I gotta git cleaned up. You go bring the people in from the wilderness. Satan a prowling. They probably already dancing and drinking and worshippin' the golden calf."

As he strained to help Posh stand, Black passed wind. Black's mortified expression caused Posh to chuckle. Posh said, "You need a healin'. How that wife live with you? What the hell she been feedin' you?"

Embarrassed, and aware another transgression was dangerously close, Black apologized.

"No need. As they say, what done, done. Who gone, gone. My Lucille is gone. Even a stink-ass fool like you know that. So, Black, bring in the sheaves. Any golden calves out there, just look the other way."

Encouraged by the driving rain, Mrs. Jacobs and the rest of the flock quickly returned to their pews, shivering and expectant.

"People o' God?"

Amen, amen.

"People o' God?"

Amen, amen, amen.

"People o' God, is this Lucille?" Posh asked, pointing to Lucille's body.

Amen.

"People o' God?"

Amen.

"People o' God, this is not Lucille. This was Lucille, but now she robed in glory. This pretty old weddin' dress ain't a robe o' glory. Lucille raised from the dead, raised to glory. I believe in the resurrection. I command you also to believe. That that."

Distant thunder growled, and heavy rain pounded on the Church roof. Elijah had finally fallen asleep.

"Black and I talked a little theee-ology," Posh cried. "He a bless man, and I lucky to have him here. We fought a hideous demon. You doubt that, go to the vestibule and take a deep breath. That a foul spirit. Billy, do you say amen to that?"

Billy amened and held his nose. "That a foul spirit, Reverend."

"Good boy, Billy. Black took a demon's punch. He a man o' God. I name him a deacon, just now. Not I, but the Holy Ghost. Black, you a deacon. That that. People o' God, Lucille with God now. That that. Now give the Lord an amen."

Amen.

"Give the Lord a hand."

The people clapped.

"You call that a hand?"

The peopled clapped and shouted. The sister and brother saints started dancing in the aisle. Sister Perkins spoke in tongues.

"Amen. Jehovah, our great God, into thy hands I commend the spirit of our departed sister. You care for her spirit, and we will bury the flesh. Lucille Posh, you with God now."

The people cheered. Posh wept.

"She my wife, Lord. Tell her I love her. Tell her she always be mine."

ROY GILES

Black Night Ranch

From April/May 2010

"SHEEP ARE BORN to die," James Carl said, pointing his syringe at Billy. "They think that's their purpose. We want their wool. They want to die. The trick is to make the stupid son-of-a-bitches think you want them dead." He vaccinated with authority, tossing sheep aside like wool blankets when he finished with each one.

"They'll spite you that way and live. Don't baby them. Make them think you're stabbing them to death."

James Carl and Billy had hanging around their necks clear bags of sheep dope with long rubber hoses attached to needles big as framing nails. The sheep were packed tight into the 20-foot pen, squirming and crawling over one another like maggots. Every time James Carl tossed one, the whole bunch erupted into isolated geysers of sheep. Billy kept losing his balance in the melee, exasperating the beasts. It was the uncertainty of it. Falling. They couldn't stand it. An old ewe leapt at Billy's head, dragging the needle in his hand with her. The chisel end of the needle carved a deep line in Billy's cheek. The ewe's front hooves clawed his back as she made her way over.

"Fucking sheep!"

"Don't baby them," James Carl said, tossing two animals at once. He was in a hurry. A group of Mexican shearers were due at his ranch by noon, and he wanted to be ready for them.

Billy had been looking forward to the shearing ever since waking up. All through breakfast James Carl had talked about it. He said they could shear a sheep in less than two minutes, and if they brought the young one called Miguel with them, then Billy would really get to see fast.

"And quit that cussing. Your parents didn't let you, and I ain't either," James Carl said.

Billy climbed out of the pen.

"Where you going? I see three unmarked backs."

Though it was more of a bad scratch than a cut, Billy touched a finger to his cheek and tongued it from the inside. He didn't know much about sheep. Before Bird Creek Bridge gave way three months earlier, taking Billy's parents forever with it, his family had run a few cows, but never sheep. He'd gotten the job and moved in with his father's old friend, James Carl, mostly because the rancher was lonely, but the official reason was that Billy knew Spanish. Or rather, he was supposed to know Spanish. James Carl owned the only sheep ranch in Hughes County, Oklahoma, and every spring he hired Mexicans out of South Texas to shear his sheep. Lonely as he'd been the ten years since his wife left, he frustrated himself into great depressions when he couldn't communicate with the only company he ever had. He'd said that very thing to Billy the day of the funeral. Billy's dad, who'd been proud of how well Billy did in school, had bragged about his son being so smart in one language that he took up another one. That had impressed James Carl. But while Billy recognized words when he saw them on paper, and he did well in class, in truth he understood little spoken Spanish. Nonetheless, Billy was fresh out of high school and fresh out of parents, and James Carl took him in.

"Don't worry about the cut. Them's antibiotics," James Carl said. He caught up with the last three sheep and had them stuck and marked before Billy could get back across the fence. "Just get the gate."

James Carl was a big man. Notoriously big. He was so big that when people saw him for the first time, they'd say out loud, "Goddamn, that is a big man." When he walked, his steps were so far apart, his gait looked like slow motion to Billy. His fists were as wide as Billy's head, and he could lift four sheep at once when their wool was thick. And since Dog, the only sheep dog on the Black Night Ranch, couldn't herd, protect, or do anything else that a sheep dog was supposed to do, that's how they often had to move them. By hand, five at a time. Billy's one to James Carl's four. It took a long time to move the animals like that, but usually, even if Dog was around, he spent more time scattering the sheep than anything else. Billy wasn't crazy about Dog because sometimes when James Carl left the front door of the house open, Dog would nose his way into bed with Billy. Billy slept heavy and never noticed until he either woke up with the mutt or else itching from the dirty black hairs, cockleburs, or ticks the animal left behind. Even thinking of Dog made Billy itchy.

Billy opened the gate at the end of the pen farthest from James Carl. To the sheep the opening must have looked like an entrance to hell because the front lines facing the gate were impenetrable. They weren't going. James Carl kicked and pushed from his end, but the gray mass absorbed him like a pond takes a pebble. Finally, letting out a series of spooky high-pitched yelps, the big man grabbed a lamb and threw him over the top of the horde. It was a half-eared lamb they called Sonny, who had only been on the ground a little over a month.

James Carl, who called every dog he ever owned Dog, named all his sheep. Few had simple names like Sonny did. Most were called things like That Bitch Ewe Who Almost Killed Me, The Lamb Who

Got Tangled in the Fence That Time, or Billy's favorite, The Ram with One Nut. Sonny was named after James Carl's father, Sonny, who, a few years before he died, had gotten half an ear kicked off by an emu. Sonny landed beyond the open gate and ran. The rest of the sheep, looking at one another for reassurance and apparently not finding it, dug in after him, emptying the pen into the pasture where the rest waited to be sheared.

After rounding up all but a few dozen stragglers hiding somewhere on the rancher's 3,000 acres, they were ready for the Mexicans, so James Carl told Billy to start plowing the upper 320 acres, the 320 for short, and he would call him when their company arrived.

Billy had barely climbed in the Big R Versatile tractor when he spotted six or seven wild dogs working the tree line to the north. They were a long way away, but he knew they were dogs because dogs don't hunch up all timid-like and prance the way coyotes do. Dogs are worse than coyotes. Braver. Smarter, too, which made them bad news for sheep. These looked especially menacing to Billy because they resembled a slow moving snake the way they slithered in and out of the timber. About 1,000 yards east and upwind of the dogs were a group of 13 sheep, five ewes and their lambs.

Billy picked up the CB handset and radioed back to James Carl, who was supposed to be preparing a barbecue pit by the shearing barn.

"Found the stragglers. We got dogs on them," Billy said, but he realized that from where the shearing barn was, he was right in the line of fire. In a hurry he added, "The dogs are behind me." He made a hard right turn so the dogs would progress past him.

Five minutes after radioing and hearing no response from James Carl, Billy saw a ewe go down. She kicked her back legs high in the air before falling. Over the noise of the tractor, he hadn't heard a rifle report, but he'd often seen deer kick the same way. It meant the ewe was likely heart-shot. It also meant James Carl mistook his sheep for dogs. While Billy fumbled for the CB, he saw another ewe collapse, and he dropped the handset. A lamb then spun to the ground. The dogs were about 200 yards from the sheep when the lead dog broke and ran for them, the rest of the pack following. The sheep stood looking in the wrong direction until Billy honked his horn. As the sheep turned toward the tractor, they caught sight of the dogs and fled into the timber out of Billy's sight. When the dogs were nearly at the spot where the sheep disappeared, the sheep reemerged and ran straight at the dogs. All but one.

A lamb separated from the group and ran flat out across the newly plowed field toward the tractor. When it got close enough, Billy saw one of its ears was half gone, which was strange because Sonny was supposed to be with the others they'd rounded up that morning. At first it looked like he was headed back to the pasture he'd escaped from and was going to cross in front of the tractor, but instead the lamb cut hard just short of the Versatile and took cover under it. Versatiles like the Big R were enormous, and though they swiveled in the middle, such tractors couldn't be maneuvered like the tiny Fords and Farmalls Billy was used to operating. The tires alone were taller than he was, and there were eight of those. As fast as Sonny was running, the big tractor must have looked parked. Billy heard and felt nothing, but he knew he got the lamb because it never came out the other side. He shut the tractor off and climbed out, mindful of James Carl's position at the barn. With Sonny coming at him like he had, Billy had lost track of the other sheep.

Shots echoed off the timberline from the north. Billy couldn't see anything that James Carl might be shooting at by that time. He also couldn't find Sonny.

"Break down?" James Carl asked over the CB. Billy climbed back into the cab to answer him.

"Ran over Sonny."

"Anything salvageable?"

"Can't find him."

"Quit plowing and go gather up what woolies you can find."

"How come you shot those sheep?" Billy asked.

"What sheep?"

"Those sheep up there I radioed about." Billy waited long for a response.

"My goddamn eyes. Who'd I kill?"

"Not sure, but three."

"Shit. All right. Just get the dead."

Billy drove the Versatile a quarter-mile across the field and parked on the timberline where he last saw the dogs. He loaded the three sheep that James Carl had killed, pulling them on top of the plow. He found some old, rusty barbed wire rolled up and looped over a fence post and used it to tie them to the frame. He had expected to find one or two more dead, or at least some evidence that a couple had been killed by the dogs, but instead, he found seven strung out along a short path on Wewoka Creek, which was the east border of the property. He couldn't believe the waste. Two went unaccounted for. He assumed they had been killed and carried off, but the fact the dogs had killed seven and let them lay was odd. And then there was Sonny, plowed under somewhere on the lower half of the 320. Billy drove the tractor and sheep to the shearing barn. James Carl looked over the dead.

"Ten? Damn. Just three were mine? I shot eight times."

"Just the three."

"The Ewe I Hate and One Eye ran with this group."

"Yeah, but I didn't find them," Billy said.

"Did a headcount. They ain't with the rest. Why'd Sonny split off from the others?" James Carl asked. Billy didn't know. He also didn't know why James Carl would ask him. He knew Billy didn't know anything about sheep. "Sheep don't split up. Don't make sense. Why'd those dogs kill so many?" Billy didn't know that either. From the recent lack of ticks in his bed, and the fact that he hadn't seen Dog around, Billy thought he'd been missing a couple of days, but he wasn't willing to mention it without something concrete to say about it.

"Instinct never failed an animal so much as a damn sheep. Untie my three. I'll skin them and hang them in the smokehouse. Take the rest to the bone yard in the pecan orchard. How's your eyes? You see good?"

Billy told him his eyes were fine, but that he was only a fair shot with open sights.

"Can't be any worse than me. I reckon you better start carrying the rifle, at least until I get a scope for it."

Billy had only been working with James Carl the three months since his parents died, and already he was used to seeing sheep do things that made no sense. He was used to seeing them get killed. They ran into barbed wire fences, off cliffs, into slow moving dirt road traffic, and other such nonsense on a regular basis. Apparently he and his boss could add running under tractors and straight at dogs to the list of stupid things sheep do.

"Maybe Sonny was retarded," James Carl said with serious wonder. "Get back to plowing. I'm going to go find the hole he slipped through. I'll yell at you when the Mexicans get here." It was his last word on the subject of Sonny.

Billy didn't say anything, but he didn't think Sonny was retarded. For one thing, the lamb had been the only one to find the hole in the fence, which Billy thought was smart. And had he not run under the Versatile, splitting off from the rest of the sheep would have proven a wise move. Billy considered it a huge oversight on the part of James Carl for him to think a lamb running from dogs pointed to low intelligence.

Sweating, Billy climbed back into the Versatile. It had been a dry year. A drought if you listened to farmers. Farmers couldn't be trusted when it came to weather, though. They'll tell you it's either too wet to get the wheat up or too dry for it to grow. Billy had never met a farmer yet who had a good year where weather was concerned. But it was dry that morning, that's for sure. The wind had blown all during the night before and dried the ground to a powder by daylight.

Dust puffed in through the cracks of the cab. Billy tied a bandana around his nose. Soon it was too soaked with snot to be of use. He took the bandana off and leaned over the gearshifts. Eyes squinting and nose dripping like hydraulic fluid, he thought about James Carl. He had never known a tougher man. For years he'd heard his father talk about *the* James Carl Henry who could lift Hemi blocks without a cherry picker and who stepped over gates instead of opening them.

When Billy was six, he and his father were fishing a roadside pond when he first saw James Carl. At that time the man wore a thick black beard. He was looking for Billy's father in order to trade him a beefalo for a .223 Remington rifle. Billy saw him step out of his Chevy one-ton and walk toward them.

Billy said, "Daddy, there's a really big man coming."

"What do you think that man wants?" Billy's father asked, casting his line.

"I don't know. He looks mad."

"Think we ought to run or fight it out?"

"I think we ought to run."

After that Billy found it fascinating to hear all the stories about the big man. James Carl once took on a band of Hell's Angels 60 miles away in Lehigh, Oklahoma, back when being a Hell's Angel had nothing to do with parades or charities. Back when all outlaw motorcycle gangs called themselves Hell's Angels. Outside the only bar in Lehigh, for fun he kicked one of their bikes to the ground. After a short chase down unfamiliar dirt roads, he wound up taking 23 stabs in a wheat field. Billy had heard his father tell the story many times.

Shortly after being hired on, and in a rare moment of courage, Billy had asked his boss about the stabbing. The courage to raise the question resulted from James Carl having burned the palms of both his hands when Billy had mistakenly tried to open the hood on the feed truck he was driving. What Billy had thought was steam rolling from under the hood, James Carl had realized was actually smoke. He had knocked the boy out of the way and burned himself instead. He had talked Billy through how to bandage his hands for him, and in the moment, though Billy had felt responsible for getting his boss burned, he'd also felt a kind of safety and trust in doctoring the man's burns. In feeling that sense of safety, Billy asked about Lehigh. James Carl said it was the prettiest stand of wheat he ever saw. He claimed it's what saved him. Said the wheat sang to him and kept him from bleeding out. Billy didn't much buy it, but he wouldn't have been the one to disagree. Two of those stabs were to James Carl's neck, and not pocketknife stabs, either. All his scars were at least an inch wide. Those bikers had used big knives.

Starting to doze into his daydream, the CB cracked. "Wake up, goddamn it."

Billy hit the brakes and looked up. He had been veering off into a cut in the timber toward the creek. James Carl must have seen him and figured he had gone to sleep.

"I'm awake."

"The Mexicans are here. Park the tractor and come on."

James Carl did the introductions. "Billy, these are the Mexicans. Mexicans, this is Billy. Tell them how many head we got and ask them how long's it going to take. Not that I care. I just like to know. I'll go get some ice for the water cooler." James Carl carried the water can to the house.

Billy wiped his nose on his shirtsleeve. Words passed back and forth through his head, but he was afraid to say them. He knew that once spoken, he'd be expected to make sense of the words that would come back at him. He pretended to spot something important on the ground, bent to pick up a rock, and stuffed it in his pocket. He wiped his nose again. A square-faced man stepped forward and handed Billy a red bandana. Billy took it but didn't know what to do with it. The man motioned to his face like wiping his nose and Billy got it. Even though Billy already had a bandana, he nodded a "thank you" to the man and blew his nose into it. It smelled of lemons. The Mexican pulled a blue bandana from his pocket to show him he had another and motioned for Billy to keep the one he'd handed him. Billy nodded again but said nothing.

A boy about 15, Billy guessed, stepped out from behind the others. The boy looked toward the sheep gathered out in the pasture.

"Looks like two thousand. He thinks you speak Spanish, huh?" the boy said to Billy.

"I can read it."

"Tell him we will do it in one day and one half."

"Okay," Billy said.

The boy leaned in close and whispered, "Drink whiskey?"

The sound of James Carl closing the house door straightened the boys. The rancher returned with a five-gallon orange water can filled and ready. He took Billy aside. "What'd Miguel say?"

"That was Miguel?"

"I've been gone ten minutes, and ya'll didn't so much as introduce yourself?"

"No."

James Carl got loud. "Did you talk sheep at all or what? Pimples and jacking off?"

"He said it would take the rest of today and half of tomorrow."

"Twenty-three hundred head? Seven Mexicans? You misheard."

"No."

James Carl thought about it. "I guess that boy's got faster."

The Mexicans rigged up, tested their shears, and donned their chaps, but mostly they waited for sheep. James Carl and Billy ended their conversation and herded in the animals from the pasture through hog panel corrals they'd rigged up for that purpose. After getting ahead of the shearers by 500 head, James Carl sat in lawn chair in the shade of an elm growing beside the shearing barn. He opened an ice chest full of beer and watched.

The shed was set up with ten shearing stalls, which were just plywood cubicles with eight-foot tall burlap bags hanging in wooden racks in the corner of each one. Each stall was six feet wide and had a back and two sides. The front was open to the outside. Billy helped Miguel's little brother stuff the bags with shorn wool, and when each bag was full, James Carl left his beer and hoisted the little boy into the sacks so he could tamp the wool down. Billy noted the little boy was wide between the eyes, and though he wasn't clumsy, it appeared he never really looked at anything. Like he looked past everything. He was a pleasant boy, though, and stayed steady.

Billy's hands, already soft from handling the wool every day, turned yellowish-brown and grew foul from the stink of it. He wiped his hands on his pants but couldn't rid himself of its stickiness.

"Lanolin," James Carl said from the shade. "Wool's got lanolin in it. Give up, you ain't getting it off. Look at your boots." Billy's boots glistened in the rich grease. "They won't be leaking for a while."

"It's like ear wax," Billy said.

"Quit stuffing a minute. Watch that boy shear."

Billy had been working so hard to keep up that he hadn't been able to watch the shearing like he'd meant to. Miguel kicked a sheep loose two-to-one faster than the next fastest. James Carl timed him.

"Goddamn." He showed the stopwatch to Billy.

"It looked fast. Was it fast?"

"The record is about 20 seconds slower than his average. That one was 27 seconds." James Carl timed again. "Twenty-nine seconds. Look how he hardly nicks them."

Miguel was beautiful. The sheep, quiet, docile in his hands, trusted the boy. Where the other men occasionally had to struggle to get the sheep positioned just right, Miguel molded them between his legs exactly the way he wanted the first time. He never repositioned until he was ready to turn them to his shears, and he never grabbed an animal that went rank in his hands, not even the moody rams.

At the day's end, 2,109 sheep were sheared. Nine-hundred and seventy-two were Miguel's alone. With less than 200 sheep to go, the Mexicans were antsy to finish, but James Carl refused to string lights in the shed. Instead, he built a great fire in the pit he'd dug earlier. A white man fire, he called it. He spit a gimp yearling and feasted them on mutton and beer. When everyone had their bellies full and their heads buzzing, he ordered Billy to get two cots from out of the shed behind the house.

"Me and you are going to sleep outside with them tonight," he said.

Billy fetched the two cots and started setting them up beside the fire. The Mexicans looked uneasy about it. It was clear they didn't know if the cots were for them or for James Carl and Billy.

"Explain it to them, Billy. They look scared."

"Explain what?"

"I don't want them thinking we don't trust them. Just tell them we feel like sleeping under the stars tonight. The fat one plays guitar. I might get my fiddle. Tell him I'm better than last year." Billy waited for his boss to walk away liked he had before, but the big man waited to see what was said.

"Well?" James Carl asked.

Billy looked for Miguel but didn't see him. Finally, he said, "They're shy, and only Miguel will talk to me."

"They've been chattering all day. They ain't looked shy to me."

"But Miguel—"

"Billy," James Carl said, raising his voice, "if the next word out of your mouth ain't some Mexican gibberish I can't understand, then I don't want to hear another word."

"*Dormir?*" Billy said.

"Good, but look at them when you're talking. They're the Spanish speakers, now ain't they?"

Billy turned to the group of Mexicans, who had grown silent as James Carl's voice had risen. Miguel walked up. Billy searched the boy's face. Finally he said, "*Dormir. Quere dormir.*"

Miguel nodded to him. "We will, too, then."

"I'm a dirty bastard," James Carl said, looking at Billy. "I had me a feeling about this." He walked off toward the house. "Put the cots up."

Watching his boss walk away, Billy thought he should say something. Anything. Explain himself somehow. He wanted to tell him how he would try to learn how to speak it and how he knows how to read it, but what came out was, "But my parents—"

James Carl turned back. "What? What about your parents?"

Billy couldn't finish his thought because he didn't have any idea what he had planned to say. It just came out. Embarrassed, he lowered his eyes and stared at the ground.

"I won't put up with a boy who'll run his parents down, particularly when they ain't here to defend themselves. Is that what you intended to do? Tell me it's their fault you lied to me?"

Billy said nothing.

"What then?"

"I don't know," Billy said.

"Well, I don't, either. But I know what trust is. Do you?"

When Billy couldn't answer, James Carl walked away.

"You better sleep out here tonight," Miguel said.

"Yeah," Billy said, but he didn't move until his boss was fully out of sight. "Why did you speak English? You got me caught."

"Already caught. I just made it hurry," Miguel said. He spoke to his family in Spanish, which Billy couldn't understand, but when the square-faced one went to the back of their truck and retrieved a blanket for him, he figured out what had been said.

Billy wrapped the blanket around himself and pulled a lawn chair close to the warm pit of embers. He sat wondering if he'd be fired, but more than anything, he was just sorry he'd disappointed the man. He'd disappointed people before. So far as he could tell, it was as much his purpose to disappoint as it was the sheep's apparent desire to die. The way James Carl looked at him when he realized he'd been lied to, Billy had seen before. He'd seen it when he let the bottom burn completely out of his mother's favorite bean pot that had been handed down three generations. He'd seen it in his father when he stumbled in one night drunk and bloody from falling. And he'd seen it in his grandmother when he'd doubted God. But he'd never seen it like it was in James Carl. It felt as different to him as the difference between killing a mouse and a horse. The bigger they are, the more it hurts. There is something in the weight of it. The size. The space a thing takes up in the world. He fell asleep in the chair feeling he had scarred a big piece of the world. A really big piece.

Billy woke, scratching the back of his neck. Miguel's little brother, springing from behind him, giggled and tossed a tuft of wool in Billy's lap. From his cot Miguel shushed him, then pulled a bottle of whiskey from his sleeping bag and offered it to Billy. Billy shook his head "no," but looking at the people sleeping around him and back at the house to see if lights were on, he eased out of his creaking chair and signaled Miguel to follow him.

Billy led Miguel and Miguel's wide-eyed little brother a half mile to the Versatile at the lower edge of the 320. They crawled under the tractor, built a tiny pit fire, and sat in a circle around it.

"How do you shear so fast?" Billy asked.

"Faster I shear, faster I finish," Miguel said passing the whiskey. Miguel's brother reached for the bottle but was passed over. "No."

"He's quiet. What's his name?" Billy asked.

"He has no name."

"I got a name. It is Carlos," the boy said.

"It is not Carlos," Miguel said.

"It is Claudio."

"Stop lying. It is not Claudio either."

"It is Pedro."

"Why did you have to ask his name?" Miguel asked.

"I know my name," the boy said, getting agitated. "My name is Jesus. It is Justo. It is Ramiro. It is—"

"*Sí*. I am sorry. It is Justo," Miguel said.

"Ramiro."

"I know. Ramiro."

"It is Ramiro."

"I heard you," Miguel said.

"It is."

Billy interrupted, "I'm Billy."

"Yes!"

"Yes, what?" Billy asked.

"We both have names."

"Oh." Billy opened his mouth to ask how old the little boy was, but thought better of it. He guessed him to be about nine or ten. That was close enough.

The little boy stretched out on the ground and fell asleep. Miguel slumped against a tire, drunk. Billy drained the bottle, stood up too fast, and banged his head on the tractor.

"Fuck!"

The little boy stirred but didn't wake. Miguel looked long at his brother. "The same voices," he said. "Day and night. Same voices all the time. I am tired listening to sheep. To shears. My hands shake all the time. It is like I am shearing when I am not shearing. I am tired listening to him talking nonsense all the time. It would be worth dying if I never had to hear sheep or shears or him or Mexicans and Americans trying to understand the other."

"Yeah," Billy said.

"You will not be fired, I think," Miguel said.

"Maybe."

"You can learn my language by next year when we come. I did not speak English last year. My brother did not. Tell him that."

"Why would he even need me to speak Spanish if you speak English? He doesn't need me."

"He will. I will not be back," Miguel said. "I am hungry."

"I am hungry, too," Miguel's brother said, waking to the suggestion.

"Too bad one of those stupid sheep hasn't walked by and dropped dead. I bet I could cook mutton better than James Carl," Billy said.

Miguel perked up. "Want to go kill one?" He pulled a cheap looking survival knife from his boot. "It is sharp. Feel," Miguel said handing Billy the knife. It was sharp. He handed it back. Miguel crawled out from under the tractor. His brother sat looking hopeful. "There are too many here. He would never miss one. I say we get one of the woolly ones still in the wood corrals. Easier." He crawled up on the Versatile to get a better look. "I think it is too far for him to hear." Miguel jumped down from the tractor and slid under it to put out the fire.

Billy didn't want to kill any sheep. He'd seen enough dead for one day, but he felt like doing something brave. He felt like taking up a greater space in the world, like James Carl. Billy helped fill in the pit, leaving no visible evidence there had been a fire. He remembered to bury the bottle.

Miguel led the way but hesitated at the timberline. "I get lost in trees," he said. Billy took over and led the boys straight through to the other side where it opened up into another field not yet plowed. Across the field lay the wooden corrals. Miguel out front, they sneaked the last quarter-mile. At the corrals, Miguel's brother put his hand through and let a lamb lick his fingers. He giggled.

"Stay on this side," Miguel said to his brother. Grinning at Billy, Miguel took the knife from his boot and bit down on it.

Climbing over the corral fence, Billy missed a step and fell into the sheep, frightening them. Bleating, the sheep scattered and ran in futile circles around the boys. Miguel took the knife out of his mouth to laugh at Billy lying in the dirt, put it back, and began the chase. Miguel lunged at one, missed, chased another, and missed again. Billy faired about the same, each boy running in drunken circles, laughing and falling, until Billy gave out and crossed the fence. He sat panting in the grass with Miguel's brother, who rocked patiently. Billy heard the gate jangle. Miguel approached carrying a tiny lamb. It looked dead, drooping in his arms. Miguel spit the knife onto the ground. The lamb raised its head, curled comfortably into his arms, and fell asleep.

"I cannot do it," Miguel said. "He jumped in my arms like I was to save him. They all ran. He jumped."

Billy, feeling big, picked up the knife. "You can't baby sheep." He tested the knife's edge, wiped it off on his pant leg, and raised the lamb's sleepy head, exposing its neck. He gripped the knife hard, felt for the best spot to cut, and looked up at Miguel. Miguel took a deep breath, closed his eyes, and turned away. Billy lowered the lamb's head. He could see there was more to it than Miguel not wanting to be the one holding the knife. He could see the boy didn't want it killed at all.

"Let's put him back," Billy said, tossing the knife in the grass.

Miguel relaxed his shoulders and stared up at the sky, his hands slipping to loosely hold the lamb. Seeing the look on Miguel's face, Billy, too, felt a sense of relief. In his periphery, Billy saw Miguel's little brother pick up the knife, but he was too slow to prevent the little boy from slitting the lamb's throat. Miguel dropped to the ground with the lamb and tried to stop the flow, but it was a good cut. The lamb was mostly dead.

"Why did you do that?" Miguel pleaded.

"Huh?"

"I said why did you do that? We were going to put it back. I have it all over me. What are we going to do with it? Shit. Shit." Miguel turned to Billy. "Do something."

The little boy put his hand on Miguel's shoulder. "We eat? I am hungry. We eat now?"

Miguel cried, leaning over the lamb.

"We could throw it in the creek," Billy said. Wewoka Creek was only 200 yards away.

"Throw it in a creek? There is blood all over." Miguel stood and walked away from them into the dark. Billy, hearing Miguel's crying intensify, ducked his head and stared at the ground like he always did when he was nervous. He noticed blood had splashed his boot. It beaded up in red half-moons that with a shake rolled to the ground.

Miguel reappeared, calm. He pointed a finger at his brother. "His name is Cordaro." The boy started to correct, but Miguel leapt onto him, pinned him to the ground, and knocked the knife from his hand. "*Cállate el osico!* I want to hear nothing from you. Hear? *Nada!*" Miguel's brother looked vacant, as if focusing on some curious point far beyond his brother. Miguel crawled off of him and went to Billy. He started to cry again but stifled it. He picked the lamb up from the ground and held it like a dead baby. "Which way?"

Billy led him to the creek. It was full of spring rain. Miguel waded chest deep and released the lamb. Watching it float downstream, he washed away the blood, then washed his brother. Billy, sitting on the bank sobering up, caught movement downstream. In the moonlight, he saw Dog slip through the cattails on the opposite side of the creek. He was after the lamb. Billy stood.

"Get," Billy yelled. Dog looked up and saw him but appeared unconcerned.

"*Que?*" Miguel asked, pulling his brother close.

Dog stretched his neck out into the water, nipped at and missed the lamb. He hunkered his haunches. Billy knew he was going to leap. He ran down the bank toward Dog, throwing anything he could grab as he closed the gap between them. Dog was brave, but he wasn't stupid. He abandoned the creek and disappeared into the cattails. Billy slowed when he saw him leave. He waded in and pulled the lamb from the water. Dripping at the river's edge, he saw Miguel staring at him.

"A dog was going to get him," Billy said.

"It is dead."

"Yeah."

Billy heard the familiar diesel cams of the Versatile hammer to a start. Though it was a half mile away, it was clearly the big tractor. When lights washed the tops of the creek willows, he knew James Carl was coming. He saw that Miguel knew it, too.

"Put it back in the water," Miguel said.

Billy laid the lamb in soft grass and walked the incline up and out of the creek to get a better look. The tractor was almost to the corrals. They hadn't bothered to kick dirt over the blood. Miguel and his brother joined Billy.

"He will know," Miguel said. Billy nodded. "Tell him that dog did it. Tell him we chased but too late." In the headlights, Billy saw James Carl standing at the corrals. "Tell him it was the dog," Miguel said again. Billy descended the slope to where he'd laid the lamb. He gathered it in his arms and climbed the rise, stopping beside Miguel. "You will tell him it was the dog?" Miguel asked.

Billy stood looking into the lights now heading his direction. "Stay in the creek bottom. Walk up it until you get to a fence. It goes right across the creek. Follow the fence back to the barn."

"You will say it was the dog?" Miguel asked.

Billy shook his head.

"It will be bad," Miguel said.

Billy nodded that it would, and carried the lamb into the lights of the Versatile.

D.E. FREDD

Steiner Requests His Hole Be Dug in Poland

From April/May 2007

The Border—April 1939

AH, POLAND! The giant, blundering cow lolling about her pasture, mindless of the fact that progress is barking at her heels. Poland—breathing in the dust of the past now ground so fine it barely grits the teeth, yet when one stands still long enough to catch a breath, there it is, visible in a thin coating over the entire land. Who knows? Perhaps she'll benefit from some good German housekeeping.

Any Hole: A general plan

The deeper the better. Level off the perimeter to reduce muddening. Keep the sides smooth. (Nothing stirs the soul more than the smell of freshly dug earth.) Calculate the hole in relation to the size of an average man. If he is German, place him feet first so as to allow him the privilege of speculation. If he is Polish, it matters little which end is where.

The Beginning of the End as Far as Steiner Was Concerned

A truck pulled itself up the hill to the edge of the trees, then stopped. There was a slight breeze. Hauptmann got out of the cab and turned towards the rear. From the back Endlich was the first out, then B., then Meyer. Some feel Steiner was already in the woods, but who could be certain in that twilight. Hauptmann gave his instructions to his men—short and to the point. B. broke from the small formation, headed back to the cab and shook hands with the driver. A signal was given; the truck reversed itself, then teetered down the hill as the four started into the forest. It was just seven. Suddenly shots were heard. Four Germans were dead in ambush and poor, bewildered Steiner was being held at bay by the Poles. So simple, yet so complex.

Steiner Tries to Explain the Entire Incident to All of Poland

I am Steiner. I wandered into your territory by accident.

—You were found two kilometers inside the border.

I had no idea where I was. I am a musician. I know nothing of politics. (These Poles are all fools as concerns interrogation. Belinski, in this case, in particular.)

—Your name again?

Steiner. I am a musician, violin.

—And the others?

I know none of the soldiers. I was on a picnic. My companion left to answer a call of nature and was overdue. I began a search. I swear it before Almighty God. (That's it, Steiner, swear. Test the breeze. Stand upwind from a Pole. Fart something divine. A Pole will smell it, then salivate his trust in return.)

Back to Those Shots in the Forest

The first—a quick, unsuspecting sound, which, had it not been so sudden and come during such a haphazard period of silence, might well have acted as a warning to the second already breaking through the underbrush and pummeling into the still crumpling body of Hauptmann. Then came the third and fourth—still distinct enough to be counted, and B. running from the rear, trying to keep low and to the side of the narrow trail and just getting up to the bend before the fifth shot rang out and he also halted, freezing in mid air until the sixth was heard and then he, too, slumped forward, a slight maroon circle visible beneath his side.

When it's all over and done with, and when "this" seems to be the choice between "this" or "that," there may not be a man there to write it down and record it the way it was, and that makes it all the more tragic, you see.

The Interrogation, 1

Each morning Steiner is asked two questions. They are pushed beneath the slotted door with his first meal in a neatly printed envelope. He feels obligated to answer each question, as it would require little more than a word or two and would be no trouble whatsoever to take care of the task preemptory to beginning his breakfast, such as it is. The questions concern objective information, but despite their simplicity, unhappily, they do not relate to him at present or to anything in his past. He would be quite happy to oblige, but they might as well be asking him the weather in the Sudetenland a year from now. This evidently angers them.

Because of grey, white always has so much more.

Interrogation, 2

From a medium distance one might think Belinski handsome, but his eyes, as one closes the gap, are set too close together, and his chin angles into his neck much too quickly. This causes him to breathe through the mouth. He has developed the habit of muttering. It's as if his brain were incapable of thinking inside itself. He reflects that punishment, to be effective, must occur soon after the offense. Yet torture often yields nothing more than a bastard version of the truth. The task then becomes sorting out the few strands of veracity within the fabric of any lie. It would take a brilliant mind to do that, and Belinski is certainly not brilliant; however, one must commend him for being aware of his limitations. He suspects torture would only further cement this German's elaborate hoax. A decent beating, just for appearance's sake, wouldn't ruffle any feathers. Therefore Steiner will remain a violinist, at least for the present.

They come each hour to thank him very much for making the best of things until they decide about the sun, for just because it's April is no excuse for May in these trying times.

Holes Again—Some Speculation

The basic difference between the German mind and the Polish may by typified by the way the two nations viewed fornication in 1939. For the Germans such an act was a highly effective and thoroughly proven method for producing more Germans. In fact their scientists did research into various aspects of the act as it might affect the resultant offspring. Unfortunately the statistical evidence was incomplete with respect to any correlation as concerns the following factors:

- position used
- temperature of the room or immediate area
- time of day or night
- food consumed before, during or after the occasion
- location of the respective genital organs
- occupation of the participants
- ability to quote Goethe or Schiller from memory

This is not to say that any of the above factors are to be ruled out, but it does mean they are not to be given as much weight as they once were.

For a Pole, fornication was an act the upper class might dabble in when time could be found for such a thing; something the middle class, God willing, might do between confessions; and, lastly, something by which the lower echelons sustained themselves because it would appear there was little reason for the poor Poles' existence once they had spent themselves in bed than to rearrange the bedclothes and proceed again as best they could. This probably accounted for the fact that time passed by much more quickly for Poland than Germany.

It Is a Very Pleasant Day So Far. The Sky Is Filled with Bundled Cloudlings, Which Edge Down to Extra-Hear Steiner Being Questioned

—Are you married?

Yes, to Frau Bremmer. I am her second husband.

—Her address?

She is on a concert tour. England at present, I believe.

—What were you doing on our border?

I was on an outing with a friend. I wandered.

—Who was this friend?

A young woman. We became separated before the shooting. I would appreciate your discretion in any report you might make.

There Is No Telling in What Situation a Man Can Find Himself These Days

Steiner is sitting in a chair. Belinski stands before him, the light from the swinging bulb gently pushing both shadows up the wall. Steiner remains firm. He is a violinist. Nothing can sway him from this point. Belinski has found a violinist two kilometers inside the Polish border. A violinist who claims he was about to ask four Germans if they had seen his mistress wander by. Steiner smiles faintly. A concertmaster's position awaits him in Gorlitz. Up to now the easy life—fame, modest fortune, success, marriage to the famous Frau Bremmer—now this! An impulsive outing, a needless flirtation with a concert hall usheress from Dresden who, as naked as Eve, suddenly sprints into the bushes clutching her skirts to her breasts. Other garments are tossed aside to mark a trail of seduction. An aging violinist stumbles after her who, having tasted of the young grape, now wishes the wine. Then shots interrupt the romp. Men break past him before toppling in death. A dog bares its teeth, and an out of breath violinist surrenders to both his passion and a Polish patrol.

No one can predict what a nose will think of its face.

What of Belinski?

Belinski is vacillating. Surely he has felt sexual urges before, and at times, they are well worth crossing a border. They are also worth being shot at, but never the trouble of being hit. Steiner is either a fool or a

German infiltrator. If he is a fool, then only the fear of God need be used. If he is a spy, then he must be killed as an object lesson to all those looking on from the west. That is the conundrum. Free of the present situation, a fool will soon expose himself. All Belinski need do is release Steiner to prove this. But Germans are wise enough to disguise such matters, so it would do no good to release him as nothing would be proven. It does no good to imprison him; what lesson could that serve? Belinski is at a loss. He looks again at poor Steiner for an answer, but the man has now assumed a position of some comfort. His head is bowed to shade the glare, arms folded across his chest, and his legs are crossed in an almost feminine fashion. He does not expect nor fear any more retribution because he is an artist. He has seen women weep at the very music he creates. A man who, in certain respects, is above other men, an *Ubermench*—gifted, respected, loved.

The Author Interrupts the Narrative to Insert Some Extraneous Material Relating to Holes in Various Countries and the Role, if any, Ascribed to Each

Ireland:

 The soil in this area is extremely rocky and coarse. One cannot sink a spade into the ground without hearing a sharp clank, the reverberation of which sends the entire body spinning. In accordance with this, there are few holes, and the people generally live above ground. This accounts for the high rate of Catholics.

Russia:

 These holes, taking precedence from their literature, are modeled, after a fashion, from the French. (It has been said, sarcastically, that Russian holes are really French holes dug by Russian *parvenus*.) They are not as deep as those in Germany and much narrower, yet several individuals are placed in the same hole without regard to sex or station in life. (This is certainly not the case in Great Britain.) Those in the holes are given little to sustain their lives and next to nothing in the way of comfort. It is considered honor enough to be in the bosom of Mother Russia. Occasional musical programs are planned and performed some distance from the aperture. Curiously, this has a soothing effect upon those involved, especially where a balalaika is used, and therefore the uproar and populous revolutions are not nearly as strident as those of their French counterparts.

Switzerland:

As strange as it may seem, there are no holes in this nation. This is because all individuals living in this location who have the need to dig a hole do so in a foreign country, bringing only the excess soil from such a hole back to their native land. Over the eons this behavior has led to the formation of a large mountain chain, the Alps, to which the Swiss attribute most of their fame and a majority of their culture. Few countries have taken note of this example, but unless one enjoys rocky, snowcapped mounds of foreign soil, there is little reason to do so.

The Narrative Resumes Only to Find That Steiner's Situation Has Grown Desperate

Steiner is escorted down a long dark hall into a small room. He is forced to strip. His large buttocks are reddened from the long sit. He is indignant but reserved. Sensitive but not shy. He has rarely exposed himself to men, and his hands show a concern for his condition. He is made to bend forward, inhale deeply, then is probed. He protests, but the search continues. A guard explores his genital area, and he, Steiner, vacillates between embarrassment and humiliation. Then, the search complete, he is placed in a cell adjoining the room under the careful eye of two guards. There is a cigarette from one of them. A simple gesture between human beings. Then Belinski enters, and Steiner is stripped again and beaten. A length of rubber tubing is used. The neck, back, and soles of the feet are targets. Steiner is rendered unconscious. Belinski orders the abuse stopped, leaving Steiner naked and, for the moment, alive.

The main supposition here is that life is somehow historical.

That Forest Again

The woods are quiet. It rained a few hours before, nothing much, just enough to ease the spades as they turn the earth. Belinski has selected the spot himself. A soldier informs him that all is ready and salutes smartly. Four bodies are placed in blankets, wrapped snugly, and secured with leather thongs. Leather takes four years to rot; blankets are never the same after three months. The bodies are placed in the shallow, roughly hewn graves. Reverence for the human being is still upheld—Belinski sees to that. There is a moment of silence. Belinski clears his throat to break it, and the deaths are now officially over. All evidence must be suppressed, so leaves are spread over the site lest the Germans discover their dead. Revenge is inherent in their kind, and whatever qualities they lack as humans beings, they more than compensate for by the tenacity to which they avenge injury to their own. Hence Belinski takes part in the cover up, smoothing the soil by hand as would a child playing in a schoolyard.

In 1939 even the very little ones looked so much smaller.

What About Belinski?

Belinski spent his lifetime in pursuit of success and fortune. Only a fool would attempt this in a bureaucracy, but nevertheless, Belinski tried. In the early years he dispensed useful information from behind a small desk in Warsaw: lavatory directions, transportation schedules, the location of various offices, that sort of thing. He did this menial job in such a way as to be noticed. He never nodded a perfunctory direction and never gave way to anger by the many redundancies of the day's inquires. No, Belinski was quite polite, his manner friendly and efficient. A train schedule always included the wish for a pleasant journey. Each day's weather carried with it a certain conversational uniqueness, which Belinski was quick to seize upon to anyone who passed by. As might be expected, important officials noticed his attitude.

From that obscure information desk, it was to the licensing bureau, and from there to the censor's office, where after a short stay, he was attached to Colonel V., the minister of the frontier. Yet Belinski was never a creative thinker. His main asset was that of plasticity, and with Colonel V. being the brute of a man he was, Belinski soon molded himself into a brute as well. Violators of V. (the famous July Papers called them traitors) were tortured and their signed confessions brought to V. by Belinski personally, further creating a bond between the two. Then V. abruptly left the scene for another post, and in his place came Gervitz, a former professor of literature. Belinski then read poetry. Volumes of Dryden and Keats were left clumsily on his desk, and Gervitz, noting this, soon took Belinski into his trust.

Times changed. Gervitz moved on. Belinski was now in charge of this section of the border, and there was no one to copy. Paperwork took up much of the time. Pleasures were few. Belinski had reached a point where his digestion limited the grand meals he sought so hard to afford. His prostate had blown to the size of a large mushroom, and his piles castigated his bowel movements, such as they were. Pleasing others was once a pleasure, but now personal safety haunted his evenings. Germany was on the move. One only had to read between the lines in the papers. Like kitchen ants they had secretly been crossing the border through these forests and fields while Poland had been tending its window boxes. Soon something would break, and Belinski would have the distinct honor of being the first Minister of the Frontier to lick German boots. He wondered if their ilk read poetry as Gervitz did. It would be of some compensation.

As fond of mercy as daybreak.

That Same Forest: In a Hole, Hauptmann

Hauptmann, the soldier, lies in the forest under a foot of earth. A worm is slowly burrowing its way through his leather boot. Hauptmann is unmoved by the matter. His dedication to life has ended. In a way it's a relief, as dedication for a German is always so much more burdensome than for another. But Hauptmann did his best. It is men like him who, with their unyielding faith in the adjective, always imbue any proper noun they come across with much more dignity than should be the case. Hauptmann was a good German. He was also a man. Many will say he dismissed the latter and concentrated solely on the former. Either way he is still dead, lying in a Polish forest with an energetic worm, the worm now free from the hindering restriction of yarn and leather, gorging itself upon his flesh. Fortunately, that good German blood is still warm.

How Is Steiner Doing?

Steiner has managed to drag himself from the floor of his small cell to the front steps of his home in Hamburg. He is dreaming of course, but it is one of the few ways his mind can maintain its sanity. He is now surrounded by comfort, including his favorite white wine, amply chilled. Suddenly the door bursts open, and Frau Bremmer enters, her face emblazoned with passion and her sultry voice filled with lewd suggestions (he taught her how to talk dirty, and now she enjoys it). She has just returned from a triumphal tour of concert halls and lovers, but at present her beloved husband Steiner is in her heart and soul. There is an embrace, something perfunctory yet essential to seasoned lovers. Then an impassioned kiss initiates a tumble of clothing, and the race for pleasure is on.

Later, when they have spent themselves, Steiner begins his story. He relates the forest and his capture, leaving out his female companion. He recounts Belinski and the terrible beating. As the past is revisited, blows rain down. He weeps, and tears stream down his face onto Frau Bremmer's breasts. She listens. She also weeps. Poor Steiner. She lets loose curses for the Poles in general. She embraces him, and like a small boy, he drifts into sleep in her arms. In the morning she will leave for Stuttgart to begin rehearsing the power of Wagner. She will make love with a French horn player. She cannot help this because sensuality is part of her artistic nature.

Belinski's Opinion of Matters as They Now Stand

Steiner's death would be a blessing, but Belinski is a bureaucrat. Accountability is the key. People never look at the act, only the papers relating to the act. Records can provide a shield during any inquiry. But instinct tells him to forgo the paper trail. It will be difficult to prove this case as black or white, and gray always has so many more forms in triplicate. So it would be better for Belinski to secretly take Steiner to the woods and do the deed himself. The more he thinks about it, he is positive, knowing his limitations, that this is the correct action. Steiner is a limitation. Limitations are generally placed in holes. Belinski knows where one can be dug.

Steiner Has His Worries Also

Steiner's mind is wandering. Things are not in their true perspective. He is a man whose life has been structured on a rococo theme, hence the bare cell and straw mattress add to his deprivation. The time was when he soaked his hands in olive oil before a performance; now they are cracked and swollen. He is only asked to confess to being a German infiltrator, a mild sin if one at all, but an affront to the dignity of any artist, let alone a violinist. The trouble with these Poles is that they have yet to forgive Mozart for overshadowing their Chopin.

What Will Become of Frau Bremmer When Steiner Is Gone?

Frau Bremmer is a beautiful instrument. Superb craftsmanship, she. A masterpiece of design: something made to be played but only by a master virtuoso. When this is done, her soul comes alive. It would be such a pity to waste something this precious on Steiner alone. No, the instrument lives on. It matters little who brings out the tone.

What Will Happen to Belinski Once Steiner Is Gone?

Belinski has a country home outside Warsaw. The road is lined with poplars and white birch, behind which and set far back into the fields sit the peasant cottages. The trip there is scenic, peaceful, and quite a change from the kowtowing, bureaucratic life to which Belinski must adhere. At his house he will greet his lovely wife and two growing sons. There will be an excellent meal: stuffed meats, wine, and fresh bread. Belinski will eat and drink his fill, then take time to recapture the exploits of his sons. After that he will spend the evening with his wife reminiscing their many years of hardship. They will go to bed, and perhaps in the morning he will confide his thoughts about Steiner to her.

A Letter Which Steiner Has Found the Time to Write

My Dearest Wife,

If those about me have their way, this will be the last time I shall communicate with you in word or spirit. If I were at liberty to explain the circumstance into which I have blundered, then I would gladly do so, but, alas, this is not the case, and I therefore must beg your forgiveness for the lack of specifics you will find in this note.

Let it be known I have tried, though failing on many accounts, to be faithful to you. My downfalls can be attributed to excesses of the flesh. It is a sad fact that throughout my lifetime I have never been able to control my appetites, though as I sense death approaching, I have seen, at long last, my folly in its true perspective. My tragedy, if one as insignificant as I can be said to have one, is that the sins for which I am being punished have gained me nothing.

In a word I became a victim of my own lust, to the extent that I not only surrendered my body to it but allowed it free reign over my mind. Hence it led me blindly (no, I cannot say "blindly," for had I given reason the courtesy it is due, matters would be different—I shall use foolish); it led me foolishly to the well-deserved edge of my destiny, where it has now become the task of others to proceed with my eventuality. The true tragedy (and this will be the last time I shall use that word) is that I am cognizant of my downfall; were it the other way, were it that I had no insight into my sins (in this event as well as others in my past), then I would not be due as much pity as you might be able to spare.

Enough then. I have rambled on, most of it meaningless to you as certain liberties in communication have been stripped from me. Let me say in closing, my sweet, that now, at the end, I realize it is you I love because I have been given a dying man's last reward, that of insight into my own soul. My death, though in vain, is deserved; your pity is my shroud.

> *Until our spirits meet, I remain your devoted lover and husband,*
> *Steiner*

As Suspected

Steiner is dead. It happened last night. Swift and without much noise. Belinski, an audience of one, was there to officiate. Steiner was calm, accepting. He asked that his hands remain free and refused a hood as he knelt. There was no moon, and the leaves on the path through the woods muffled any undue attention. Steiner spoke at great lengths of music. Mendelssohn in particular. He recalled his performance of the E Minor Violin Concerto, opus 64 at the Concertgebouw in Amsterdam. The applause. The encore. Death.

The Aftermath, September 1939

It has begun to rain in Poland. It is a hard rain, one with a rigorous, relentless persistence. At times the westerly wind rises and scatters it in flying shards that knife through the nation. It is the type of rain that, with the aid of time, will fill up all the holes Poland has had to dig and will soon cover the land with a thick brown mud. From now on no Pole can safely tread across an open field without fear of dropping to a watery death in the abyss. All is lost.

SOMA MEI SHENG FRAZIER

Maybe I Should Call This Fiction

From October/November 2014

MAYBE I SHOULD put on the red dress. Or the soft black slacks that hug my ass, paired with a sheer silk blouse. Who am I fooling? I don't have a sheer silk blouse. Maybe I should fly my Chinese colors— red, orange, purple, yellow, whatever, in bright floral patterns—rather than mixing and matching in a way that is synonymous with classic American style.

Maybe I should tell the story of falling up the concrete stairs outside our two-bedroom apartment when I was young: describe the unit's cheap interior, and how our cabinets were stocked with Doritos instead of oatmeal. Tang in the fridge instead of real juice.

Conversely, I might recall the splendor of the elite private school I attended: its gothic chapel with a 1928 Cram and Ferguson addition, and how I stood in the pew licking my lips slowly enough to give Jason Shelton a hard-on underneath the largest Aeolian Skinner pipe organ in the tri-state area.

Maybe I should recount the time my ex-girlfriend Brianna and I were followed for a quarter-mile or so down a rural road in Bronxville, New York, where we were taking an early evening stroll. Before pelting us with 32-oz cherry Icees that made me cuss and Brianna gasp (perhaps not at the cold, but the tragic loss of two 32-oz Icees), then peeling away, the ~~white~~ guys in the car shouted *Ugly nigger! Dirty Puerto Rican,* oblivious to my actual ethnicity. Ha! Joke's on you, ~~white~~ guys in the car.

Maybe I should put on the "boyfriend jeans." These are jeans made for women, but designed to look like borrowed men's jeans. Or I could borrow one of the elegant velvet jackets my mother paired with frowsy wool skirts, clogs, and other odd American items in an ill-fated effort to look less Chinese. Except none of them would fit me. My mother, already short, has shrunk further with age. Apparently in some states, people under 4'10" can request handicapped placards from the DMV. But in other states, being short isn't a disability.

Maybe I should tell you about the black students I've taught here in Oakland: how an extremely skilled debate team champion pulled a gun out of his waistband during a field trip, saying, *I'm so sorry Ms. Frazier. I forgot to ask how you felt about firearms.* Or I could deconstruct the ~~white~~ students. Last week, they spent half an hour arguing over neologisms—whether it's valid to make up one's own words—while I sat silently at the head of the table. Of course it's fucking valid. How do you think language is created?

Maybe there's no need to explain. You understand what I felt when the debate champion pulled his gun out (an intense fear for him) because you understand the intersections of race, history, oppression, and poverty. Or maybe you expected I would fear for my own life instead? Maybe you think all these black kids in Oakland are dying from gun violence because they're inherently violent and criminal. Well, it's one or the other, isn't it?

Maybe I should put my hair in a ponytail. With, like, a poof in the front? I don't know what it's officially called—the poof—but I do know some women actually insert a little piece of foam underneath their hair to form it. Maybe I should do this, and maybe I should also get breast implants, cadaver skin to plump up my lips and surgery to shorten my pinky toes so I can wear slim stilettos. Then, when my daughter asks why we look so different from each other, I'll tell her it's because I didn't like the way I looked back when I looked like her. Or maybe I'll say *Because you're black, and I'm not.* Clearly I wouldn't say *Because I'm half-white, and you're not,* because white is the norm and therefore needn't be remarked on. And I've said enough about Chineseness already!

Should I try and analyze why it is that I'm so fucking angry when I write—being a generally peaceable person? Oh. Now I remember. It's because I'm a generally peaceable person. When I'm not writing, I lie my ass off. See? Like many other Asian-Caucasian mixes, I've got no ass at all. *No, no. I get what you're saying. Of course I didn't mean it that way.*

Maybe if I actually had zero ass, my father wouldn't have raped me! Should I describe the way he made me hold a mirror to my private parts when I was young and "home-schooled?" The way that Planned Parenthood clinician pulled me aside to talk about internal scarring? Or how valuable I think Planned Parenthood is, although sadly they can only hold onto medical records for seven years? Damn. Too late to put pops away.

No, no, that's too much. I've told men about those things before, and they've backed slowly toward the door. In the metaphorical sense, of course. And when I've told women about it, they've rocked me in their arms. In the come-here-and-I'll-genuinely-rock-you-in-my-arms sense. Obviously, after that embarrassing moment, I've dumped them. So then, what if I just describe the frantic thrashing of the sapling outside the café where I sat writing earlier today? It could be a symbol.

The entire western wall was a window, and inside the café there was low, soothing music—while outside, a storm was fucking everything up. Making people run to their cars. It was hard for me to fathom how a barely-there pane of glass could render such lovely music mute out there, and such a feisty storm nonexistent in here. *What kind of tree is that?* I thought, sipping my frappuccino. *The city bans poplars due to their shallow root systems, but I'm pretty sure it's a tulip poplar.* Wait. Maybe it was more of a magnolia?

Anyway it was a tree getting thrashed by a storm. The newscasters sometimes talk about how America is destroying its wildernesses, but I'd rather that than the other way around. Have you seen *Naked and Afraid?* It's a show that drops people out in harsh landscapes, naked. And afraid. The things ~~white~~ folks come up with, ha!

Maybe I shouldn't have written that. But hopefully it's okay, seeing as how I'm half ~~white~~? Also, I'm not someone who supports fracking or environmental violations or what have you.

Okay. I should just wear some yoga pants, probably, with a big tee shirt and basketball shoes. Agh! Unlike my mom, I was born here, but I still don't know how to fit in at an important and possibly life-changing event. I don't know what to wear with my elegant velvet jackets. Who am I fooling? I don't have elegant velvet jackets.

After the ~~white~~ guys in the car drove away, my girlfriend and I went home and undressed and lay on our cheap air mattress and licked one another's tears, and then fast forward we moved back to Oakland, California, fast forward she received something spurious in the mail, fast forward she kept asking me to hit her so finally I did and our dog was so upset he ran in a circle around us and shat on the floor, fast forward we broke up, fast forward became friends—the type of very close friends who talk rarely because talk is irrelevant, but yesterday we did speak, and she told me that if I intended to publish this story, I should remove every instance of the word ~~white~~ because the publishing industry is very ~~white~~.

So maybe I can explain the race thing as follows: no, it's not like I'm black or Native American or even the type of Asian American that negates racial privilege or anything, but I grew up fat and mixed-race in rural New Hampshire where my not so affectionate nicknames were *Chunk* and *Chink*. Also, as you may have discerned from the news, Oakland is a war zone, and it's hard to live for decades in a war zone and avoid writing about the war. Especially when your husband is a black man and you have a little daughter whom, no, you did not adopt. And okay. I get it: it's not fair to drop that kind of bomb about my father, Floyd, either, and then just let it sit there ticking. But most bombs don't really tick. Do they? (Maybe you know.)

Last week, I wrote a story about a gang rape set at the elite private school where I gave Jason Shelton a raging boner underneath the largest Aeolian Skinner pipe organ in the tri-state area. (No, he's not really named Jason. Nor is my ex-girlfriend named Brianna or my father Floyd, but the names are very close.) Actually, it was a story about a young woman coming to grips with her parents' relationship as she considers her own engagement to a kind and generous guy named Jack. (The guy in the story is really named Jack.) But my mom only read up to the gang rape scene. Then she set the manuscript down on her office desk and phoned me. *Did you send this story out yet?* she asked. *If not, I think you should remove the school's name. You could get sued,* she advised.

I don't think I can get sued, I said. *Because it's fiction.*

Sometimes people disguise reality as fiction, she said.

Well, if it's reality then I won't get sued, either, right?

I could hear her chewing her cud. Or maybe it was peppermint gum; she likely still favors peppermint gum over cud. *The other reason you should change the name,* she added, *is that kind of thing doesn't happen at the school.*

What? I said. After some small talk, we hung up. Then I sent her the Clery Act-mandated public log of crimes recently reported on the campus of the high school in question. The rapes averaged about four per month. The next day, she called again.

At first we didn't talk about the gang rape story, which was really a story about what's-her-name and Jack. But then, very casually, my mom said, *The reason I think you should change the gang rape scene in your latest story is that the dialogue isn't realistic. How can I trust that this ever really happened?*

It was at that moment that I understood she wasn't talking about my story. She was talking about my father. Actually, we never talk about my father. And in the larger sense, she was in fact talking about *my story.* So maybe I got all that backward?

Oh! You know about the Clery Act? No, they haven't extended it to apply to secondary schools participating in federal financial aid. The rape in the story wasn't really set at the school I attended at all. I feel like even more of a traitor telling you this, but in fact it was set at the cushy private college where my mother works. But—look—I've omitted the names of *both* schools from this piece, at my mother's advice. (No, I haven't really asked my mother for advice about this piece. What do you think I am, suicidal? Don't answer that!)

Anyway I don't have much to say about the school with the pipe organ, as we could only afford to enroll me in a six-week summer program. Beyond that I attended—and graduated from—a low-ranked public school whose wayward students may or may not have set another low-ranked public school on fire.

In conclusion, my husband and I now live in a very nice house, with oatmeal in the cabinets and real juice in the fridge. And as for falling up the stairs, our daughter has only done so on cushioned Berber carpet. But I did write a long and rambling bit about the concrete stair incident:

I died as a toddler, at the bottom of a community swimming pool in Amarillo, Texas. The water was cold and soft. I saw limbs and bodies gliding by and, sinking, tried to copy their movements. I remember being surprised when that didn't work. Taking my first breath underwater was tough, but after that it got easier, like stealing, surviving, betrayal, and other things that should remain difficult but become easy once you've done them enough. The floor of the pool was prickly as a cat's tongue, and I grew heavier and dimmer there while my lungs filled. It would've been the last growing I did, but a skilled teenage lifeguard saw me. I guess by now he's a grandfather, but once he was an angel of mine, and who knows how many others'—all before turning nineteen.

Afterward I was returned, dry, clean, alive, by the aunt who had misplaced me, to my father's arms (another soft suffocation I would narrowly survive), and she said, *I'm sorry for the pain I've caused you, Floyd.*

My father, selfless martyr, corrected, *Caused her, not me,* but as he would turn out to be in so many irreversible ways, he was wrong. Dying was not painful. The pain came later, after I'd died, when I punched my girlfriend in the gut; aborted the first baby; felt the pulp of my family slide through my hands; attempted clumsy teenage suicide but only succeeded in shattering both knees; was the fat kid; asked my mom what *Chink Chink Chink* meant and read her face; went falling up our concrete stairs, knocking out two baby teeth; ran my finger down the business end of a butcher knife—and my eyes flew open, and I saw my angel's focused grace—his blond, wet hair, his steady gaze—as he pushed the water up and out. Yes, how it hurt coming back to life.

See? I told you it was long and rambling!

Maybe I should go with the red dress after all. I've got a great ass, and the dress shows it off. Maybe I should describe the enormous, flying cockroach I encountered in Tokyo once. Maybe I should be more whimsical in print, dress, and comportment. Wait. Am I deciding what to write, here, what to wear, or what to talk about once I get there? And I haven't even stated where it is I'm going. I'm sorry.

Leave it to me to confuse things so terribly. Maybe I should wear the tuxedo pants with ~~white~~ shoes. After all, it's still four days to Labor Day.

ALFREDO FRANCO

Song of the Jet

From January/February 2011

MOST WEEKENDS I spent with my mother. There wasn't much difference between her rectitude and that of the nuns at St. Mark's, where I boarded during the week. Saturday mornings after breakfast she would confine me to the dining room to do homework. Then she'd quiz me on the *Baltimore Catechism* in preparation for my First Communion, followed by pitiless drills of the multiplication tables, which I still did not master though I was seven-and-a-half years old.

Weekends when it was my father's turn were very different. My father would pull up to the school on a Friday evening in his two-seater Lotus Elan, with the top down if the weather was good. It was a white roadster with a black racing stripe down the middle and a well-stocked Executaire travel bar in the trunk. My father would leap out of the leather seat lithely. He worked for Bendix, The Tomorrow People, and made an ample salary.

Sister Magdalene, who had acne red as a third-degree burn, would hand me my little Scotch-plaid suitcase, and Sister Anne-Sophie would remind me to do my homework and to take suppositories if I got a fever. "I've packed some in his bag," she'd point out to my father. My dad would scoop me up with a "Hey, buddy!" and I'd suck in his invigorating scent of Bay Rum and Vitalis. We'd rush out to his car; he'd loosen his tie and rev up the engine. The other boys peered through the barred dormitory windows in awe and envy. And away we tore.

My father lived in a modern high-rise near the airport, with an endless supply of airline stewardesses and jet-setting women as his house-guests. In those days airports were cathedrals of aviation, sleek and spacious with sloping walls of glass. My father's building was airport-like, international style, with contrapuntal cantilevers and pristine white walls. From his bachelor's suite you could watch the planes coming and going, so close you could read the logos on the tail rudders. I could identify them all—Eastern, Piedmont, Pan Am, TWA.

His efficiency had a galley kitchen and a bar, bottles and shakers arranged to suggest the Manhattan skyline. He owned a Clairtone stereo system with futuristic round speakers and an Ampex reel-to-reel tape machine. But his most unusual toy was the Wurlitzer Elektrika Music Lounger, a white, horizontal bed made of fiberglass that looked like a coffin with the ends rounded. You could connect it with a cable to the record-player or the reel-to-reel component and listen through internal speakers. A small, red bulb on its outer side lit up like an angry eye. Inside it was lined with wadded white satin. It had just enough space for two to make love to "The Girl from Ipanema." I was afraid to lie in it, but my father often chose it over his actual bed when fucking his girlfriends.

Regarding music, my father rejected the rhythms of his Cuban homeland. Loud, wild Cuban music wasn't my father's style of seduction. His was Brazil, the subtle strains of Tom Jobim and Astrud

Gilberto. He particularly loved Brazil 66 doing "So Many Stars," the understated rhythm fading wistfully at the end, like a plane disappearing in the twilit distance, by which time the woman had melted in his arms and would be eased into the Wurlitzer Elektrika. It worked like a charm.

My dad's girlfriends were my girlfriends. The stewardesses were trim, wholesome, clean, all-American women with healthy complexions, flip hairdos, and an impeccable work-ethic. They had names like Beth, Mary Ann, and Linda. When they spoke, they sounded like the telephone lady, Jane Barbe, with vibrato-less, crystal-clear enunciation. I loved their crisp, simple uniforms, their satin scarves, their pillbox hats emblazoned with silver wings, their conch-shaped vanity cases, the efficient, economical grace of their every movement. They were like the planes themselves, cool and brave and thrilling. After nights of vigorous lovemaking, they would rush off conscientiously in fine stiletto heels to work early-morning flights to Cincinnati, St. Louis, or Rio de Janeiro.

The other women were foreign and less meticulous about hygiene. Their bodies gave off earthier smells. There was Lupe, the bronze Brazilian, who suffered temper tantrums; she had killed her husband in Bahia, we later learned, breaking his skull with an iron skillet. There was Anna, the melancholy Italian, who had thick, pouting lips like Monica Vitti; there was Amanda, the English swinger, who wore black leather jumpsuits with multiple, tantalizing zippers; and there was Huan-Hui, the delicate Vietnamese with black hair hanging straight down to her tight little butt. While the American stewardesses liked to ply me with candy, the Italian held me close as she read *Being and Nothingness*, and Amanda tried to teach me judo. For a time it was the doll-like Huan-Hui I loved most of all. I remember the day my dad, Huan-Hui, and I went on a cruise along the Potomac and got off at an abandoned islet. I went down on my knees before her, as if practicing for First Communion, and declared: "I hereby name this island Huan-Hui."

There wasn't a bedroom in my father's apartment, just a big walk-in closet. My father kept his Brooks Brothers suits there, his several pairs of Allen Edmund shoes, his dozens of ties and monogrammed shirts. His actual bed was placed outside, facing the window; you could count planes instead of sheep. Above the bed hung crossed medieval swords. When a woman spent the night and it was time for cognac in snifters, I was told to go into the closet, where my father would roll in the TV to distract me. But it was impossible to pay attention to anything on the screen. I could hear the rustling of garments as they fell to the floor, the escalating sighs and moans. I always knew if he was using the Wurlitzer Elektrika because it creaked when bucking movements began, or if Lupe was reaching climax, because she'd scream hysterically. (My father once showed me the pink lacerations on his back from her fingernails, boasting how he had wrestled her down like a tiger.) And there I was, sitting in the closet, fuming, because, after all, they were *my* women, too. I hated being left out. I hated being a child. Sometimes, though, one of the women would take pity on me and knock on the closet door to offer me candy or a hug, not minding if I saw her in a slip or panties.

Every time I returned to St. Mark's from weekends with my father, I would compare the nuns to his lovers. The nuns were hulking horrors in black habits; they smelled of dirty feet, Oleum Infirmorum, and the sad, buttered toast served in the convent for breakfast, lunch, and dinner. Sister Aubel, the Mother Superior, had stubble on her upper lip—the light would rake it when she glared down at me at report card time. Sister Anne-Sophie would box me on the ear for the slightest infraction. Sometimes she threatened to lock me in the school basement with a Negro. He'd beat me and make me his slave, she'd warn with a chilling smile.

My mother also compared negatively to my father's women. I hated the peasant scarf she wrapped over her huge hair rollers at night. Though educated by American nuns in Havana, she could not get rid of her embarrassing accent—she'd say *oh-ven* for oven, and "beach" always came out as *bitch*. She wore big-buttoned, woolen blouses in red plaid that were scratchy and smelled like a dog in the rain. Her face was gaunt, joyless; she was flat-chested, with thin, ungenerous lips; she had a mannish aggression when it came to arguing a bill, defending the Republican Party, or competing for a parking space. Although I sensed my mother's deep loneliness, I sided with my father.

One Saturday night I was dispatched to the closet as usual, but this time I peeked out. Instead of sex I saw Mary Ann in her TWA uniform, powder blue with a round, white, Catholic schoolgirl collar. She stood very still and quiet, looking at my father, who also said nothing. He held a martini glass, empty save for the eyeball of an olive pierced by a little plastic sword. The single sound was the white hum of the central air-conditioning.

There was so much space between, around them. My father smiled fatuously, his tie a crooked noose. He made a gesture toward the Wurlitzer Elektrika, but Mary Ann just stood there, unblinking, firm, self-possessed, her fine features and perfect brunette flip sculptural in the stillness. "I feel sorry for you," she said finally in her clear, even voice. "I mean, living this way..." She picked up her handbag and pivoted toward the door as I receded into the closet. *Don't let her go, Dad!* American happiness was leaving us forever. I heard the door of the apartment click shut.

Another weekend, no women appeared. My father was vague when I asked about them, especially about Mary Ann. I went back to St. Mark's sullen, kicking against everything that the nuns asked of me.

I didn't see my dad again for over a month, what with First Communion practice and my mother tightening her discipline as report card time approached. I spent my classes dreaming of Mary Ann, of flying away with her to Rio on a Boeing 707, leaving all of these ugly nuns and my insipid mother behind.

I couldn't wait for Dad's next visit. On his appointed day he called, but to cancel. I started crying right there in the office and developed a fever. In the infirmary Sister Anne-Sophie shoved a suppository up my ass.

Dad canceled for my First Communion, too. I went through the motions in my white shirt, white jacket, knee-length white pants, white socks, and white shoes. The Host tasted like cardboard. I was careful not to bite down on it. The nuns said I'd be biting Jesus.

Finally, one Friday afternoon, my father reappeared. Sister Anne-Sophie handed me my suitcase packed with two days' worth of clothes, my arithmetic book, a *Jane's Guide to Passenger Aircraft*, and three suppositories wrapped in tinfoil. Dad took me in his arms. I hugged him especially tight. As we went down the front steps, I looked for the Lotus Elan. Instead a pus-yellow Ford Falcon awaited us. It was a used '63 model, the grille and headlamps reminiscent of a depressed dog.

"Where's the Lotus?" I asked with alarm. I knew the boys were watching expectantly from the windows. My father ignored me and kept walking. I repeated my question. "Hey, Dad—what about the Lotus?"

He turned on me with sudden ferocity: "Were you waiting for *me* or for the *Lotus*?" I looked down, withered.

At his apartment we started talking again. I asked him to make me a Roy Rogers on the rocks ("And don't be stingy with the grenadine!"). He replied with unusual firmness: "No drinking today." He didn't mix himself a martini, and I noticed that the Manhattan skyline was broken up, missing several bottles. In fact the whole apartment was a mess, clothes lying everywhere, dirty ashtrays, newspapers, and ties like dead snakes hanging over the rim of the Wurlitzer Elektrika. He didn't cook that evening, either. I'd been hoping for steak tartare or herring soup with strawberry jam and champagne. Instead we had a drab fried chicken dinner at the Howard Johnson's.

Surely after dinner we'd drive to the airport. We usually did, if none of our women were with us. Maybe we'd meet Mary Ann just back from Rome or Tallahassee. Then I remembered a pencil case I'd seen months ago at the airport shop. I don't know why, but suddenly I just *had* to have it. It had a map of the world on the plastic lid and two narrow windows at either side, one for the names of countries, another for the capitals. By turning two dials below, you matched up each country to its capital. Not all the countries were on it, just the big, important ones. Cuba didn't qualify.

"Are we going to the airport, Dad?"

"Not tonight, buddy."

"But... Dad? Ya see... There's this pencil case that Sister Anne-Sophie said I have to use in class. She told us all to have one by Monday. I *really* need it and the only place they sell it is at the air—"

"I said *no*. Now finish your milk and let's go home."

My father had never denied me anything. This was a different person from the sunny, generous man who'd been my father. Perhaps this wasn't my father at all but Sister Anne-Sophie's Negro wearing a mask of my father. I wanted my mother. The Ford Falcon smelled like linoleum and old vomit.

When we got home, he poured himself a tumbler of Seagram's VO, forgetting his earlier injunction against drinking. I hoped we'd settle on the couch and watch the star-like planes and listen to Brazil 66 on the Clairtone or the Ampex, but instead he turned on the TV. We lay in the unkempt bed, fully clothed, squinting in the flickering TV light. He didn't say a word. His right arm was locked around my neck, the cuff-button branding my cheek. He drank VO and smoked a chain of Winstons with his free hand. I peered up at the crossed swords directly over my head, worried they might fall and impale me. To the right the Wurlitzer Elektrika's evil eye stared at me. I tried to remember some of Amanda's judo to loosen my father's hold.

Bonanza came on, an episode in which Lorne Greene punches one of his sons, Little Joe. Suddenly Dad spoke, his voice lit with VO. He said Lorne Greene reminded him of his own father back in Cuba, and that his father, too, had punched him once.

"What for?"

"I got the crazy idea," he said, "of starting my own conga band."

I did not know what a conga was. It sounded like King Kong. He took another gulp of VO.

"I invited all the niggers in the neighborhood. My dad came home earlier than expected and found us all there, beating the *shit* outta those drums. He pulled out his revolver, a goddamn *revolver*, yeah, like a cowboy, and the niggers ran for their lives. Then he knocked me out with a single punch, right in the kisser. How 'bout that, buddy, huh?"

I knew little about my father's Cuban life. I thought of him as American, cool as Stu Bailey from *77 Sunset Strip*. He wasn't like those Cuban men who ran the Hispanic grocery—puny, brownish men with pencil-thin moustaches, reeking of goat-cheese. No, my father was tall, clean-shaven, sandy-haired, fair of skin. Unlike my mother, he spoke General English without a Spanish accent. When he said "back home," people thought he meant Peoria. He worked for Bendix, The Tomorrow People, not in some *bodega*. He was at the cutting edge of the future; thanks to him, someday there would be cities beneath the sea and passenger flights to the moon. He lived in a world of beautiful women, slide-rules, Microtomic pencils, electronic music loungers, transcontinental jets, and—except for the inexplicable Ford Falcon—fast cars.

His lock relaxed. I rubbed my cheek to erase the button branded on it. I twisted my neck this way and that, grateful to be free.

"What do you think, buddy?" my dad asked, pouring himself another VO. "How 'bout we call your grandfather? Wouldn't you like to talk to him, all the way in Cuba?" He lit another Winston and squinted at me through the brown, acrid smoke. He seemed far away. There were bags under his eyes and a big, damp stain on his shirt under his arm, where my head had been trapped. He did not look like the fresh, well-groomed man I loved.

"But how? Does he speak English?"

He put the drink down angrily and pulled the Winston out of his mouth. I held my breath.

"Does he speak English? Come on, buddy! He used to go around Havana in a fucking Stetson *hat*. Why do you think he made me spend seven years at that military school in Ohio, not even letting me go home at Christmas? So I'd forget Spanish, *that's* why. Jeez, I don't even remember how to say *cunt* in Spanish. Well, at least I don't talk like a spic like your mother."

He took another mouthful of VO and looked at me, daring me to contradict him. I felt a new allegiance to my mother, but I was too scared to stand up to this transfigured father. He might make me lie in the Wurlitzer Elektrika.

Dad walked over to the Wurlitzer—my heart stopped—and mashed his Winston into its side, leaving a permanent black burn in the white fiberglass. He wiped his lips on the sleeve of his sweaty shirt and went into the walk-in closet. He came back with a dog-eared, leather address book. It held the precious numbers of the world's most beautiful women, but also, in fading ink, of people left behind in Cuba. In those days it took a long time to connect to Havana. You had to go through the operator. I waited patiently for the first hour, intrigued but also frightened to speak to the man who had punched my father. By midnight my eyes burned with sleep. My father just stood there, the receiver at his ear lodged in place by his right shoulder. He smoked, guzzled VO, and gazed at something on the horizon of his memory.

Struggling to keep my eyes open, I said, "Can I hear, Dad?"

He extended the receiver toward me. I heard the blackness of watery depths, waves of muffled static, wires or cables shifting... The murky sound was like an impenetrable wall of rain, soot, and smoke.

"I can't hear anything, Dad."

I fell asleep, dreaming that crucifixes were departing every three minutes for Rio, Rome, and Oklahoma City. Sister Anne-Sophie was forcing me to eat a dish called Cuba that consisted of suppositories mashed on buttered toast, and she was crying because I refused to eat it and there was no money for other food, or for pencil cases, and I was, she said, the most selfish little boy in the world. I saw my mother dead in the Wurlitzer Elektrika Music Lounger, and I knew I was now completely alone. Crucifixes took off from runways, landed, roared through the skies...

I woke up in tears and saw my father with the phone still at his ear. All he kept saying was "Hello?" in a different voice each time, as if he were searching for the one voice that would impress his father most. Some of the hello's were swaggering, others clipped like a hardboiled detective's, another cheerful, expansive, even forgiving. It was frightening to hear his multiple voices. I went under again, heavy with sleep.

I awoke with the telephone cable stretched tight across my throat. I wriggled out from under it; it descended, a tensed umbilical cord, into the Wurlitzer Elektrika.

My father's voice came from inside the berth, hollowed out, as if in a cavern. "You bastard," I heard. "You fucking bastard."

My father's voice buckled with a sob, then went on.

"I lost my job at Bendix. Ever hear of them, Bendix, The Tomorrow People? The Tomorrow People—isn't that what you called Cubans? *Mañana, siempre mañana,* you'd scream at the niggers in your lumber yard... Can you hear me, Dad? You wouldn't even let me come home for Christmas. Not even for a lousy Christmas..."

Then his voice sprung like a panther.

"I hope that Castro hangs you from piano-wire. I hope that Castro castrates you. Do you hear me? I hope you shit in your pants! I hope you—!"

"Dad!" I shrieked. "Is it your dad? Is it *him*?"

There was a long silence. I feared he'd died, like my mother in the dream.

"Dad, where are you? Dad, I love you... Dad? *Please!*"

Slowly my father sat up in the Wurlitzer Elektrika and looked at me with a sad smile. His hair was disheveled, his shirt crumpled as if he had been in a fight. He climbed out of the berth shakily and came toward me, cradling the telephone receiver in both hands.

He held the receiver before my face—it smelled of liquor, cigarette breath, and the dried-out spittle of rage. I took it, careful as an altar boy handling a ciborium. I raised it to my ear, but holding it just a little away, as if the invisible grandfather might hit me from faraway Cuba.

"Hello?" I asked in a trembling voice. "*Hello?*"

Muffled static. Blackness. An oceanic moan.

RICHARD DRAGAN

The Builder of Invisible Bridges

From July/August 2012

AS A CHILD, he was often visited by angels, their susurrant wings churning the dead air in his dark attic room over his mother's crowded apartment where he tried unsuccessfully to sleep—wings like the ears of a herd of elephants flapping on the quiet savanna, something vast and terrible and delicate all at once. At moments like this in nightscape and near dream in a sad child's world, Malak was happy enough.

He had returned to his small, terrified country after the fall of the Communists. He had studied in England and briefly in the United States. He was a now a middle-aged structural engineer who worked in an architectural firm run by new and eager capitalists. Originally, thinking it would be safe, Malak had planned to help build his country up from its humble architectural doldrums, to make it into a new country, to create shining cities of glass where once there were none.

He knew the hidden forces in bridges were always in motion, that a good bridge distributed its weight like the human frame, its musculature cables and steel instead of bones and sinew.

Everywhere he had been, they said he was a sad man, but that was because he was often alone. He now lived with his old Aunt Beier, the sister of his mother, who had passed away before all the fighting began. Perhaps he seemed sad because he was unlucky. He was always ten minutes late for his appointments. He had never in his 41 years gotten a proper seat on a bus or a train. The instant one opened up, it was occupied by someone else, usually an elderly person, not that he minded. Nonetheless, every day, Malak went to work over his draftsman's table with his rulers and pens, collaborating with the architects to give flesh to their designs, to make sure their shining new cities would last for decades.

At first, there was optimism. Four new office buildings were going up, as well as the restoration of old buildings after years of totalitarian neglect. Then the fighting started, and those projects were abandoned, if only temporarily. Then Malak's firm was hired by the new government to take over the clean-up of buildings damaged by the civil unrest. He saw photographs of buildings torn from within and without. Had he been a surgeon and the structures human torsos, he would have been justified in his sadness. But then he remembered how people lived inside these buildings once, and so it was quite gratuitous to worry about mere edifices in such difficult times. But anyhow, most of the casualties could not be salvaged, so he became an expert in the mechanics of demolition: how to bring down a building cleanly without it toppling over in unexpected ways, using its own bulk against itself, severing key bones and tendons to set it crumbling inwards, safely, as simply as possible.

A few months later, the shelling became so commonplace that no one had time to think of dead buildings. The generals were doing his work for him, creating a more unpredictable rubble, but rubble all the same. So, outmoded by the efficiencies of warfare that made building unnecessary and did a better job of tearing down, Malak's firm closed for good.

Malak was forced to find other work to avoid being conscripted. So he toiled in a government office filing microfiche, the documents of 40 years of surveillance of a people by its police. He spent hours a day photographing mountains of files containing the minutiae of a citizenry's life.

"Do you want to see your files?" Horst once asked.

Horst was a former party official who had grown fat and bald with profit during his association with the ruling faction. When it had fallen out of power, he was given a sinecure position in the same operation where Malak now worked. As children, Horst and Malak had often played together, before Malak had escaped to England to live with his cousin.

Despite his recent demotion, Horst still liked to pretend he commanded influence. His wide face was open and joyful as he tried to entice Malak with the offer of his dossier.

"Do I have files?" Malak asked.

Horst only chuckled to himself. "Oh, everyone has a file," he said.

The belly of the building was gorged with paper, as if it had, with a growing and obsessive appetite, consumed as much as it could for 40-odd years. (It was known that in the last days of the regime, the security police had chronicled everything about the movements of so-called dissidents in such great detail that they had not realized the entire country was afoot.)

The proverbial forest had been consumed by fire, Malak thought. And after all, that was why he had come back, to experience this newly discovered flame.

"I can get your file if you want," Horst said. "It would take some time, but I could get it."

So Malak agreed. It did not concern him so much what he would find. He knew he was not a happy child. His father had moved away to Germany, and his mother had been left behind. Then he had escaped himself.

"I can't believe it, my friend," Malak said, "that I would have been of interest to anyone."

"In the East, we were surrounded by angels," Horst chortled. "Don't you know each of us had a guardian, in fact a team of guardians, all listening in?"

By then, Malak did not suspect he had ever had any sort of protector, angel or otherwise.

In the free zone of the city, free from the regulation of the authorities, it was easy to see how the black market flourished. You wouldn't think, of course, of the danger involved in going to the market to buy food and other household necessities. You wouldn't think it a luxury of the civilized world, but it was. Malak knew this because he had bought groceries in London many times, and it was never like this.

When the shelling started, you heard only two or three thunderbursts before realizing the impending tragedy you were about to become a part of—that the next one was for you, and there was little to do except dive under the nearest stall with its collection of lettuce or turnips or cabbage. Or more likely, you didn't hear the thunder at all because you were hurled through the air at the speed of sound, made unconscious, the shrapnel in its approximation of God or the science of chance cutting the flesh for some, cutting vital arteries, nerves, or large organs, whether mortally or no. The shells were ruthlessly stochastic, rooted in chance, despite their outward appearance of being attached to one's usual sense of morality, in the crisscrossing lines of political or cultural forces here in Malak's small and terrified country.

The fortunate ones like Malak got a chance to think over things, lying in their hospital beds recovering, lucky enough to have morphine as the rent flesh tried its best to heal itself with whatever improvisatory skills the makeshift surgeon could offer. The victims thought to themselves how ill-fated they were, or even how lucky they were, trying to discern what great forces were at fault for the missing foot which now so insistently reminded its owner it once was there, in dreams calling out its presence in images of running through a field covered with tall summer grasses which scratched both bare feet and legs. The wounded thought to themselves, *Who was really at fault here?* It was the military on both sides, the archaic feelings of nationalism. It was the brutal history of the people. More generally, perhaps it was human nature itself, as selfish and power-hungry as it was.

But to Malak, the real fault belonged to his Aunt Beier, who sent him to the square that morning to buy provisions as the old woman was too tired, she said, to wait on the queues that inevitably formed in front of any vendor with any decent goods to sell. It was just such a line that Malak was caught in.

Yet Malak could not blame Aunt Beier. She was old and quite infirmed, badly arthritic now, but with the bright intelligence shared with his late mother. If Aunt Beier had gone, perhaps, she would have met with his fate, losing a limb like he did. But he was undoubtedly hardier than she was, he knew, and so she may have not pulled through the surgery.

Resting in his makeshift bed, a cot really, clear fluid diffusing into his blood and under what medication they could afford to give him, Malak tried not to torture himself with hypothetical sentiments of what might have been, for it was every kind of tragedy that had conspired to relieve him of his foot. It was political, historical, the confluence of local and specific accident that had worked together to accomplish this.

In real life, he was always a bit off-schedule by a dozen minutes at least. If only he could have been late that day in the square when the projectile came whizzing—or, he corrected himself, not actually whizzing since it was traveling faster than the speed of its own sound, exploding before its victims could have possibly perceived it with their ears, except of course if they ruptured an eardrum in the instantaneous change of pressure. Malak and the other five victims were too busy traveling at the speed of impact to their separate destinies, the few milliseconds that would separate the lucky from the unlucky, both in varying degrees, the survivors from those pulled lifeless from the wreckage: a relief, it would seem to Malak, to the rescue workers since they could proceed at their leisure. For Malak, it was a short and transforming half a second. Wasn't it strange to realize that unlike an anatomical drawing, the human body was not inviolable? When dropped from a high place or impacted with a piece of metal moving almost 1,000 feet per second, it did not give way like those American cartoons that showed the flesh bend and bounce comically back to the original shape. The real body, and one's special sense of it as perfectly adequate, despite one's aches and pains and imperfections of shape and texture and size, was easily broken.

When something like this happened, one's special sense of wholeness as a being separate from the cosmos and at once having a special place in its orders was eliminated, as simple as exhaling a last panicked breath enroute to a thankful unconsciousness. One saw the error of one's previous thinking, its fragility. In fact, Malak thought to himself, from his cot at the hospital, it was that material inside one's head that was particularly responsible for the accident of perception that led to such a betrayal about one's sense of the world and one's station in it. The brain was the culprit, thinking in its pride that because it seemed to possess a solid anchor on the substance of what existed around it, it was its master. When confronted with the errors of its previous life, of its subsequent shell-shocked descent from earlier bliss, Malak's brain reacted with a gnawing vehemence. Even though his injuries were obviously more severe in other places, evidenced by his bandaged leg and the single hump protruding underneath the covers at the end of the bed, he found now his head ached most of all, and his eyes and ears, too—though his hearing, mercifully, had been spared. He would have done anything to rid himself of these discomforts so he could ponder his new body, now that the old one was gone. Though he still had a body, it was different physically now, and his sense of it would be different as well.

His mind would never be the same, now that it saw only grotesques in the world's shapes. A bluish light of twilight made its way weakly through the tiny rectangular windows there at the hospital, and dim though it was, it only made Malak's head throb. The gruel they fed him, for he was still to unable to sit up and eat for himself, with its flavorless consistency, only made Malak more aware of his previous failings.

As a student in the university, he had read the story of a man who was wounded in battle during the Crusades. He had forgotten his name by now, though the man in question might have been French. While this man was awaiting the decisions by his surgeons—whom Malak guessed were just as likely to kill him by accident as to cure him as his own doctors were, their lack of supplies making up for their lack of skill—this medieval Frenchman had thought of converting his life over to something of value. It might have been to give himself over to the church, or to pursue wild success as a wealthy trade merchant, or to become—if it were still possible—a great lover to the women of the courts across Europe.

Likewise, Malak's mind ranged over a wide list of possibilities when he considered the fallen man thinking of what he would become now that he might not be able to do anything. (But of course, Malak would manage. Others had, and he would, too.) Malak thought of his own life, beyond the present conflict, which had to exhaust itself sooner or later.

Things had not gone well for the Frenchman in question, though. His war lasted 30 years, eventually. That man was miraculously healed by his surgeons, who were themselves surprised by his splendid recovery. But since he was a man of great imagination but little diligence, he did not choose to become a monk, or a merchant, or a great lover of the ladies of Europe. Instead, out of habit, he went back to battle for the glory of France against the pagan Turks and was killed in the war the following year.

As for Malak, he knew he would leave the country if he could, even though that was nearly impossible since the army, as a matter of course, controlled all the border towns. And he suspected that in his state now, he wouldn't be able to move very fast, at least for a while. In any case, he felt lucky when his mind and his body were put at rest for an evening or two during those weeks of convalescence.

One afternoon—it was a Saturday—Malak was awakened by a familiar though still unpleasant voice.

It was Horst, who said hello and expressed suitable sympathy regarding Malak's recent injuries and how he was he hadn't visited before, but he had been quite busy. Horst was now a capitalist, albeit a very cynical one, who worked in both the black and gray markets selling whatever he could to whomever would buy it.

He had brought some smuggled Russian vodka, and soon both of them were into their cups, though it was only about two in the afternoon.

"Do you remember the mausoleum keeper?" Horst asked him, quite abruptly.

"Yes, of course," Malak said.

They were drinking Russian vodka and talking about the meaning of life. It was not absolutely clear what factor was cause and which was effect in the present matter.

"Do I remember the mausoleum keeper?" Malak mused out loud. He thought of their place on the beach on the Adriatic Sea in the summer, decades ago, when the two boys had vacationed together, a certain luxury because of Horst's father's affiliation to the party.

Malak recalled a time of simple innocence. He recalled that summer was warm and particularly humid.

"The mausoleum keeper asked us along. He wanted to show us his work, up on the hill," Malak recalled.

"We were young and carefree, and so we turned him down."

"After thinking about it, perhaps he wanted to give us a good scare," Malak said.

"He was a suspicious man, I remember. Too much time spent with the dead, polishing their crypts," Horst continued.

"He kept their secrets."

Horst bent down into a battered black satchel, his bald head appearing round, a dull moon in the afternoon light.

"But we know better now," Horst said. "There are no secrets."

And he revealed a thick dossier, upon which was written Malak's original name, before it was anglicized, before he had escaped to a better life in England.

"You found it," Malak said, his voice steady, his hands shaking as he took it from him.

"I never disappoint," Horst replied. "But don't read it now," he went on. "Wait until you have some time to yourself."

And so the two men continued an uneasy celebration of other times, sitting together in the dull light of the hospital.

Malak was surprised, finally, to see that as the world saw it, he had experienced a happy childhood, full of promise and delight.

There were photographs of him and his family taken before he had left for England.

There were reports from his earliest teachers. He had always been a horrendous speller, but he was surprised to see he had earned good marks for his spelling and grammar.

"Subject leaves his flat every day at 06:00 for his state school. He is perfunctorily dressed in uniform. He is well-liked by his teachers and gets along with his classmates. He is no good at football, but is an excellent swimmer."

Malak remembered hating group swimming lessons and being terrified, as a rule, of water.

"Subject's family are good citizens." As proof, the report listed his parents' devotion to several party organizations. He himself remembered cleaning up trash with other boys as a part of a state-sponsored program.

He also remembered his father and mother arguing late at night. His father wanted to escape his country, and his mother argued they should not. And he remembered sleeping in his attic room and listening to the apartment building groan in the wind, sure beyond everything that the slanted walls would tumble in on him and extinguish him right there in the darkness.

A later report said that because of his aptitude, Malak was being considered for military service.

Then his father was discovered to be a dissident.

But the dossier did not say his father ran away to Germany as Malak and his mother always thought. His father had been arrested and sent to prison. The report said he had passed away not long before his mother did. Both of them had seen the better days after the party's fall but had not seen the latest phase.

His father had disappeared just before Malak turned ten, he remembered. Because of this, they stopped celebrating his birthday.

"Germany," his mother had said, crying.

Not knowing the truth, she claimed to be angry with his father. After that, she had become secretly very religious. Malak remembered his attic and the beating of wings. Those wings had appeared quite soon after, he was certain.

That week, Malak was to be fitted with a new foot. They were waiting for a batch of medical supplies to arrive, and prosthetic devices were to be included. There were arms and legs and hands and feet. Just in case, they had asked him, if the shipments were late, would he mind a temporary replacement?

"Already used?" he asked, astutely.

"That's right," the doctor nodded, and Malak understood what he meant. He said he didn't care, that one limb was as good as another so long as it was in working order and provided a sound fit.

So Malak, with his dead soldier's foot in place, left the hospital on crutches. He went home to Aunt Beier, his mother's sister, who was happy to see him.

He had decided that despite everything, he was one of the lucky ones. The angels, of course, were not with him then at the moment of impact, but now they were. Now they hovered around him in droves. Soon he was back at the Archives Office, where he busily catalogued the minutiae of a nation, taking the rolls of microfiche, putting their names and descriptions on the cartons and tucking them away onto the dim shelves.

One day, on the way home, he decided his luck was changing. His bus wasn't particularly crowded. This in itself was one miracle. That no one else got on the bus was another. There it was, Malak's single chance at simple relief. He would get his seat on the bus. And now, with his sympathetic cane, he would get a perfect seat. He would sit and ride in comfort now and look out the window onto the short, squat, gray apartment buildings and the factories with their smokestacks and their intermittent black plumes sent out against a sky of glowing gray. And beyond that was the countryside, mountainous and still unspoiled with its rough-edged beauty. Malak would look out the window in comfort. He could relax and daydream a little. He would spend the ride in comfort, contemplating the countryside and whatever architecture confronted his eye.

There was a seat on the bus, now, a good one, next to an old woman wearing a worn blue coat. All he had to do is make his way past the people standing in front of him. There was a burly man with a large parcel. There were three tallish children. There were two old women dressed almost identically, with long undertaker's black coats and similarly rigid, wrinkled faces.

Malak was about to sit down to enjoy his simple comfort. He would be fulfilled. Aunt Beier would be waiting for him at home with a hot stew. She was walking all right today. Her rheumatic joints had freed up. She was cooking for her newly recovered nephew.

But as Malak was about to sit down, as he was approaching from the aisle of the bus, he felt a tap at his shoulder. It was a small disturbance, as though it came from somewhere else, some other place entirely. Malak turned around and saw a small, flaxen-haired girl, about five, who did not say anything. She just looked out imploringly past the vacant seat and out through the window that opened onto an open stretch of country. Malak saw she was bandaged over her right eye. He had no idea of how badly she had been injured. So Malak, of course, letting his cane fall, picked up the child and set her on the seat, taking care she was situated so she could look out onto the terrain beyond.

She stared out of the window, and Malak watched her looking. On her knees she could just see out over the window frame as the bus moved on, roughly, over the potholes and gravel marking the roadway. He pointed out several bridges to the girl, one by one. She looked on carefully, not sure of what she was seeing.

"A bridge is a living thing," Malak began.

The little girl nodded and wanted to know why.

The bus jolted this way and that. He made sure she did not topple over as he began to explain.

KAVITA DORAI

India, September 11th, 2001

From January/February 2004

Writer's Note: I travel frequently across India by train. Most passengers trade stories—life stories, adventures, and myths—as readily as they share their food and drink. The following was narrated by an oldish-young man whilst courteously proffering his paper screw of roasted peanuts. He had a sad, faraway voice and was interested in my forthcoming trip to New York in the autumn of 2003. He got off the train rather abruptly at Nagarawadi, a dusty station in rural Maharashtra, before I could ask him what became of Usmaan Ali, Shantabai, or the foreign tourists.

BEING A PIMP in Bombay (or Mumbai, as the New York of the East is called now) is a lucrative business, if you are reasonably pleasant to all, reasonably unpleasant to a few, and have no overt interest in climbing the Mafia ladder. Usmaan Ali was one such minor player, an urbane, *paan*-chewing pimp on the payroll of Shantabai. The Shantabai in question being a top-of-the-food-chain *gharwaali* in Kamathipura, Mumbai's oldest and Asia's largest red-light area. A hulking-buffalo of a woman, her ominous rages were muttered uneasily about, and in the pockets of her silences lurked a ShivSena acolyte, a Deputy Inspector General of the Mumbai police, and most chilling of all, the *Capo di tutti capi* of Mumbai.

Like everyone else in Kamathipura, Usmaan, too, had a dream. He did not dream of escaping to stark poverty in a Bihari village like Champakali did, or of finding a rich patron to set him up in a Malabar Hills apartment like Rukhsana did. He did not dream like Shankar did of appearing on the "Kaun banega Krorepati" show and shaking hands with the movie star Amitabh Bachhan.

At nine, Champakali's brat Shankar was a poet of some promise. Perhaps it was the result of the opium Champakali drugged him with as an infant, before shoving him under the rented 8-hour cot on which she serviced her customers. He was being taught the metrics and the intricacies of Urdu poetry by Maulvi Sahib, one of his mother's regulars. Maulvi Sahib claimed he had been present during the filming of the advertisement for Brittania biscuits, the one that goes "*Gabbar Singh ki asli pasand*—Brittania glucose biscuits," and had taught the film star model to give the word *pasand* a graceful flourish. He dreamed of doing likewise for Madonna someday.

Usmaan's dreams were not so lurid, though his canvas was grander. He dreamed of becoming an assistant to a god-fearing butcher in a delicatessen in New York city. A distant cousin, Khalid Bhai the butcher, had almost promised him the position on one of his trips to Mumbai, provided of course Usmaan could save the money for his fare and then some. "New York," Khalid Bhai had explained, "was a "Badaa Seb," a Big Apple, full of people eating and drinking, mostly eating. He made a good killing during Id-ul-Fitr and Id-ul-Zuha, when families were desperate for sacrificial goats. He could afford to employ a helper-boy, especially now that he was growing older and it took him longer to say his prayers.

These days at night, when furious fights broke out between the mangy street dogs and the whore-children squabbling over fish-scraps from the rubbish dumps, Usmaan would wake up disoriented at finding himself in the sweaty squalor of Kamathipura, instead of in the freezing courtyard of a New York mosque listening to the muezzin's call float high above him. Usmaan ran side-errands for Shantabai's mafia contacts, and as a reward was given part shares in Phoolmati, one of Shantabai's whores. She was a throwaway, a half-price bargain, unlike the fair-skinned, light-eyed Nepali whores who were smuggled in from across the Himalayan border. Dark-eyed, dark-skinned Phoolmati was from nearby Nagarawadi, a small town steeped in the sense of its own nothingness. Brought up on a steady diet of Bollywood films, she ran away to Mumbai with her lover, who predictably abandoned her in Kamathipura after he had gambled away her jewelery. It was tacitly understood that Phoolmati had no dreams, and Usmaan was careful not to corrupt her with his own.

Usmaan ran a side-business as well, its profits like everything else in his life depending on Kamathipura. He arranged guided tours of the whore-cages for groups of foreign tourists. They paid quite handsomely, for without his protection, their cameras would be smashed and they would be stoned by the denizens of Kamathipura. The tourists stood out in the crowd: burnt-red and ungainly in shorts and sweaty tee shirts and the all-important camera, gawking at everything. "Say Jaawhn, did ya get a load of that!" "Lil ol me's for a tall cool beer right now." "OK folks, let's get this show on the road..."

Sometimes, to while away the tedium, he would ask one of the tourists for his address.

"I'm coming next year to Amreeka for my cousin's marriage to attend, Sahib. I am visiting you in your home? Or your church if suiting you? I am bringing fresh-fresh photos for you of dirty-Indian-womans, yes?" he'd say and watch their eyes bulge out as the veins in their foreheads turned purple.

The New-York-Girl was different. Emboldened by the fact that she was a native of his magic-city, he had asked for her address. She studied him awhile before answering in a curious twang, "Sorry Ozman, no can do. I never mix business and pleasure." At first Usmaan was apoplectic with rage that she thought he wanted to pleasure her. What dirty minds these women have, Allah Tobah! Then with a rush of hot pride, he understood she was acknowledging him as a business contact. Indeed, he reflected, they were in the same line of business. The Human Trade one could call it. Though personally he drew the line at traffic-light beggar children.

The New-York-Girl took lots of photos of them though, all big eyes and rags. She took lots of photos of the women in Kamathipura too. Not just the ones he herded and arranged in a group for her in their fluorescent greens and oranges, posing behind the bars of their cages. No, she stuck around with her cameras hanging about her neck, talking to the women before and after their customers, smoking their *beedis* and eating their greasy *biryani*. His mind winced away from the memory, but he had tried questioning her once. "Why you are always wanting to photo these gutter-people? All foreigners coming to India, why for? For looking at hungry, dirty, naked *loag*. I know in Amreeka you are not having such peoples, so always you photo-photo here. But you are not having Taj Mahal also, not having Lakshmiji temple also. Now we're having many Computer-*loag* for customers, and we're having Cable-TV also with Baywatch for them. Why you not want photo them?" he asked while she continued to pack her cameras in a flat silence. In frustration he caught her arm and stilled her for an instant, forcing her to face Tulasa, who was unbuttoning her blouse with a lewd wink for a passing customer. "These womans not having shames are forcing to do such things for *rozi-roti*," he said. "Why your mother not teaching you shames also? Not teaching you respecting other peoples shames?" He spluttered as his words made spit patterns in the lane.

She touched his cheek with a long white finger. It felt like a stinging slap. "See you tomorrow Tulasa Bi," was all she said over her shoulder, before walking off in her dirty-yellow tee-shirt. He never saw her again.

One of the new-fangled computer-*loag* liked watching CNN instead of the usual soft-porn flicks while being serviced. The whorehouse was happy to oblige. It was much quicker and more hygienic. So it was that, on the 11th of September, 2001, while on his way to Shantabai's den to make arrangements for the latest across-the-border consignment from Bangladesh, Usmaan Ali saw New York city burn to cinders and crumble to dust. He watched in stunned disbelief as his dreams were buried forever under a million tons of metal, glass, concrete, and burnt human flesh. The blue skies of his beloved city turned black as the twin towers of the World Trade Center crashed and rained death and debris on the city and its people on that sunny September day. The observation deck of the WTC had been the first landmark he was going to visit when he finally arrived. He would stand there all alone and look far ahead into the future and far beyond into the past...

Strangely enough, he could hear a keening voice rising above all the strange American accents on TV, moaning "*Ya Allah, raham kar. Ya Khuda raham kar,*" and with a cold shiver he realized it was his own.

"Not to worry, Usmaan Bhai, the Amreekans will take revenge," said some of the customers who had come running at the strange sound of a pimp wailing. "Arrey, they will throw atom bombs and hydrogen bombs on Baluchistan and Pakistan and Hindustan. They will make a "Kabristaan" of the whole Afghanistan. So please do not disturb yourself, Usmaan Ali," blurted one over-excited man.

"Will the Amreekan-*loag* come and bomb Nagarawadi as well?" Phoolmati asked no one in particular, with a puzzled expression on her vacuous face.

"Oh yes, indeed," sneered Usmaan in a white-hot rage. "The most powerful man in the world, the Amreekan President Sahib himself, is going to come in his jumbo jet airplane and bomb everyone in Nagarawadi. All the 10 Rupee whores like you that one can buy in the dingy grocery stores of Nagarawadi, and all the bowlegged rickshaw-wallahs and all the municipal school raggedy children." The iron buckle of his belt left angry red weals on her torso, and purplish-red blood oozed out of little punched out holes. Hot tears of shame made dirt tracks down her cheeks.

"I was only asking," she whispered. He whipped her with his belt and punched her with his fists and kicked her with his boots and slapped her with the palm of his hand, all in a mesmeric rhythm.

"What do you have in Nagarawadi that is so precious? So great, that when New York is attacked you think Nagarawadi is next, *do-takiye-di-randi!*" his fists rapped out his words on her body in a fast, furious tempo.

Phoolmati did not answer. It was dark in the room, and the shadows grouped around her thick and fast. Through the slit of the bloodshot eye she had left, she could see, framed in the sunlit doorway, a little girl chasing a butterfly down a dusty mud path.

"*Qatl: Qatl bin Qatil bin Qatil Maqtool nahin. Ishq: Ishq bin Aashiq bin Aashiq Mashooq nahin.*" Shankar's reedy voice learning his Urdu lessons aloud could be heard long after Usmaan's footsteps had faded into silence.

Three first-year medical students at the Lokmanya Tilak Municipal Medical College got first hack at Phoolmati's cadaver. They sawed diligently at her purple, bloated stomach, unaware of the ghosts of sad-eyed village children clustering around their knees, or of the butterfly-ghosts fluttering around them, or of the firefly-ghosts dancing frenziedly around the naked light bulb above their heads.

SARA CATTERALL

The Artist's Conk

From April/May 2011

WE DON'T ENJOY each other's company, but once a year, family is family.

Nearly all of us arrive the Friday evening before Labor Day to claim our assigned rooms, most of them in the lake house, a monstrous old Adirondack-style lodge. This is our own carefully managed ancestral wilderness, larger than the nation of Andorra. There is no cell reception or internet access, and those of us with seniority have banned any obvious use of modern technology whether for work, amusement, or escape. So, once we have slept in and gotten through lunch, most of us are hellishly bored.

We organize elaborate group meals on the long open porches, pick blueberries in the high meadows, empty the boathouse onto the lawn and into the lake. The boats give the children something to do, give the rest of us an excuse to flee each other, and allow couples to find a little privacy for a conversation, or a fight.

Whenever talk dies or darkness gathers too closely around the breakfast table, we all know the list of ritual activities we can brightly suggest to skip the day forward. There is the attic crammed full of relics. There are the outlying houses, which younger subsets of us have raided for first editions, prints, and collectible porcelain. There are lawn sports, indoor games, and trips to the nearest towns for ice cream and an impoverished semblance of shopping. And there are other family relics to examine and explain at too much length to newcomers and children. One of those is the tree mushroom collection.

For generations we have collected tree mushrooms, the hard, flat kind that grow out from the side of certain large forest trees, as if the tree had decided it needed a little shelving and pushed a segment of itself out into the air. The underside is a buff color, velvety to the touch, easily bruised. You can scratch your name in them, draw pictures on them, hence their common name, the artist's conk. Delicate and responsive when fresh, they dry hard as oak and keep forever if, as Aunt Judy will say, the woodworms don't get them. We have an honored collection of more than 50 prime specimens, decorating the 12-foot stone mantelpiece over the fireplace in the log cathedral of the main sitting room. The most impressive one is right in the center, a monstrous plate that must be 30 inches across—none of us may bring it down to examine it closely. No other mushroom can approach it in size or quality. A skillful, many-toned impression of our lake with the boathouse and the pine trees around it is scratched into the buff side, and though there is no signature, in a corner is scratched the date: 1924.

We are all desperately individual, of course. We have all been, as most of us would not say, very well educated. Private schools, tutors, boarding schools starting as early as 11, pick of the Ivies, the Sorbonne and Oxford, every advantage, every opportunity. We are all top dogs in our various ways, brilliant and well-connected. Only when we abandon work to come up here, only when we are standing around the lawn in the morning with coffee mugs, or in the late afternoon with alcohol or surreptitious highs, trying to stroll away from each other while Frank, the groundskeeper's border collie, tries to herd us back together in a lump, then we feel our shine dim and sputter, and we can't be together a moment longer without some kind of purpose.

Late one frosty Saturday evening after a jarring dinner, we were mostly in and around the central sanctum of the lake house. A large fire of maple and apple logs burned in the blackened maw of the fireplace, and several of us were staring at it, brooding, sunk in old feather cushions in the dark wood furniture, while others read, fidgeted, or lay on the threadbare rug to work a large puzzle of the Matterhorn that may or may not have had all its pieces.

Someone, looking at the mushrooms displayed on the mantel like crooked teeth, wondered aloud about the giant in the center, a bright attempt at conversation that seemed likely to swamp in the general fog of gloom and boredom. But then someone else commented that of course that was a long time ago, when the earth was new, and now what with global warming and acid rain... which of course sparked an irritated rejoinder and denial from at least two others, with a reattribution of blame to the anemic lethargy of current generations. Our blood rose, and within minutes we had ratified a plan to hunt down an equally large or larger mushroom on the following morning.

In the depths of the night, one of us woke. Rather than lie there waiting for the clutch of old demons, she got up, pulled her coat over her nightshirt, and went out on the front porch. Her bare feet cooled instantly on the smooth floor boards, cold air slipping up her sleeves, up her legs, insinuating itself around her waist. A high breeze rattled the shadowy tops of the trees. The old moon shone in the sky above the lake, a "C" tilting on its back, and there above it were the Pleiades. She hadn't seen them in years. Peering at them she could still see all seven, not bad for 48, not bad at all. There they shone, faint and high, forever bonded in... was it death? Grief? Exile? Not a comforting story. The thought sent her back to bed.

Sunday morning dawned warmer and brilliantly sunny. There was actual cheer in the kitchen over the coffee, the toast, the high fiber cereals and fruit. Tree and mushroom guides cluttered the dining table. Some of us were wearing technical hiking gear, leaning telescoping walking sticks against the walls and the porch railing, organizing sandwiches and flasks and bug spray into day packs.

Melissa is an oddity among us, a classics professor with a nine-month contract. She spends her summers here with her daughters and their visiting friends and father, from May until the end of this mass gathering. If classes started earlier, she would never stay this long, but she has no airtight excuse, and she does stay for us, year after year. She sits all the long weekend doing fine needlepoint in Byzantine colors while her unwanted family eddies around her. On this morning we found her sitting in the sun on the porch, working a cushion cover with a geometric puzzle of crimson and gold, dark green, deep blue and black.

"Come on, you have to go. Everyone is going," we cried. A bee zigzagged over her work, mistaking it for blossoms, and landed on her arm, crawling briefly over it to reach the field of colors. She paused for it, but she didn't flinch. Tasting the wool, it withdrew and rose, vanishing high over the lawn.

"What's so exciting?" she said, smiling wide-eyed for the children, black eyes shining in her pale face, black hair loose around her throat.

When we told her, she said, "No, you're welcome to it. I'll hold the house down. Don't get lost!" and waved us off with an overblown show of gaiety.

Some of us took off, individually and in small groups, for far corners of the estate, determined to rely on intuition and paths less traveled. Most of us drove up to an old mixed beech and sugar maple forest, full of ancient giants and scattered with boulders the size of SUVs.

Silver-gray trunks gleamed over a sea of russet gold, the ground more thickly covered with leaves than the branches above, the air rich with the smell of warming pine branches and decay. We wandered through the underbrush, drifting apart like an aging universe, breaking the fearful silence with our rustling and snapping, our voices and thumping feet. Birds sang in distant trees with underwater voices. High above us, scraps of brown and gold fluttered against the deep blue sky, and around us a dank chill breathed out from the boulders and up from the mossy ground.

One of us was 16 and not sure whether this purgatory was any improvement over the one that waited for him the other side of Monday. He was only here because of his father, who dragged him up every year, saying he would have his cousins to play with: Melissa's five- and seven-year-olds, and a pair of arrogant twin girls, aged 11, suspected of allergies to everything, pale and hollow-eyed from a willful lack of sleep and food.

Cold and bored and depressed, he drifted off, skidding down the sides of a bowl everyone else had skirted, his sneakers sliding on the mulch of leaves until he came up with a jolt against the trunk of a huge sugar maple, rooted near the bottom of the basin. He edged down around it and bumped his knee on what at first he thought was a bench. It embraced the sunny lower half of the tree, a thick-ringed, brown monster, edges pooling out into the air. He let himself down next to it, slipping a little, griming the seat of his jeans. It was wicked huge. He thought about keeping it a private secret, and for a while he sat chilling himself at the roots of the tree, hugging his knees and his luck. Then he heard a scampering in the leaves above him and delighted little girl whispers that turned to shouts of his name and a tumble of questions. Ignoring them, he stood and shouted for the rest of us, and shouting to each other, we converged on the basin, gathering around the prize.

It had to be three feet across. There was admiration, awe, and debate. The old maple was dying on the mushroom side, withered leafless twigs in clear contrast to the remnants of a blazing red-orange canopy. Aunt Judy leaned on her walking staff, her wrinkled fingertips going white with cold, and stared up at it.

"Grandpa used to say they were bad for the trees. They turn living wood to rot, year by year."

"So we're doing a good deed," said an uncle. "Who has the tools?"

We tried a lot of things, including futile efforts with a screwdriver and a hatchet. Feeling re-diminished, the finder wandered off from us, clambered onto a mossy boulder, and pulled himself up into a red oak tree to watch uncomfortably from above. Finally the groundskeeper arrived with a case of wood chisels, and we took the largest to the base of the giant fungus with the help of a mallet. The hammering set up an echo in the woods that seemed to return from miles away, surrounding us with a reverberating onslaught of our own uproar.

Later, some of us were sure it was the vibration that stirred up the bees. Of course not, said others. The bees weren't in that tree at all. They were in the big, old, half-hollow beech tree right behind us on the opposite slope. They came out of the hole near the fork. Most of us in fact (among those who had gathered there) never saw them. We only heard the yips of the first two people to be stung, the cry of *Bees!* and then the shout of the groundskeeper: *Run! Get in the cars!*

Nobody liked to mention later on if they had noticed the pale twins hunting for rocks to throw up at that hole. One of them was the first to be stung, the other was up on the rim of the bowl and ran when she heard her sister shriek. When their uncle looked up and saw the black storm of insects descending, he yelled and grabbed the marked girl, scrambled up out of the hole, was stung himself, ran downhill stripping off the child's shirt, brushing at bees and shouting over her screams, ran for the road, passing her mother and sister who pelted after them as we all scattered for the cars.

The boy was still up in his roost. At first he thought the bees would follow his flailing relations and leave him if he stayed still against the trunk, but then he heard a high-pitched insect whine, and they were on him. Bees filling his hair, pouring into his collar, up his sleeves, a thousand needle stabs of poison in his skin. He covered his face with his hands, drove his forehead into the bark, pressed himself against the tree, and yelled in desperate agony, but no-one heard him. At least, no-one mentioned it later. There was a lot of yelling going on.

Once at the cars, the uncle slammed himself into the back of a minivan with the little girl and slapped off every crawling insect he could find, stamping them to the floor, crushing them with fingers, grimly not listening to her melodramatic screams, which were starting to catch in her throat.

Her mom slammed into the van, pushing the other, miraculously unstung sister ahead of her. She had the Epipen right there in her hand. She had never used it, but she had been trained. Everything would be fine. But then she froze. Forty-five minutes to the hospital—she saw the red number flash across her vision—45 minutes. We'll never make it. One of us snatched the Epipen from her and uncapped it, but the mother screamed, "No, give it back," and grabbed for it, knocking it out of his hand and under the seat as the driver stamped on the accelerator.

Back at the lake house, nobody missed the boy. Not even his father, who had hardly seen him that weekend and was used to it. Those of us who wanted lunch ate it standing up in the kitchen. Some of us went to our rooms to pack. Others hung around the dining room, near the only working phone.

When the call came, there was a sigh of relief and a general dispersal. The girls were fine. They would be back for their things in the morning. We were all eager to leave, and our annual last dinner around the bonfire by the lake was more lively and generous than any of us would have normally expected. Halfway through the evening, the boy's father wandered among us, asking casually if anyone had seen his son. When we said no, he said, "Well, he's probably off by himself somewhere. I'll go check his room in a while." It was going to be a long drive the next day. His ex-wife had insisted he deliver the boy to school on his way down to Boston, and he wasn't looking forward to it. He drank wine, he drank scotch, he went to bed and slept in.

Early the next morning, when the groundskeeper cautiously returned to the forest to look at the nest, he found the cold body of our boy, hanging by one ankle from the cleft of the oak tree, its crown blazing dark red against the white sky above him. None of us were there.

KRIS BROUGHTON

The Black Folks Guide to Survival

From July/August 2007

MALCOLM X ACTUALLY did once say, "The chickens have come home to roost." Nice, evocative image from an ex-farm boy turned pimp turned convict turned religious leader turned civil rights activist. But most of the younger black folks I know have never seen a live chicken. The ubiquitous Nextel chirp holds more meaning for them than the clucking of a brood of hens, waddling back to the chicken coop as nightfall approaches. These days, it's our own chickens who have begun shuffling back into the fold—our demands for racial equality, for equal access to opportunity, for fair playing fields, have created a modern America that has learned to accommodate us by saying one thing and doing another.

I've used the imaginary title *The Black Folks Guide To Survival* for so long when I am trying to emphasis a point, I can picture this book in the African American section of Barnes and Noble, with a black cover (what else?), its white-lettered title emblazoned across the top, an unfocused picture of two modern day black professionals, their bodies framed from the waist up, their shoulders shrugged as if they are lost, centered below the subtitle, "In the New Millennium." I'm supposed to be a writer, I said to myself, so why not write this one?

Survival in White America for Dummies was a strong second choice, but the legal wrangling, although a sure-fire publicity generator, was more than I could stomach. So I've got a title, I've selected a free form way to communicate the storyline to the reader, I've dug through my personal collection of modern day black folk do's and don'ts...

Let's get this show on the road.

Prologue

...you think they'll buy this? Hasn't somebody already done it?" Rocky is a motor mouth. He had once asked seven rapid-fire questions in a row before the guy mugging him had enough and broke his jaw three years ago. He's been at General Motors long enough to know he isn't going to go far with them. "I mean, I've got this MBA, I went to an Ivy League college, I wear the right clothes... shit, I even go to hockey games. What is it I'm doing wrong?"

Rocky was my college roommate 15 years ago. Since then we've gone down separate career paths. He's worked at three of the country's largest manufacturers since grad school, but he seems to be stuck at the director level—not even assistant vice-president. He's been married and divorced, a brief union with an ebony socialite who didn't think he was getting to the top fast enough. I am still single, with a little nest egg from a failed Internet startup about to run out and a book deal whose advance is close to disappearing if I don't get a manuscript in the mail by the end of the month.

It was Rocky who suggested I write about racism. "It never goes out of style. Black will always be the new black."

"What about the Mexicans? Isn't brown the new black?"

"Hell, no. They've got to work their way up to being full-fledged minorities. Subjugation isn't what it used to be, you know." What the hell did Rocky know about subjugation? I liked his racism idea though—very meaty. All I had to do was draw from my experiences...

Which brings me to where I am now. Three days have passed, and I am still stuck on the first page.

"Man," Rocky says, "just throw some shit down. How hard is it to follow up that 'chickens come home to roost' quote? Just write something like... like... like, uh..."

"NOW do you see what I mean? I need a tone. A voice really, even though it's a non-fiction book." I look at Rocky standing in front of me, a child of the suburbs, whose harshest racial incident was back when he was four, when he realized the Santa Claus his mother had in his living room was the only black Santa in the neighborhood. He is oblivious to the racial Cold War America has been in for the last 25 years. Cats like him, they need a wakeup call. Yeaah, that's what I'll do. I'll wake his ass up.

Introduction

White folks, and white men in particular, have always found ways to alter, bend, or just totally ignore the rules they've made up when something doesn't suit them.

Finally, a sentence that says what I want it to say. It's bold and direct, with a presumptive stance that assumes the reader will possess a point of view sympathetic to one of the oldest themes in the book: power corrupts absolutely. This will be the page-one header of *The Black Folks Survival Guide.*

"How does that sound, Roc?" I say, reading the sentence out loud to him.

"Damn, man. Don't you think that's kind of in your face?"

"To whom?"

"It just sounds like you're pandering to the 'us versus them' thing."

"Didn't you tell me you're the only black guy in your B-school graduating class who isn't a VP yet?"

"Well..."

"My ass. Nobody ever fires you. You know why? 'Cause you're too willing to work too hard for too little for them to let you go. So they give you the 'not in the budget' okie doke when you ask for a raise. The 'what can I do, I gotta take care of the CEO's nephew first' spiel when you try to slide into a new position. They'll give you any line in the book to keep your ass from rising up."

"But I..."

"No, you need to hear this. I mean really hear this. Your parents thought they were hooking you up by keeping you out in the 'burbs. By not mentioning anything negative or derogatory about white folks. By striving to create an oasis of fairness and racial harmony.

That shit might work in the minors, but you're in the big leagues, Roc. These white folks you work with are playing for keeps. For stock options. For fat-ass bonuses so they can take the family to Europe, or put a pool in the backyard. And your dumb ass is still coming in to the office on Sundays." I look at him. "I'm writing this book for all the clueless young negroes like you."

"Clueless? Who you calling clueless, motherfucker?"

"Who? Overeducated people like you, who think the NAACP doesn't do shit. Blind, black bastards who refuse to believe the FBI and the CIA have secret agendas. Motherfuckers who," I say, my voice hot, my motor running, my mind crackling with possibilities, "take their voting rights for granted. Stupid assholes who believe we can stop asking so many questions of our government, the same government that still thinks it fucked up when it raised you up from three-fifths of a man to a whole. Easily led astray son-of-a-bitches, like you, who accept blindly the need to accumulate the trinkets and trappings of the *nouveau riche*. And especially black folks like you, Rocky, who turn their noses up at those of us who haven't made it."

I haven't done an imaginary roommate before. This character Rocky, whose name I've borrowed from one of my college drinking buddies, is an amalgamation of some of the more privileged black students I went to college with. The real Rocky used to be a straight up nigga from "up the way," who had to learn the exact opposite set of skills from my make believe persona—how to operate in the sterile corporate environment without looking like a bull in a china shop.

Digressions, as you can see, are a weakness with me. I forgot I was in the middle of telling you how this book came to be written. Another chunk of prose comes to me while I am ranting at Rocky. The paragraph is kind of dense, but I think it does a pretty good job of setting up what is to come:

A subject like racism is hard to parse into discrete sections, ready to be analyzed under a microscope like a slice of skin, or subjected to a centrifugal force that separates the whole into its components, with a goal of recording repeatable phenomena in order to consider whether it is real or not from the standpoint of the scientific method.

"Who do you think you are," Rocky says, "Henry Louis Gates? That mumbo jumbo sounds like a college professor reading from his dissertation."

"What I'm saying is that racism is subjective. And I threw the microscope reference in there to imply it's the little tiny things—the nuances—that matter these days."

"Well, why didn't you just say that?"

"What's wrong with what I've got?"

"I'm a smart motherfucker, but I don't like to read that type of shit if I don't have to."

"You know what you need to do? Go stand in a bookstore next weekend for a couple of hours and tell me what you see. The people who buy books for pleasure can read, Rocky."

"When this shit ends up at Books-A-Million for a $1.99, you can say I told you so."

"Dude, it's starting to flow. Listen to this:

We live in a world where we want measurable, quantifiable, scalable action plans that will tell us, if we devote a certain amount of hours and a particular amount of money, that these problems will go away.

Now this shit is starting to come together.

"Not bad," Roc says, his eyes wandering. "Now the beginning makes more sense."

I don't think he notices I've cheated a little with that one—I deliberately threw in some of the buzzwords he uses all day in his meetings. "Aw shit! Check THIS out," I say.

Our Otherness is irredeemable, indestructible, unbreakable, indelible. It is not symbolic or imagined. It is real, in a physical sense, its mass and volume at once immeasurable but distinct.

Roc stares at me. "Man, you need to go ahead and do your thing. It's starting to get deep over here. I gotta crunch some numbers tonight anyway."

I don't hear him leave, my mind focusing on these few paragraphs I've strung together. I come up with the lead-ins to the first few chapters practically overnight.

Ex-Crackers

"Gated communities now, forever, and always."

If you're like me, you probably live in the suburbs. What you need to realize is all white folks are not alike. Here in Atlanta, for example, a substantial number of the people you will live next to are ex-Crackers. Some of them are descendants of genuine Ku Klux Klan members. But these people have made something out of themselves, have risen out of the muck and slime of abject intolerance. How else could they live next door to you?

Neighbors

"Can't we all just get along?"

Most of your neighbors are Babbitts, boosting ideals because, well, because they just feel they ought to be Boosters, good Solid Citizens, ever on alert for the hint of crabgrass in their neighbor's yard or the garage door down the street that has been left open, for these are perversities and imperfections that will bring down the all important Property Values, values upon which mortgages lean heavily, mortgages shoring up credit card debt that has been consolidated into equity lines of credit, enormous sums whose principal balances are humored by monthly payments designed to leave small dents in these carcasses of debt masquerading as houses, whose structures have already, just a few years after being so proudly erected, begun to decay and rot and leak.

If you've lived in the suburbs long enough, you are probably a Black Babbitt, a peculiar distillation of Babbittry, which is prone to be more prejudiced than your ex-Cracker neighbors. You look down your nose at all Asians, Mexicans, and Indians who invade the inner sanctum of the sacred cul-de-sac. You save your most potent vitriol for other blacks who move into your neighborhood who don't have as many degrees as you do, whose skin is darker or lighter than yours.

Talk to your neighbors. Believe me, they are talking *about* you if they are not talking to you.

Colorblindness

"I don't see color. I only see people."

We've all heard this one before. For someone to say they don't see color is to say we don't exist. They have remolded the reality of our existence into a likeness of their own choosing.

DO NOT BLOW THIS STATEMENT OFF. You need to be extremely concerned about this obsession with defining your existence according to the standards of outsiders. To listen to others dictate why you should or shouldn't feel the way you do is not much different than a slave master keeping his charges in line. This colorblindness thing is a cop out. We look different. It is an empirical fact, although the degree of difference may vary between individual black people. So why are we supposed to pretend these things don't exist?

Diversity

"America is one big, racial melting pot."

You know where you came from. You know who you are. Hanging out with black people exclusively isn't going to make you any blacker. Hanging out with white people all the time isn't going to make you any whiter. What you need to do is reevaluate who YOU are and decide what is really a part of your ethnicity, and what is really just some baggage from the past.

These days, whether it's a group where you have a history with each other or the people on the other side of the fence, WHATEVER COLOR THEIR FENCE IS, you want to ultimately get along with them. So learn a little about NASCAR. Memorize a few country western tunes. Sit through a performance of *Rigoletto* at least once.

Study the rules of hockey. Because if you don't have any way to connect with anyone outside your own group, you are fucked.

Dating White Men / White Women

Can white be alright?

There will be times when you find you are not attracted to anyone who looks like you. It may be because you don't live around many of us or work around many of us, or you have just gotten tired of all the drama that can go along with dealing with some of us.

If you grew up in the suburbs, white people were your childhood friends. Your high school classmates. Your college roommates. You may have gotten out of sync with their internal rhythms in the last few years, but it's just like riding a bike—you never really forget how to do it.

DO NOT de-Negro-ize yourself if you are in one of these relationships.

DO think about shit before you do it. Taking your white significant other to a Nation of Islam rally, for instance, is a sign you are in the process of de-Negro-izing yourself, a period during which your brain only functions in a limited capacity.

The "N" Word

When ex-Crackers have had enough of your ass.

What are you supposed to do when you hear someone white call you a nigger? If you're a rich black, they are beneath you. You expect used-to-be Crackers to be uncouth and unsophisticated anyway. If you're one of the mass of middle and lower class blacks, something will snap, and they'll get an earful. You are not going to risk going to jail just to prove a point to some ex-Cracker asshole. But if you happen to be one of that ten percent of us who is always pissed off, whatever strata you inhabit, it might be time for them to start getting their mouth measured for dentures. You can already feel the handcuffs around your wrists, but you will still try to break something—an arm, a leg, a couple of ribs—so these ex-Crackers understand you are not to be played with. By the time the police arrive, you will have already counted how many meals you're gonna have to eat behind bars. You will have already made a couple of calls to arrange bail.

NOTE TO EX-CRACKERS WHO MAY BE READING THIS ON THE SLY: This person may be found in Armani or Adidas—do not be fooled by the restraint of a $1,500 dollar suit.

"So what's going on with your book deal?" Rocky looks pensive.

"Aw, these fuckers are scared. My agent almost jumped through the phone. 'This isn't the book I thought you were writing,' she said. I told her, 'You know, I was kind of surprised myself. But I like it.'"

"And?"

"She started hemming and hawing about my unnecessary, caustic, disrespectful commentary about white folks."

"I thought you said she was okay with the idea?"

"She was, when she thought it was a funny book aimed at us."

"So what are you going to do?"

"Fuck her. I already did it. Sent that shit straight to the publisher. Son of a bitch editor Myron Reinstein called here laughing his ass off. I figured most of the vitriol in the book was about ex-Crackers, and there's nothing a New York Jew likes better than to make fun of southern bumpkinism. You gotta read between the lines in these deals."

"I might need to take a class in reading between the lines."

"What's wrong, Rocky?"

"I, ah, I tried some of the things you said at work. You know, about being more aggressive and stuff. Now people are looking at me funny. No one wants to eat lunch with me anymore. They think I've gone militant because I've started questioning the things they tell me."

"Did I say it was going to be easy? The only two reasons Buckwheat was in *The Little Rascals* was because he didn't challenge Spanky and the gang could laugh at him all they wanted. Is that what you want—to be a modern day Buckwheat?"

"The, ah, the thing is, if I do this, it basically means the life I've lived up until now has been... has been a sham."

"No, it doesn't. Didn't I tell you them damn TV shows have fucked your brain over? Life is NEVER as simple as people want to make it out to be. The thing is, you couldn't know until you knew. So what you didn't know before is irrelevant. Now if you keep doing what you were doing AFTER you know the real deal—then you're talking sham existence. But you wouldn't be the only one."

"So what do I do now?"

"Well, now that you've got some extra time alone, use it to plan how to get from where you are to where you want to be. Walk around the office when everyone has cleared out. You'd be surprised at what just 15 minutes of surveillance a day will yield to an ambitious brotherman like yourself."

The character Rocky faces the same age-old dilemma most of us have: how to deal with the unknown and unknowable. Now you understand why Muhammed Ali is seen as a hero. Writing "white folks" and "ex-Crackers" today carries nowhere near the personal costs for me that it did for him, or Dick Gregory, or Malcolm X, or Stokley Carmichael. And yet there are office buildings sprinkled with up and coming young black execs who can see their six-figure salaries disappearing if they make too many waves, if they don't laugh at those inappropriate jokes, if they don't take into account how the white men they work for might view them at review time, at raise time, at option grant time.

Out of the frying pan and into the goddammed Neiman Marcus fireplace. Oh, well. Back to the *Guide*...

Religion

"And they sware unto the Lord with a loud voice, and with shouting, and with trumpets and with coronets."

You don't have to drive all the way across town to go to the kind of church your grandmother attended. It's okay if the members of the church near your home wear shorts and tank tops to worship service. Its okay if you don't get the willies during the sermon because the white guy behind the podium sounds like a late night talk show host.

Guess what? The pastors, reverends, and preachers behind the podiums all over town are reading from the same book. Howling a sermon as if one of your feet is caught in a bear trap does not consecrate The Word any more thoroughly than if it is delivered in a measured monotone.

Condi and Colin

Are Amos and Andy back on the air? Are they "simonizing" their watches in D.C.?

There are ex-Crackers out there, especially the ones you work with, who wonder why we all can't be like Condoleezza Rice or Colin Powell: smart but not uppity, aggressive but not angry, ambitious but not power hungry.

As unpopular as some of the decisions are that Rice and Powell have made in our community, they are still two black folks in blue suits using complex language on television to articulate their thoughts.

DO NOT FALL FOR THE OKIE DOKE! Condi and Colin don't want to get to the top spot in their organization. You do. If your goal is to be "The Man" in your organization, you are going to have to take the gloves off and duke it out sometimes.

Being The Boss

When your minions won't comply.

You've been a desk jockey since you entered the workforce. You started out in middle management and never looked back. Your clothing is tailored. Your memos are exquisite creations, succinct and direct and cogent as hell. But there are those below you, and those at your level, who do not feel you are supposed to be there.

Nip that shit in the bud. If you have any ex-Crackers in your employ, immediately resort to MBWA (Management By Walking Around) combined with MBBA (Management By Being an Ass). Tell their ill-mannered, overindulged asses to quit eyeballing you so damn much and do some work for a change instead of complaining about how unmotivated they are. Snort at them through your broad or narrow brown or yellow or beige nostrils—there is something visceral about that sound, something that conjures the image of a charging bull in the minds of your staffers that is more effective than ten terse emails.

Last Resort

"Break glass in case of emergency."

There are going to be times in your life when shit just doesn't add up. When even the advice in this book can't help you through. If that happens, you need to resort to one of our age-old skills that used to serve us well in the past.

Denial

If we as black people didn't have the power of denial to depend on, our progenitors would have lost their minds generations ago. We who have been or are being discriminated against often arm ourselves with hair-trigger reactions for protection, but the price for such vigilance is an overly testy personality and blood pressure that is off the charts. *The Black Folks Guide to Survival* recommends taking a "chill pill" once in awhile, instead of blowing a gasket at each and every instance of racism. Rome was not built in a day, prejudice will not be eradicated overnight, and some people do not have the capacity to change.

Epilogue

Rocky isn't as nice a guy as he used to be. But he is a senior vice president now, and he will be the first one to inform you that my book made all the difference. He told me that ever since the company put him on the cover of their annual report, he's been having this recurring nightmare. In this dream a reporter finds out he was adopted. The reporter prints a story revealing Rocky is the secret love child of Martin Luther King, Jr. and Strom Thurmond's illegitimate daughter.

My know-it-all posse of agents, editors, and marketing experts all held their noses as they launched the book. "It's too offensive." "It's not universal enough." "No self-respecting black person will buy this." They were right. Very few black people bought it. On the other hand, white folks loved it. Well, not all of them. Ex-Crackers were incensed. Many of the copies purchased right after the book was released were never read. They fueled bonfires held by the more radical ex-Crackers to denounce their portrayal. There were enough fires around the nation in the first 30 days, though, to push *The Black Folks Survival Guide* onto the *New York Times* Best Seller list.

Now my know-it-all posse wants another book. Fast. They'd like to get it out in time for the holiday season. But I've already told them the one I'm working on, *C. P. Time and Other Lies and Untruths,* is... well... is going to be late.

SEFI ATTA

A Union on Independence Day

From October/November 2003

IT IS NOT a good day to tell her. This morning she quarreled with Dr. Darego again. They were upstairs in their bedroom on the second floor; I was on the sofa bed in the basement where I sleep every night. I heard their voices clear as if I pressed my ear to their door. Mrs. Darego called him a selfish man. Dr. Darego said, "Listen, I work very hard." Mrs. Darego said she was overworked. "What are you harassing me for?" Dr. Darego asked. "You wanted help, I got you help. You have your nanny downstairs. Call the girl, tell her to get the kids ready, take the keys to the jeep. All of you, drive to wherever you feel like spending your July Fourth. I'm not going. Finish?"

Mrs. Darego must have been the one who slammed the door.

Perhaps this is why houses like theirs in America are called "dream homes." They are not built with unhappy couples in mind; their walls are too thin.

I fold up the sofa bed and replace the cushions, which are in a pile by the concertina-shaped floor lamp. I untie my black satin scarf to let my braids down, slap lint off my shorts, then listen to a world news broadcast as usual. It is Independence Day here in America. Hopefully, there will be an update on the demonstrators from my hometown.

Forty years it took for our story to reach the front pages of the *Times*: *Nigerian Delta Women in Oil Company Standoff.* The women had occupied Summit Oil's terminal, the report said. They were clapping and singing. If their demands were not met, they would strip naked, and this was a shaming gesture, according to local custom.

I did not know of any such custom in my hometown. I only remembered old-fashioned Catholic women who would consider knee-length shorts like mine a taboo. We Kalabaris were an overdressed people. You had to see our men in traditional attire, with their long tunics, staffs, and black bowler hats. Women wore bright silk head ties, lace blouses, and layers of colorful plaid wrappers down to their ankles. Why would they bare their bodies for a cause? I thought the newspaper report was a hoax, designed to ridicule Africans and trivialize our protest. I wondered who in my hometown had joined the demonstrators, what had happened to my friend Angelina who was one of them, whether Val had since been found, and if Mama now agreed with Papa when he said that on the arrival of the foreigner, the native must learn to sleep with one eye open.

The broadcast ends without a word about my hometown. In a cowardly way, I'm relieved. I pull the floor lamp to its proper place by the wall, push the sliding doors open to let warm air in. My goose bumps shrink. Outside, the Daregos' small lawn is bordered by flowers I can't name. They are pale compared to hibiscus and bougainvillea, muted like the rest of the house. Indoors, there are beige walls, bronze carvings, ebony masks, mahogany tables, and batiks. African-inspired, I've heard Dr. Darego say about their choice of decor. I've never seen a house in Africa that resembles theirs, so consciously and deliberately African, so beautifully coordinated. To me it is highly westernized.

"Eve?" Mrs. Darego calls from upstairs.

"Coming," I say.

Fresh air from outside chases me as I hurry to her kitchen. Living in a basement is like living in an underground tomb.

When I was a girl, I was in love with every expatriate I came across in my hometown, Catholic priests especially. I thought they were as pure as God in their whites. I couldn't wait to hop on their laps. I was envious that they seemed partial to boys. My class teacher, Sister, I didn't understand why no man had spoken for her. I would have married her myself. She was as beautiful as the Blessed Mary with her red hair and freckles. She was decent enough to spank with rulers, unlike the tree branches our mothers favored for beatings. She taught us about Mungo Park, the Scottish surgeon who was killed on an expedition trying to find the source of River Niger. He was trapped in swamps, fell ill with fevers, was ambushed by natives who stole his equipment and shot at him with bows and arrows. The textbook said he eventually jumped into the river to save himself, and drowned.

I cried for Mungo. I thought natives were wicked people, too ugly in the book illustrations. I grew up, and missionaries like Sister left town. The only expatriates I came across worked for international oil companies—British, Dutch, Canadian, Italian, and American—like the human resources director of Summit Oil who interviewed me for a nursing position at Summit Oil Clinic. He signed the rejection letter addressed to me. Most nurses I graduated with were selling bottled water, bathing soap, tinned milk for a living. Few people in town could afford to buy such provisions. We were one of them. Papa was an electrician; Mama had a Coca-Cola consignment. Still, I was lucky to come to America to work as a live-in nanny.

Mrs. Darego is wearing a flowery housecoat. Her face looks freshly washed. She has the kind of dark skin I admire, almost indigo. This morning she appears gray under her fluorescent kitchen lights. She narrows her eyes as she speaks.

"I'm sorry, Eve," she says. "It's me and you today. We have to take the children to the barbecue. Their father doesn't want to go, and I don't know what else to do."

She was going to give me a day off and spend her time shopping for groceries and cooking. I was looking forward to doing nothing useful.

"Shall I get them ready?" I ask.

"Yes, please," she says. "I'll pack the cooler and make sandwiches."

I head for the children's room, but she stops me by the fridge.

"Is everything all right?" she asks.

I smile to assure her. She has sensed my mood.

I arrived in America in February of 2002. I saw snow for the first time. To me it looked like granulated sugar, this white sprinkle on trees, streets, buildings and the expressway to the Daregos' house in New Jersey, so pretty I reached out in their yard for a handful and licked it. I loved snow more once I was indoors and warm. Through the sliding door in the basement, I watched the flakes fall. I stepped outside one night to feel them settle on my head and thought the wind was playing a terrible joke on me, the way it cut through my cardigan to my bones. In Nigeria, we had a dry season most of the year, rainy season in summertime, harmattan winds over Christmas and New Year. None compared to the chill of winter. Out there, under the black-blue New Jersey sky, I thought that living in America was exactly what it was like to live in a mortuary.

In my first week, I caught a flu so severe I wished for mere malaria. I sweated from fevers; headaches pounded my temples. Mrs. Darego worried because I had no health insurance. She treated me with lemon drinks and vitamin supplements. I was meant to relieve her, but already I was a burden. I recovered and found I was down to my weight as a teenager. In my spare time, I went for walks to the mall to increase my strength. There, I saw shops for underwear, shops for pets, and thirty types of breakfast cereal. Pancakes with blueberries, raisins, honey, nuts, chocolate chips. Disinfectants and air-fresheners for every germ and odor. Scented toilet paper!

"Where are you from?" Americans often asked. Sometimes they smiled, other times they looked at me with suspicion. I was from Africa, I ended up saying, because I quickly learned they didn't know Nigeria. They asked, "Algeria? Liberia?" I started to say West Africa, to make things easier for them. They said, "Oh, South Africa!" I met people in New Jersey who had never been to New York. I began to understand their sense of the world.

"Hello, Auntie Eve," Alali says as I rub her back.

"I had a bad dream," Daniel groans.

They sound like frogs whenever they get up. Daniel is five and Alali eight. They have their mother's half-moon eyes. I untangle their legs from their Disney bedsheets and notice new lumps on their skin from mosquito bites. Here, there is no risk of malaria.

"Bathtime," I say.

When I met them, their expressions were Who-are-you? and What-d'you-want? Their accents were wanna, gonna, shoulda. "You talk funny," Alali said, once she was comfortable with me living in the basement. "Are you one of those people who call candy sweets and cookies biscuits?"

"Yeah, are you from Africa?" Daniel Junior asked through his missing teeth.

Alali pointed out imaginary locations on the tablecloth. "Now, my mom is from this little village here in Africa. My dad is from this little village here in Africa. Which village are you from?"

"A town," I said. Her parents were from cities. Her father grew up in Port Harcourt in the Niger Delta, and her mother was from Lagos, though she was raised in Tanzania and Cuba—her parents were in the diplomatic service.

"I sawed the picture of Africa," Daniel said. "And the boy had no hair, and his belly was all swelled up, and he lived in a hut, with, um, no windows, and I don't like Africa. Africa women have droopy boobies."

Alali laughed. "Huh?!"

"My dad's name is Daniel," Daniel said, ignoring her. "That's why I'm called Junior." He paused as if contemplating a serious political issue.

""And my mom's name is Pat," Alali said, pushing her chest forward. "She's a doctor, but she hasn't got her papers, so she can't work yet."

I smiled so she wouldn't be envious. Between them they would reveal all their family secrets.

Daniel shook his head. "My mom really wants her papers, because my dad is controlling."

"Come on," Mrs. Darego says. "Out of the tub, both of you, or someone is going to get smacked today." She claps her hands as she leaves the bathroom. She never hits her children. She shouts at them, especially if they are reluctant to get out of the tub. "I'm not playing," she warns from the corridor.

She is recovering from her call the night before. On a day like this, she has little patience for nonsense.

"You heard your mother," I say. "You want trouble?"

Alali plants a big foam ball on Daniel Junior's head.

"I'm telling," he whines.

"So?" Alali retorts.

Daniel crosses his arms and turns his back on her. His bottom cheeks are clenched. In school they think he has Attention Deficit Disorder. He won't listen; they want to medicate him. His mother says the teacher who suggested this must be on drugs herself. Cheap ones. Alali continues to gather foam with her bloated hands.

In my hometown we had rainbow-colored water. It tasted of the oil that leaked into our well. Bathing water we fetched from a creek. This smelled of dead crayfish. Our rivers were also dead. When rain fell, it rusted rooftops, shriveled plants. People who drank rainwater swore that it burned permanent holes in their stomachs. Our roads had potholes as big as cauldrons because of the rain. Only in the villages on the outskirts of town did we have one smooth road. The road ran straight from a flow station to Summit Oil's terminal. The villages had perpetual daylight once the gas flaring started. The flare was where cassava farms used to be. Summit Oil bulldozed those farms and ran pipelines through them. The land was now sinking. The gas flare was as tall as a giant orange torch in the sky, as loud as a hundred incinerators. It sprayed soot over coconut trees. From the center of town we could smell burning mixed with petrol. People complained that their throats were as dry as if they swallowed swamp mahogany bark. Elders feared the gas flare was like hellfire. Children wanted to play. Sometimes they played near the flare. Their mothers cuffed their ears if ever they caught them. We'd all heard the story of one little rascal nicknamed Boy-Boy. Boy-Boy wore glasses that belonged to his dead grandfather. He was always with his homemade catapult trying to kill birds. He burned in a gas-flare fire. His family held a funeral for him. They had nothing but his ashes to bury. They buried them in a whitewashed wooden casket.

I help the children out of the tub after the bathwater runs out. Their bodies are warm and slippery. I throw towels over their heads to make them laugh.

"Oh, Auntie Eve," Alali says, hugging me. "I'm so glad you're staying. If you left, I would just die."

She smells of raspberry bathwash. She hugs me too tight.

"My dear, don't curse yourself," I say into her ear.

She knows her mother is angry with her father again.

During the months I was out of work, I stopped at Summit Oil Clinic to see my friend Angelina. She too was a nurse, and she got her job because her aunt was the midwife there. I'd pass the line of patients sitting on benches in the admissions ward. There were the usual malaria cases and children with stomachs bloated from *kwashiorkor*. There were also patients with strange growths, chronic respiratory illnesses, terminal diarrhea, weeping sores, inexplicable bleeding. We had too many miscarriages in our town, stillbirths, babies dying in utero, women dying in labor. People blamed the gas flare. They came to the clinic and sat for hours. The nurses turned them away. There were not enough beds, so patients slept on raffia mats on the floor, even women in labor. New nurses were quick to develop lazy walks. If a patient called out for help, they snapped, "What?!"

One old man who was a regular, he came by canoe from a hamlet on the other side of our main creek. He lived in a bamboo hut near mangroves. In his youth he was a member of the Ekine Society, those masqueraders who paid tribute to Ekineba. Folklore said Ekineba was this beautiful Kalabari woman who was kidnapped by water spirits, and she returned to the land to teach the masquerade dance. People said this man was over a hundred years old, and his body was refusing to die. Some claimed his soul was possessed. He would sit on the admissions bench cursing and prophesizing disasters. The land was our mother, he said, and we would suffer for allowing foreigners to violate her. One afternoon, I went to the clinic, and he was there again, naked from the waist up. His chest hairs were white, and his skin clung to his ribs.

"Nurse," he said, to Angie, "I'm choking here, can't you see? There is something terrible in the air. Our seasons are not as they were. Our ancestors are spiting us." He held his hands towards us. "Deliver me."

Angie whispered that we should get as far away from him as possible.

He stood up. "You turn your backs on me? Oil is a curse on the land, you hear? You will suffer for your complacency. Your fathers will cut off their penises to feed their sons. Disease will consume your mothers. Daughters will suckle their young with blood. Nurses! Prostitutes in white!" He spat with such force he staggered.

Angie and I rushed to his aid. We sat him on the bench.

"He's senile," Angie said with a smile. "Honestly, Eve, we all pray that he will die."

The man's bones were as strong as iron.

"For goodness' sake, be quiet," Mrs. Darego says for the second time during our drive. Daniel and Alali are asking if we are there yet.

"We'll be there soon," I say. "Alali, don't put your hand out of the window."

It is cool enough for us to drive with the windows down and the sunroof open. The jeep is as big as a hut, with three rows of leather seats and a DVD player. I've heard people on television complain that vehicles like these use up too much fuel. I wonder why they are built so large, considering Americans have such small families; why they are so sturdy when the streets I see are flat and wide. The critics on television say that people buy them for status. They have no idea what status is. Nigerians, given a chance, would drive jeeps as huge as mansions for show. But at least we have plenty of children; at least we have appalling roads.

Unfortunately, no one asks my opinion. Instead, I end up arguing with television pundits, after I get tired of the soap operas and their never-ending dilemmas; the talk shows with cheating lovers, cross-dressers and women who are miserable because they can't stick to diets; reality shows; infomercials. Twenty-four hours of programs to entice me into one studio-produced existence or another. It is a struggle not to click on the television in the basement and be transported into a Hollywood movie. Fuel consumption is not the only indulgence in America, and at least the supply of fuel is limited.

The barbecue we're going to is for a community of Nigerians who live in New Jersey, mostly doctors and their families. Mrs. Darego is in a yellow sundress. She wishes her stomach were flatter. She had both children by C-section. Today, they are in their usual coordinated Old Navy and Gap clothes. We stop at a traffic light. This part of New Jersey is all mountains and expressways. She taps the steering wheel.

"Eve," she says, "you forgot to give me your passport again."

"Sorry." But I didn't forget.

Her nails are clipped for work. She is not wearing her wedding band.

"No, no," she says, "don't worry. I just need to send off your renewal by tomorrow, understand? Immigration is tough these days. Me, myself, when I came, I made the mistake of applying on my husband's visa. Seven years, and I'm yet to see a green card. Everything is delayed since September 11."

She has just started a pediatric residency program and needs me to be at home with her children. She is hoping to have my visa extended. I can't tell her I am looking for a green-card sponsor now. I am ready to work as a nurse. What will she say to that after flying me over to America?

"I'll give it to you today," I say. Here in the land of free speech, I've learned to keep my mouth shut.

"You too talk, Eve," Mama used to warn me. "You no see your friend Angelina how she quiet so? If Val marry you, make you no carry dat mouth go 'im house, oh!"

My nickname at home was Tower of Babel because my legs grew long before my torso. I was never mouthy; I just wasn't fluent in silence like most women I knew. I envied them, the way they expressed their opinions and emotions clearly, without opening their mouths. Elderly women especially, they terrified me with their shrugs and side glances. I thought they were dishonest. Why couldn't they just say exactly what they were thinking? I felt compelled to explain myself with words. I couldn't trust people to understand me otherwise.

I never told Mama the source of my vexation, though, which was Val. He was my boyfriend from secondary school, tall and fine, except for his pointy ears, and brilliant. The whole town celebrated when Val was accepted at the University of Port Harcourt. He never returned to town after his graduation. He stayed in Port Harcourt and got a job with Summit Oil as a public relations clerk. He moved into his uncle's servants' quarters to save on rent money, kept telling me about the man's Spanish-style villa, the man's Benz, the man's golf-club membership, yacht and trips to Europe. What was my concern? Was the man willing to hire me as his private nurse? I attended nursing school in Port Harcourt or PH, as people called it, or Garden City. Val was my shadow there. We rocked to the days of jazz funk. We disvirgined each other. I cried when I couldn't find a job and had to return to our boring town. All we had was a bungalow ambitiously called the Grand Hotel, one main road called Mission Way, a marketplace, Summit Oil Clinic, and one of the oldest Catholic churches in our country. Val never asked me to visit him after I left Port Harcourt, much less talk of marriage. We argued whenever he bothered to come to town to see me. Yes, I provoked him. Sometimes I wondered why he chose me and not Angelina. They were friends from church. Angelina was the sort of person who smiled at everyone, and everyone loved her for her dimples. She would have made him a perfect wife: the quiet, graceful sort of woman who was praised for the peace she brought into a man's home. The sort of woman my mouth would not allow me to be.

The barbecue is in a park. People have set up picnics in separate territories the way folk in America socialize within their communities. We find our group under a tree.

Nigerians don't appreciate the sun beating down on them. Next to us is an African-American family all wearing the same yellow T-shirts saying, "Knight Family Reunion." There is also a Hispanic family, and their music sounds like the music we call highlife at home. I seesaw my shoulders to the rhythm of salsa and observe our small gathering. We are homogenized in our T-shirts, baseball caps and sneakers. What gives us away as Nigerians is the way we barbecue our hotdogs and hamburgers. Women are manning the grill. Nigerian men have their limits to being Americanized. Some have not quite mastered their wannas, gonnas, shouldas. Everyone laughs loudly and talks as if they haven't been out in years. They are lonely people, I think.

In the Daregos' house, friends rarely drop by. When they do, they telephone first. Dr. Darego once said that the fewer guests he has, the better anyway: Nigerians gossip too much and wish bad on others. He complains about Americans the same way, saying how rude they are, how arrogant and prejudiced. I've heard him call the Indian and Filipino doctors he works with a bunch of ass-kissers. My father would have said to him, ""Young man! Check your own stinky armpits before you walk into a room full of people and begin to complain about foul odors!"

Dr. Darego works all week and moonlights in his spare time to pay for his dream home. He is too tired for his family. He has no intention of returning to Nigeria. The place is a jungle, he says. But does he like America, the land and people? He loves his children, and they are American. He loves his dream home in America, but America the place is nothing more than a giant mall and workplace to him.

Will living here be different for me? Sometimes a shop assistant follows me in a store, and I want to turn and scream, "If not for the havoc your people have wreaked in my country, would I be here taking shit from you?!" Then, on a day like this, I think of the guerrilla politicos in my country, petroleum hawkers, who treat the land and people of the Niger Delta like waste matter. I look around the park, see trees I can't name, clear skies, smell the clean air in New Jersey that is supposedly polluted, and think, "Well, Gawd bless America."

Alali is teaching Daniel Junior the pledge. "I pledge allegiance," she says, with her hand over her heart. "To the flag. Of the United States of America. And to the republic for which it stands. One nation under God, indivisible—"

"I'm bored," Daniel says and runs off.

He has two boys his age to play with. Alali watches her new friend who looks like a giant Bratz doll. Such a pout on this new friend, and she seems to know all the hip-hop dances. She dips, rolls her head and pumps her skinny arms. Her jeans are riding low, her navel is exposed, and her fingernails are sparkly blue. I know Alali will demand a bottle of that as soon as we get home: "Aw, I wanna have nail polish!" Her mother will certainly say no. Mrs. Darego believes girls should not be little women.

There was a girl who lived on my street; her name was Amen. Amen was Teacher's daughter. She was sixteen and in secondary school. She bought Coca-Cola from Mama and looked like a bottle of it: small, shapely, slim and dark. Amen liked to style her friends' hair. She wanted to be a hairdresser. Her father was against that. He asked me to encourage her to apply to nursing school. Amen said, "But look at you, Eve. Since you graduated, you have no job."

I used to watch her whenever she passed our house. She wore jeans and funky fake imported T-shirts: Calvin Klein, Fruit of the Loom. She giggled and showed off her pretty dark gums. Towards the end of her school year, I noticed how Amen started walking on her own. She relaxed her hair and started wearing it in a tight ponytail. She shaved her eyebrows and painted her nails bright pink.

"Something is going on with Amen," Mama said after she'd sold her a bottle of Coca-Cola. "She's just growing up," I kept saying. I thought Mama was being critical like other women in town. "No," she insisted. "Something is going on with Amen, I tell you. She is looking too advanced." We argued over this. I told Mama she should leave the girl alone. Did she expect her to be sweet sixteen forever?

Then one day I passed Amen on our street. She turned her face away from me and started to cross over to the other side. "Amen, you can't greet somebody?" I asked, jokingly. Perhaps she was expecting another lecture from me about nursing school. She eyed me. ""You yourself, can't you greet somebody?" I stood there with my mouth open as Amen strutted off.

Mama was the one who told me. Amen ran away from home and her father thought that she'd been kidnapped or murdered. He rushed to the police headquarters in Port Harcourt to file a missing person's report. There, he learned that Amen was one of the girls arrested by the Naval Police off Bonny Island, where the Liquefied Natural Gas project was based. Amen was now a resident of Better Life Brothel in Port Harcourt. Amen's father came back to town without her.

Teacher was a skinny man and he stood with his hands behind his back. His shoes had holes, and yet people called him a dignified scholar because he spoke big English. Whenever someone asked,

"Teacher, where is Amen?" he answered, "Amen? Amen expired. Most unfortunate. Ah, yes, it was unanticipated. A great loss to our family. A tragedy of calamitous proportions."

Amen should have gone to nursing school. She ended up hanging around the port, edging local customers, looking like smoked fish. Prostitutes with college educations had better chances of finding expatriate customers who would keep them.

Mrs. Darego has her sunshades on. I can tell her eyes are wandering.

"You're upset about something," I say.

"Me?" she says. "I'm just thinking. Why?"

"You're not mixing much."

She raises her brows. "Me? I came because of the children. They need to play. I want them to meet other Nigerians. In this country it's so easy to forget your identity."

I've been to birthday parties with both children at places like McDonald's, KidZone and Chuck E. Cheese's, places with contraptions to distract them. They have soccer practices, ballet lessons, and karate lessons after school. Their mother says they have no time to play.

I dust sand from my sandals. "Everyone is so excited to be here."

She shrugs. "These people, they are my husband's friends, not mine. Most of them I would never have met in Nigeria."

She is someone I would never have met in Nigeria, a diplomat's daughter. Back home, for the amount she's paying me, she would have a housegirl for each child, a cook, a washerman for her laundry, a driver to take her to work. Here, she worries about who will look after her children while she's in a hospital taking care of other people's children.

Mrs. Darego is a "butter-eater." I know this because she eyes her husband when he crunches on chicken bones. He grinds them to the marrow, flexes his jaws, spits the pulp on his plate. She watches him as if she would like to punch him in the mouth. Dr. Darego won't clear the table, load the dishwasher, cook, or bathe his children. One day she joked that he should add these initials to his medical qualifications: B.U.S.H.M.A.N.

"Do you have picnics for October 1st?" I ask.

"It's too cold in the fall," she says.

October 1st is our country's Independence Day. It is hard to imagine America as a former British colony. That is, a country like mine, broken down and forever recovering from military coups.

She takes off her sunshades. "Eve, I want to tell you something personal. Please, and I don't want you to tell anyone else."

Everyone found out what happened between Val and me; that Val had a woman in the city, a woman who was pregnant by him, a woman who was older than him. At first he claimed it was a vicious rumor spread by those who resented his success. I forced him to confess, slapped his head as if he were my son. "Tell me the truth! Tell me the truth!" Then I cursed him and cursed the woman. I stopped short of cursing their child. Val lowered his head until I finished shouting. He was probably thinking, someone please get this lunatic away from me.

I could not leave home for a while after we broke up. Whenever I did, people stopped me to give advice. "Go there and fight her, Eve." "Sit on his doorstep and refuse to leave." Cook him a good meal, one old woman said. There were people who blamed me for breaking up with Val. He was intelligent, so his head had to have been turned by this other woman. And I, to let a man like him go, a man with a job in an oil company, something had to be wrong with me.

When I heard about the interview for the nanny job, I saw it as a way to escape our scandal. I went to the man who was hiring. He was Dr. Darego's grand-uncle, the head of their family who lived in our town, but he had no money, and no one really respected him. He sat in his cement compound, on a varnished cane chair, cooled his face with a raffia fan. Behind him was his bungalow with a rusty corrugated-iron roof. The man was almost blind. He kept calling me Helen. "Are you spoken for, Helen?" "Do you have a clean reputation, Helen?" He said he chose me because I didn't look like someone who would run wild in America and chase after men. I told him I was very grateful for his commendation. Some of my colleagues said it was below my qualifications to apply for such a job, a mere housegirl. I knew they were jealous. Angie hugged me, and then she burst out crying in the clinic. She said she could never leave her mother.

Angie was her mother's only child. The rest died as babies. Her father was killed in a motor accident on Mission Way. Her mother was always in church saying novenas. People said she was paying for the sins of her fathers.

I couldn't imagine such a burdensome love between mother and daughter. I was Mama's last born, her only daughter. Mama said, "Go. You're unhappy living here anyway. Everyone knows how Val disgraced you, and they won't employ you at Summit Oil Clinic. Nanny is not what we sent you to school to study, but it's not as if you're going to Heaven and you can't come back."

There was a time I thought going to America was as fantastic as going to Heaven. When I was a child and I used to sing that song, "Come and see American wonder. Come and see American wonder." When I fell in love with Michael Jackson. I was twelve and walking around town saying I was going to be Mrs. Michael Jackson, and Mama would tell people, ""Leave her alone. The Jackson family is coming to ask for her hand soon." I had my white church glove, I had a poster of Michael with his glittery glove. I wrote to Neverland. The post office clerks used to laugh at me. I thought they were all mistaken. But accepting the job was a question of common sense. Dr. Darego offered me ten times the salary I would earn working as a nurse.

Nothing else mattered, not missing my family, or standing in line at the American embassy in Lagos, being ordered to step forward, step back, answer only when I was spoken to. Certainly not being held up by a gap-toothed Nigeria airport official who was looking for a bribe: "Where you get dis? Dis passport is fake!" Least of all being inspected and questioned at Immigration and Customs at Newark Airport. "How long are you staying?" "May I check your baggage, ma'am?"

"I'm moving into hospital accommodation," Mrs. Darego says. "Yes. I've been thinking about it for a while. My commute is long. I'm in the hospital most of the time. Would you mind being alone in the house with the children and their father?"

I say I'm not sure. Her voice is insistent.

"It will only be for the next six months. I have to. I mean, you're not going to be with us forever. I supported my husband when he was in residency. I stayed with the children, but now I'm Dr. Darego, too. He has to learn how to support me, see?"

I saw.

"Do you think you can manage?"

"I'll try."

She taps my shoulder. "What you've done for my family, I cannot tell you. The children are so fond of you. It puts my mind at ease when I'm at work."

Please, I want to say. Don't sweet-talk me today.

One evening, I took a shower after the children went to bed. Mrs. Darego was on call and Dr. Darego was out. I was sitting on the sofa in the basement with nothing but a towel wrapped around my body. I was rubbing Vaseline on my elbows and knees. The kitchen door opened, and I heard footsteps on the stairs to the basement. I stood up and held my towel tight. It was Dr. Darego. He had shoulders like a football player, and his head was shaved. At first I was angry he didn't seem embarrassed. Bastard, I thought, in fluent silence, and my expression must have given me away. He walked down the stairs without saying a word, searched behind the sofa bed and found a magazine. He rolled the magazine up like a baton and walked back up the stairs. As if I wasn't there. He lost favor with me after that, even though he never did it again.

"You yourself," Mrs. Darego says. "You seem quiet today."

"My mind is at home."

"The demonstrations?"

"Yes."

"Have you heard from your people?"

"No."

She pats my back. "Don't worry. At least women are involved this time. The world is focused on their cause. No one can harm them with this much media attention."

"I hope not."

"Definitely not," she says. "And it is good that women are involved this time. Women, we are always the first affected and the last heard."

Who knew the women's union would start with Madam Queen? Madam Queen, the drunk who talked too much. I used to pass her house on my way home from school. She was one of those we called half-castes. Madam Queen's mother was Kalabari and Italian. Madam Queen herself, her father was German. She was the color of beach sand and over six feet tall. She couldn't find shoes to fit, so she wore men's sneakers. Divorced and no children, and she drank like a man. People said that had to come from her foreign blood. I was always a little scared of her. She had bluish eyes, black hair down her back. In the afternoons, she sat on her veranda with her wrapper pulled up to her knees. Her varicose veins were thick. She couldn't bear the heat. Sometimes a few women gathered in her compound like disciples.

Madam Queen told folklore, and I found such stories boring, so I never really stopped to listen. The first time I did, I was coming back from school and heard her booming voice: "Hurrah! Congratulations! We celebrate when someone we know gets a job at Summit Oil Clinic. We hope they will bring us into the fold. We forget about what the company is doing to our land. Kalabari people, we are not like that. We come together. We don't allow foreigners to rule us by dividing us, or we are no better than those who sold their own for bounty when the Niger Delta was the Slave Coast..."

I thought she had to be drunk to talk like that. I stayed to hear more.

"The oil companies," she said, "they drill our fathers' farms and they don't give we, their children, jobs. We eat okra, cassava, grown in other parts of the country. We use their yam, plantain and palm oil to cook our *onunu*. There are no fish in our rivers, no bushrats left in our forest. We don't use natural gas in our homes and yet we have gas flares in our backyards. We can't find kerosene to buy and we have pipelines running through our land. Some of us don't have electricity. Some of us don't even have candles to burn. Are you listening, women?

"Young men are kidnapping expatriate employees and demanding ransoms. They are locked up. We call them thugs. Young girls are turning to prostitution to service expatriate employees. They are locked up, too. We shun them. We say they bring AIDS. Meanwhile, the oil companies spill oil on our land, leak oil into our rivers. They won't clean up their mess. All they do is pay small fines, if they pay at all. Our community leaders write petition letters to their directors and they don't give us the courtesy of replying. When they do, they call us liars. We protest because they continue to breach regulations and they call security forces to handle us. Women, listen to me. I'm telling you this, as we speak we are dying. We are dying of our air, we are dying of our water. We are dying from oil. We are not benefiting from it. Must we continue to stand by in silence and wait for men to fight our battles?"

I went home feeling like I'd fallen under her spell. Superstitious people said Madam Queen had such a sweet mouth that she could hypnotize her listeners. At home I saw Mama and Papa sitting under the framed poster of Jesus. Jesus was nailed to a wooden cross and his eyes were raised heavenward. Around the frame Mama had stuck photos of my brothers, Solomon, Benjamin and Ezekiel, to protect them because they'd left home. Papa was in his cane chair, taking a pinch from his snuffbox. Mama was sitting on the chair next to his. She wore her hair in a neat plait. She thought untidy hair was a sign of inner turmoil.

"I listened to Madam Queen today," I said.

Mama frowned. "Queen?"

"Yes," I said. "She is speaking against the oil companies."

"That old drunk?" Mama said.

Papa raised his pinch of snuff. "Yes, indeed, Queen does that. She speaks the truth about the foreigners on our land. She has their blood and she detests them. She is fearless, that woman." He sniffed and sneezed. "Just like a man."

Mama pouted. "That's why she can't keep a man. Please, Eve, don't listen to Madam Queen again. She is trying to get people killed. Remember what happened to the Ogoni people?"

Papa and his pronouncements. My brothers laughed at him behind his back. He was short, with a nervous twitch from the Civil War where he narrowly escaped a detonating landmine, but no one dared challenge him.

Mama, whose idea of a major fight with Papa was to make his *onunu* extra lumpy, so that he might ask, "Ah? My wife, your *onunu* is not smooth today. What have I done to deserve this?"

They actually argued that day. Papa gave his usual proverb about natives sleeping with one eye open. Mama said she would rather trust a foreigner than an Igbo, knowing full well Papa's mother was Igbo.

"My good customer Mr. Obrigado," she said. "He's never done any wrong to me. He's perfectly charming."

She didn't know his real name. He was a journalist with the biggest nose I'd ever seen on a white man. Sometimes he said "obrigado."

"Foreigners," Papa muttered. "They can't keep their hands off our women."

"Obrigado doesn't stray," Mama said.

"He strays to our town center," Papa said. "He's lucky no one hijacks him. He should speak to the Americans at Summit Oil and find out why they keep away from us."

"Obrigado comes here to take photographs," Mama said.

"What for?" Papa asked. "How would he like it if a group of us went to his country to take photographs?"

"Obrigado thinks it's unfair that our government attacks us," Mama said. "He thinks our government should do more to protect our land."

"Obrigado should clear off our land!" Papa shouted. "Is he deaf and blind?! Isn't it the oil companies who arm our government? Now, every useless man in uniform has the gall to attack us! I must not see that foolish fellow in your shop again!"

Yes, I heard about the Ogoni people, how they protested against Shell. Security forces came and shot at them, burned down their homes, beat up women and children. Ken Saro-Wiwa and others who led the movement were tried by a secret military tribunal and hanged in Port Harcourt. I was in nursing school when General Sani Abacha detained oil and gas union officials after the strikes. In Port Harcourt people queued for days to fill their car tanks. Students from Val's university marched to the governor's house and threw petrol bombs through his windows. Kill-and-Go police came and opened fire on them. Eight were struck, five were killed. One had a bullet through his forehead. The governor shut down the university and our nursing school for public safety. Val and I returned to town. No kerosene to buy, was all we heard. Women from the gas-flare village tapped a burst pipeline one morning. There was an explosion. The women, all seventy-three of them, perished. The villagers refused to accept the mass grave Summit Oil offered. They blocked access to the flow station in protest. Summit Oil called in soldiers. The soldiers threw tear gas at the protesters, butted their heads with rifles, kicked a pregnant woman in her belly until she miscarried, beat up one old man until he was comatose. The government said the reports were grossly exaggerated, the dead people were illegal scavengers and lawless rioters, ordered a dusk-to-dawn curfew. I'd never demonstrated in my life. Why would I?

"We should go home soon," Mrs. Darego says.

It is getting cloudy. The sun has disappeared and there is a cool breeze. I call out to the children, "Alali! Daniel! Time to go!"

"Aw, man," Alali says and stamps her foot.

"I don't wanna go," Daniel whines.

They never want to. The word "go" sounds as terrible as "die" to them.

"Not now," I say. "Soon."

A white man and his son are flying their multicolored kite. The son laughs and twirls.

We arrive home early in the evening. Alali and Junior have to stop their Harry Potter DVD, and as we drive into the garage, they complain that they are bored.

"I work all night," their mother says, yanking her car key out. "I go to a . . . a picnic on my day off because of you. You can't even say thank you, and now you're bored because you can't see the end of Harry Potter? Get out of my car. Get. Out."

Her voice is too low to trust that she won't smack them. I make them apologize. They scamper. Their pupils are dilated from a DVD overdose.

Dr. Darego opens the door. "Hey," he says. "What's going on here?"

Alali jumps on him. "Daddy! We went to a park! You should have come!"

"Hi, Dad," Daniel says and hugs his knees.

Mrs. Darego and I walk past carrying the empty cooler and tray. She is still not speaking to her husband. Me, I avoid looking at him; I don't want trouble. We reach her kitchen and she says, "Eve, please don't forget your passport."

We hear Dr. Darego laughing with the children. Sometimes I believe every child needs two mothers: one who gives birth, and another who can easily forgive fickleness.

The sliding doors in the basement are shut. I search my suitcase for my passport and find Angie's letter first. I've read it many times before.

Dearest Eve,

I hope this finds you in good spirits. If so, splendid. We miss you terribly here. Your parents send their greetings. My mother sends her greetings. We are all fine, but unfortunately I don't have good news for you. You won't believe it, Val was sacked from his job shortly after you left. That woman he thought was carrying his baby was well-known for targeting men at Summit Oil and feeding them the same story about being pregnant. She was going with Val's direct boss, a married man. The man found out about Val and wrote him such a bad appraisal that Summit Oil sacked Val. He came back to town.

He was bitter, Eve. He talked about revenge. He said Summit Oil's terminal is like Hollywood. They have a clinic, cafeteria, video games, watch television from overseas. He said that not one person on the senior staff in Summit Oil headquarters is from the Niger Delta and from day one he was treated as an outsider. Now, he's missing. The police have charged him as an accessory in a kidnap case involving an expatriate employee. They arrested him and no one knows where he is. We are all waiting for news. I hope you've forgiven him. He made a mistake and he's paid a huge price.

I go to meetings at Madam Queen's house regularly now. I've even recruited my mother because of what happened to Val. Madam Queen says we will get him released. She may drink but the woman is a force. She says we should not be afraid. She is rallying as many of us as she can to join other women of the Delta to demonstrate at Summit Oil's terminal. We will block their airstrip, jetty, helicopter pad and storage depot. We will demand that they give us electricity, clean water, better roads, schools, clinics, jobs. Pregnant women, too, and mothers with babies on their backs. She said Summit Oil may send the security forces to stop us, but we will not be stopped. We will carry nothing but palm leaves in our hands and respond to their threats with songs.

Eve, you can't come back. There is nothing here for you. You must take your nursing exams while you're there. I hear they need nurses over there in America. You can always come home to visit. A nurse here told me of her friend called Charity. Call Charity. Her number is . . .

Charity lived in the Mississippi Delta. I called her the day I received Angie's letter. "Who sent you to me?" she demanded. She was angry that I had her telephone number. Then she said parts of the Mississippi Delta were as bad as the Niger Delta, but there was a strong possibility of finding work there and getting a sponsor. She advised that I kept my plans secret from Mrs. Darego meanwhile. "Who knows? You know how women can be. She might frustrate your career to further hers. Study in private, take the exams. Once you find work, take off without giving her notice."

I said I couldn't do that.

"Why not?" she asked. "Did she feel sorry for you when her husband brought you here to work illegally? Are they paying you minimum wage? Are they declaring your wages in their taxes? Do you realize you can have them jailed for breaking federal laws and sue them?"

I told her that wasn't my intention, to ruin the Daregos' lives, only to find a legitimate way of staying in America and earn enough to continue sending money home.

She said, "Ah, well, you will soon learn how things work over here. We Africans, we only get attention when we need help, when we have no hope, and oh yes, most especially when we are naked."

"Eve?" Mrs. Darego calls from upstairs.

"One moment," I say, reaching for my passport.

"Come here! Please! Now!"

I drop my passport. She is never rude or impatient with me. I find her standing by the computer desk in the family room, under the mud-cloth painting of two gazelles. She hands me a photograph printed from the Internet.

"Aren't these the demonstrators from your hometown?"

The photograph is clear, although greenish. I recognize Madam Queen, Angelina's mother, Angelina with her big dimples, and—
"Mama!" I shout. Her beautiful, troublesome face. What is she doing there?

"Your mother is one of them?" Mrs. Darego asks.

I nod. Amen's mother is there, Val's mother and his older sister, Sokari, who counseled me. Never lose hope in men, she said.

Mrs. Darego hugs me. "They've brought Summit Oil's operations to a standstill! Can you imagine? Can you? The company is negotiating with them. See?"

The women are dressed in traditional attire: lace blouses, plaid wrappers and head ties. They are waving palm leaves. Mrs. Darego laughs. Her body feels warm. Why am I afraid? I think. We hold each other for a while, and then I pull back.

"I have something to tell you, but you may not want to hear it."

"Eve," she says. "What can be worse than me abandoning my children to you?"

Contributors' Notes

Sefi Atta was born in Lagos, Nigeria, in 1964. She was educated there, England, and the United States, and she now divides her time between those three places. A former chartered accountant and CPA, she is the author of *Everything Good Will Come* (2005), *Swallow* (2010), *News from Home* (2010), and *A Bit of Difference* (2013). In 2006, she was awarded the Wole Soyinka Prize for Literature in Africa and in 2009, the Noma Award for Publishing in Africa. In 2010 she was on the jury for the Neustadt International Prize for Literature. Also a playwright, her radio plays have been broadcast by the BBC, and her stage plays have been performed internationally. A collection of her plays is forthcoming in 2017. "A Union on Independence Day" was named one of the top ten stories of 2003 by *StorySouth's* Million Writers Award and later republished as "News from Home" in her collection of the same name.

Kris Broughton has had stories published in *Carve, Exquisite Corpse, 3AM Magazine,* and *Mipoesias.* He received a Pushcart nomination in 2004. Originally from South Carolina, Kris lives in Atlanta, Georgia, where he toils ceaselessly in software sales. He is at work on a contemporary novel about "brown men thinking real hard." He says, "At some point in a good story (hopefully, near the beginning) the words rise up from the page, wrap a metaphorical arm around the reader, and make him a co-conspirator."

Sara Catterall was born in Ankara, grew up in Minneapolis, and lives with her family outside Ithaca, New York. Her writing has been published in *Bluestem* and *The Sun Magazine.* She interviews authors and reviews books for *Shelf Awareness.*

Kavita Dorai is a physicist whose research focuses on nuclear magnetic resonance techniques and quantum computing. Her writing interests are diverse and include fiction, science communication, cinema studies, and issues of sustainable development.

Richard Dragan teaches writing and journalism in New York City at CUNY / LaGuardia Community College, where he is an Associate Professor of English. After getting his MFA at Columbia, Richard earned a PhD in English from the CUNY Graduate Center. A magazine journalist for many years, he has written in depth about topics such as emerging technologies and the digital humanities. His recent writing has appeared in *Snow Monkey* and *The Journal of the Short Story in English*.

Victor Ehikhamenor is an award-winning visual artist, writer, and photographer who draws influences from traditonal African motifs and religious cosmology. Born in Udomi-Uwessan, Edo State, Nigeria, he lives in Nigeria and the United States. He has held numerous solo art exhibitions, and his poetry collection, *Sordid Rituals,* was published in 2002.

Alfredo Franco has appeared in *Blackbird, failbetter, Euphony Journal, Breakwater Review, Crack the Spine, Prick of the Spindle, The Tower Journal, Gulf Stream, Permafrost, Midway Journal, The Pembroke Magazine, Ragazine*, and *Compass Rose*. He is a graduate of Johns Hopkins and received his MFA from New York University in creative writing, a subject he now teaches at Rutgers University.

Soma Mei Sheng Frazier is an East Coast Native living in the San Francisco Bay Area. Her debut fiction chapbook, *Collateral Damage: A Triptych,* earned praise from Nikki Giovanni, Daniel Handler (AKA Lemony Snicket), Antonya Nelson, Sarah Shun-lien Bynum, Molly Giles, and others, and it won the RopeWalk Press Editor's Fiction Chapbook Prize. You can find her work online at *Carve Magazine, Eleven Eleven,* and *Kore Press.* New work is available in *Salve,* a second prose chapbook just released by *Nomadic Press,* and forthcoming in *Glimmer Train* and *ZYZZYVA*. She is at work on a novel and a screenplay.

D.E. Fredd lives in Townsend, Massachusetts. He has had over 200 short stories and poems published in literary reviews and journals. He received the Theodore Hoepfner Award given by the *Southern Humanities Review* for the best short fiction of 2005 and was a 2006 Ontario Award Finalist. He won the 2006 Black River Chapbook Competition, was nominated for three Pushcarts, and was included in the *storySouth* Million Writers Award notable stories list four times.

Roy Giles has published poetry and fiction in *Ninth Letter* and *C4 Fiction Anthology,* among others. His critical essays in theater won him a fellowship to the O'Neill Critics Institute at the Kennedy Center in Washington, DC, and he has had numerous plays produced regionally. He serves as senior editor for the literary magazine *Arcadia*.

Stephen Healey holds degrees in Religion and Society from Eastern Nazarene College, Andover Newton Theological School, and Boston College. He was named director of the University of Bridgeport's Program in World Religions in 1998. An associate professor, Healey's research and publications have focused on religion and human rights, globalization in religion, religion and conflict, and religion in the post-9/11 era. He explores religious motivation, charisma, and community building in his fictional pieces, and he is concerned to understand the impact of big ideas on little people. He serves as the University's provost and vice president for academic affairs.

Thomas J. Hubschman is the author of *Look at Me Now, My Bess, Song of the Mockingbird, Billy Boy, Father Walther's Temptation, The Jew's Wife & Other Stories,* and three science fiction novels. His work has appeared in *New York Press, The Antigonish Review, The Blue Moon Review,* and many other publications. Two of his short stories were broadcast on the BBC World Service. He has also edited two anthologies of new writing from Africa, Asia, and the Caribbean. He is a regular essay contributor to *Eclectica* and maintains a blog. He lives in Brooklyn, New York, which remains his chief inspiration.

Joan Shaddox Isom has served as an associate fiction editor of *Nimrod International Journal* in addition to working as a writer-in-the-schools for the Oklahoma Arts Council and teaching at the university level. Her work has appeared in numerous literary magazines and anthologies, including *What Wildness is This: Women Write About the Southwest, storySouth, Southern Scribe, Senior Women,* and *The Indian Historian.* Her book for young readers, *The First Starry Night,* was a finalist for the Oklahoma Book Award, and she was nominated for the Indian Historian Award for *Foxgrapes: Cherokee Verse.* "Remade Tobacco" was named one of the top ten stories of 2004 by *StorySouth's* Million Writers Award.

Tim Keane has been awarded fellowships in fiction from The National Endowment for the Arts and The Bronx Council on the Arts. His stories have appeared in *Alaska Quarterly Review, Quarterly West, Other Voices, Golden Handcuffs Review, Rosebud,* and many other publications. "Greta Garbo's Hair" is excerpted from a novel-in-progress presently entitled *The King of the Birds.* He lives in Brooklyn, New York.

Thomas Kearnes is an author from rural East Texas, now living near Houston. His fiction has appeared in *PANK, Word Riot, Sundog Lit, Necessary Fiction, Gulf Stream Magazine, Five Quarterly,* and elsewhere, including numerous LGBT venues. He turns 40 this summer.

Caroline Kepnes is the author of *You* and *Hidden Bodies.* Originally from Cape Cod, Massachusetts, she now lives in Los Angeles. A long-time contributor to *Eclectica,* she reports being thrilled to see her work in this collection.

Will Lasky has had his fiction published in *Eclectica* and the *Ampersand Review.* He lives in Brooklyn.

Svetlana Lavochkina is a novelist, poet, and translator, born and educated in Ukraine, now residing in Germany. In 2013, her novella

Dam Duchess was chosen runner-up in the Paris Literary Prize. Her debut novel, *Zap*, was shortlisted for Tibor & Jones Pageturner Prize 2015. Svetlana's work has been published or is forthcoming in numerous literary magazines and anthologies in the US and the UK, including *Poem, Straylight, Circumference, Superstition Review, Witness, Cerise Press, Drunken Boat, The Literary Review,* and *Chamber Four Fiction Anthology.* Her experimental mono-musical, *Tumbleweed,* scored by Patrick Flanagan, was broadcast on *Radio Blau* in May of 2016.

Rachel Maizes is a writer based in Colorado. Her short stories have been published or are forthcoming in *Witness, Bellevue Literary Review, The Barcelona Review, Blackbird, Slice, The MacGuffin,* and other literary magazines. Her essays have appeared in *The New York Times, The Washington Post, Spirituality & Health,* and other national publications. She is working on a collection of short stories.

PD Mallamo appears regularly in a variety of international literary journals, most recently *Sukoon* (Dubai), *Don't Do It* (UK) and *Kikwetu* (Kenya), not to mention *Futures Trading* (Kansas) and *Los Angeles Review* of Los Angeles. He is a MacDowell Fellow and holds degrees from BYU and the University of Kansas.

Louis Malloy works as a computer programmer but prefers to write fiction. He has had over 40 stories published in a range of magazines and anthologies and has won various prizes, most notably first prize in the University of Plymouth Short Fiction Competition. His work has appeared in *The Edinburgh Review, The New Writer,* and *The Middlesex University Press Anthology,* among others. He earns sufficient money to command an average annual writing income of £136.55. He lives in Nottingham, England, and like everyone, is writing a novel.

Eric Maroney is the author of two books of non-fiction, *Religious Syncretism* (2006) and *The Other Zions* (2010). His fiction has appeared in over a dozen journals. His non-fiction has appeared in the *Encyclopedia of Identity, The Montreal Review,* and *Superstition*

Review. He is a regular reviewer for *The Colorado Review.* He has an MA from Boston University and lives in Ithaca, New York, with his wife and two children. "The Incorrupt Body of Carlo Busso" was *storySouth's* Million Writers Award runner up for best story in 2011.

Roger Mensink was born in Belgium and grew up in the Netherlands, Seattle, and Southern California. He received his MFA from UCLA (in painting) and has no plans to get another one soon. He lives in Los Angeles but would like to move as soon as possible—perhaps to Bozeman, Montana, perhaps to a hilltop village in the south of Italy. Recent fiction appears in *Revolver, Your Impossible Voice,* and *Literary Orphans.*

A. Ray Norsworthy is a well-traveled playwright and author who has lived in places as diverse as New York, Las Vegas, and the mountains of Idaho. He has been influenced by his encounters with a wild bunch of characters, such as Sam Peckinpah, Ken Kesey, and Larry McMurtry, and he spent his rural Oklahoma childhood on hardscrabble Indian leases and sharecrop farms between the creeks of Big and Little Beaver. "All the Way to Grangeville" was *storySouth's* Million Writers Award runner up for best story in 2007.

Raul Palma earned an MA in Writing and Publishing from DePaul University. Presently, he is a PhD student in creative writing at the University of Nebraska-Lincoln, where he is also pursuing a specialization in ethnic studies. He is an Assistant Editor of fiction for *Prairie Schooner* and a contributor to *Watershed.* His work has appeared or is forthcoming in *Alimentum, Alaska Quarterly Review, decomP, Midwestern Gothic, NANO, Rhino, Saw Palm, Sonora Review,* and elsewhere.

Anne Leigh Parrish was *Eclectica's* Fiction Editor from July of 2012 through November of 2015. Her debut novel, *What Is Found, What Is Lost* was a finalist in the Literary Fiction Category of the 2015 International Book Awards. She is also the author of two story collections, *Our Love Could Light The World* and *All The Roads That Lead From Home*. She lives in Seattle.

Padma Prasad is a writer, painter and graphic artist. Her fiction has appeared in *The Looseleaf Tea, Reading Hour, ETA Journal,* and *The Boiler Journal.* Her poem received Honorable Mention in the Palm Beach Ekphrastic Poetry competition, 2016. In her writing, she tries to capture stillness; in her painting, she tries to paint narratives. She lives in Northern Virginia.

Gokul Rajaram lives and works in Silicon Valley. He dabbles in writing on the side, and he has most recently focused on writing about entrepreneurial and product development lessons he's learned in his career. "The Boy with the Hole in His Head" was named one of the top ten stories of 2003 by *StorySouth's* Million Writers Award.

Ethel Rohan is the author of two story collections, *Goodnight Nobody* and *Cut Through the Bone*, the former longlisted for The Edge Hill Prize and the latter longlisted for The Story Prize. Her debut novel, *The Weight of Him*, will be published by St. Martin's Press in early 2017. Her work has appeared in *The New York Times*, *World Literature Today, PEN America, Guernica Magazine, Tin House Online*, and more. Born and raised in Ireland, she lives in San Francisco.

Nancy Saunders is a lover of all things books. She has worked in libraries, Waterstone's (when they still had the apostrophe), written short stories (published a few) and is working on her first novel for young adults. She's also been a conservation volunteer leader, a support worker for adults with learning difficulties, a yoga teacher, a traditional music fiddler, and a home educator of two now grown-up lovelies.

Anna Sidak was named a *Pushcart Prize* Outstanding Writer, and her work has appeared in *Storyglossia, Linnaean Street, Pindeldyboz, Ink Pot, Gator Springs Gazette, Beyond Baroque, Papa Bach*, and other journals.

Paul Silverman was the Chief Creative Officer of Mullen Advertising. Holder of a MA from Brandeis in the history of ideas, his writing and creative stewardship built Mullen into one of the country's premier creative agencies and among the top 25 in overall billings. Throughout his 26 years of leadership, the agency garnered hundreds of advertising awards and Mr. Silverman was named a Legend of Advertising by *The Wall Street Journal*. He retired in 2002 and returned to his first love, writing short stories. He published over 100 short stories in a wide range of small press publications, and was nominated for the Pushcart Award four times. He passed away unexpectedly in 2009.

Elena Tuparevska was born in Macedonia and now lives in the UK. She has worked in NGOs, universities, and schools in Europe, Africa, Asia, and South America.

Chika Unigwe was born in Enugu, Enugu State. She is the author of three novels, including *On Black Sisters Street* and *Night Dancer*. Her short stories and essays have appeared in various journals. Her works have been translated into many languages including German, Japanese, Hebrew, Italian, Hungarian, Spanish, and Dutch. A recipient of several awards, she lives and works in the US. "Dreams" was named one of the top ten stories of 2004 by *StorySouth's* Million Writers Award.

Recommended Online Fiction Publications

The 2River View
3AM Magazine
52 Stories *
AGNI online
Alice Blue Review *
anderbo.com
Annalemma Magazine *
Apple Valley Review
Barcelona Review
Barrellhouse
Bartleby Snopes
Big Bridge
Blackbird
Bodega
Carve Magazine
Cha: An Asian Literary Journal
Contrary
Cortland Review
decomP
Exquisite Corpse *
Failbetter
Five Chapters *

Fwriction *
Guernica
Hobart
Kudzu House Quarterly
McSweeney's
Monkeybicycle
Narrative
One Throne Magazine
PANK Magazine
Pif Magazine
Pindeldyboz *
Quarterly West
The Rumpus
Spartan
Stirring: A Literary Collection
storySouth
The Summerset Review
Twelve Stories *
Virginia Quarterly Review
Witness
Word Riot
Words Without Borders

* Publication no longer active, but archives may still be available online.